SOUTHERN STOCK

SOUTHERN STOCK

A Novel

GENA ELLIOTT

GREENLEAF
BOOK GROUP PRESS

This is a work of fiction. Although most of the characters, organizations, and events portrayed in the novel are based on actual historical counterparts, the dialogue and thoughts of these characters are products of the author's imagination.

Any product names, logos, brands, and other trademarks featured or referred to in this book are the property of their respective trademark holders. Neither the author nor publisher are affiliated, associated, authorized, endorsed by, or in any way officially connected with such trademark holders.

Published by Greenleaf Book Group Press
Austin, Texas
www.gbgpress.com

Copyright © 2025 Southern Stock LLC

All rights reserved.

Thank you for purchasing an authorized edition of this book and for complying with copyright law. No part of this book may be reproduced, stored in a retrieval system, used for training artificial intelligence technologies or systems, or transmitted by any means, electronic, mechanical, photocopying, recording, or otherwise, without written permission from the copyright holder.

Distributed by Greenleaf Book Group

For ordering information or special discounts for bulk purchases, please contact Greenleaf Book Group at PO Box 91869, Austin, TX 78709, 512.891.6100.

Design and composition by Greenleaf Book Group and Mimi Bark
Cover design by Greenleaf Book Group and Mimi Bark
Cover image by © Gary Isaacs/Trevillion Images

Publisher's Cataloging-in-Publication data is available.

Print ISBN: 979-8-88645-389-8

eBook ISBN: 979-8-88645-390-4

To offset the number of trees consumed in the printing of our books, Greenleaf donates a portion of the proceeds from each printing to the Arbor Day Foundation. Greenleaf Book Group has replaced over 50,000 trees since 2007.

Printed in the United States of America on acid-free paper

25 26 27 28 29 30 31 32   10 9 8 7 6 5 4 3 2 1

First Edition

To my father, Stick, who charged through life, as we Southerners say, "like a bat out of hell."

And to my beautiful mother, Charlotte, who cruised carefully and gracefully in the slow lane.

I love and miss you both.

> "Prestige don't pay the bills or put food on the table."
> —STICK ELLIOTT

January 17, 1920—The 18th Amendment forbade the "manufacture, sale, and transportation of intoxicating liquors." Fueled by a culture of proud heritage, grit, and rebellion, many in the southern United States saw Prohibition as an opportunity.

Small-town farmers in the southern Appalachia region relied on the production of illegal liquor at home for decades, passing recipes along to the next generation. Because illegal alcohol couldn't be taxed, moonshiners enjoyed high profits, which continued throughout the '50s, '60s, and '70s.

To avoid getting caught, men modified their cars to outrun the law as they transported moonshine to points of distribution. Some of these bootleggers were the earliest stock car drivers who raced in an organization created by Bill France and known Georgia moonshiner Raymond Parks. The organization later became known as NASCAR.

CHEROKEE COUNTY, SC
-- 1980, 11:42 P.M. --

A layer of white enveloped his body. Blue eyes burned as they fluttered open. Clouds like cotton tops, rays of light puncturing through dense bolls. Sparse cirrus revealed a faint hint of gray. A husky cough was the only sound in the void.

Anchored. Arms and feet in the wrong place. Hands dangled, touching a smooth surface. Feet suspended, shaking in open space. If he could only see what was holding him there. But the white fog prevailed. Tingling in the toes, a rush, a head heavy, heartbeat slowing. He took a deep breath and choked. His eyes closed. Blackness.

Chapter 1

LAWNDALE, NC
– 1950 –

The sirens were closer. Just around the bend, Gene saw a chain-link fence. To the right, a ravine. There was nowhere to go. He slowed. Three Cherokee County cops sped down the straightaway. A hundred yards away, the cars lined up, side by side, blocking the road. Gene waited until the first door opened, then jammed his foot on the gas and headed for the fence. Not a meter from the metal lattice, he spun around, off-road. Weaving between two trees, he sped past the cops who had slammed on their brakes at the dead end. He glanced in his rearview mirror and saw Sergeant Adams throwing his black patent hat across the hood of his dented car. He couldn't hold back the grin spreading across his face.

The police had been chasing Gene Daves all over North and South Carolina for years. They never caught him. But they sure tried.

He had been bootlegging since his foot could reach the pedal, weighing his granddad's Ford down with over seven hundred pounds of homemade whiskey and mulberry wine. It was the '50s, and those cars were built like tanks. Smugglers like Gene modified the car, adding more carburetors, increasing the diameter of the cylinder for more horsepower, and stiffening the suspension so it could carry more weight without bouncing around. Gene drove mostly at night without any headlights, so the cops couldn't see him coming or going.

Even when he wasn't hauling, he sped around in the Ford Model A Coupe, practicing his 180-degree spins and off-road techniques. The backwoods were where he learned the art of aggressive driving, foot-to-the-pedal mechanics, and balls-to-the-wall tricks no one else would dare try. He would speed up on the curves, jump the ditches, and play chicken with the cops. It was what made him the best driver around.

Gene made his delivery to Anderson Farm, dumping wooden boxes in the shed out back and covering them with bales of hay, just as he was instructed. The Andersons were prominent members of the community, and didn't need law enforcement snooping around in their business. He switched out his plates and turned on the car lights, then headed over to the town of Bostic to pick up his granddad, who worked the late shift as yardmaster for Clinchfield Railroad.

Gene pulled into the yard and flashed his lights twice as the old man waved. At six foot, Jake Elliott was almost as big as his grandson. The old man's striped overalls were faded so the white lines blended into the light-blue fabric. He had a scruffy beard and the same piercing blue eyes as Gene. Jake took off his conductor's hat and wiped his brow with it. He hung his clipboard on a peg in the wall, deposited his night stick in a bucket, and saluted his crew.

"How'd it go?" he asked, climbing into the passenger seat.

"'Bout as expected," Gene said. "Adams was pissin' mad. Thought they had me down off Hickory Road on account of the ravine. But I got by."

His granddad let out a deep, guttural laugh. "I bet you did, son."

"I heard they opened up a dirt track down at the fairgrounds for stock car racing. I was thinking I could try my hand at that."

"I don't know. Might call attention to the car. You've eluded the cops thus far. Why risk it for a game?"

"They know the car already. Hell, they know exactly who I am. They don't care. I think they kinda like the chase." Gene grinned again.

"What if you wreck the car?"

Gene had anticipated that objection. "The purse is five hundred dollars."

Jake's left eyebrow raised like it always did when he was thinking. "Okay, but you can't drive the A Coupe."

"But that's what I'm used to."

"The best drivers can drive anything. Adapt to the situation. Rig up the Chevy."

"The Impala? That thing's a piece of junk. Won't top ninety, and the back end drags the ground."

"Fix it. You know how. Go down to Virgil's junkyard and find the parts. He'll give you most of 'em. Or trade for some whiskey."

"A'ight," Gene said, pulling out of the station.

"And I get half the profit."

"That's fair. Now, you wanna get home fast?" Gene asked, fixing his granddad with another smile and revving up the engine.

"Hell yeah."

Shelby, NC

Gene pulled the cylinder from a mound of metal and tossed it to the side.

"You don't want that. It's crap," said a voice behind him.

"Well, this is a junkyard." Gene turned to see his granddad's old friend. "Virgil, you son of a bitch," he said, bear-hugging the old man.

"Good Lord, son, what's Jake feeding you? I swear you're a monster. You've already passed your granddad by a head. What are you, six-two?"

At sixteen, Gene was brute strength, tall, and muscular. Jake always joked his grandson had inherited good genes, but his time spent tossing bundles of hay and lifting barrels of whiskey had developed every muscle in his body, shaping him into a modern-day Spartan.

"Six-four," Gene replied.

"Good God," Virgil said, laughing. "Them girls still chasin' you?"

"Everybody's chasin' me." Gene ran his fingers through dark brown hair, stopping to feather his sideburns.

"Whatcha lookin' fer?" Virgil asked, pulling on his overall straps.

"I don't even know. Gonna go race down at the fairgrounds. Granddad gave me the old Chevy to drive, but I think it won't stand up to those Fords."

"Naw, don't matter. People think it's the car, but it's all about the driver, and I've seen you drive. You ain't got nuthin' to worry 'bout. Those cops drive Fords, don't they? And I ain't seen one catch you yet."

"Yeah, but I'm driving a boosted Ford. Extra carburetors and all."

Virgil cleared his throat. "'Member that one time the Ford was in the shop and you had to drive the Chevy? Did pretty good that night, I heard."

"Yeah, guess I did. Had to get creative, but I left 'em befuddled over by Rickety Creek."

"Exactly. Now let me tell you what you need. Is it the fairgrounds over your way?"

"Yeah."

Virgil took a soiled red cloth from his pocket and wiped his forehead. "Them boys been racin' V8s. They don't allow no modifications, but I don't think they check real good, not that you need it. No, strip the interior. You don't need nuthin' but a seat, steering wheel, brakes, and a gas pedal."

"I don't use brakes too much."

"True," Virgil said, laughing. "You gonna need a good seat belt."

Gene tilted his head. "Seat belt? Who needs—"

"Trust me. Most been puttin' in aircraft seat belts. They're sturdier. I think I got one or two in the office. We get the darndest things 'round here."

Gene riffled through some junk parts, moving lug nuts and bolts around, clanging metal spokes together. He picked up a stacked metal piece that looked like a 3D jigsaw puzzle.

"I'm tellin' you, you don't want those old carburetors. Will bring too much attention on account of the extra noise. But I know a guy who makes cams by hand. No one can tell the difference between those and the factory ones, and they might give you an extra bump. Helps to make the engine valves efficient."

"And what about a roll bar, hoops?" Gene asked.

"Roll bar? Some boys down at Greenville-Pickens been experimenting with the roll cage. Gives a lot of protection. You can use water piping."

"Heard 'bout that, but think I'll use exhaust pipe and cover it with something soft."

"Smart," Virgil said as he walked around the junkyard, Gene following. "You got somebody good to remove the windshield?"

"Why the hell would I remove the windshield?"

Virgil laughed. "The dirt here's red clay, son. How you think you gonna see when that stuff gets all caked up on the window?"

"Wouldn't it just get in my eyes anyhow?"

"You gonna wear goggles."

"But—"

"You bring a rag along and wipe 'em clean when you need to."

"Huh." Gene hadn't thought about such things. He was sure glad Virgil had.

"What ya looking for now?" Gene asked as Virgil stopped by a row of wrecked cars headed for the smasher.

"A steering wheel."

"But I got a steering wheel."

"Yeah, but those Chevys have fancy-looking wheels. You need something sturdy, not too big. With a grip." He reached inside an old, black four-door. "This here's your wheel."

"What kinda car is this?" Gene asked, bending down to look for a name or insignia.

"Ah, this here's a mash-up. Buncha different cars put together. Got a lot of those. Boys playin' in their garages on the weekends, tinkering with stuff they don't understand, so they don't run too long. The parts don't all work together, and they end up here."

"How much do I owe ya?"

"Nuthin'. Just be careful." Virgil's voice shook a little.

Gene squinted at him, confused by the sudden concern. "Aren't I always? If I can drive through these backwoods full of dips and turns, kudzu and gravel, I can handle a circular dirt track. Don't do nuthin' but go round and round. How hard can that be?" He put his hand on Virgil's shoulder.

"I've known you since you was born. Not afraid of a damn thing. But them boys at the track, they're a different breed. They'll do anything for that checkered flag."

"So will I," Gene said. "Plus, how much trouble can I get into? I'll be encased in metal, and with all these safety enhancements, I'll be fine. I'm a big boy, Virgil."

"Okay. Give 'em hell."

"You know I will. Fire and brimstone."

Love Valley, NC

The black Chevy door swung open, and Gene stretched his long Wrangler-clad legs. He dug the tip of his steel-toe boots into the mud and lumbered out of the car, uncurling his body to fit the open air. *Need to move that seat back a hair*, he thought, rubbing his achy knees. He hadn't anticipated the Chevy to be so cramped. He slammed the door, and the newly built cage rattled, reminding him to ask his friend Butch to weld it shut. Gene squinted in the sunlight, the corners of his eyes crinkling upward as his heavy eyebrows scrunched to form a perfect V. A black-speckled Palouse trotted through the middle of town, trailed by a slow-moving mare and a chestnut foal.

Love Valley, a small Western town built around a rodeo arena, just happened to have the best leatherworker in the area. Gene needed a new pair of square boots, so the toe box wouldn't get stuck under the pedal. He'd noticed while driving at higher speeds he got a better feel when he wore his granddad's snip toes.

As Gene stepped onto the wooden sidewalk, he gazed over the small Western town that wasn't big enough to hold him. Shoulders back yet relaxed, he maintained a wide-legged stance, one thumb tucked casually in his belt loop. A blonde beauty tying up her horse looked up momentarily, and that's all it took. Gene made eye contact, touched one finger to the brim of his cowboy hat, and nodded. The blonde blushed and dropped her rope. *This is so easy*, he thought.

"Slick as usual," a voice said, and Gene turned.

"Roy?"

"The one and only," said a man in a checkered shirt, rolled up at the elbows.

"Roy, I haven't seen you since—"

"That night down at Rickety Creek when they was shooting at us. Damn hillbillies making hooch out of an old bathtub in the middle of nowhere. How were we supposed to know? Still can't figure out how they got it out there," he said, stroking his short, clipped triangular beard.

Gene laughed heartily. "Shot straight through my hat. Good thing I was wearing a Gus, otherwise I woulda been missin' half my brain." Gene shook Roy's hand vigorously with one of his while grabbing his elbow with the other. "Good to see you. You workin' up here?"

The flustered young blonde finally got her horse tied up and sauntered past the men, batting her eyelashes like an extra in a Hollywood movie. Gene let his eyes follow her briefly. He always appreciated a beautiful woman, but there was no sport in it, no chase. He could have his pick of the litter, and he knew it.

"Man, if I had half of what you . . ." Roy shook his head. "Anyway, I'm tending to some of these horses, got a little room above the General Store. Go to service on Sundays." Roy pointed to the small wooden church at the top of the hill, the beacon of Love Valley.

"Sounds like you got a good setup."

"What you been up to? Still workin' for your granddaddy?"

"A little. But I just worked up that Chevy over there, and I'm gonna try my hand at stock car racing."

"Oh, I heard they was doin' that at several venues round here. You'll be good at it; you was always good at working the stick shift. 'Slick Stick' we called you. I might have to come see you sometime. What you doin' up here anyhow?"

Gene stuck his foot out. "Need a new pair of boots."

"Old Silas is the best leatherworker around, so you won't be disappointed going in there. Well," Roy said, hitching up his pants like he'd been studying Westerns, "I better be on."

"See you, Roy."

"See you, Gene, or should I say Slick Stick?"

Gene smirked. He rather liked that nickname. It made him seem cool.

The makeshift sign above the leathergoods store advertised cowhide, alligator, and snake, and when Gene stepped inside, he was overcome with a musty, sweet smell.

"You know you can tell where a man's been by the wear on his boots," a crackly voice said from behind the counter.

"I imagine so," Gene said, eyeing the rabbit and raccoon skins hanging from the rafters. "Especially if they're well worn."

As Gene walked toward the desk, he could see an elderly man with shaggy hair and a long gray beard, smoking a pipe. The man grinned, revealing a mouth full of yellowed teeth. He rocked in a spindled rocking chair, his rippled black boots clonking on the floor.

"I need a new pair," Gene said.

The old man stood up—a good seven feet tall. He never looked at Gene but rather turned his back and rummaged through boxes filled with various animal skins. "I'd say. Those steel toes are for kicking, not racing."

"How'd you know—" Gene began.

"I know by a man's walk. Yours is confident. Maybe too much so." He put his finger up in the air as if to stifle an objection. "It will do you well in your line o' work but not with them fighting shoes. You may have kicked a few barrels or ribs with 'em, but you need a sturdy short box for racing."

Was this man prophetic? Surely someone must've given him some background information. "Okay, so what would you suggest?"

The man's long black coat swayed just past his knees as he continued to dig, tossing aside leather, skins, and metal studs. He finally stood full height and turned around holding a pair of square-toed boots in the darkest leather Gene had ever seen. The man placed them on the counter. They had distinctive scales and deep ridges along the instep and vamp. The rest of the boot was elaborately stitched with thread two shades lighter, in an intricate maze pattern.

"These are amazing," Gene said.

"They're perfect for you," the man said, and Gene noticed he had one glass eye.

He slipped the boots on and walked around the room. They were sturdy yet soft and supple. "What these things made of?"

"Python, strongest material out there. You'll have 'em as long as you need 'em. Do you know anything about pythons in Greek mythology?" he asked in a raspy voice as he leaned against the counter, long spindly arms grasping its side.

Gene took a step back, uneasy. *This weirdo probably has pythons slithering up his pantlegs.*

"I don't know nuthin' 'bout mythology, period. Or the Greeks."

"The python was born to the goddess of the Earth as protector of a precious stone at the Earth's center. It drew on the energies of oracles, trophies if you will, and became more and more powerful with each energy it sapped. So powerful in fact that every time it died, the python rose even stronger in each new life."

This guy thinks he's a wizard, Gene thought. "That's interesting. I do like the boots. You were right, perfect fit. I'll take 'em. How much?" Gene asked, sliding his wallet out of his pants pocket.

"Gimme thirty-two dollars."

That was a lot for a pair of shoes, but everybody kept saying this leatherworker was the best, so Gene figured he'd have them for years.

"They'll last you a lifetime," the old man said, as if reading his mind.

Gene threw the money on the counter and tipped his hat. "Thank you, sir. I'll wear 'em out," he said and made a beeline to the door. He couldn't get out of there fast enough. What was that old freak talking about snakes and Greek gods?

Gene climbed into the driver's seat, turned on the engine, and slowly backed out. He pressed his toe into the gas pedal, and the charge snaked up his leg as if the boot was an extension of himself. Maybe the old man was onto something. *A python. A powerful creature. Just like me.*

Chapter 2

SHELBY, NC
– 1951 –

Gene almost missed the hand-painted sign advertising the race. A quick turn and he was on the bumpy path leading into the woods. He dodged potholes and puddled water from rain the night before. The track at Cleveland County Fairgrounds would be slippery, but Gene wasn't nervous. That's when he did his best driving. When everybody else was sloshing around and slowing the curves, he would speed up, handling that water like a boss.

After a good stretch, the forest opened up. A modest chicken-wire fence circled the half-mile oval track. Copper clay created a flat racing surface four cars deep. A concrete wall guarded stadium seats on one side, and a makeshift concession stand advertised burgers and beer. Tall wooden poles were dotted sparingly around the track, their lights just beginning to flicker on. Cars lined up in the pit, all Fords.

Gene pulled onto the grass, one arm hung out the opening where the window used to be in his painted black-and-red Chevy.

"Spectators not allowed in the pit," said a hefty bald guy in an oversized shirt smoking a cigar.

Gene laughed. "I'm not here to watch. I'm here to race."

"In that thing?" the man asked, waddling over to the car. "No offense, mister, but boys here drive Fords."

The youngsters around him snickered.

"Yep," Gene said, crawling out the window and standing a full head above the rest.

"A'ight, son, it's your funeral," chubby pants said, walking away.

The rest of the boys just stood there, all scrawny copies of each other in white T-shirts and rolled-up jeans.

"Where do I sign up?" Gene asked.

"Thataway," the redheaded one said through gapped teeth, nodding to the left.

Gene walked past all the Fords. A few looked like they'd seen better days—dented and rusted—but most looked like they were driven right off the lot. A small bespeckled man with a clipboard sat under a makeshift tent strung together with twine and tarp, a stark contrast to the glossy paint jobs surrounding him.

"I'm here to sign up for the race," Gene said.

"Good Lord, son, how old are you?" the man said with genuine curiosity.

"Sixteen."

"Wow, you from 'round here?"

"Yeah, Lawndale."

"They grow 'em big in Lawndale, huh?"

"Guess so."

The man handed Gene a clipboard. "Fill out the top part and sign the bottom. Heats start at eight. If you qualify, you'll move on through. The big race is at eleven. Prize money for that one only. The purse is five hundred fifty dollars tonight. Your crew can take the left side, near that blue Ford down yonder."

"Crew?"

"Yeah, you know, your team that helps with the car."

"I don't have a crew," Gene said as he filled in the form.

"Well, hell, son, who's gonna change your tire if it blows?"

"Guess my granddad can do it."

"Just one man? Lord, these kids got three or four to help 'em. They drive dirty out here on account of little to no rules. You gonna need a team."

"Naw, I'll be all right," Gene said, handing the clipboard back.

"A Chevy? Son, you sure 'bout this?"

"Pretty damn sure. It's all I got."

"You might, uh, well, good—"

"Don't say it," Gene interrupted. "Bad luck."

Gene didn't know exactly where his superstitions came from, but he figured it was an answer to all his mother's preaching on how God commanded everything. He learned early that was a pile of horseshit and decided he would take control of his own life, because if God loved mankind, then why the hell did he toy with his mother's brain so much?

He looked the guy square in the eyes. "I don't need luck no how. I'm gonna teach these boys a thing or two about drivin'."

"First heat, line up." The announcement came through the loudspeaker above Gene's head as he buttoned up his stark white racing suit.

The raceway roared to life as sixteen cars lined up in staggered rows of four across the track. Drivers revved their engines as the slowly forming crowd cheered and waved homemade flags with their driver's number on it. Drivers still in the pit fine-tuned their cars or paced and scolded their nervous crews. A thickset boy with a crew cut opened up his trunk, then slammed it shut, fast. A man, with the same stocky build, bopped the kid upside the head, then opened the trunk, removed the wooden crate, and ordered two guys in skinny black ties to take it away. Somebody forgot to unload their lightning. Gene walked over to the edge of the grass and climbed up the pillar. It was as good a seat as any to watch the race.

The green flag dropped, and they were off. At first, cars stayed in their respective lanes, but after a few rounds, a white car painted with a blue #8 on the side pulled away from the pack. He cruised past three cars easily. Gene noticed he hung close to the inside of the curves, hugging them tightly. By the end of the race, white #14 had weaved its way in and out on the straightaways enough to pull into first place just as the checkered flag was thrown.

In the second heat, green #4 started at the back of the pack, pulling ahead quickly by jerking his wheel toward the cars on either side of him. They flinched, and he passed, bullying the next set of cars. A few ran right off the track into the cornfield, cursing and spitting as their car came to a slow stop. Soon, #4 was alone at the front, easily taking the flag.

"Final heat," the announcer said.

Gene tapped the top of his red-and-black #77 three times, then crawled inside. His starting position was in the last row, since he was a newbie. He looked left and right. *What a jumbled mess.*

He surveyed the track. The dirt was packed down pretty good, but the muddy slush a quarter mile up the track would be trouble. If he got stuck on the outside, he would slide. A few small puddles meant spinning out was also a possibility. The car in front of him, a gray #18, had a large back fender that stuck out a foot behind the car. To the left, blue #42 was sitting a little sideways, its tire pressure unbalanced. And to his right, a sleek, freshly painted coupe with #13 emblazoned on its side in crisp white paint had its front end fitted with a shiny grill, the hood of the car rising steeply to a rounded point, like a nose.

The ground beneath him shook as the cars came to life, the smell of fuel filling the air. Gene put both hands on the wheel.

The green flag dropped, and all fourteen cars stepped on the gas at once. Gene hung back for the first couple laps, taking it all in, studying the other drivers. This was high-stakes chess, and if he could anticipate the others' moves, he'd win, pure and simple. First, he focused on specifics. Numbers 15, 17, and 72 clung so tight to the inside lane, he figured they must've been coddled too much by their mothers. Car #26 tended to switch gears too hastily, causing the automobile to slack halfway through the bend. A strange yellow car that resembled a cucumber beetle had no number at all but sped around the track in a zigzag motion, losing precious seconds on the stretches. *He's scared of others passing him, so I'll be able to slip right through.* As Gene's eyes zoomed in on his opponents, he created a personality for each driver, so when the time came, he would know what made them tick. Next, he analyzed the macro picture: the way they bunched into a tight group, jotting in and out, inches from one another, leaving the entire outside empty. A swarm of bees, they stuck together, forgetting to utilize key components of the track, like the banks. The corners seemed to mystify the drivers so much that they lined up one behind the other, especially on turn three. A dip in the back straightaway forced them all to dodge left, drivers caught in the rut of brainless forward motion. Gene had the whole thing mapped out in his mind, and on lap number five, he let loose.

With an aggressive turn to the right, he cut in front of #17, claiming the outside lane. Passing cars, he made his way up to the second row. Gray #18 drifted in front of him, blocking his clean path to the front. Gene waited until the bend, then floored the gas with his new square-toed boots. Number 18 slowed down, but Gene trudged on, tapping the back fender ever so slightly.

Tap. Tap. Tap.

"Come on, asshole, move," Gene said. *He's stubborn, but he'll crumble under pressure.*

The driver wouldn't move, though. Gene tried to get around, but #18 quickly drifted left. Gene saw the straightaway coming up. He got inches from the back bumper and made a fluid side-to-side motion, so the car in front of him didn't know which way Gene planned to go on the next curve. Then, at the slightest bend, he went straight into #18.

Tap. Tap!

He clipped the back bumper, and the gray car spun out as Gene passed him on the left. Cars behind him slowed, but he pumped the gas even harder.

Gene glanced in his rearview mirror. No yellow flag. Meant no one was hurt. The path to victory was clear. Now he would only look ahead. Gene caught up with the stragglers and quickly passed them, double lapping all the other racers. Number 26 was in front, and Gene knew he would be shifting gears soon. He waited for the hiccup, then sprinted around him right up on the blank yellow car weaving around like a drunk on the track. Gene could get past him easily, but if he got caught in one of the puddles, he would spin. He knew the other drivers would overcompensate to avoid the muddy slush at the quarter, so when the beetle zagged far left, Gene moved to the outside, his right tires just catching the edge of the mud. He clipped the sharp nose of #4, who braked in surprise. Gene never let up as he taunted the passing cars with the wave of his hand or a quick salute. The checkered flag dropped, and Gene cruised through it, far ahead of the pack.

"Woohoo!" he yelled, pounding on the steering wheel. A rush of excitement flowed through his body, and he knew he'd found his calling. The thrill had always been there, lingering deep within the pit of his stomach as he coasted through the backwoods, slipping through the brush to narrowly escape law enforcement. But this, he thought, this adrenaline was purer than any hooch. *This feeling is liquid gold.*

He slowed down long enough to grab the winning flag from a beauty queen waiting on the sidelines. He gave her a wink and was off again, waving the black-and-white cloth in the air.

A newspaper reporter was waiting in the pit as Gene pulled in. "Mister, that was amazing! What's your name?"

Gene thought for a minute. His real name, the name he was given at birth, was boring. And he didn't want to give credit to the father he never knew, so he'd honor the one who'd raised him.

"Last name Elliott."

The reporter scribbled on his pad, then looked up. "First name?"

Who's going to remember Gene? It sounds kinda dorky. I need something much cooler, a racing name. He thought for another second, then remembered his meeting with Roy. *Stick.* Smooth with the stick shift. And the ladies.

"Stick. You can call me Stick."

"All right, Stick. How'd you do that? In a Chevy nonetheless."

"It's not the car; it's the driver," Stick said with a smile, then jumped out the window and pointed over to a group of young ladies smiling, waiting with racing programs. "Now I gotta get to those beauties over there. Seems they want an autograph."

He pulled off his helmet and fluffed his dark hair with one hand.

"This line of work is gonna suit me just fine," he said and strolled off.

Chapter 3

BERKLEY COUNTY, SC
-- 1952 --

The old red farm truck stopped just short of the railroad tracks. The sandy road to Hell Hole near Charleston was flooded from the swamp that lurked on either side.

"Think we can make it through?" Jake asked.

"Nope," Stick said, surveying the mucky water before them.

"We could get out and walk the rest of the way. It's only yonder past those tracks."

Hell no. "Eh, the water's stagnant, no more than a couple feet deep," he said, backing the truck up a bit. "We've got big tires. If I drive real slow down the middle, we should be fine."

"I figured you'd speed it up and leap over," Jake said.

"I want to, believe me, but this'll do it."

Stick shifted into low gear and proceeded through the nasty swamp, water stirring like a pot of steaming witches' brew. Warted toads hopped from their resting places as mosquitoes flitted around, sticking to the windshield of the truck.

"No wonder they had so much moonshine coming out of this place. Who the hell would ever come down here?"

"Al Capone," his granddad answered.

"What?"

"Well, I don't know if he ever visited this way, but they sure did ship a lot of liquor from this area."

"How?"

Stick had never really asked about the particulars of the business. He had heard bits and pieces over the years, but only when Jake wanted him to know. The less Stick knew, the better.

"They loaded the stuff in boats, trucks, horses, whatever, but mostly railroad."

"And you—"

"Well, I started working at the railroad. Innocent enough at first. Then I noticed these crates comin' through. I'd been experimentin' with makin' my own 'shine for months but didn't know what to do with it. Mostly just consumed it myself. Me and my buddies. But when I saw these crates, thousands of mason jars filled with dark, sweet-smelling liquid, I knew there was money to be made. Those bundles, they were headed up to Chicago. I didn't want to get involved in that, knowing how dangerous it could be and all. Plus, the family farm didn't have those kinda yields. But I'd figured out the stuff I had was a hot commodity, and according to the amounts packed in those boxcars, it would be more profitable than the corn I kept trying to sell at the market."

They continued through the water and over the tracks, finally settling back onto a somewhat dirt path.

"So that's why you kept working at the railroad all these years?" Stick asked, eyeing the forest closing in ahead.

"Not exactly. I wasn't using the trains to hide 'shine—didn't need to. I had a whole farm to do that. I kept the job so the cops wouldn't come nosin' round my place. Working at the railroad did two things, see. It gave me a legitimate job. That way, nobody was questioning where I was getting my money. Second, when the authorities came to raid the boxcars, I cooperated. I never tipped them off, course, just gave them full access to what they needed. Why would they suspect I was booting the same stuff just a few miles down the road?"

"Smart," Stick said, impressed by his granddad's logical scheme. Stick knew Jake was a shrewd businessman, but he didn't realize just how astute and composed his granddad really was. *I wouldn't've gone within a hundred yards of the railroad, but he knew the pigs were comin' and used it to his advantage by leading them right through the door.*

The road had come to an end. In front of them was a makeshift footbridge spread over the musty swamp. The first part was composed of four flat pieces of lumber laid side by side, followed by two thick round logs in the center, followed by four more pieces of flat lumber. The design was less than practical, and Stick wondered why the unstable logs were laid over just the deepest part of the swamp.

"Guess we got no choice but to cross that?" he asked, hoping there was a different path.

"Yeah, and there's another part you ain't gonna like either."

Stick should have expected this. His granddad had been quiet on the drive to Hell Hole, not saying much about the enterprise they were about to venture into. "Remind me why we're here again?"

"I never said. But guess it's okay you know now. These folks down here make some of the best 'shine around. Why do you think Capone wanted it? But since it ain't illegal no more, business has slowed down a bit, and I guess the boss has gotten soft. He's gonna let me sample what they been doing for years. We never competed anyway, not in the same area."

"So, you're gonna start selling this 'shine?" Stick was confused. He thought his granddad was ready to slow down.

"Aren't you the least bit curious?" Jake smiled, knowing full well he was answering the question with another question.

"'Bout as curious as a mouse before it gets gobbled up by a gator."

Jake pursed his lips together and drew a breath as if he wanted to say one thing but was going to say another. "I'm gonna retire from the railroad. Business is slower than in the glory days, for sure, but we still got some customers who like to keep their mouths wet with backwoods hooch. Hell, they'll pay premiums for the stuff just 'cause it's different. And this stuff down here, it's in a class all its own. Some say it cures their ailments, though I'm sure that's just an excuse to be addicted to the way it makes them feel. At any rate, I'm getting old, and I don't need to monitor the comings and goings of the boxcars no more. The bull don't even come down there most of the time, and when they do, they're looking for marijuana. I'm gonna live off my retirement and push a little 'shine on the side."

"But you still gotta be careful," Stick warned.

"Yeah, I know. The local police are out to get the moonshiners, but I don't know if the G-men care much anymore."

Stick shook his head. He begged to differ but didn't want to argue. He opened the door to the truck and stepped out into the hottest, muggiest air he'd ever been in. The makeshift bridge was creaky and unstable, so he went first. As he stepped upon the thick round logs that made up the middle portion, they rolled, and he had to steady himself by squatting and grabbing hold of a nearby tree branch. The swamp below was murky and stank of rotten eggs. When he made it to the other side, he motioned for Jake.

"Be careful in the middle. Them logs ain't attached right. You might want to hunker down a bit."

He prayed the old man wouldn't slide off into the swamp and become some gator's meal. But Jake proceeded carefully, with a slow, purposeful heel-toe step, his long legs bent slightly at the knees, the tan leather satchel he wore over his shoulder getting caught on the chipped trunks of tupelo swamp trees. Stick was relieved when Jake finally stepped onto the dirt on the other side.

"Now comes the hard part," Jake said, bending over to roll up his pantlegs.

"That wasn't the hard part?" Stick asked, not really wanting to see what else this hell on earth had to offer.

Jake didn't say a word, just continued down a dirt path until they came upon swamp so deep it was impassable.

"What do we do now? Surely, we're not wading in that stuff?" Stick said with disgust.

Jake laughed. "There are water moccasins in there, rattlesnakes, gators too. We're taking a canoe." He pointed at a small, pointed brown-and-green boat propped against the side of a cypress tree.

"You gotta be kiddin' me," Stick said. "In that thing?" He walked closer to inspect the canoe. "There's only one oar."

"Then we'll take turns paddlin'," Jake said calmly.

Stick sighed, and they lugged the canoe from its resting place and pushed it toward the edge of the water. The grass was tall there, and Stick felt an itchy, burning sensation on his ankle. He looked down to see a tiny bright-red bug.

"What the—" he flicked it off only to reveal a row of swollen, pink dots. He pulled up the other pantleg. Same thing. Dozens of tiny bites.

"Chiggers," Jake said. "They live in the grass. Ain't nuthin' you can do about 'em. They'll even dig through socks. We'll put a little calamine on when we get home. They itch but are otherwise harmless. Now, let's go."

They crawled inside the canoe and sat upon its slats. Jake started with the oar. It took him a bit to get the motion down—every time he pushed one way, the boat turned another. They mostly rowed around in a circle, pushing themselves deeper into the tall grass. Finally, he got the hang of it and started making progress. Stick kept his hands in his lap. He couldn't wait to be out of this place. Invisible creatures moved in the otherwise still water. The cypress and tupelo trees pushed up from the depths and surrounded them, stifling all sunlight so the swamp was shadowy and noxious.

"Are you sure there's actual civilization out there?" Stick asked.

"Yeah, but not much. Just some old moonshiners and a small Gullah community."

"Them poor people brought over as slaves?"

"Yeah, their job was to work in the rice fields of the Low Country. Because of all these Goddamn mosquitoes," Jake said, swatting one with his hand, "the European settlers died from malaria and yellow fever, but the Africans were immune. The White folk got the hell out of Dodge, and the Africans stayed, retreating farther into the swamps. It was a good place to hide. When they were freed, years later, they continued to take up residence here, keeping their culture intact."

"Huh. Are they friendly?" Stick asked, looking around.

Jake laughed. "Yeah, though I don't think you'd understand much of what they're saying. It's English, but Creole vernacular, so takes a trained ear to zone in on the words. But they ain't gonna bother us. I worry more about the rednecks living down here."

"Great," Stick huffed.

They rowed for several more minutes before Stick noticed a structure in the distance. Gray stone, it appeared to be the front skeleton of a church. A set of steps descended into the water as if Jesus himself would come walking right up. The ornate front wall was completely intact, right down to the cross on top. One partially standing side wall had two Gothic-style windows the size of an adult man. The rest of the church was gone, but the way it rose up out of the water like a dark shrine made Stick shudder. A family of foxes lurked near tall columns by the steps, peering around as if to say, *How dare you come here.* Beyond the church was a forest. Jake rowed the boat right up to the large rocks surrounding the island and, holding steady, pushed the nose of the canoe into the mud.

"Get out," he said.

Stick stepped onto the rock formation, then helped his granddad. He looked upward. The large stone structure was even more ominous up close. A curved space where a door must have been was at least twenty feet tall. Above that was a tiny oval window no bigger than four hands across. *There's gotta be bats up there*, he thought.

"Looks more like a house for vampires than a place to worship the Lord," Stick said, and Jake gave him a shush.

They walked through the opening to a gray stone floor only to find another set of steps on the other side that led to more swamp. Jake pointed to a large tree covered in moss. "There," he said.

The tree had an enormous base, enough to fit eight men around if it wasn't for the wooden spikes coming out of it. As they walked, Stick's weight sank his feet, plunging the toes of his boots into the swampy mud. Swarms of mosquitoes buzzed around his head, and once or twice, he felt something slither across his foot. When they made it to the tree, Jake hung his bag on one of the spikes and whistled.

Stick looked around, half expecting some band of hillbillies bearing shotguns and crossbows to surround them. But instead, a small mustached man appeared from the hollow of the tree. Stick jumped back. It was so dark, he hadn't even seen the opening in the tree's base.

"Howdy," the man said as he stepped into the one beam of sunlight coming through the branches.

He was barefoot and carrying a musket, wearing a faded blue button-down, frayed brown pants, and a black hat wrapped with raccoon fur.

"Here to see Trigger Law," Jake said. "Gold dust," he added, and it was clear that was the code word, because the man moved aside.

"You'll have to bend down a bit—you mountain boys pretty tall," he said in a twang that wasn't entirely Southern, but recognizable enough.

Stick and Jake walked through the hollowed-out tree, which rattled with tin cans on strings attached to its innards.

"Security," the man said, noting Stick's surprise.

On the other side of the tree was a tall wooden fence and a large pile of leaves and sticks resembling a beaver dam. An owl hooted above, and Stick looked up to find dozens of camouflaged men hidden in the moss-covered trees. They had rifles and nets.

"More security," raccoon hat said, nonchalantly.

Stick touched the Colt in the waist of his pants. *Lotta good that's gonna do.*

They were led around the side of the fence to a clearing where a shed with a rusted-out tin roof spanned the space of four boxcars. Underneath was the biggest distillery Stick had ever seen. Jake let out a gasp.

"Impressive, ain't it?" said a booming voice from behind a large stone furnace.

A man, who appeared to be practically as tall as he was wide, stepped into the clearing. He had bronzed skin, gray hair in the shape of a crescent around his head, large lips, and bulging dark eyes. But his most notable feature was a matted chest-length gray beard with two white streaks right down the middle.

"Trigger," Jake said.

The man shifted on his feet, pulled his hands from the deep pockets of his overalls, and spread them wide. "Jake," he said. Then he smiled.

"For fuck's sake, you scared the shit outta my grandson over here," Jake said with a low belly laugh. "And he don't get scared often."

It was mostly true, but Stick didn't want to admit to it. Trigger Law approached him, and he forced himself to hold his own. Trigger stood eye to eye with Stick and held out his hand.

"Good to meet ya," he said.

They shook. His palm was warm and clammy.

"Well, come on over and we'll do a little tasting," Trigger said. "Your grandfather helped me a lot back in the day, keeping an eye on my freight. We sure shipped a lot of 'shine outta here."

He walked over to a large wooden barrel with a copper siphon straw sticking out of the side. Holding up a tin cup, he turned the siphon a bit, then pinched it to control the flow. A dark, thick substance poured out, very unlike the clear, peach-tinted stuff Stick was used to.

"Have a sip," Trigger said, handing the cup to Stick before pouring another for Jake.

Stick looked inside, then sniffed it to be sure. It was 'shine all right, but it had a different smell: mustier, stronger.

"Looks like maple syrup, don't it?" Jake said. "They did that on purpose, so if anybody cracked open a crate, they woulda thought they'd discovered a whole bunch a sweet stuff. Course, they never got that far," he added proudly.

Stick took a tentative sip. It was hard stuff, and he was glad there wasn't a fire within twenty feet, because he woulda gone up in flames. But it was undeniably smooth.

"Rum," Trigger said. "We add rum. Gives it a kick and its color."

By then, ten other men had gathered, sporting shotguns, knives, and arrows; one even had an axe.

"This here's my main posse," Trigger said as he began introducing them. "Crank, Shortie, House, Boomer . . ."

The names were as interesting as the people themselves. Most of the men were Jake's age, with the exception of two younger fellas who were probably offspring. They had shaggy, oily hair and long, dirty fingernails. A few wore camouflage bibs and steel-toe boots. The rest had ill-fitting jeans, long-sleeved shirts, and waders. They were all missing teeth.

When Jake and Trigger walked to the adjoining shed, the posse stood in a semicircle around Stick, as if guarding not only Trigger but the 'shine itself. Stick sat down on an overturned log. He was used to his granddad having private business conversations without him, but never under such dire circumstances.

"Ain't gonna finish it?" the one named Crank asked as he motioned toward the tin cup Stick was clutching.

"I'd love to. But I'm driving, and we got a long way back."

"You a runner?" a younger boy he remembered as Jimmy asked.

"Yeah."

"Me too," he said, puffing up his chest. "I'm the fastest south of the Mason-Dixon."

I doubt that, Stick thought, but he didn't dare say it.

"Uh-huh," he muttered instead.

"Wait a second," House, an apt name for a man of his stature, said. "You look—you that Stick Elliott boy?"

Shit. "I reckon I am," Stick said, afraid of what was next.

"Ha ha. That's the one I was tellin' y'all about," he said as he nudged a few of the men. "You ran a hell of a race up at Cleveland. He's better than you, Jimmy."

Stick knew that wouldn't go over well. Runners didn't take too kindly to other drivers claiming to be superior, especially, he would guess, this crew, who looked like they really didn't take to outsiders in the first place.

"Ain't nobody faster than me," Jimmy said, stepping forward with his hands now on the holsters at his waist.

But House egged him on, much to Stick's dismay. "Ah, yeah, he is. He got the trophy to prove it. Plus, this cat been driving up in the foothills and mountains. That terrain's difficult."

"Ain't no more difficult than—" Jimmy started, but House interrupted him.

"Driving on a flat road?" House roared with laughter, and the other men followed.

Shit.

Jimmy was mad now. "This here's swamp. It's hard to drive in on account of the water and all—"

But nobody was listening. They were all too busy laughing. Jimmy reached into his holster and pulled out a gun, held it straight up in the air, and fired. The sound ricocheted through the swamp, and Stick was pretty sure he saw vampire bats flying from the creepy armed trees.

Trigger and Jake came running.

"What the hell is going on here?" Trigger screamed, his nostrils flaring.

Stick sat forward on the log, his hands folded neatly while House explained.

"We figured out this here's Stick Elliott, the racer from Cleveland I was tellin' you about. Jimmy got mad 'cause we said Stick's faster."

Trigger let out a huge belly laugh. "Boys will be boys."

"Let's race to settle it," Jimmy said, not wanting to give up so easily.

Stick's eyes shot over to Jake. He was sure of his abilities, but he didn't want to race this joker. Not today. Not after consuming a half cup of hard liquor. Not in the pickup truck.

Trigger was quiet for a minute as he stroked his beard. "No, you dumbass. We been hiding out here for decades, and you wanna go rev up some engines just to prove a point? In the middle of the day, no less? Go sit down. And take them guns off, you fool."

Jimmy bowed his head and removed his guns. He laid them at Trigger's feet and skulked away. Stick exhaled in relief. He hoped Jake had brought his spectacles, because as tipsy as he was feeling, he wasn't sure he could drive home.

"All right, enough nonsense. Shortie, help these boys find their way outta here. And take this pint with 'em," Trigger said, handing Shortie a brown clay pitcher wrapped in sweetgrass.

"You giving some 'shine? You always said—" Jimmy shouted from beside the shed.

"It's rum, you idiot. Of course we don't give up the full 'shine recipe. Not that Jake here would try to copy it anyhow. They ain't got the same kinda ingredients we do down here."

Jake and Trigger shook hands. Shortie led them out through the tree, and Jake placed the rum into his satchel that still hung from the large thorn on the tree.

"Walk ahead a couple feet to the edge of the grass," Shortie said. "Keep going. Don't turn around for no reason."

It was a warning. Jake and Stick did as they were told, and when they got to the edge of the grass, they heard a loud boom as if something had dropped from the sky. Jake smiled and pointed forward, toward the church. "Stop and pray?" he said jokingly.

"Coulda used it before we went into that crazy place," Stick whispered. "I ain't never seen nuthin' like that. It's like they're—"

Jake put a finger up to his lips, and Stick looked around. No doubt they were listening.

Stick rowed the canoe this time, choking on mosquitoes and the heaviness of the air, the journey feeling three times longer this way around. When they finally made their way across the footbridge and safely back to the car, he examined his body. He was eaten up by chiggers and deer flies, and his boots were drenched. He removed them, emptying water and mud slush onto the ground. He stepped into the truck barefoot and settled into the seat. He was feeling better and drier, and he could feel the liquor wearing off a bit.

"Did we really come down here just for a bit of rum? We coulda bought it."

"Not like this, you can't. They make their own rum. Lots of sugarcane down in Monks Corner and Charleston. Good stuff too, real sweet. Plus, I ain't seen Trigger in a long time. He used to send a small jar every other week for your mama. Was the only thing that helped her sleep. I tried a hundred times to treat her with the lightning, but she wouldn't drink it because she said it made her delirious." He gave a little laugh. "Imagine that. But the Low Country stuff, it put her right out when she was having a bad spell. Trigger's a crazy fella, but he ain't all bad."

There was a lot Stick still didn't know about his mama, nor the man who raised him, but he knew better than to ask too many questions. They didn't talk about her much. Jake would get real low, and Stick didn't want his granddad suffering like that.

"The rest of them's pretty mixed up," Stick said instead.

"Yeah, they spent all their lives there in the swamp. I guarantee you'll see that Jimmy boy again, though. He thinks he's the fastest, and he ain't gonna let that go."

"I'll be ready," Stick said. "'Cause he's gonna have to come to my turf eventually. And as far as I'm concerned, I'm faster than the devil."

Chapter 4

LAWNDALE, NC
– 1953 –

The barn was lit by four lanterns, one on each corner, well away from the bales of hay. The woody scent of firewood, the pungency of feed, and the sweet richness of leather commingled, creating an altogether satisfying smell. As Stick stepped past the horse stalls, empty for some time, he noted a saddle propped against the wall. He had traded most of Jake's horses for car parts years ago and now felt guilty about it. His granddad had refused to get any more after the last one died, an old quarter horse that had run mule on moonshine for years. Maybe the old man had reconsidered. He loved his horses.

As Stick neared the back stall, he heard Beethoven. The heavy sliding door was cracked, and he could see his granddad inside, holding the contents of a mason jar up to a lantern atop an old curio. He swished the jar around, then glided over to a large barrel, the music guiding his movements. Siphoning a slightly clearer liquid, he put one drop on his tongue, then immediately spit it into the brass spittoon at his feet.

"You know we have electricity," Stick said as he stepped into the room and pointed at the single lightbulb overhead. "We're one of the lucky ones."

"May as well have a beacon advertising *moonshine this way*," Jake said as he swayed his hands to the melody emanating from the player in the corner.

"What, you gonna start wearing cow shoes, too?" Stick laughed, referring to the hoof-shaped shoes moonshiners would wear to throw the police off their scent. "If the classical music didn't give it away, I doubt a single lightbulb would."

"Okay, so I like it better this way. Something serene about this dark, dusky space. I figure it's what it must be like in those monasteries in Italy. And they produce some good stuff."

Stick smiled. "Okay, Granddad." He raised his hand in the air. "What's this one? Beethoven?"

"None other," Jake said. "Sonata Number One in C. There's more to it than that, but you wouldn't know the difference."

"Probably not."

His granddad had listened to classical music for a long time. It must have started sometime after Stick's mother had her breakdown, because he didn't remember it much before then. Music was probably better therapy than how Stick used to deal with his mother's chaos—running clear out of the house and into the woods as fast as he could. Little Gene didn't know what was going on with his mother; he was barely three. Viola would be folding laundry when suddenly she would drop the clothespins, hike up her flowing white skirt, and sit right down in the water basin. Gene would join her, happy to bathe in the soapy bubbles, until she dunked him clear under the water to baptize him in the name of Jesus. From that point on, he hated baths, sometimes going weeks without one, until his granddad noticed the red ring of dirt around his neck and made him wash off in the sink. That night when he stayed at his granddad's house, he heard gentle notes and flutters of strings. Gene figured the music soothed the old man's soul, but now as he watched his granddad flit around the room, he could see it inspired him as well.

"I was thinking," Jake said. "I could mix the corn with a bit of barley and see if that would stiffen it up a bit." He tapped a wooden spoon on the side of a jar. "And I was thinking you could do runs starting in the wee hours of the morning from now on. You still get the night cover . . ."

Stick listened as his granddad enthused about this new plan, waiting for the right moment to interject. He'd been thinking on the matter for days but just couldn't break it to the old man. But as he watched, he realized this symphony could go on for hours. Now was as good a time as ever.

"Granddad, I don't want to moonshine no more. I just wanna race," Stick blurted out.

He immediately felt guilty. Jake had quit the railyard and was producing some of the best 'shine he'd ever made, for a handful of loyal customers. The old man would be crushed.

Jake carefully picked up the needle from the record, and the room became silent. "Son, you ain't winning purses big enough to stop running. Plus, who else am I gonna get? No one drives like you do."

Stick had known he'd get some pushback, and although he felt bad about it, it's what he wanted. He'd just have to prove to his granddad that driving was as important to him as moonshining was to Jake.

"I'm doing pretty good. Racked up another win last weekend. I love the dirt track, but it don't pay. Thinking of trying my hand at this new NASCAR race in Darlington. The purse is big."

His granddad removed his straw hat and scratched his head. "I heard about that, but it's a lot different. Those guys drive real fancy cars. And there's lots of rules. And driving on hot asphalt is different."

"I know. You think I never drove asphalt before? I'm gonna give it a try. It's real high profile, though, so I can't be running no moonshine anymore. I got to stay clean."

Jake bowed his head. "I can see there's no talkin' you outta it. When's the first race?"

It was just like his granddad to put his emotions aside for the sake of someone else's. Plus, Stick knew Jake would be his biggest fan from the get-go. It made him feel even guiltier.

"Qualifying is three weeks from now. It's a five-hundred-mile race, so I better get to practicing. Not much blacktop around here. Thought I'd drive down to Atlanta and race some of those big city roads."

"Go up to Charlotte; it's closer. But be careful. Policemen everywhere. Those folks'll lock you right up if you go weaving in and out, speeding down them streets."

"I'll be safe," he said as the left side of his mouth turned up slightly in a sly grin. "Or at least not get caught."

Jake pulled a cotton square from his pocket, wiped his face, and put the hat back on his head. "Now, are you gonna help me with this?" He handed Stick a jar and a piece of mesh and restarted the music.

"All right." Stick sighed, but he was glad his granddad wasn't dwelling on the issue. *Or is he covering up his real emotions with sonatas?* Some men chose whiskey to drown their sorrows; Jake chose Beethoven.

As they worked, Stick noticed how the distillery kept tempo with the music. Steam released with a whistle as string instruments stretched the limits of their pitch. The thumping inside the still pounded like a bass. They dipped, siphoned, squished, and stirred until the wee hours of the morning. All the while, a beautiful symphony played among machine and man.

Darlington, SC

The track at Darlington was black as tar. Stick walked to the front of his car and sat on the hood.

"It's a Goddamn egg," he said, referring to the elliptical shape of the track.

"Yeah, damnedest thing I've ever seen," Butch said, crossing his arms as he leaned into the side of the car.

Butch was a tall guy, just a few inches shorter than Stick, but you couldn't tell on account of his girth. He was square, as big at the top as he was at the bottom. He was Stick's best friend and the new crew manager. Stick thought since all the fancy NASCAR drivers had a crew, he better get one too. So, he recruited Butch and a few other buddies, promising them a small portion of the earnings, should he win.

"That first corner's pretty tight."

"All them corners are tight, but the first two will be a beast."

"You think I can't do it?"

Butch shook his head. "Naw, I know you can. Problem is, I know you'll wanna speed up on 'em, and if you do, you gonna crash right into that white wall out yonder."

"What makes you think I would do that?" Stick said with a lopsided grin.

Butch stepped up to face his friend. "Look, I don't think you need to speed up, that's all. Just maintain. All them other boys are gonna be slowin' down, drivin' cautiously. I've been studyin' these races. They talk a big game, but they don't play that dirty."

"All right. What about corners three and four? Speed 'em up?"

"Still don't think it's necessary."

Stick trusted Butch. He wasn't a driver, but he knew his way around a racetrack. Smart as a whip, he studied statistics, calculated speed and velocity, and knew race cars like the back of his hand.

"You shoulda gone to college, Butch. You're one smart motherfucker."

"College is for preps. Plus, where's it gonna get me? I like working with these cars. Don't need no education for that." He smiled and shook his head. "You ready? You're playing with the big boys now."

"Course I am. I'm the biggest boy of all. Gonna teach these city boys a thing or two."

"Good Lord, you've got confidence."

Stick smiled and slapped Butch on the shoulders. "Now, let's go. There's a bar downtown that's been calling my name."

The cars were flashier, and the drivers were dressed in Hawaiian shirts, collared button-downs, white pants.

"Is this a car race or a fashion show?" Butch asked.

Stick smirked and reached for his cowboy hat. "What kinda car is that?" He nodded toward a large car with a dipped, pointed rear end, like the tail of a wasp.

"A Hudson Hornet."

"Appropriately named," Stick said. "Never saw one. Funny lookin'."

Butch pointed up to the sky. "So are those clouds. Looks like rain."

"Ah, rain ain't never hurt nobody."

"First off, you're the only one here that ain't got no windshield."

Stick looked around again. He hadn't noticed that before. "Well, I'll be damned." The other cars had windshields, but they were wrapped in cellophane. "Why the—"

"I guess so it don't crack and ice-pick the driver."

Stick let out a *humph* and shook his head. "Still, the rain won't stop me."

"Rain on a dirt track makes for a sloshy, messy race, but rain on asphalt . . . Well, that's a different story. You'll go slip-slidin' all over the place. You'll have to slow down."

"The hell I won't." Stick fixed his gaze to Butch.

Butch just shook his head and walked around the back of the car. "Gonna put a little more air in the left tire, then you're good to go. I checked everything out this morning. Also," he said, pointing to the front of the car, "had to cover your lights. It's a rule."

Stick noticed the front lights were crisscrossed with silver tape. "Couldn't found something that looked better?"

"It's all I had last minute."

Stick looked at his watch. "Two hours. Guess I'll take a look around." He pulled his sunglasses down to eye the competition. "Hey, all these cars got the owner's name on 'em."

Butch was squatted by the back tire with an air compressor. "You mean the garage name? There's room right behind your number."

"No, not the garage name. I mean, by the looks of these fellas, these drivers don't own their cars. Someone else does. Maybe some rich guys finance 'em?"

"Yeah, probably."

Stick cackled. "Well, I never. Now I get why all these boys can drive such fancy cars. Hell, I'm paying for my own hunk of metal—slap my name on there." He hit the side of the car.

"Ain't got no paint."

"What about that half pint you got in the truck?"

"Stick, that's pink paint for the nursery."

"Is it enough?"

"Well, yeah, but—"

"If that boy Elvis can wear pink, I can paint it on my car."

"That one from the ghetto that wiggles his hips?"

"The girls are goin' crazy for that boy."

"Stick, racin's a lot more—"

"Butch, just do it. But make it nice block letters. No fancy swirlies or cursive."

"You got it, boss," Butch said as he stood, shaking his head.

Stick turned around, adjusted his belt buckle, and walked right up to the first trailer he saw. Three guys in matching brown jumpsuits immediately hopped from the back.

The shortest one waved his hands in the air. "Hey, bud, what do you think you're doing?"

"Just came to say hello," Stick said with a disarming smile.

"Oh, well, hey. You an owner?"

The other two crew members joined the first, each placing his hands on his hips.

"Owner and driver," Stick said.

The crew snickered, but Stick ignored it. "What kinda car you got in there?" He peered into the trailer.

"You can't go in there," one of the boys said.

Stick couldn't tell one from the other but could tell they all knew something about keeping secrets.

"Hell, I don't want to go in. I'm just asking about the car."

"You'll find out during the race," said the small one, looking up at Stick, who was a full head taller.

"See you out there, then."

Stick wondered why the NASCAR boys cared so much about keeping things under wraps until the race started. He was used to everybody showing off their Frankenmobiles, boasting about how much power they had under the hood. After strolling around and getting dirty looks, he figured it best to head back and leave the other drivers to their own devices.

Butch was finishing up the *k* on Stick's name as he approached. He dropped the paintbrush in the bucket. "You'll be memorable, all right. The pink's real cute."

"I'm gonna drive so hard they'll never forget."

The track might've been the wrong color, the drivers too uppity, and the cars too polished, but one thing was the same—the need, the downright craving, for speed. The country boys wanted it. The crowd wanted it. And Stick was willing to give in to their appetites.

The cars lined up just as the first drops of rain fell. Stick could see Butch pacing on the sidelines. He hopped out the window and ran over to him, much to the dismay of the other drivers. Butch pointed up at the sky.

"Ah, don't worry about it. Last race I drove on a wet track, and that turned out well."

"This'll be different. You have to slow down if the rain comes in too much. I mean it, Stick. The wall on that first turn, it's a death trap."

"And so are half the roads back home."

"Please."

Stick looked into his friend's eyes and saw the fear. "Okay. I'll slow down."

Stick ran back to the car, past the drivers shaking their heads, and gave a thumbs-up to the announcer.

"Glad you could join us. Hope you don't drive as slow as you start," said cocky #14.

Stick laughed and launched his legs into the car window with the ease of a much smaller driver.

"Cute color, fairy," said the driver next to him.

Now, normally, Stick would've decked the guy, but today he was feeling confident. He fastened his helmet and popped the collar of his race suit up, just for kicks. *Let 'em think what they want*, he thought. *They'll be lost in my fairy dust by the fourth lap.*

The flag dropped, and all forty-eight cars jolted at once. The squeal of tires on the asphalt brought the crowd to its feet. They stomped thunderously, yelled at the top of their lungs, and beat on their chests. Stick wondered what he'd gotten himself into, but then he heard the clanging of cowbells and was reminded of the first time he drove a car right through a pasture.

It was Jake who had taught him to look at the whole picture: the landscape, the livestock's movement, the fence that could split him in two if he hit it the wrong way. So, Stick sat back in his seat, draped one arm over the top of the steering wheel, and studied the track and other drivers. He noticed they didn't turn the wheel much, probably because the track was smooth, not dimpled and potted like the tracks back home. By the tenth lap, he had their driving styles down, and by the twentieth, he'd figured out just how those tires glided. The rubber stuck to pavement, making driving much more predictable, boring even. Stick was used to being the king of car control, constantly changing strategy, adjusting based on the condition of the track. He could spin his back tires more than the front, causing traction on the dirt, but it wasn't needed here. All he needed was steadiness—steadiness and thinking of every possible scheme to pass.

I could tap them, he thought. *Nah, the suits in the box won't like a spinout.*

He noticed the driver beside him was panic-stricken when his rear end jumped. He pressed the brakes and attempted to control the car with the wheel, which Stick knew wouldn't work. *He doesn't know what to do. I could jump in front of him, real close like, and cause that rear to jerk. Especially around the curves. Butch won't like it, but Butch isn't driving this car.*

The next lap, Stick picked his first victim. Yellow-and-black #22, with the name Hank Bee on the side. *I'll just buzz around bumble bee here until he lifts off. He's already oversteering, so it'll be easy.*

Catching a break to the right, Stick punched the gas around the corner to snap in front of #22. The driver did exactly what Stick knew he would—backed off the throttle, sending the tail end up into the air. Swerving in and out of his lane, #22 lost control. The cars around him slowed, turned, braked. Stick sped up, passing a dozen cars in a matter of seconds. The straightaway was clear, with only a few cars ahead of him. He steadied the next few hundred laps, satisfied with his progress. The cars he'd passed struggled to catch up, clipping one another and going nowhere. He was sure they'd be pretty pissed to be outsmarted by a newcomer.

As he surveyed the front competition, he noticed a skinny kid in a Chrysler, #92, fighting for the lead. *Relax, boys, there's plenty of time.* They stayed tight on the turns. There would be no sneaking around these guys. They knew what they were doing.

Around lap 250, the rain picked up. Light at first, a million delicate droplets sprinkled on his goggles. Then the showers started, streaking his sight, but the rubber gripped the track. It was unlike anything he had experienced on dirt. He let out a whoop and bore down on the gas, betting the others would slow. Numbers 8 and 12 spun out early. Red #15 slipped and slid its way into #42, but #92 trudged on, taking the rain in stride.

With ten laps to go, the sky opened up to a downpour, and Stick looked up at the stand. No flag. *These guys aren't stopping the race.* They were going to let them fight it out. His goggles were now an intricate series of spiderwebs, water branching off in different directions. The summer heat made the lenses fog and the cars blur. Stick grabbed the rag tucked into the neck of his suit and wiped at his eyes. Number 9 had ricocheted off the wall, leaving a trail of midnight paint. Number 14 was directly in front, so Stick approached the outside. When #14 shifted to the right, Stick got so close, he could see the driver's surprised face. Giving a delicate wave, Stick passed him, cutting him off for good measure.

"Guess the fairy doesn't drive so slow, huh?" he yelled.

Now in fourth, Stick knew he didn't have much time. He could see the finish line, the checkered flag. Ahead, the other cars were avoiding oil that had spilled onto the track, guaranteed to cause havoc. Stick knew he didn't have the luxury of going around it. He'd lose if he did. The only way to win was to blast right through. He stepped on the gas and hit the oil like a sheet of ice. His car went spinning, but he never braked. He held the wheel firm, his muscles bulging and tensing under the strain. As the car slowed, he was pointed right at the fence, so he whipped the car around and gunned it to the finish line. He cruised past for a split-second finish behind the mint-green machine. When he slowed to a stop, the first-place driver, a small man with a pencil-thin mustache, stepped out of the vehicle in Bermuda shorts and argyle socks. He walked hastily over to Stick, his hand outstretched.

"That was the damnedest thing I've ever seen!" he said, smacking a mouthful of gum and shaking Stick's hand vigorously.

As the marshal handed over the first-place trophy, the driver pulled Stick to his side.

"Take a picture. Take a picture. The crowd loves you," he said, smiling big for the cameras.

Not wanting to take another man's glory, Stick said, "No, I didn't earn that. They're cheering for you, the winner."

"Nope. Listen . . ."

The whole crowd hissed with the sound of a snake.

"They're saying Stick. I may have taken the prize, but you won their hearts."

Stick looked up into the crowd. The grandstand seemed to swell, bulging at its seams with exhilaration. Men whipped their hats overhead. Women clutched their chests, hearts in their eyes. Gene wasn't used to losing, but this frenzy took the sting out of it. He knew it would be a cold day in hell before he came in second again, but he'd relish the fame for now. *I created a fire in the bellies of these fans. There's no stopping this fever.*

Chapter 5

LAWNDALE, NC
-- 1954 --

"We got some celebrating to do tonight," Stick said, passing around cups of foul-smelling liquid to his newly formed crew.

They were in the basement of Jake's main house. He'd let Stick use it on occasion, as long as the guest list was approved and they didn't wander out to the barn.

Butch walked over to Stick. "Man, that race was your best one yet," he said, referring to the race earlier that night, where Stick beat out half a dozen seasoned drivers to capture the purse.

"See seventy-two's face when I passed him on the left? Son of a bitch thought he could shut me out by huggin' that curve on the inside. I was so close I coulda damn near reached out and wiggled his ears."

"You've got quite a pot now. Maybe time for a new paint job? These boys would love to shine that car up for you."

"Naw, I'm savin'. Wanna get outta moonshining and do this racin' thing full-time. It's legit."

"And Jake?"

"He's not happy, but he can't argue with a man making his own way."

"Yeah," Butch said. He picked up a pair of dice from the redwood table and jiggled them in his closed hand. "You decide about that dirt race Saturday?" He released the dice with a flick of his wrist.

"I'm doing it," Stick said, looking down at the pair of twos Butch rolled.

"It's rough on the car, especially the suspension."

Butch was pragmatic; that was one of the things Stick liked about him. He would lay out the facts as he saw them, no ruffles.

"I know, but we'll fix it before the next smooth top. I love the dirt."

Butch picked up the dice again. "You're playing a game of chance," he said, tossing them down.

Stick caught the dice before they rolled off the table. "We're all playing a game of chance, Butch. May as well have fun doing it."

Butch sighed.

"Born from the dirt, live in the dirt. When I die, they can return me to the dirt," Stick said.

"Well, get your rest. You got another race in two days."

"You don't want to stay? Might go down to Shady's later."

"Lord no. Margaret would kill me."

Stick liked the good ol' days when Butch would hang and shoot the shit, but ever since he'd met Margaret, he was whipped, always rushing to get home. Stick couldn't understand why any man would want to stay with the same woman for the rest of his life. Too much responsibility in that, too much to risk.

"I gotta get home to the baby," Butch was saying. "Margaret still says she don't know what to do with a boy. She was fully expecting a girl, you know." He leaned on the table. "Besides, an old married man would slow your game with the ladies."

"Nuthin' slows my game."

Butch let out a belly laugh. "Stick, you'll never settle down."

Stick smiled. "What's the fun in that?"

Gaffney, SC

"It's time for a new car, fellas," Stick said, sliding out from under the Chevy. "Brakes are salvageable, but the transmission's shot, and engine sounds like hell. And I'm pretty sure we're leaking oil." He pointed to the black puddle near the front.

Tommy, a young mechanic of seventeen, leaned on the side door. "Well, if you'd stop with the dirt and just focus on NASCAR—"

"I didn't ask for your opinion, now did I?"

"Nope," Tommy said, pulling his hat over his eyes.

Butch shot Stick a look. "All's he's saying is the dirt's messin' up the car. The purse is bigger for NASCAR anyway. You're barely making pay with the clay, just covering entrance fees."

Stick threw the rag he was holding on the ground. "We've been through this. I'm not givin' up dirt. Why can't y'all get it through your thick skulls? That mess of dust makes me a better driver. It's the only reason I'm as good as I am."

Finnegan, a new crew boy, snickered. "Not the only reason," he said in a hushed tone.

"What was that?" Stick rushed over and grabbed him by the collar.

"Nuthin," he said timidly.

"He said it's not the only reason," said Tommy, rubbing the diagonal keloid on the top of his hand.

"Oh really? And what's the other one?" Stick said, his face inches from Finnegan's.

"The moonshine, sir," Finn said, his voice cracking.

Stick locked his jaw and stared stone cold into the Irishman's eyes.

"You're Goddamn right the moonshine," he said finally, belting out a laugh as he released Finn's collar.

The whole crew released a collective sigh of relief.

"But, Finn, don't ever say that aloud again. Got it?" Stick said, sure that with a bit more pressure Finnegan would have pissed his pants.

"Yessir."

"And, Tommy?" Stick said, turning to face the brown-haired boy. "Don't rat out your crewmates."

Tommy swallowed hard as Stick continued. "We're a team, guys. Act like one. And someone find me a new car. I don't care if we have to build it ourselves. Put some thought into it, and get back to me by Thursday. In the meantime, fix this thing up enough to get me through Shriner's Classic."

"But, Stick, the purse on that one's low. What's—"

"There you go again, Tommy. I just need a car for Friday."

"Okay, Stick, you got it. But it won't be pretty."

"I don't need it to be pretty. I just need it to drive."

A patchwork of black and gray, the beat-up Ford resembled a hearse.

"What did y'all do, steal this thing from the mortician?" Stick asked, walking around the vehicle. He'd told the crew to have the car waiting for him at the track. He hadn't expected the monstrosity before him.

"You said to find something to race in," Finnegan said. "This is all we could find."

Tommy, whining like a schoolboy, piped in. "And you said it didn't matter what it looked like as long as—"

"I know what I said, but by the looks of this, I woulda been better off in the torn-up Chevy," Stick said, slinging his hat across the roof of the car.

"Nah, you wouldn't have," Butch said, giving the tire a good kick. "You were right, the car was shot. This one's in good shape, despite its appearance. All the major parts are working. It's heavy, yeah, but you know how to get past that."

"Where'd it come from?" Stick asked. He was still skeptical, but knew Butch wouldn't put him in something that wasn't solid.

"Virgil. He assured me of its safety," Butch said. "And its speed," he added before Stick could inquire. "Tested it myself. She gets up there. Was an old—"

"I know," Stick said. He recognized an old runner car when he saw one. "This is fine for now, but we gotta get our hands on a new car soon. I mean, I do have an image to protect," he said, tilting his head toward the eyesore beside him.

"Yeah, I'll work on it, boss. Win this one, and that's more money toward a new car."

"Newberry Speedway welcomes you to the Shriner's Classic," boomed the voice over the intercom. "The race will begin in about thirty minutes."

So much for warm-up laps, Stick thought. Smaller tracks didn't run according to any type of organized schedule. There was a race time, but that was more of a suggestion than anything, with drivers often showing up minutes after lineup. And if the crowd got wary, the race would start early, just to appease and keep fights at bay.

Stick had known this, so he'd shown up in his racing suit. He dipped his hands in a bucket of clean water that previously housed beers and ran his hands through his unruly locks, smoothing the hair back from his face. He slid his helmet on, pulled his goggles over his eyes, and made his way into the car.

"Good to see you, ol' friend," he said and patted the dash. "You're not looking so good, but I know you got the guts to win this. So, work with me, all right?"

The lined black leather seats, the perfectly circular speedometer, the legroom—it was all as familiar to Stick as the back of his hand. Minus the seats and dash, the interior of the Ford was royal blue. Stick tapped his heel on the floorboard and heard the echo. It was hollow, a hidden compartment to hide extra car tags, 'shine, or guns.

"Whaddya think?" Butch asked, leaning in, both arms on the windowsill. "Just like riding a bicycle, right?"

"Yep," Stick said, running his hands over the wheel. "It's a monster."

"It's only a half-mile oval, and they got y'all running two hundred laps. Just push through everybody if you have to." Butch shook Stick's arm and walked away.

Stick dragged the cage net across the window and lined up in a mess of cars. There had been no heats or qualifiers, so it was to each his own. He felt like he was in a tank, sitting up higher than the other drivers; he figured he could roll right over them if he wanted.

The race commenced, and Stick easily barreled through the first row. The old Ford had some get-up-and-go, and as he settled into a rhythm, Stick thought of his early days riding through the backwoods. He hadn't even been old enough to drive, that's for sure, but he'd been hauling, nonetheless. He'd found it so freeing, twelve years old, all alone in the woods, behind the wheel of a powerful machine he commanded. He had that same feeling now. He somehow managed to ignore all the cars around him and just drive. It was fairly easy, considering he'd taken a considerable lead, and there was nothing in his way.

He drove like this for a while, enjoying this kinship with the Ford. He knew its motions, the sway of the underbelly, the fierceness of the engine. He knew the quirks too: the way the pointed back end tended to drag and how his fingers rested between the crescent in the oversized steering wheel. He plowed right through all that dirt like a tractor tilling a field and watched as frustrated drivers tried to catch him, only to fall short by several car lengths.

He was now a full lap ahead. As he rounded the third turn, the one farthest from the grandstand, Stick felt something hit the roof of his car. *Acorn*, he thought. Newberry Speedway was surrounded by rich brush and oak trees. A few clapboard houses and sheds butted right up against the track, and he even saw a few chickens pecking around. *Thump, thump.* There it was again. Stick figured there was a squirrel creating havoc in the tree that branched clean over the third turn. He looped the track again, sliding back in his seat because he knew he would win.

Thump, thump, thump, thump. Thump, thump. Thump! That was no squirrel, and those were no acorns.

Stick glanced up at the dents in his roof. He was being shot at. He snapped out of his reverie and stepped on the gas. Fuck! Stick knew there were some rough hillbillies out in the sticks who got territorial, but this was a racetrack. They had to be used to it by now. As he pushed down the straightaway, he glanced in his mirror. The other cars went through the third turn with ease. No panic. No extra push of speed. They were shooting at him and only him. *Who . . .*

He had to either pull out of the race or deal with whoever was trying to kill him. *I'll be damned if they'll scare me away*, he thought, as he rounded the danger zone again. Just two laps to go. This time, Stick pushed to the inside, figuring whoever the gunman was didn't have the balls to step from the brush for a closer view of his target. Stick hugged the curve so tight to the inside, he had two tires in the grassy center pit. Even then, he still felt pings, this time on the passenger side. *Pop, pop, pop, pop, pop.* One, two, three, four, five shots. *Fuck me.*

On the last lap, he could see the flagman pulling yellow cloth from his back. *Don't you stop this race. It's one Goddamn lap!* Stick figured he could dodge the bullets; he'd done it before in the backwoods, in town—hell, he'd dodged so many bullets in his lifetime he may as well have been a mob boss. He rounded the second turn as fast as he could and barreled down the straightaway so fast the flagman didn't have time to wave a yellow. *Bring out the checkered flag, asshole. Squares of black and white. That's all I want to see.*

This time at the risky third turn, Stick moved to the outside, so near the bushes he felt them rustle and scrape against his front end. *I'll knock you clean outta that bush, you son of a bitch.* Of course, the gunman could also hit Stick dead-on at such close range, but that thought only crossed his mind when it was too late. Plus, Stick was no pussy. *Pow!* One shot straight into the back right tire sent the Ford flailing toward the inside. Stick pushed the gas to the floor, knowing he was risking the whole tire exploding. He spun around, creating spirals in the dirt until he could no longer see anything—except that checkered flag flying in the wind, like a beacon bringing him home. He adjusted the throttle and shifted his weight to the damaged side of the car. And spun right through.

"Stick Elliott wins the Shriner's Classic!" the announcer said. Pause.

"And it appears there's damage to the car, beyond the usual—are those bullet holes?"

The crowd gasped as the Ford rolled to the left side with a loud creak. Stick banged his elbow a bit but hopped out the passenger window like nothing had happened.

"Why are there bullet holes in the car?" "How did that happen?" They were all asking the same questions at once.

They hadn't seen it. How could they not have seen it?

Stick did a quick scan of his body to make sure he wasn't hit. His arm was bleeding a bit, but that was it. He looked back at turn three. Of course, no one would have known. The turn was too far away, and the cars too loud. *And I was going too fast for them to notice*, he thought with satisfaction.

"Somebody was shooting at me out yonder," he said. "Coming outta turn three."

"Who?" a Shriner with a tall cylindrical red hat asked.

"Hell if I know," Stick said, his elation turning to anger. The cowardly prick was still out there, and Stick would find him. He put his hand up as he eyed Tommy and Finnegan in the distance. They had packed pistols and run toward the third turn, much to Butch's dismay. Stick had to stop them. As far as he knew, the boys' only experience with guns included shooting deer in the wee hours of the morning.

He shoved his way through the crowd. He whistled loudly between two fingers then yelled, "Finn, Tom—stop!"

The boys turned around and looked at Stick. "We saw that son of a bitch sneaking back behind that shed yonder," Tommy said as Stick neared.

"Let's us get him, boss," Finn said, desperate to please.

"No."

"No?" they asked in unison.

Tommy picked up a shell casing from the ground. "But them was real bullets, not BBs."

"I know it, but—" Stick stopped when he heard snickering from one of the other drivers.

Stick turned to see a whirly fella in brown racing overalls smiling through gapped teeth. He leaned against the tree on the other side of the shed, rolling a casing in his hand. Removing his goggles, he squinted, and his ruddy face wrinkled up as if the sun had dried him up like a prune. This guy knew something.

Stick grabbed a crowbar out of Finnegan's pocket and strode over.

"You can't go over there with just a—" Tommy started.

Stick spun around. "I can't very well go shooting people on the track," he spat, his face full of fury.

"They did—" Tommy started, but then looked back at Butch, who'd cautiously made his way over.

"That's before anybody knew. Now they're watching," Butch said.

The crowd had dispersed a bit, but a few stragglers, curious about the commotion on turn three, had turned to face the action. Stick marched over to the punk and pushed the bar into his chest.

"What's so funny?" he asked.

He smiled up at Stick. "Oh, I was just thinking about how your mama lived off swamp hooch," he said, flicking the tip of his tongue through the gap in his front teeth. "Musta taken a whole bunch to rock that bitch to sleep."

Jimmy. The hillbilly bootlegger from Hell Hole. He'd changed, his hair shorter, his nose a little crooked. Anger boiled inside Stick, and he wanted to beat the life out of the swamp trash right then and there. He glanced over his shoulder at the dozen people still lingering around the track. He grabbed Jimmy by the collar and shoved him into the brush. Jimmy stumbled, and a pistol fell from his pocket.

Stick picked it up. "You don't talk about my mama, you inbred hillbilly," Stick growled and hit Jimmy square on the knee with the wrench.

Jimmy fell to the ground, and Stick heard a rustle in the trees nearby. He peered into the thick kudzu to see four more guys bearing guns, all pointed at Stick. He pulled the newly acquired pistol from his back pocket and swung it around.

"Buncha cowards," he said, just loud enough for them all to hear. "That's what you do—hide. In the bushes. In the swamp."

"You pretty used to hidin' too," said a voice belonging to a pair of tired hazel eyes.

He was right. He'd been running and hiding his whole life—under the veil of the forest, the night sky, the protection of the farm. But he'd been out in the open as of late and was trying to make an honest living. You couldn't outrun your past.

Another rustle, the snap of twigs.

Tommy appeared behind Stick, rifle in hand. Finnegan popped up beside him, two pistols pointed straight from his hip like a gunslinging cowboy. And Butch, over his left shoulder with the biggest gun he'd ever seen. Now, it was an even fight. Stick was glad his friends hadn't listened to him.

"You're on our turf now, boys. Why don't you go on back to that mire you crawled out of?" Stick pressed the heel of his boot into Jimmy's crotch and snarled when he winced.

"Trigger's gone," a stocky one said. "Died in the spring. So, we've decided we're expanding our boundaries."

"Ain't much business up here anymore," Stick said, knowing damn good and well there was plenty, but not in the amounts the swamp monsters were used to.

"We ain't talkin' 'shine," Jimmy said.

Stick momentarily released the pressure from Jimmy's groin, and he scrambled to his feet.

"We got some money saved up, and we're investing in some real nice cars. We're gonna prove who's faster."

Stick slid the crowbar behind his head with both arms, resting it casually on his shoulders. "Aw, shucks, boys, this is all about lil ol' me?"

The three other men emerged from the bushes. They all stood in the dry, brittle, yellowed grass near the shed, in a circle, swamp boys on one side, mountain on the other. Their guns were raised, except for Jimmy, who didn't have his, and Stick, who was no longer bothered by the rednecks. It was rather funny now, knowing these boys made their way all the way up to the foothills just to help him lose a race. They certainly didn't want to kill him. Not yet, anyhow.

"If this is all about winning, why were you shooting at me? Can't beat a dead man. Not that you coulda got me. Your aim was shit."

The stocky one in army fatigues spoke up. "We wasn't tryin' to kill you. Just slow you down a bit, scare you. If we wanted to hit ya, we would've."

His words were thick and garbled, and Stick could tell his crew didn't quite understand what had just been said.

"So, you're scared of a fair race?" Stick asked, mocking the accent.

That set Jimmy off. He jumped around like a jackrabbit. "We ain't scared of—"

"We got a problem here, gentlemen?" Two armed police officers walked into the clearing.

"Naw, no problem at all," Jimmy said, but Officer Marty Taylor, a veteran, kept his gun up.

"He said no," Stick repeated, interpreting.

"Then put your weapons down. All of you."

They dropped their guns, and the second officer, a rather large linebacker-looking fella, collected them.

"You too, Stick," the officer said, eyeing the crowbar resting at his side. Stick handed it to the officer. "Okay, Marty."

"Now, y'all get on out of here. Stick, take your crew back to the pit and go home. I'll bring you your guns." He looked at the swamp boys. "I know the green Pontiac is yours, and now it's marked. I'm gonna have my entire police force on the lookout for you boys. We're gonna run these races nice and clean, or you're all gonna end up behind bars."

"When do we get our guns back?" Jimmy asked, smiling a wide crocodile smile.

"You don't. You're lucky you ain't in the paddy wagon already. Now git!" he yelled.

Stick, Tommy, Finnegan, and Butch walked alongside Officer Taylor back to the track. He noticed Tommy and Finn didn't say much, and Butch looked damn near scared shitless.

"Marty, you transferred to Newberry County?" Stick asked.

"Naw, I'm still up where you are. Just came to see you race."

Stick laughed. "In full uniform?"

"Never know when you're gonna need it," he said. "Plus, just off a shift."

"I knew you liked me," Stick said, his mouth forming a lopsided smile.

"You're the Goddamn best driver I ever seen. But my job is to keep the law, and if that means chasin' you all around to stop you from delivering illegal goods, I'll do that."

Stick smacked him on the upper back. "You like it, the chase. Admit it."

Marty didn't say a word, just gave a knowing smile and handed the Southern boys their guns.

Chapter 6

LAWNDALE, NC
– 1955 –

"What the—get up!"

Stick rolled over to see his granddad standing over him, baseball bat in hand.

"Good God, Granddad, what—" He untangled himself from a blanket and fell onto the straw floor. "It's the middle of the night."

"And we've got work to do, but you gotta get rid of that mess first," he said, pointing to two girls clothed in nothing but panties, arms draped over each other on the right side of the mattress.

Stick turned beet red and grinned. "Oh, yeah, I forgot. That was, I was—"

"Never mind, boy. I don't care what you're doing or who you're sleeping with. Rule number one is you don't bring anyone in this barn. It'll compromise my whole operation." He smacked Stick upside the head, hard.

"Ouch! They won't say nuthin'. They didn't even see nuthin'. The distillery is over—"

Jake smacked him again. "Shut up! And get these girls outta here. Through the front doors," he said, pointing toward two large barn doors. "You gotta stop with the liquor. It's gettin' to your brain."

"Okay, okay," Stick said, reaching around in the dark for his pants. "Let me just—"

The bat hit hard on the ground. "Now!"

He'd never seen his granddad so mad. Stick crawled onto the bed and shook the girls. "Hey. Get your stuff and—can you drive?"

The girls stirred and looked around, confused.

"It's the middle of the night," a petite, tangle-haired blonde said.

"I know, I know, but I'll call you tomorrow, okay?" Stick said, but he didn't mean it. He never called the girls. He didn't have time for the idiosyncrasies of relationships. He had driving to do.

"Get going now." He threw a floral blouse at the blonde's chest. He found his white T and handed it to the brunette. "Here. Wear this. Don't know where yours is."

She sat up. "You sure? I'll cherish it," she said, hugging the shirt like a kid with a new toy.

He handed them their keys and asked again, "You okay to drive? If not, I can call Tommy to take you."

"Who's—never mind. This is messed up. I can drive. It's fine."

The girls stalked off, and as soon as the car started, Jake closed the doors and looked around. The place was a mess—bottles and cigarette butts among the piles of hay.

"The barn is no place for a party. It's my business—the only one I got right now. And why were you smoking? Never mind the fact that you coulda burned the whole place down, that nicotine is bad for you."

"I wasn't smoking. The girls were."

"Only trashy women smoke. Now get up there and get me two cases."

Stick looked over at the crooked ladder. Red maple rafters extended up to form a V above a loft filled with mason jars. He lumbered over and carefully climbed to the top. The place was spotless. His granddad took pride in his work and always made sure his customers got the cleanest, purest moonshine around, and that meant the jars were sanitized and as clear as a crystal wine glass. Stick felt even worse now.

"Eight ounce or twelve ounce?" he yelled down to his granddad.

"Twelve."

Stick gathered two cases, placed them on the makeshift dumbwaiter, and climbed back down the ladder. He unwound the rope and pulled until the cases reached the first floor. Carrying both boxes at once, he made his way over to the polished steel drums beyond the door at the back of the barn. It was only then he noticed how his granddad was dressed.

"Granddad, why are you wearing a suit in the middle of the night?"

"People respect a man in a suit," Jake said, sticking his hands in the pockets of his charcoal pants so they fanned out on the sides.

"But no one's here."

"I'm here," he said as he siphoned golden liquid from drum to jug. "Always dress above your station to be taken seriously. No matter the time of day, people know I'm boss. You should do it too. Stop showin' up to races in ridiculous cowboy outfits. Wear a suit. You'll gain some respect."

Stick took the jug and poured moonshine through a mesh strainer that funneled pure liquid into each mason jar.

"I already have their respect. Besides, the cowboy hat and boots are my signature."

"Your signature is your drivin', son. Wear the hat and boots, just do it with a suit, no worn-out Wranglers and God-awful rodeo buckle. The fans love you, but you need sponsors. Them rich folk like to see someone polished, refined like this here moonshine. Perfection," he said, kissing the side of the jar.

"I ain't perfect."

"No one is. But they need to believe you are. You're unstoppable on the track. Now, show 'em you got brains and class."

"Okay, Granddad," Stick said, screwing the lid on the last jar. "Where these going?"

"Down Crawmond Lake."

"In Cherokee County? The old Teasters' house?"

"Yeah, long story. You're meetin' the son at the bottom of the hill. They won't let no one past the gate. Lucas is five-two on a good day, but he's got attitude. Take your gun just in case there's trouble."

Great.

Stick threw on a shirt, loaded the cases in the back of the Ford, and laid the leather seats right back on top. He threw a flashlight in the back and a pistol in the glove compartment.

Stick loved driving back roads in the dark. He was in full stealth mode, a black car in the pitch-black night. Down the hill he wound, like a villain emerging from his lair. He wanted to avoid town, so he drove ten miles out of the way through backcountry. As he pulled up to large iron gates, he felt exposed. *This is too out in the open. No tree cover.* A green pickup made its way down the gravel drive and parked at the gate. A short man in an oversized trench coat popped out and peered through the gate.

"Stick?"

"Yep. Hey, Lucas. I got some stuff for you, but I'll need to come in."

Lucas ran a Colt over the railings, the wooden handle clanging against the grates. "You can't come in. Nobody gets past the gate."

"Well, Lucas, I don't feel comfortable exchanging goods here." Stick opened his arms wide. "Is there somewhere else we can go that's a little more private?"

"Nope. Your granddaddy said the drop is here," he said, pursing his lips. "There ain't nobody out here."

"As far as you know. Cops hide in them kudzu vines pretty well."

"Drop is here, and that's it," Lucas said, crossing his arms haughtily and holding them all the way up to his collarbone.

"I guess there's no drop, then. If you don't want to let me in the gate, there's a thick brushy area just a quarter mile down the road. Passed it on my way up. Nobody gonna see us there."

"I ain't going nowhere."

Stick turned and headed back to the car.

"Hey, hey!" Lucas yelled, waving the gun around. "Get back here."

Stick put his hand on the pistol in his pocket. He heard a chain and the creak of the gate opening. Lucas was right behind him, aiming the Colt.

"Gimme my moonshine," he said.

Stick stepped close to Lucas so the barrel of the gun was in his chest. "Or?"

"Or I'll shoot you, that's what!" Lucas screamed, his voice cracking.

Stick rolled his eyes. "Okay, let me—"

In one swift movement, he grabbed Lucas's gun and twisted his arm behind his back.

"Oww! You're—"

"Shut up," Stick whispered. "I'm gonna let you go, but I'm keeping your gun. If you want what I have in my car, you're gonna let me through that gate. Otherwise, I'm driving off and you got nuthin'."

He let go of Lucas's arm and twirled him around like a marionette.

"Did you piss your pants?" Stick said, looking down at the stain on Lucas's trousers.

"I—I'll open the gate, but only a little. Dad needs his 'shine."

He opened the gate while Stick pulled in the gravel drive and parked behind a tall hedge. He grabbed the two cases of mason jars and set them in the back of the pickup truck.

"Nice doing business with ya, Lucas," Stick said, closing the car door.

"I want my gun back," Lucas said, puffing out his chest.

"What's that?" Stick asked, patting his pocket.

"I need that gun back. Please. It's Poppa's. He don't know I took it," Lucas said meekly.

"Well, I guess you'll have some explaining to do, won't you?" Stick said, driving away and leaving Lucas addled by the gate like a lost orphan.

Stick decided since he had unloaded his packages, it was safe to go through town. Plus, he had a mean headache and wanted to get back to bed quickly. As he pulled through Gaffney's singular city street, it was deserted. Like the Wild West, brick and wood buildings rose only two stories high, misspelled advertisements painted on the sides in basic faded colors. The entire downtown was lit up by four lampposts, two of them flickering to be changed. The one traffic light bore solid red as Stick approached. Glowing halos around each illumination made his head pound. He slowed, looked left, right, then proceeded at a crawl through the stoplight.

The black car was on him fast. Blue lights flashed, blinding his rearview. He looked over at the guns lying in the passenger seat, the bag of cash on the floor. He'd be damned if this was what brought him down—not when he was so close to getting out for good. Calmly, he pulled to the right of the road into an open parking space and watched as the cop did the same. Tapping his fingers on the wheel, he waited: *one, two . . .*

"Three," he said, stepping on the gas.

Startled, the officer forgot to shut his door as the chase began. It slammed shut with a bang as Stick took a quick right turn toward the trees. *Sucker.*

"Let's see how you do, new guy," Stick said, as he cut through the pharmacy parking lot.

Stick drove head-on toward the bank. *I'd rather slam right into that brick box than let this pig take me in. Go down in a blaze, and, hell, they'll remember me forever. The one the law could never catch—but then again, I'd be dead. Got a lot more records to break.* Sideswiping the curb, Stick spun the car around, so he was now facing the cop, back tires lifted by the bottom stair. The black-and-white Chevrolet Bel Air slowed to within yards of him. *Time to play.*

Stick worked the gas and brakes at the same time, so the back of the car lifted off the step, trunk in the air. The paddy wagon was idle. Releasing the brake, Stick sped past his pursuer and back down Main Street. *Where are you? Give up yet?* Stick's mind raced through all the possible scenarios, none of which involved him losing this game of cat and mouse. As he rounded the corner onto Maple Avenue, the cop car was so far in the distance the blue lights were but a sparkle the size of a firefly in the night. *He never had a chance.*

Stick stuck his head out the window and let out a howl. He cruised back up the hill, stopping by the creek bed to hide in the brush in case the patrol car happened that way. *Enough games for tonight.*

Stick got out and splashed his face with water. Crickets sounded all around him, an orchestra of stridulation. He sat down on the riverbank, letting his mind finally wander in the quiet.

I need to get outta here. I'm no longer a big dumb lug, hauling spirits in the dark. I'm right there, under the bright lights. I'm what the people crave: speed, spectacle, a hard-charging SOB who doesn't abide by rules. I create my own. And I'll make my own place the way I want to. He looked back at his granddad's car, dirtied from the mud. *And I need to do it without you, Granddad.*

He got back in the car, turned off the lights, and drove the last few miles home. He pulled into the drive and saw his granddad on the porch, rocking and smoking a cigar.

"Must've been one hell of a night," he said. "You can fix that scratch in the morning."

Stick noted the white marks, like chalk, along the side of the car. "Will do," he said, tossing the cash bag at his granddad's feet. "I'll fix it, then I'm done."

"Done?"

"Done bootlegging."

"Let's not do this again. Gene, I don't trust no one but you. Who am I gonna get that can drive like that?"

Stick shook his head. "I don't know, Granddad, but I've made up my mind. That was my last haul. I've saved enough to buy me an RV. I'll park it by the barn and pay you rent if you want. Otherwise, I found a nice spot down by the creek."

Jake nodded and tapped his cigar on the side of the chair.

"All right then. I knew this day was comin'. Gonna be a racing man full-time, huh? What if it doesn't work out?"

Jake's tone was conversational, slightly mocking. *He doesn't believe me.*

"It has to work out. I want people to take me seriously. You said it yourself. I'll put the suit on, but I gotta know the man underneath that suit is legit."

Gaffney, SC

The tall hats of the Shriners moved around like maroon thimbles on a Monopoly board. Stick stood on the top rafter and watched businessmen milling below. His brown suit fit tight across his chest and shoulders, restricting movement as he latched the flimsy belt. He slid two fingers into the collar of his shirt to adjust the pencil-thin tie that cut into his neck.

"You look great," Tommy said.

"Yeah, well, the only comfortable part of this gitup is the boots," he said, glancing down at his worn-in Fryes. He placed a tan cowboy hat on his head with one hand and pushed it down to his brow. "Let's get this over with."

It was time to sell these folks on the new Stick Elliott image. The swamp boys had been pumping cash into brand-new cars with souped-up engines, so Stick needed monetary flow to compete. The race began in two hours, but the uncomfortable work of finding a financier started now.

"Well, look at this guy. You clean up well," said Francis Smith, owner of the second largest car dealership in the Carolinas.

"Not for long. He'll be slinging dirt in a few hours, and we'll all be covered in his dust," said a round-faced man Stick did not recognize. "David Cooper, down from Pennsylvania. Word up north, the streets are hot down here. Everybody's talking about you burning up the track."

He talked fast like all the other Yankees who ventured down South. His words were scratchy and cool, like jazz, but had a sincerity to them.

"I had to come down to see for myself. Even the kids have drag races on their bikes now. And they all fight over who gets to be you."

"Well, I do the best I can," said Stick.

"You win at all costs. I like that. We should talk later."

Mr. Cooper handed Stick a business card, and Stick stuck it in his pocket. *That was easy enough.*

"Let's see how tonight goes before we start placing bets on this young man," Francis said. "There's a whole lotta good drivers here, some we brought in from Atlanta."

"It doesn't matter," said Mr. Cooper, straightening his bow tie. "I'll place my bets now. It's on this fella," he said as he casually pointed at Stick and walked away.

Stick made the rounds like a natural, smiling, shaking hands, gathering business cards. When Tommy came over to announce it was time for warm-ups, Stick was relieved. He didn't like parading around, making small talk for the rich folk. It made him feel like a cow at market. He shed his suit jacket as he approached the 150 Utility Sedan. This Chevy was lighter than what he'd driven in the past, but it had a Super Power V8 that packed a punch. *The car looks great—except for the huge oil spill under the front.*

"Didn't fix that?" Stick asked as he bent to examine the spill.

Tommy popped open the hood. "We did the best we could, boss. It keeps leaking. Just take it easy."

Stick stood up, his jacket thrown over one shoulder. "I don't even know what that means. This is a race. By definition, I can't take it easy."

"If you don't, you'll damage the car. You might get three-quarters through the race," Butch warned.

Stick loosened his tie. "We all knew this car was on its last leg. It just needs to make it through this race. So, no, I'm not slowin' down. What else can we do?"

"You could come in halfway through, and I'll fill the oil to the brim," Finnegan said.

"That takes too much time. Anything else?"

No one said a word.

"All right then. I'll come in, but clock it. You better have me out of the pit in thirty seconds."

"Thirty seconds!" they all said at once.

"Okay, twenty-five, then. I can make that up, no problem."

"Okay, we'll do what we can," Tommy said.

"Twenty-five seconds or you're fired." Stick hit the hood. "Let's do this, boys."

Butch leaned into the car. "If you smell smoke, you come in. If the car starts jumpin', you come in. If—"

Stick put his hand up. "I got it."

"But will you do it?"

"I think you know the answer to that." Stick patted the side of the car with the palm of his hand. "Now move, Butch. I got a race to run."

The strong smell of gasoline filled the air, penetrating his nostrils. *Is the gas stronger than usual? No, don't let it get in your head. Ain't nuthin' wrong with this car. I've been through worse obstacles. Hell, I've jumped ditches and bottomed out on the ravine. I can drive this clunker round a circular track. As long as it don't blow . . .*

The starting shot rang through his head like an alarm waking him from a dream.

GO.

Stick let off the brake and at the same time hit the gas.

I could shoot right past all these jokers, but I'm gonna sit back and watch a bit, figure out the newcomer game. Half a dozen here from Atlanta, so let's see what they've got. It's fun making them think they stand a chance.

Stick cruised around the track, careful to stay just far enough back to observe, but not so far he couldn't make it up in one lap. He noted how #12 rode midway. *Safe.* Blue #43 drove his car jerkily, like he didn't know quite how to work the clutch. Four others crowded in the front, jumbled together like a pack of M&Ms. *They're gonna scatter like marbles when I go through the middle.* There was no competition. *Not tonight. Long as my car holds up.*

Stick waited until the forty-fifth lap before knocking, passing his way to the front. The next fifty laps were easy, Stick a good lap in front of everyone else. A little smoke blew in on the hundredth, but he ignored it. The car shimmied a little on the 125th, but he didn't slow down. *Twenty-five laps to go.* "Come on!"

On lap 148, the car sputtered. Stick grasped the wheel and switched gears, but he didn't slow down. The last lap of the race, his lead was shrinking. As he rounded the final bend, sparks flew from the engine. A thick fog of white smoke surrounded the car so he couldn't see. He knew he was in the homestretch. He hit the dashboard, floored the last of the gas, and stared into the abyss.

He hit a familiar lump on the track as the announcer yelled something he could not discern. The car slowed, then came to a full stop. He waited a moment, then stepped out of the smoking vehicle. Butch came running over.

"You okay?"

"Yeah, I'm fine. But the car gave out at the last minute. I know I was near the finish, but it wasn't enough."

"Enough? Stick, you won the race! Nobody could see you on account of all the smoke, but you crossed the finish line a full fourteen seconds in front of the next guy. How did you know where the finish line was?" Butch was talking so quickly he was tripping over his words. "How did you not hit the other cars? How did you see where you were going?"

"I know every turn and bump in that track. I could drive it with my eyes closed."

"Well, you just sealed yourself a sponsorship deal, I'm sure of it. A lot of heavy hitters here, but Cooper seems the most determined. We need the money for a new car, but it's all up to you, boss."

"Them suit types make me uneasy. Can't explain it. What if I sign on, then they think they own me? I don't want nobody telling me what kinda car I should drive or trying to get me on some team."

"I hear ya, but we need funding. We just bought this car. And if you're still considering NASCAR, you'll need a second."

"'Cause of the windshield?"

"Rumor is they're gonna start requiring it."

"It don't make no Goddamn sense," Stick said, shaking his head.

"I know, but ain't no use in—"

"Can't you just take the windshield out for the dirt races?"

Butch sucked in a breath of air and blew it out slowly, like a parent about to explain some simple concept to a child who just wasn't getting it. "Every time, Stick?" Butch didn't wait for Stick's response. He pursed his lips together, then continued. "I could, but there's always the chance it could crack. But if that's what you want, I'll do it."

"That's why you're the best, Butch. Just for a little while, until we can finagle another car. We'll get there."

"You ain't got enough in savings, Stick. We're runnin' through cars like candy as it is."

Stick thought for a moment. He didn't like the idea of a bunch of strangers controlling him. There had to be a better way.

"Butch, would you and the boys want to put some money in? We all buy the car, and we all own a piece of the Stick Elliott brand? I'll share earnings with everybody."

Butch considered the proposal for a moment. "I think it's a real smart idea. These boys believe in you. But collectively, we don't got much."

"I can come up with the rest. I've got money saved up to buy an RV. I'll put it toward the car instead and live at Granddad's."

"I thought you was done hauling and all?"

"I am, but if I live there, I can protect his assets without having to run legs."

"You'll be security."

"Something like that," Stick said as he trotted off toward the trophy stand.

He didn't have to moonshine anymore, but there wasn't any sense in abandoning it altogether. The trade had made him what he was, so the least he could do was protect it.

Chapter 7

DAYTONA BEACH, FL
– 1958 –

Stick peered out the pastel curtains to see lizards sunning themselves on the pavers. Two sabal palms moved rhythmically in the Florida breeze, and he caught the smallest glimpse of ocean waves. As light filtered through the window, his room at the Tropic-Aire Motel filled with brilliant hues, like someone had turned the color dial all the way up. He pulled on a light-blue linen shirt and white shorts that were way too short and too tight in the crotch.

"Oh, hell no," Stick said, pulling the shorts off and replacing them with a worn pair of flat-front pants.

He grabbed a cream Panama hat and, tilting it slightly forward, placed it on his head to hide limp, matted hair. He grabbed a pair of sunglasses, a notebook, and a pen and walked out the door to find Butch, dressed in a brightly colored striped shirt and printed shorts.

"You said you was wearin' the shorts," Butch said, tugging at the back of his shorts in an attempt to pull them down more.

"Didn't fit. But you look real cute," Stick said with a laugh.

Butch grumbled as they walked to the convertible they had borrowed from Virgil.

"I still can't believe they buildin' a racetrack down here," Butch said as he placed a pair of sunglasses on his face.

"Well, they been beach racin' for years. It's about time. But a tri-oval? I don't know . . ." Stick's voice trailed off as he became distracted by a group of ladies in bathing suits strutting along the side of the road.

"Geez, they don't wear much round here, do they?" Butch said.

"Fine with me," Stick said, lowering his sunglasses to wink at one of the women.

They continued down the avenue to US Route 92. Crews knocked down palm trees and burned brush as bulldozers wheeled down a steep embankment.

"That's gonna be one helluva track," Stick said, parking along the side of the road. "Gonna be hot as hell, though, drivin' in this weather. Don't it ever git cool down here?"

"Not really," Butch said. "But let's go have some fun. That's what we came here for anyway."

It had been Stick's idea to go down to Florida for a vacation. The crew had been working hard, and he thought they could all use a break. They'd saved up enough in winnings to treat themselves for a day or two. Butch had wanted to save up for that second car, but Stick convinced him it was better to spend the little they had on crew morale, seeing as the process of taking the windshield in and out hadn't been as laborious as they'd anticipated.

"How you gonna walk on the beach in them pants?" Butch asked as they pulled back up to the hotel.

"Thought we'd go to a bar instead," Stick said, waving to Tommy and Finnegan, who jumped in the back seat.

"In the mornin'?"

"Always a good time for a beer. Besides, I can't drink before practices,

I can't drink before races, I can't drink before autographs or press appearances. When am I supposed to drink?"

"All right," Butch said. "But let's go to a sandbar at least."

"Now you're talkin'," Tommy said.

They drove to the boardwalk and pulled right up beside sunbathing beauties in large-brimmed hats.

"How's this?" Stick asked.

"This'll do just fine," Tommy said, smiling as everybody exited the car.

"I'm gonna grab a beer from that stand," Stick said, pointing to a red-and-white canopy near the Ferris wheel. "Then, I'm gonna park myself on the end of that pier and just stare off into the never-ending turquoise."

"Sounds like a plan. I'll come with you," Butch said. "I got a wife at home. I don't need all this temptation."

"Not me. Nuthin's stoppin' me today," Tommy said as he sat down in the sand. "Ain't that right, ladies?"

The women next to them giggled. One turned on her side.

"Hey, aren't you Stick Elliott?" she asked, looking up at Stick.

"Yes, ma'am," he said.

"Heard you were the fastest around," she said, shielding the sun from her eyes.

"Nobody can beat this man!" Tommy pumped his fist in the air.

"Thanks for the confidence, Tommy, but let's not make a scene," Stick said. "Ma'am," he said, nodding to her as he walked off.

"You think you're better than everybody else, redneck?" a voice said, and Stick whipped his head around.

"Ah, shit," Butch muttered under his breath.

"There ain't no need for that kinda talk in front of the ladies," Stick said, cracking his knuckles and scanning the crowd for the loudmouth son of a bitch who wanted to pick a fight.

A lanky man stepped forward. Stick barely recognized him with his fresh new cut, a number one shaved into the side of his head. But with a square jaw, bushy eyebrows, and some missing teeth, Stick knew it could be none other than Jimmy from Hell Hole Swamp.

"The ladies can bear witness while I kick your ass," he said in that same choppy, mashed-up dialect.

Stick stepped forward, but Butch pushed him back. "No," he said.

"What's your problem?" Tommy asked as he and Finnegan stood shoulder to shoulder.

"My problem is that you foothills boys shoulda stayed up on your farm."

"Listen, man," Butch said. "We're just tryin' to vacation here. Just let us be."

"Nah, don't think I will," Jimmy said as four more guys joined him. "We been g'ttin' ready for you, but you don't run with the big boys much. Lo and behold, here you are. Again. You might be good up in the sticks with all those Frankenstein cars, but down here with the sand and water, you don't stand a chance."

"Stick, let's just—" Butch started, but Stick was already pushing past him.

"You an official driver now?" Stick asked, getting right up in Jimmy's face.

"Yeah, the best in real racing. NASCAR. I don't bother with small-time tracks no more."

He was just as cocky outside the swamp. Stick had heard of a driver named Jim who was making a splash in Florida and Georgia, climbing in the Grand National rankings. He also knew he had a reputation for being a dick. But he didn't know it was the same asshole who had tried to shoot him years ago.

"You're good," Stick said, surprising everyone. "But the best? I don't know. Care to place a little wager?"

"Oh, no, no, no," Butch said. "We're not—where would we race?"

Stick spread his arms wide. "Right here. On the beach."

"Yeah!" Tommy and Finnegan exclaimed at the same time.

"Dear Lord," Butch said, rubbing his head.

Jimmy squinted down the beach. "There's enough room. But you gonna drive that thing?"

"Ah, man, I could beat you on a bicycle. You should know it's the man, not the machine."

"Glad you agree. I'll be racing in that." He pointed to a teal Mercury Monterey.

Stick swallowed hard. The Monterey was the fastest car around, so he would need to figure out how to get an advantage in the sand.

"Got any ideas?" he whispered to Butch. "Sand dynamics, velocity? Wheel traction?"

"I ain't got no idea! There's no sand in the foothills. This harebrained idea just might land you right in the ocean. Christ, it's like having a second child—" Butch continued to mutter as he wandered off.

Stick bent down and picked up a handful of sand and filtered it through his fingers. It was soft but filled with pebbles and small shells. He walked down to the sea and squatted, rubbing his hands through the wet ground. He noted the texture was much coarser closer to the water. Standing up, he took in the shallows and dips of the beach. *A soft track with hollows the size of sinkholes. I may as well be driving in quicksand.* He looked back at Tommy, who was hastily putting the roof back on the convertible. The car was low to the ground—much lower than the Monterey—which meant the sand would pile up underneath. *I may have gotten myself in too deep this time,* Stick thought, then smiled at the irony. He did love a good challenge. *Think. Soft, sinking dirt filled with tiny rocks. How the hell do I drive on that? I'd be better off with a sled . . . That's it!*

Stick approached Tommy just as he was clicking the last roof clasp back into place.

"Deflate the tires," he said.

"What? Are you nuts?"

"Not all the way," Stick said. "Just real low, like twelve or fifteen PSI."

"Okay, but I think you're losing it."

Maybe. I'm not a hundred percent sure this will work, but I can't let him know that.

Butch walked up, taking deep breaths. "No way I'm talking you out of this one, huh?"

"Nope. I've got a plan."

Butch sighed. "Can't wait to hear this one."

"I got Tommy taking the tires down to twelve or so. Spreads the circumference so the tire—"

"Rides more on top of the sand," Butch finished his sentence. "Brilliant. A full tire will just sink right in."

Stick cocked his head to the side and spread his arms, feeling confident.

"Ready, redneck?" Jimmy asked from behind him.

Stick scoffed. "Ready, but we never identified the prize."

"Winner gets Dixie braggin' rights, and loser has to shave the winner's car number in the side of his hair."

"Fine. But those stakes aren't good enough for me. Are you doubting yourself, Jim boy? What about loser has to pay for winner's car damages and new engine upgrade for their race car."

"Deal," Jimmy said, and they both climbed in their cars.

"Stick, we ain't got enough money to pay for all that!" Butch said out of Jimmy's earshot.

"That's why I better win," Stick said, grinning.

A blonde in the smallest pair of shorts Stick had ever seen stood on top of a pickup truck and blew a whistle. Stick tapped the gas pedal carefully, unsure how the car would react. He trudged forward, tires gliding across the sand. Jimmy had taken off quicker and left Stick in a sandstorm that piled up like cumulus clouds around the car, impairing his vision. *All I gotta do is drive straight. No sharp movements, otherwise it'll be like applying the brakes, and I'll flip.*

Stick pressed on the gas a little more and gave the car more throttle. *That's it.* The ride got smoother. Stick saw taillights in front, a beacon in the storm. The dust cleared as Jimmy's Monterey stalled, tires spinning but going nowhere. *This is the one place speed is not an advantage, my friend.*

He came up right beside Jimmy, who was aggressively pressing the gas pedal and madly hitting the steering wheel. *Just digging your sea grave.* Stick backed off the gas a smidgen to plow through dips in the dunes. The finish line was just yards ahead, and there was a host of people waiting on the sidelines. Stick could see Jimmy coming out of the mound and gaining traction near the water. Stick was driving in wetter sand now, digging the tires in and slinging pebbles. But he was making up lost time. Stick pushed the throttle more as Jimmy sped up again, but this time Jimmy's right tire spun while the left one dug in. The Monterey tipped on its side into the water, just as Stick crossed the finish line.

He didn't know what made him do it, but Stick jumped out of his car and ran down the beach toward the car.

"Jimmy! Jimmy!" he yelled as water lapped around his ankles. "Somebody help!"

Stick wondered why Jimmy didn't get out of the car. The soft impact couldn't have knocked him unconscious. As he approached, a hand reached out of the passenger window.

Stick pulled the door open for Jimmy to spill out onto the beach.

"Congratulations, redneck," Jimmy said, spitting sand out of his mouth. "I have never seen someone win a race driving so slow."

"It's not always the speed, boy; it's the skill," Stick said, as he offered him a hand.

"You was comin' to save me? Why?"

"'Cause I can't see no man die without deserving it," Stick said.

He'd have drawn faster than a sheriff in the Wild West had Jimmy been toting a gun, but there wasn't any use in letting a man drown for no reason.

"I got new respect for you, Stick," Jimmy said as he stood up and began to walk away. "I'll be in touch on that new engine of yours."

Stick wondered if he had earned Jimmy's respect by beating him in a sandy, watery landscape as similar to a swamp as you'll get, or if Jimmy had softened over the years, a result of maturity and honest defeat. He figured it was the latter. Or embarrassment. Whatever it was, he'd take it.

"Ah, man, that was one crazy race. Let's go have a beer." He'd bury the hatchet once and for all. He was tired of making enemies.

Jimmy smiled an alligator smile, teeth pointed, gapped, or missing. "I thought all you mountain boys only drank moonshine."

Stick stopped and crossed his arms. "I don't know what you're talking about."

There was silence, then Stick let out a laugh. "Let's go get a drink, swamp man. I'll take hops over fermented peaches any day."

Chapter 8

LAWNDALE, NC
– 1960 –

Stick walked into the barn, past stacked bales of hay in search of the noise beyond the pig enclosure. He held his nose as he stepped in among the pink, speckled hogs snorting and grunting about. Just on the other side of the fence, his foot hit something hollow. He bent down and moved his hand along the ground, brushing away dirt and bits of straw until he uncovered a latch. *That's never been there before. What's the old man up to?* He pulled. The trap door opened to reveal wooden steps that extended deep into the earth. Stick peered down and saw a dim light, a flicker at the bottom of a well. The banging continued. *Boom, boom, clang. Boom, boom, clang.*

"Granddad?" Stick yelled, knowing no one could hear him with all that racket. "Granddad?" he yelled one more time before stepping onto the makeshift ladder and balancing himself. The smell of rotting earth mixed with a pungent acidity as Stick carefully made his way down.

"Who's that?" a voice asked, startled, and the noise stopped.

"Who do you think it is?" Stick answered as a lantern shone up through the hole, cutting the darkness.

When he reached the bottom rung, his granddad was there waiting for him. Stick looked around. "Good Lord."

The room was two hundred paces long and almost as wide. Pipes creaked and banged through an enormous copper cooker and snaked their way through a polished fermentation tank. A seven-hundred-gallon gas tank gave off a faint sulfur smell. Three large barrels stood in the corner along with a bucket, a table, and a few dozen mason jars.

"When did you do all this?" Stick asked, amazed at his granddad's ingenuity.

"At night mostly, while you was busy racin'. You ain't been out to the barn in a while. Good cover, puttin' it behind the pig sty, don't you think? Ain't no law man gonna trample through them hogs to find an underground room they don't know nuthin' about. And that ain't all. Take a look over here," Jake said as he opened a steel door on the left-hand side of the room.

He ushered Stick inside a smaller room packed with canned and pickled vegetables, jams and jellies. Jugs of water lined the walls, and in the middle of the room a table with chairs. In one corner, a mattress with blankets and in the other a hole in the ground, covered by two wooden planks: a makeshift toilet.

"What the—"

"President Kennedy said we should be making bomb shelters on account of them Soviets—you didn't see that? So . . ." He spread his hands open in a circle.

"You're ready."

"Bet your sweet ass," Jake said, walking back into the distillery room.

"Well, I'll hand it to you, this is about the most detailed underground operation I've ever seen."

Jake checked his pipes and lightly tapped on barrels. "Ah, this ain't nuthin'. Them big cities got all kinda underground operations. Speaking of that: I heard old Jimmy Hoffa was puttin' together a meeting to unionize professional stock car drivers. You can bet Bill France won't have any of that. He don't want to get involved in all that mess." Jake turned to face Stick. "Wait, you ain't going down there, are ya?"

"No. I ain't unionizing nuthin'. Hell, I don't even want to be part of a team, much less a whole union. I'm a loner, you know that."

"And it's served you well so far."

"Yeah, I guess so. Been doing pretty well, which is why I came to see you today." Stick paused, his lips forming a flat line.

"What's on your mind?"

Stick took a deep breath and waited. *This is it.*

"I saved enough money to get me an apartment in town, closer to the garage. And seeing as you seem to have this all under control here, I thought it'd be a good time for me to be movin' on."

He stopped and let his words settle in the air for a moment. Stick had been more nervous about telling his granddad he was moving out than any race he'd ever entered. He wasn't worried about Jake. His granddad was tough, the kind of man who could take care of himself, but Jake had devoted his whole life to raising Stick. Would he think his grandson was abandoning him for a little independence? Stick fiddled with his shirt cuff, torn between making his own way and staying close to the man to whom he owed everything. Jake picked up a bucket and moved it to a different corner of the room, no doubt wasting time to collect his thoughts.

"Well," he finally said, "I reckon you helped this old man enough. And I don't blame you for gettin' a place of your own. Makes it a whole lot easier on you too. You don't have to be sneaking them girls in all hours of the night."

Stick laughed, glad Jake had finally accepted his guilt-laden decision. "Thanks, Granddad."

He knew kids left their childhood homes all the time. It was only natural. But his relationship with Jake was different, and that made this so much harder.

"Just promise me you'll visit every now and again."

How could Jake ask such a question? Did his granddad not know how much he loved him?

"Well, of course. I'll be here almost every day. You think I can cook for myself? Hell, I can barely boil water. And you keep coming to the races. There's always a free ticket for you at the gate."

"I will. Hey, you want to do one last run for me?"

"Granddad, I—"

"It's for old Mrs. Thompson. She's got cancer, and my branch water's 'bout the only thing that takes her pain away. It's just two bottles."

"Well, in that case . . ." Stick was a sucker for a sad story. Mrs. Thompson had been his third-grade teacher, so he had a soft spot for her. His granddad handed him two ceramic jugs with cork tops. Stick put them in a velvet bag and headed to the ladder.

"Thanks, son," Jake said.

"Good thing I love you, old man," Stick said as he mounted the ladder, the bag around his shoulder.

"Love you too, shortie," Jake said with a laugh.

Stick packed the bags under the passenger seat of his personal truck and headed back through the woods to Mrs. Thompson's house. She lived down in Gaffney, near the old limestone quarry. As he crossed the railroad tracks, he saw a cop sitting in the parking lot of First Baptist Church. There was no service that day, so Stick was sure the cop was out to hit somebody with a speeding ticket. *Not today*, he thought as he paused at the tracks and looked both ways before crossing. He drove thirty-five past the church and made a right onto Limestone Avenue. Just as he rounded the corner, the cop was on his tail. Knowing he hadn't done a thing, Stick kept driving until he got to a mailbox at the end of the lane. He pulled over and sat in his truck as the police officer stopped behind him.

"Whatcha doin', son?" the cop asked as he walked up to the driver's side.

Stick wondered why all policemen called him "son," since he was clearly the same age as most of them.

"Visitin' an old friend," he answered.

"Really? Mrs. Thompson's your friend? She's a whole different generation, don't ya think?"

The cop had beady eyes and pursed lips.

"She was my third-grade teacher, and she ain't feeling so well. So, I brought her a gift."

"Oh, and what is that?" he asked with arrogant suspicion.

Stick reached under his seat and brought out a jar of strawberry jam and a crusty bag of bread.

"I was warned about you, so I'm gonna take a look around your vehicle."

Stick had been careless on this run, and he knew it. The bottles weren't well hidden, placed under the seat, just waiting to be found. He slid his hand right onto the cushion to feel the gun handle but knew this wasn't his best course of action.

"Sure, Officer, but what do you think I'm hidin' in this old pickup truck?"

"I've heard the stories. You gonna make a run for it?" he asked as he stepped back from the truck.

He wants me to flee so he can give chase. He figures he can catch me in this old clunker and brag about how he's the only lawman to ever bring in Stick Elliott.

Stick looked back at the police car: a Ford, probably with a good engine. If he were to get away from this one, he'd have to do some pretty smart driving, and with a bed full of old car parts, it wouldn't be the easiest task.

"Naw, I got nuthin' to run from. I'm just deliverin' jam."

The policeman's expression shifted from one of wide-eyed wonder to disappointment. He probably didn't get much excitement in a small town, writing a few tickets every now and then or saving the occasional cat from a tree. *This guy needs a good story he can tell his friends.*

"You know," Stick lied, "Vincent—I see that on your name tag—after I deliver this package, I was going down to the track for a few laps. It's always good to have coverage in case there's trouble."

"What kinda trouble?" Vincent asked, his eyes lighting up.

"Oh, the usual kind. Teenagers comin' down to get drunk and drag race."

"That's illegal."

"Don't I know. They trash the place up real good, broken bottles and all. And sometimes the city boys show up tryin' to start a fight." Stick was improvising, but it all seemed plausible for a racetrack in the middle of nowhere.

Vincent was eating it up. "Well, I better head down there with you. Especially since"—he patted his holster—"I got the authority to take care of things, if you know what I mean."

"Oh, I do. Give me a few minutes to make a delivery to Mrs. Thompson, and we'll be on our way."

The policeman nodded. Stick headed down the driveway, dropped the bags in the flowerpot by the front door, rang the doorbell, and left.

Driving to the track, Stick saw a split road up ahead: one side dirt that continued deep into the forest, the other paved toward town. He slowed at the stop sign, glanced at the police car behind him, then with a rumble of the engine, swung left toward the trees. *He wants a chase, I'll give him a chase. I'm feeling a little rowdy after all.*

The truck swayed and grunted with the extra exertion, and Stick could feel every bump jolt up his spine. Vincent was caught off guard and fishtailed through the turn. Stick made a quick right, then another left that took them deeper into the woods. He could see the Ford about twelve paces behind him, no sirens. *He's enjoying this. And so am I. It's been a while.*

Stick bounced around inside the truck, banging up against the door, knees against the dash. The truck bed seemed to have an identity all its own, leaning in the opposite direction anytime he took a curve, scraping the brush as he funneled his way through the dense forest. For the hell of it, he off-roaded by the creek, splashing through a foot of water as the police car hovered at its edge. *Oh, he's done. Chickenshit.* He could see Vincent outside his car, waving his arms around and whooping up a storm. Just then, Stick's back wheel slipped on river stone, causing the front end to crash right into a beaver dam. Branches flew everywhere, but he corrected his steering and managed to get the truck up the hill. Weaving in and out of trees, he couldn't help but think how easy this would be in the race car.

The snapping of twigs, the sliding of leaves on the forest floor, the scampering of scared animals, the crisp click of crickets. And among it all, the hum of the engine like a consistent drumbeat. The forest was his song, Stick the virtuoso. This is where he learned to drive, where he thrived.

He slowed as he approached the highway, staring at the gray stretch, and thought it looked like a road to death: hard, cracked, and permanent. The brown and red of nature's racetrack, however, was alive with color, texture, personality; dusty and harsh at times, sloshy and unforgiving at others, it had schooled him in the art of driving. As he eased out, Stick knew the paved roads may take him to the places he needed to go, but it was the dirt roads that would take him all the places he wanted to go.

Chapter 9

SPARTANBURG, SC
– 1961 –

A deer grazed in the only patch of grass that grew outside the circle at Piedmont Interstate Fairgrounds. Its sinewy neck elongated as its ears perked up to the noise on the track.

"Shoo! Shoo!" A woman wearing a crown yelled, her hands waving in the air.

"What is she doing?" Tommy asked.

"I guess she's making sure them boys over there don't get no ideas about shootin' that deer," Stick said, cutting his eyes over to a group of drivers where one had already taken his rifle out of the trunk.

The beauty queen walked stiffly past the drivers, who stared at her ass. She had a smile on her lips, the kind that was a bit unsure, but faking it well. She was pretty in an overdone way: candy-apple-red lipstick, caked-on mascara, and big curled hair. She paid no mind to the men as they whistled and grunted, but as she passed by Stick, who wasn't really paying her much attention other than glancing in her general direction, she batted her lashes as her smile demurred. He wiped his hands on a fresh cloth.

"Ma'am," he said, with a tip of his cowboy hat.

"How do you do that?" Tommy asked.

Stick didn't have to ask what he meant. Every woman in town threw herself at Stick, to the point where he was almost getting bored of it—almost.

"It's probably the car," Stick said, his attempt at humility.

"I don't think—"

"Speaking of—whose sky-blue Chevrolet is that parked all by itself on the other side of the track? Near the cotton field."

"That," Tommy said, walking over to Stick, "is a new driver. Some boy from Virginia."

"Why's he parked all the way over there? He don't know the pits are on this side?"

"They won't let him over here."

"Why not?"

"'Cause he's Black," Butch said, coming up behind Stick.

Stick paused a second. South Carolina was at the heart of the segregation fight. Racing was as White a sport as any, and certainly everybody at the race was in favor of Jim Crow. *This guy has guts*, he thought. *I like him already.*

"What's his name?" Stick asked.

Tommy shrugged.

"Don't know," said Butch, as if ashamed.

"Well, we better find out," Stick said. "Let's go, boys."

The crew all looked at one another.

"I said, let's go," Stick said, more forcefully this time.

The other drivers stared as Stick's crew walked across the track to the blue #34 Chevrolet. The driver was working on his engine, half his body leaned into the front as he poured oil from a canister. He stood up abruptly when he saw them and almost hit his head.

"I ain't—" he began.

"You a new driver?" Stick asked.

"Yes, sir."

He was average height, with skin that looked like he'd baked too long in the sun, curly, black hair that was receding at the temples, and a downturned V-shaped mustache.

"What's your name?"

"Willie Southers, sir."

Stick put his hand out. "Nice to meet ya, Willie. I'm Stick Elliott. And you can drop the sir; I'm younger than you."

Willie shook Stick's hand hardily. "I know who you are."

"You from Virginia?"

"Round about, but done some work in Greensboro and Winston Salem, too," Willie said, then cleared his throat. "Drove a taxi."

"Why'd you drive that far?" Stick asked, then a smile crept across his lips. "Oh," he said.

Finn murmured, "What?" and Tommy jabbed him with his elbow.

Willie was a bootlegger, and from the sounds of it, a pretty good one, too, considering the size of his territory. *And he drove all the way up from Virginia to race in hostile territory. Hell, this man has some fight in him.*

"I knew I'd heard your name somewhere. You been cashin' some checks in the Dixie Circuit," Stick said.

"Barely."

"I don't race much in Virginia, but I've done plenty in North Carolina. Wonder why we haven't run into each other."

"We did, once: 1952 at Southland."

"In Raleigh?"

"Yeah, you was just getting started, but I could already tell you was gonna be one to beat."

"That so? Wonder why I don't remember you?"

"You were pretty cocky back then," Butch blurted out, then crossed his arms and rolled his lips in like he knew it was the wrong thing to say.

"I was," Stick said. "But still."

"I showed up right before the start of the race. That way there'd be no trouble. I kept my helmet on from the time I got there till I left. Racing gloves, too. And I placed dead last, so I got outta there pretty quickly."

"Well I'll be," Stick said. It was a downright shame this man had to go to such lengths to protect his identity in a sport he so clearly loved.

"Man, that's rough," Tommy mumbled.

"Excuse me?" Willie asked.

"I just—I was wondering—" Tommy stammered, "why do you do it if they don't want you here?" The question tumbled out of his mouth as if he would lose his nerve if he didn't say it quickly.

Willie stood tall. "They don't want me nowhere. I learned to drive out of necessity, but I fell in love with the sport. The power, the escape—it's the only thing I've ever had a passion for."

Stick smiled. He could relate. This guy was a true racer, not some punk with a discombobulated vehicle posing as one on the weekends.

"Where's your crew?"

"There," Willie said, pointing to a beat-up truck hidden in the woods.

"Race startin' soon. Why don't y'all come on over to the other side?"

Willie wrung his hands. "We're not welcome over there."

"You are now," Stick said. "Butch, hop on in the driver's seat of that truck."

"What you want me to do, Stick?" Butch asked, confused.

"I want you to drive that truck over and park it next to our station, so these boys can get Willie's car ready."

"But what if—"

Stick looked sternly at Butch. He patted his pocket and looked back at Tommy. Tommy didn't go anywhere without protection.

"Don't be a wuss. Willie ain't. He's got more balls than all you put together."

Stick liked people who didn't make excuses. Willie had all the excuse in the world to give up, but he didn't. He showed up, put in the work. Nose to the grindstone, as Jake would say.

"And what are you gonna—" Butch started.

"I'm gonna ride shotgun with Willie here," Stick said, looking over to Willie. "If that's okay with you?"

Willie's stunned face looked unsure. "All right then," Willie said, and they climbed into the car and headed over to Stick's station just as the announcer's race warning blasted through the loudspeaker.

"Line up in twenty minutes!"

As Willie and his crew got out and began to check his car, a couple of redneck boys sauntered over with wrenches in their hands. "Go on back to the cotton field!" one of them yelled, then started taunting Willie until Stick walked over holding a lug bar.

"Guess his stick's bigger'n yours," Tommy said, taunting them right back.

The rednecks fumed, swearing from clenched teeth as they held their weapons in the air. Stick laughed and revealed his gun. "Don't come over here with those pitiful chunks of metal."

They 'bout near ran back to their sections.

"You don't have to do all this," Willie said. "You really gonna piss 'em off."

"I piss 'em off every time I pull up to the track anyhow. Ain't no different than any other day."

"Line up!" the loudspeaker rang.

"Willie, this is where the kindness stops. From here on out, I have one goal: to win this race. That may mean takin' you out."

Willie laughed. "May the best man win," he said as they crawled into their cars.

Right at the start, Stick could see these drivers were out for blood, particularly Willie Southers's blood. They slammed him into the wall on the first lap and ganged up on him in every lap after that. Stick was running up front the whole time, but he could see the commotion behind him. Part of him wanted to drop back a bit, spin out one or two of those aggressive assholes to teach them a lesson, but the competitor in him didn't want to lose time. Plus, he figured a proud man like Willie wouldn't want some big ol' White boy trying to be his savior. *He can take care of himself.*

Willie drove a hell of a race, and when the dust settled and Stick cruised through first place, he could see Willie giving it all he had to pull past the last guy in the field. Stick gave his fist a little pump as Willie crossed the finish line fourteenth in a field of eighteen. *He beat those sons of bitches. A few of them, anyway.*

Stick was happy to rack up another win, but this time the victory was bittersweet. His blood boiled as he thought about the other drivers ganging up on Willie. Would the result have been different had Willie had a chance to drive without having to fend off attacks? *How I'd love to go beat the daylights out of every one of those drivers who pushed Willie around.* Stick rolled his right fist into the palm of his other hand.

Cameras surrounded Stick just then, and he climbed out of the car. A beauty queen, with freshly applied lipstick, waited atop a platform, holding a bouquet of red roses and a large golden trophy. Stick made his way up to the winner's circle, pausing only to answer yes or no questions from the press. When he got to the top of the platform, the girl took his arm and pulled him to the center. It was customary that the winner receive a photo and a kiss. But just as she was puckering up, Stick glanced down the track to see Willie and his crew hurriedly packing their things as a group of angry drivers yelled obscenities.

"Excuse me," Stick said and, taking two steps at a time, descended the platform.

He marched steadfastly over to Willie, who wasn't reacting at all to the bitter racism surrounding him. He couldn't believe the inner fortitude of this guy.

"Hey!" Stick yelled when he got within earshot.

Everybody turned.

"Hey, Willie! You didn't say goodbye, man."

Willie wrinkled up his forehead, sweat beading up in the fold and running down his sideburns.

Stick reached out and side hugged Willie. "Not saying goodbye just 'cause you didn't win, huh? Just kiddin'. You drove good tonight. I hope to see you at more events. Racin's lucky to have you."

"Thanks, Stick."

"Now get on outta here. I gotta a beauty queen to kiss," Stick said with a wink.

Willie packed up his things.

"Come on down anytime. We'll have a beer. Or I'll just kick your ass on the track again."

Willie nodded and drove off. Stick looked at his crew. "Let's go, boys," he said.

"You ain't gonna go get your trophy?" Butch asked.

"They'll send it to me."

"What about that beauty queen?" Finn asked.

"There'll be another one next race."

"Then can I go kiss her for you?" Tommy asked.

"Be my guest. I'm too bothered by all this hubbub. I'm going to see my granddad."

Stick had seen racism, but never had he seen it so virile. *It ain't right*, he thought. *Bet none of them dipshits thought twice about takin' spirits from Willie when their cellars were unstocked.* They created him, fueled his passion for speed. Now they needed to let him race.

Chapter 10

GAFFNEY, SC
– 1963 –

All the important people in Stick's life were at the garage that day, doing nothing, just sitting around shooting the shit. Finn shined the hood of the Chevy, concentrating on a dull spot near the front fender. Tommy tightened lug nuts on the tires. Jake sipped burgundy Cheerwine from a glass bottle as he flipped through a motor magazine. Butch stuffed his face with a pineapple mayonnaise sandwich as he focused on the television set plugged into the floor socket.

"How do you even see that?" Stick asked, adjusting the foil-covered antennas on top. "There."

The grainy black-and-white picture was visible now, with only one line running through the center of the screen.

"Why are you watching that junk anyway?" Jake asked.

"*As The World Turns* is not junk," Butch said, knowing full well how ridiculous it sounded. "My wife watches it while she dusts. She got me addicted. I don't know how to stop," he said, as if admitting he had a drinking problem.

The whole garage erupted with laughter. Stick glanced out the window and noticed a man dressed in pinstripe slacks and a white button-down emerging from a black Buick Riveria. Stick walked out the door to greet him.

"Willie," he said, shaking the man's hand. "What brings you round?"

"Thought I'd look you up. Grab that beer."

"Well, it's a long time coming. But better late than never. Good to see you. Come on in." He led Willie into the garage.

"So, this is where it all happens?"

"Naw, this is where we fix what happened," Tommy said. "Stick's always makin' a mess of the car."

Willie walked around and let out a whistle. "She's a beauty. Shined up real good and everything. You even racin' this thing or just cruisin' round the circle like a parade?"

"I'm racin' all right. Could kick your ass all the way back to Virginia with this beauty," Stick said, a sly grin creeping across his face.

"Care for a wager?"

Butch stood up abruptly. "Stick, don't even—we just got her tuned up."

But Stick couldn't back down from a challenge. "Cherokee?"

"Sure," Willie said.

"But you're in that Buick."

"It's the man, not the car, right?"

Stick had never met someone he agreed with more. All the boys down at the track showed up in the dumbest cars he'd ever seen—big ol' engines and all—but didn't have a lick of real driving experience; just pressed the pedal and assumed the car would do the rest. Willie understood.

"All right then. Let's go see what you've got."

Stick was curious what kind of driver Willie really was, since the last time he saw him, he could barely drive on account of the pressure around him.

They drove to Cherokee Speedway, where Stick cut the lock with a pair of pliers. Once inside, they lined up on the start line.

"Ready?" Stick asked as he pulled his helmet on. "Ten laps. First back here wins."

Willie nodded, and Stick held up three fingers, then two, then one. He pointed and simultaneously pressed the gas pedal. He easily cruised the track on the first lap, Willie a full car length behind.

I knew that Buick couldn't hold up, no matter how good he is.

On the third lap, however, Willie hung to the inside within a foot of Stick's bumper. *Ah, he took a page out of my playbook, sitting back, studying my style.* Just then, Willie maneuvered from the inside lane to position himself right beside Stick. His arm hung casually out the side of the Buick, but his eyes were focused ahead.

He shot around Stick so fast Stick wondered if he was driving the Batmobile, complete with turbo boosters. Stick moved to the right to avoid a collision with the Buick that was now within inches of his front fender. *Son of a gun, how did he . . .*

Stick tapped Willie lightly, but he wouldn't budge. *This man is used to bullies of the worst kind. These tactics won't work on him.*

The fourth, fifth, and sixth laps went the same: Stick hot on Willie's tail, but with no way around. He tried maneuvering to the right, but Willie blocked him every time. On the seventh lap, Stick noticed Willie would drift right on the straightaways, probably anticipating Stick's eagerness to pass, which gave him mere seconds when the left side was clear a few feet at most. Just enough for Stick to squeeze through, albeit partway in the grass pit, where scattered trenches lurked from the slow sink of past rainfall. *If I time it right . . .*

Just as Willie began his drift, Stick gunned it and slid to the left. Metal on metal screeched as the Buick's thin paint coat peeled like unraveled ribbon. Stick hit a ditch a few inches deep, and his left front tire tilted, causing the car to lift off the track, diagonally parallel to Willie's. In wide-eyed surprise, Willie shifted left only slightly, only briefly, but enough for Stick's car to come bouncing back on the ground. They raced through the final laps neck and neck, not taking their eyes off the road. As they sped through the finish line, neither could tell who'd won. Stick came to a stop in front of the flag stand and immediately jumped out of the car, leaving it idle.

"Holy shit! That was some drivin'!"

Willie crawled out of the car and removed his helmet. "Yeah, man. That was exciting. Finally, some real racing. I feel like I'm always playing defense, not enough pure driving."

"And ain't it a shame, 'cause you're one of the best I've seen. Pure skill. I was surprised on that outer lane maneuver."

"I know. I've watched you. You favor the right side. If a driver wants to pass you, it's about timing and precision, not brute force."

Willie was right. There wasn't a damn racer out there who could bully Stick off the track, but with the right timing and dynamic, they could get a leg up. Willie had revealed Stick's weakness. *And now I can correct it.*

Stick grinned like a fox who'd just found its way into the henhouse. "And you, my friend, are like a cat. You sneak up, then at the right moment, pounce."

He leaned in and raised his hands claw-like, causing Willie to jump. They both laughed, and Stick could tell Willie was a stand-up guy. He'd given advice that could very well give Stick an advantage in the next race. *That's because he's confident in his abilities*, Stick thought. *And he should be.* Stick could tell he and Willie would be rivals and friends.

"Make this a regular thing? We could learn from each other."

"Sure, under one condition."

"What's that?"

"You get me that beer you promised."

"Sure thing, Willie. Sure thing."

Stick had respect for Willie in a way that transcended his driving. He was the underdog, someone who had every reason to give up but refused. He fought to stay in a sport that didn't welcome him, and he did it with neither fists nor bold words, but a quiet reverie of intelligence, patience, and pure unadulterated skill.

Jacksonville, FL

Stick reluctantly pulled into Speedway Park, on the west side of Jacksonville, and was immediately met with protestors. Not even a month after the assassination of President Kennedy, NASCAR had decided to hold the Grand National Series Race as a way for the country to get back to normal, but also because parts of the South needed mending. Stick thought it was a risky move, considering most of the White South had despised Kennedy's politics, particularly his progressive views on civil rights. Stick had tried to avoid any hostile situations by not racing anywhere down near Alabama or Texas until things settled down. But this was a points race, and Stick wasn't about to miss it.

Right away, Stick noticed the signs. Some were catchy, like the one that read "Flags are at half mast, but we country boys gotta go fast," held up by a grown man clad in an American flag onesie and red cowboy hat. Then there were the virulent, foul-mouthed rednecks, dressed in ragged, sleeveless T-shirts, waving the Confederate flag and carrying signs filled with nothing but hate.

"Shoulda driven faster."

"Guess what happens to Yankees when they drive slow in the South?"

"NASCAR is a white sport."

And plenty of "No blacks allowed" signs dotted the crowd, held by men and women alike. Stick thought of Willie and prayed he wasn't racing today.

He was glad he'd decided to drive the pickup instead of Jake's old Ford. Nothing said *I'm from the South* more than a pickup truck. Not that he would be intimidated; he just needed to get through the gate without too much fanfare. He'd brought along his Colt, as was customary when he raced local dirt races. Those crowds got rowdy, and there were still a few bootleggers out there who didn't take well to Stick constantly winning. In NASCAR, the weapons weren't usually needed, but today was a different story. Stick pulled into his designated garage and noticed a blue race car already there.

"What the—" he began, as he slammed the truck door shut. "Who—"

Tommy came running over and threw his body in front of Stick.

"It's Willie," Tommy said quickly.

Stick stopped, a look of curiosity across his face.

"Butch thought it would be a good idea. They had him all the way at the end there." Tommy pointed across the track. "Everybody woulda known what, um, who he was. Butch figured we could protect him here, at least until the race starts." Tommy said Butch's name like he was a mob boss no one should cross.

"Where is he?" Stick asked.

"Butch? He's over—"

"No, Willie."

"Oh, he's in the box," Tommy said, referring to the square truck they'd turned into a base of sorts, complete with a cooler, spare parts, and a bed for long nights on the road.

Stick grimaced but knew Butch had been right. They had to take attention away from Willie till the race started. Then he was on his own.

Stick slung open the back doors of the box without knocking—it was his, after all—to find Willie Southers rifling through the cupboard of shelves they'd installed.

"What in tarnation are you doing?"

Willie whipped around, a Coca-Cola in his hand. "Looking for this," he said, as if it was only natural for him to be in a competitor's truck.

Stick beamed at him. "Help yourself to anything," he said, taking Willie's hand. "Good to see you. I'm awful surprised you'd come down here."

"Got seven children. This here's a chance at some real money. I couldn't miss it."

"Seven, huh?" Stick shook his head. "That's a lot of mouths to feed."

Willie nodded, taking a sip of the soda.

"How'd you get in here? Surely you didn't go past all those protestors?"

"Only way in. Your boy Butch helped, though. We all sat in the back of the truck while he drove. Don't guess nobody recognizes my truck. Yet."

Stick blew a strong breath out. "Jesus, Willie, I'm sorry 'bout all this. You're a good man. You shouldn't have to deal with this bullshit."

"Ah, been dealing all my life," he said. "I don't even want to think about it. I just wanna race."

"All right, well, we need to get changed. How 'bout you take the space behind the curtain back there? I'll change here. Seeing your lucky underwear might ruin my night."

"What do you mean lucky underwear?"

"Oh God, Willie, you don't have a special pair for racin'? Hell, that's why you're havin' such a tough time getting the checkered flag." Stick chuckled.

Willie scrunched up his face in confusion.

"When I was little, I used to have these little metal cars, remember those?" Willie nodded. "Well, I kept them lined up on the windowsill, until one morning my mother comes through there with a feather duster and knocks the green one off, breaking the wheels. I tried to prop it back up on the window, but the damn thing would fall off in the middle of the night and scare the bejesus out of her. She came in one night and tripped over it, spraining her wrist. I threw that damn green car away and still won't go near that color on racin' day."

"Sounds crazy to me." Willie shrugged and turned toward the faded blue curtain.

"Just make sure you put that helmet on before you leave the rig," Stick paused. "Not for my sake, mind you. For your own."

"Yeah, I know," Willie said quietly as he walked back.

Willie exited first, while Stick stuck around to have a chew of his lucky orange candy. Today's race was sure to be a doozy. Richard Petty had been dominating the sport and was sure to make a win difficult with his fancy car, paid for by all the endorsements he'd so aptly earned. Banky Bledsoe was a cat from down in Louisiana with a smooth style that most drivers didn't give much credence to, until he crept up on you at the last minute. There was Nate Livingstone in a Ford, Nile Castillon in a Chrysler, and

Possum Jumper (yes, his real name) in his privately owned Pontiac. The field was a mixture of racing's top teams, sponsored by fat, rich guys with endless wallets, starving self-made guys like Possum and Stick, and then there was Willie, the dark horse of the entire race.

The race began with a bang as Possum's car backfired, blowing so much smoke in Wayston Hallock's eyes he had to pull over and rinse them out with a carton of milk. Petty took off at an almost unnatural speed, leaving everyone else at least two car lengths behind. Stick was running in fourth place but was having a hard time getting past Stockton Weatherly, who must've installed a new engine in his #92 Ford because he was usually at the back of the pack. About halfway through the race, Stick had to pit due to a wobbly tire on the left front.

"Goddamn it! I'm going to lose time!"

Some drivers liked to pit to refresh tires and fuel; it was a kind of insurance for the rest of the race. But not Stick. He didn't need reassurances. He just wanted to drive. The tire was shaking quite a bit, though, so he knew it would pop off any minute, and he'd be in a heap of trouble.

He pulled into the pit mad as a hornet. Tommy rushed to the ground with a jack while Finn inspected the tire.

"Stick, press on the brakes for me," Butch said, watching the front end.

"It ain't no warped rotor or locked-up caliper. I don't use brakes," Stick said, leaning his head out the window.

Butch didn't answer, so Stick rolled his eyes and pressed on the brakes.

"Found it!" Tommy yelled. "It's a bulge near the side tread. I gotta remove the whole sticker."

"Fuck!" Stick could feel his face turning red as he spewed expletives. "Goddamn it, I'm losing time. Hurry the hell up!"

The crew rolled out a new tire, and Tommy bolted it into place. The drilling sound of lug nuts made Stick's knees bop up and down with nervous energy. He banged his hand on the side of the car. Twenty-four seconds . . . twenty-five seconds . . . an eternity.

"If y'all don't get me outta here in five seconds—"

"Done!" Tommy yelled and jumped out of the way.

Stick didn't wait to test the new tire. He took off around the second turn, making up lost time with the slip of a wrist, a shove of the throttle. But he was distracted. In his rearview mirror, he could see Willie getting slammed around again. Willie was gaining, though, pushing through a tight pack and positioning himself just behind Stick. Stick smiled, thinking Willie would push him to victory, but with twenty-six laps to go, Willie sprinted around Stick, almost knocking him against the wall. He passed Livingstone, Castillon, and Bledsoe to run neck and neck with Petty. *Son of a gun.*

On the next lap, Willie passed Petty and never let up, cruising past the finish line, but Stick never saw the checkered flag drop. *Did they lose it?* A second later, Bledsoe crossed the finish line to a checkered flag.

Stick raced past Butch, who was gesticulating at the sidelines, and parked his car, still running, by the trophy stand. A brunette beauty waited patiently among the chaos of yells, laughs, and taunts that ensued.

Stick saw Willie standing quietly at the bottom of the platform. Bledsoe walked up to him, whispered something in his ear, and proceeded to the winner's circle. He kissed the beauty queen and raised his fist to the sky.

"Willie, what's going on?" Stick asked when he finally made his way through the crowd.

"They're sayin' Bledsoe won."

"He didn't, though. I saw it with my own eyes."

"You and everybody else."

"What the—I'm gonna go up there and—"

"No," Willie said. "Leave 'em be. I know I won."

"How can you be so calm? They're cheatin' you, Willie!"

Stick looked around at the other drivers, some with tools in their hands, ready to pounce. Stick pulled the gun from his suit, making sure the officials didn't see it. He waved it low. "Got something to say?" he asked loudly, and they all retreated.

"Ah, Stick, don't go gettin' in trouble. They'll work this out," Willie said.

"The hell they will. You know damn well what's goin' on here."

"Course I do."

As the fans began to leave, Stick saw NASCAR officials, owners, and drivers huddled by a table, reviewing timecards.

"See, they'll make this right," Stick said to Willie, who had removed his helmet by this point. No use in hiding anymore.

"We'll see," was all he said.

Stick and Willie sat there, on the bottom step of the platform, while the officials took their sweet Southern time reviewing the timecards. After a two-hour huddle, a big yeti-looking man with white hair and a round chin stepped up to the microphone. The fans were gone, as were the press, though most of the drivers had stuck around to find out who won.

"Looks like a mistake was made," he said as he cleared his throat. "After reviewing the scorecards, it has been determined the winner of today's race is Willie Southers. It appears Mr. Southers came in a full lap ahead of the rest of the pack. Mr. Bledsoe will take second place."

Bledsoe stormed to his RV and slammed the door. The remaining drivers and owners began to stir, shouting protests and insults at the official. He responded by putting his hand up. "That is the result of the race, and I encourage you all to accept it. Mr. Southers will be presented with the trophy at a ceremony to be determined at a later date. No further comments."

He stepped away from the microphone, and four armed policemen escorted him to a four-door black Ford that quickly sped away.

"Well, I'll be damned. They did the right thing. Waited too long, but did the right thing," Stick said. "You want to go out and celebrate, Willie?"

Willie sighed and shook his head. "Naw, I don't think that's a good idea, Stick, though I appreciate the gesture."

As Stick and Willie made their way back to their shared garage, they noticed the chaos had subsided. Drivers and owners who had been shouting were now quiet. Officials who had argued just moments before stood aside. A hush of disbelief—or was it respect?—settled on the crowd.

"Willie, you see this?" Stick whispered.

Willie nodded. "They're probably planning their revenge," he said, half-jokingly.

"I don't think so," Stick said, and he meant it. This felt different. "There are only two times I seen the world stand still. The death of President Kennedy. And tonight."

Willie looked at him quizzically as if to say, *You're comparing my win to the assassination of a president?*

"With all due respect, this ain't nuthin' like that. President Kennedy was a great man. A man who not only saw past color, but decided to do something about it, to take on a whole nation if he had to. I ain't got guts like that. I just drove a car faster than anybody else. That's all I've ever wanted to do."

"What you did was more than just drive a car. Hell, you had everything thrown at you tonight, and you made history as the first African American to win a NASCAR race in the fucking South. You taught them other drivers you're just as good as they are. That no amount of money, class, or privilege can stop you. I admire you, Willie, I do."

A tear fell from Willie's eye. "Thank you, Stick."

"No, thank you, my friend. Today, you reminded us all where we came from. Black, White—it don't matter. We all started runnin' moonshine in this cluster of Southern states. And what tied us together is we were doing something others told us we couldn't."

As Stick and Willie neared the pit, he could see the two crews drinking and laughing, shaking hands and slapping one another's backs.

"See," Willie said. "The world ain't standing still. In fact, it's movin' in just the right direction."

Chapter 11

BYRON, GA
– 1967 –

A sweet smell filled the air as Stick rolled onto the half-mile paved track of Middle Georgia Speedway.

"She don't look like much," Stick said to his granddad, who rode shotgun. "How'd you get Lamar to let us in here after hours? That's not something he normally does. I hear he's pretty tight with security on this place."

"Oh, I've got my ways. I wanted to give you a chance to at least take a look at this son of a gun before the Grand National Race in November. I heard Petty signed up, Robby Allister too."

"Tough competition for sure. And he won't let me take a few rounds?"

"Naw, said he'd be checking out the tire patterns 'n such. But we can walk it," Jake said, stepping out of his old Ford.

"Butch is gonna be so pissed we came without him," Stick said, closing the heavy door behind him.

"I know. He has good input, but Lamar was clear: you and me only."

They began their walk around the track, two towering figures, one with a slight curve in his back, a lean in his step. Stick didn't expect too many challenges with the track. It looked basic: oval, decent width. If he could avoid the retaining wall on the outside near the bleachers, it would be smooth sailing. Having opened the year prior, the track was in good shape. Stick didn't need to walk the whole thing but didn't want to tell his granddad that. He loved spending time with the old man and figured the more Jake moved around, the longer his ticker would last.

"You hear about the amateur races here?" Stick asked.

"No, what about 'em?"

"Seems they get groups coming up all the way from Miami for just a hundred-dollar purse. They must really like the roughness of the drivin' up here. Word is they come up so they can learn to be better drivers."

"Is that so?" Jake said, distracted by a swarm of flies near the far end of the track.

Stick had noticed the old man's mind drifting these days and could almost guarantee he was stuck in the past.

"Hey, remember when Mama chased that one fly all around the house?"

Jake let out a titter. "You remember that?"

Stick nodded. "She tried the broom, the big soup spoon, and every towel in the house."

"For hours." Jake chuckled. "Never did get that damn fly. It drove her—well, never mind."

Stick ran his foot along a seam in the track. "You think about her still?"

"Course. I wonder if I did the right thing, puttin' her in that place and all."

"You had no choice. You couldn't've taken care of her. You had to take care of me."

Jake stared past the ticket booth on turn three. They never talked about his mother much. Stick figured Jake shied away from the subject all these years to protect his grandson from a world of hurt. But now he realized it was because the memories were too painful to face.

"Granddad," Stick said, placing his hand on the curvature of Jake's upper back. "You did the right thing. She needed help—the kind only doctors could provide. And the way it ended . . . Well, no one could've predicted that."

Jake wiped a tear from his face.

"And look what a good job you did raising me," Stick added, stepping in front of the old man. "I mean, look at me. I'm a stud," he said, holding his arms out. "And I wouldn't be the driver I am today without you."

Jake placed his hands firmly on Stick's shoulders. "That's exactly what I'm afraid of."

"Listen, there's nuthin' to be afraid of. Sure, I chose a dangerous field of work, but I would've gotten there on my own anyway, to some adrenaline-pumping venture that coulda landed me in jail or worse. It's who I am. What you did was give me skill, and I'm damn good. I know it looks like I'm takin' unnecessary chances out there, but I'm not. Everything is calculated; all my moves have purpose. I'm in charge. I promise."

"You are good. All right," Jake said, and as he resigned to reality, the tension in his face released.

Stick clapped his hands once. "Enough of this mushy stuff. I got this track down. Ain't much to tackle. What do you say we get some beers?"

Jake didn't answer. He was too busy eyeing a big yeast truck that had pulled up and parked around the back of the concession stand.

"Well, that explains the flies," Stick said, and they both laughed, but Jake had a look in his eyes. It was one Stick had seen before.

"Yeah, uh, we better go," Jake said, suddenly in a hurry. "Want to grab a beer?"

Stick didn't mention he'd already asked this very question. "Sounds good," he said as they started to walk back.

"Know why your mama hated flies?" Jake asked as they climbed back in the pickup truck.

Nobody likes flies, Stick thought. *They're irritating.* "Same reason everybody else hates 'em?"

"They feed on rot," he said, his hand quivering on the door handle. "I think she knew her brain was deteriorating. And the flies—she thought they were there for her." He paused. "Maybe they were."

It was the first time Jake had opened up in that way, providing a glimpse into Viola that Stick had never known existed. It explained why sometimes his mother was normal and others, well, not so much. But Stick needed to lighten the mood, bring his granddad back to the present.

"Flies are also attracted to sweetness. I like to think it was that," he said, hoping this inadequate explanation would be enough to change the mood.

Jake smiled, understanding. "Maybe," he said, shaking his head as if coming out of a daze. "I got a better idea. I just made a batch of peach wine. How 'bout we go home, put on some music, and drink to your mother?"

"I can think of nuthin' I'd rather do," Stick said.

Gaffney, SC

Stick and Jake were feasting on sandwiches in the garage office when Butch came running in. Stick had been bringing Jake to the garage a lot lately. He figured if he involved him in even the most mundane tasks, he wouldn't spend so much time in the past.

Butch lifted the pin from the record player, and the piano sonata stopped. He waved a newspaper wildly in the air. "I take it you haven't seen this?" He threw the paper on the table, and it unfolded before them.

RAIDERS FIND STILL UNDER RACE BOOTH

Stick and Jake looked at each other. The flies.

Stick scanned the article, then read aloud. "Agents discovered a sophisticated moonshine operation at Middle Georgia Raceway hidden in an underground bunker next to turn three. A dummy ticket booth was disguised as a trapdoor, which led to an illegal distillery 17 feet underground. Capable of producing 200 gallons of moonshine every week, the still had an electric exhaust system, lighting, a 2,000-gallon cooker, a 1,200-gallon box fermenter, and 750-gallon gas fuel tank all in the space of a 125-foot tunnel just 4 feet wide. One federal agent said it was the most elaborate moonshine operation he'd come across. Agents were tipped off when the track's owner, Lamar Brown Jr., signed for 24 pounds of yeast just days before. Brown said he'd purchased the yeast to make bread for concessions."

"That'd be a whole lotta hot dogs. You could feed all of Byron and Atlanta with that much yeast," Jake said.

Stick continued reading. "Two sheriffs and federal agents discovered the still, then arrested the track's owner immediately. Agents plan to destroy the distillery with acetylene torches instead of dynamite so the track will not be damaged for the upcoming race."

"Well, that's good," Jake said. "It's a wonder nobody ever smelled those fumes. They can be strong."

Stick shot him a look. Butch most certainly knew about the business, but Stick and Jake had promised to never speak of it aloud.

"So I've heard," Jake added.

Butch sat down at the table. "You wouldn't smell it on account of the car fumes."

Stick put the paper down and took another bite of his sandwich. "Now makes sense why them Miami boys were drivin' all the way up here for races."

Butch scrunched up his face, confused.

"They were taking the moonshine back to the Sunshine State," Stick explained, wiping his face with a paper towel.

"Now why would you go transportin' so much hooch that far away?" Butch asked innocently.

Jake had been looking down, tearing pieces of bread from his sandwich.

"Greed," he said in a deeply serious tone.

"Or all them fumes gettin' to him, makin' him crazy in the head," Butch said.

Jake stuffed the remainder of his meal back into the brown paper bag, folded his napkin, and stood up. "Thanks for the lunch. I better be goin'."

Stick knew the bust must have made Jake nervous. "I'll walk you out," he said.

Jake opened the office door just as Finnegan was coming in.

"Did y'all see the news about Middle Georgia—"

"Not now, Finn," Butch said, and Finnegan stepped aside, allowing the Elliotts to exit.

"Granddad, don't worry," Stick said in the privacy of the parking lot. "Your operation is much smaller, much more discreet."

"Oh, I ain't worried 'bout the law findin' me. Seen my share of busts, and it's usually 'cause somebody got stupid or greedy."

"Well, what is it then? You seem bothered of late," Stick said. He knew something was on the old man's mind, and he had to find out what it was.

"I just worry 'bout you, that's all."

It wasn't like his granddad to worry, but it seemed to be all he was doing lately. "We've been over this. I'm a good—no, great—driver. Nuthin's gonna happen."

Jake's eyes glazed over, and he took a step toward Stick.

"It's not—look, I'm not worried about the racin'. I'm, it's just—do you know what was wrong with your mama? Why we had to put her away?"

Stick had never really asked those questions, mostly because he didn't want to know the answers. The way he had found her that night—as young as he was—it had scarred him. Viola's sweet, luminous face replaced by one Stick didn't recognize, a face distorted and confused. It had always been clear his granddad struggled with it, praying and asking the Lord to heal her brain. When she was gone, Jake turned his prayers to his grandson, whispering his name late into the night, though Stick never knew what those celestial wishes were for. Stick averted his eyes. "Mental illness. I don't need to know more."

Jake leaned against his black Ford. "She had schizophrenia. They said it was caused by a combination of genetics and bad parenting."

Stick's heart sank. He could see the old man was in a world of pain. He'd carried this burden around for years, and it had finally got the best of him. "So, you think you probably gave it to me, and since you raised both of us, I'll get it too?"

Jake nodded.

"Granddad, that's not how it works."

"What if you got that gene from me, and I raised you wrong, too? I didn't know what I was doing. I was distracted with the business, with your mother's treatment, with—I didn't know what I was doing. What if you bang your head too many times, and it triggers something?" His words were quick, shaky, desperate.

Stick steadied Jake's hands. "You were the best father anyone could hope for. What you did for me, I could never repay. You've got to let this go. Mama was sick. It was nobody's fault. Besides, you always said she was a bit of a strange child. She probably had that disease all along. You didn't cause it, and I don't have it. Unless you think I'm a bit strange too?" He attempted a laugh but could see Jake was not in the mood.

"She . . ." Jake pressed on his hands so tightly the knuckles cracked. "She talked to herself when she was little, but kids do that. She'd say she saw this and that, and I, well, sometimes she'd say she saw her mama. But that couldn't be. She never knew her mama. And she was a normal teenager—moody and all, but normal. Sometimes I'd have to give her a little 'shine to calm her down. Not a lot, just enough to make her settle a bit. The doc said it was okay. We'd always been given whiskey and honey for the cough, so what was the difference? But I can't help but think—did I miss the signs? Then when I—you—found her that day . . ."

Stick's mind returned to the cold, hard floor.

It was dusty that day, because Viola thought the dust would be good for her son, to build up his immunity. But all he did was sneeze. He'd gone into the living room to find a handkerchief and saw her there in the middle of that dirty floor. All the furniture had been pushed to one side of the room, blocking the singular window. She was curled under a white sheet, rocking back and forth. "Mama?" he'd said, but she hadn't answered. When he lifted the sheet, she was wild, a mad creature—red eyed, wearing only underwear. "Hurry," she said, "get under. The bad men will be here soon." She plucked at her matted hair and grabbed the sheet, covering Stick with it. He felt as if he would suffocate, so he ran from her, sneezing the whole way to the yard.

"You can still see it, can't you?" Jake's voice cut through, and Stick realized his eyes were shut, hands atop his head.

"Yeah, I—it's not the same. I'm not her." His heart was beating fast, so he took a deep breath and pinched his own arm. "We're here now, and you have to stop living in the past. I'm as strong and clear-minded as they come. Do you think if I had some sort of brain condition, I'd be able to drive the way I do? Plus, I got roll bars and a helmet. I ain't gonna get no brain injury. Would it make you feel better if I stuffed my helmet with toilet paper?"

Jake laughed.

"I love it, Granddad," Stick said. "I couldn't live without it even if you told me it would kill me. It courses through my veins just as surely as that moonshine does yours."

Jake let out a shush and looked around. "Ain't nuthin' better," he said.

He pulled Stick in and gave him a big hug, then put his hands in his pockets and began to walk.

"Where you goin'?" Stick asked.

"Walkin' to the General Store," Jake said as he turned away. "To buy up all the toilet paper."

"Grab me a soda while you're at it," Stick said, and the old man threw his hand up in affirmation.

The dirt kicked up, and Stick let out a sneeze. He looked up to the sky. "I ain't ready yet, Mama. Got a lot of livin' to do."

Charlotte, NC

Stick rounded the second turn at Charlotte Motor Speedway and cruised past the cameras on the straightaway. This time, as the white flag dropped, he didn't wave. He didn't celebrate, even though he was a good lap ahead of the others. The race had been too easy, as effortless as stepping one foot in front of the other.

He pulled on the strap of the ill-fitting helmet. The sun glinted in his eyes, so he adjusted his goggles, barely making out the checkered flag. The crowd stood all at once and threw their hands in the air, right on cue for the big finish. He glanced in his mirror briefly, then—

He slammed into the wall, making sure the side of the white-and-red Chevrolet made just enough contact that sparks would fly. He turned his steering wheel, crossing his right hand over the left as he commanded the car to do his bidding. With the impetuousness of a wrecking ball and the precision of a surgeon's scalpel, he coaxed the Chevy to revolve into the interior circle, lifting the back right tire off the ground as dirt and chunks of green grass went flying in all directions. Stick had sabotaged the race. On purpose.

He stopped after a few dramatic spins and sat awaiting further instruction—something he wasn't used to. *I'm the one who usually gives the orders*, he thought as he kneaded his hands anxiously around the steering wheel.

"Cut!" a voice boomed through the loudspeaker, and Stick broke pose, removing his helmet.

MGM had contacted Stick a couple months earlier to stunt-drive in a new movie called *Speedway* they were working on, starring Elvis. The Hollywood hoopla hadn't impressed him much, but Stick figured it was a good way to make some extra cash. And MGM paid well.

A gray-haired man in rose-colored glasses jogged across the track with a clipboard.

"Good job, Stick!" he yelled as Stick crawled out of the car and walked around to the other side.

"It's a damn shame, Norm," Stick said to the director.

"What is?" Norm said, removing his headphones.

"Wrecking these cars on purpose."

"I thought you'd like that."

"Me too. Hell, I wreck more cars than most, but it's for a win. This . . ."—he pointed at the scraped and dented side—"This is . . ." Stick shook his head, discouraged at the sight of the car.

"That's Hollywood," Norm said. "Hey, we're both in the entertainment business."

Stick got the point the director was trying to make, but he knew it was a whole lot different. What Stick was doing was real, a tangible outcome based on years of grit and survival. Hollywood was fake, all staged to re-create what real people were already living.

"What do you do with these cars anyhow?" Stick asked, rubbing the hood of the car.

"We send them to the junkyard."

"You could rework 'em, use 'em again," Stick said, surprised a huge movie studio would give up on a good vehicle so easily. "The way I hit the wall, the insides ain't damaged. Just needs a little body work."

"We got lots of money, Stick. We don't need to salvage these old beaters."

Stick thought about asking for the beat-up cars. He could sell them, whole or otherwise, for a decent amount. He certainly needed the money for car repairs, parts, garage costs, his crew. Hell, he hadn't bought a new fire suit in he didn't know how long, and the one he had was turning a sickly shade of yellow no matter how much he bleached it. But Stick figured big companies like MGM wrote all that stuff off on their taxes. He pressed his lips closed. Stick didn't want to seem desperate. He had an image to uphold.

The director's headset beeped, and he put it back on, adjusting the mouthpiece. He tapped the side. "Yes?"

Norm listened intently for a moment, his eyebrows sunk in the middle, creating a series of worry lines above his nose.

"I don't know if that's such a good—" He put one hand up to his face and blew out a waft of air. "All right then. Can't argue with that, I suppose. Send him down." Norm removed the headset again and let it drop to cradle his neck.

"Elvis wants a few laps around the track," he said in an exasperated voice.

Stick leaned back on the hood. "*The* Elvis?"

"Yes. I don't think it's a good idea, him being who he is and all, but he insisted on you taking him around."

Stick was stunned. As much as he wanted to play it cool, he just couldn't believe the biggest celebrity on the planet wanted to take a ride with him. He hadn't even seen Elvis, Nancy Sinatra, or any of the actors during stunt filming, as the studio took precautions to protect them.

"I have to say yes, don't I?" Stick asked. He'd never really driven with someone else in the car before, except for his granddad.

"They don't call him the King for nothing."

A blue van shuttled down the track and parked right by the car. Out stepped the god that every woman dreamed about. Stick had seen his fair share of uncontrollable fanfare, but what Elvis evoked was sheer hysteria. As he walked toward the car, a smile creased his lips, lifting his cheeks without narrowing his eyes. He was tall, slim, a few inches shorter than Stick, and his jet-black hair was the color of shoe polish, a tendril falling along the top of his oversized sunglasses. Elvis extended his hand. "I hear you're a legend around these parts," he said in a deep baritone.

Stick found himself humbled. "I just drive," he said, remembering Willie's words.

"The South needs heroes," Elvis said, removing his glasses to reveal long eyelashes.

Stick laughed. "Man, you're even more handsome than I am."

Stick had rugged good looks, but Elvis was more refined, beautifully crafted, as if God himself had reached down and chiseled him.

"I owe all that to my mama," Elvis said with reverence. "Now, can we take a ride?"

"Hell yeah. Pop in that side window," Stick said as he pulled his helmet back on.

The director handed Elvis a shiny white helmet, but he hesitated. "Are we going to ride in that?" he asked, pointing to the damaged passenger side.

Stick reached in through the window and felt along the interior. It was a little bumpy but otherwise intact. "Got a hammer?" he asked Norm.

The director spoke into his headset, and moments later, a pimply-faced teenager came running across the track with a hammer. He handed it to Stick, who reached back inside the car and banged out the indentions.

"There you go. Good as new," he said, handing the hammer back to the teen. "You good to crawl in?"

Elvis nodded and climbed in the car with the stealth of a cat and promptly buckled the seat belt. Stick jumped in after him, started up the car, and eased into first gear, barely pulling his foot from the clutch. He didn't want to scare the daylights out of the King right away. They cruised around the track at fifty miles per hour for the first lap.

"So, when you going to drive this race car?" Elvis asked slyly.

"Oh, you want to go faster, huh?"

"Yes," he said with a slight curl of his lip. "You don't have to handle me with kid gloves. Show me what this car can do. It'll help me get in character."

"You sure?" Stick asked, figuring Elvis didn't know what he was getting himself into. "This thing tops out at one twelve."

"Get her up there," Elvis said.

Stick wasted no time. He shifted gears and pressed the pedal to the floor. The car shot down the straightaway, wind whipping through the windows with a low howl. As he rounded the first corner, he glanced over at Elvis, who was gripping the dash.

"Want me to slow 'er?" Stick shouted.

Elvis shook his head no, but his face was as pale as a ghost. Stick got close to the outside wall, then kicked the passenger tires off the bank until they lifted slightly. Then he took turn one as a double apex, hitting the inside, going wide ever so slightly, then hitting the inside again, increasing speed. He tackled the second turn aggressively as he clipped the hairpins tightly, then shot out with light, late braking, causing his passenger to jostle around. On the final lap, Stick came through the finish line with a fishtail, then spun in tiny circles through the infield. When he brought the car to rest, he threw his helmet out the window and let out a whoop.

"That was fun, huh?" he asked, then looked over at Elvis.

His pretty face was devoid of color, his hands pale as they stuck like glue to the sides of the bench. He leaned his head back on the headrest and blew air from his lips.

"That was—man, I'm not going to lie. That was terrifying." He removed his helmet with shaky hands and didn't even bother to fluff his dark hair, which was now flat upon his head.

"Oh, man, I—I mean, I thought—" Stick didn't know how to respond. He'd taken Elvis for a thrill ride and scared him to death. Would he be fired?

"It's all right, Stick. I told you to. I guess I just wasn't as ready as I thought." He wiped his glistening face with a clean towel from his pocket. "I have a whole new appreciation for what you do. You always runnin' at top speed?"

"Most of the time."

The director rushed up to the side of the car. "Elvis, you okay?"

"I'm fine. Just a little shook up."

"*All shook up?*" Stick asked, giving him a look, then drawing in his lips in fear.

But Elvis laughed. "Good one. Yeah, like a Pepsi bottle."

Norm put one hand on Elvis's shoulder. "I thought you Southerners like to take things slow as molasses?"

"Only when we're sittin' on the front porch," Stick said, to which Elvis nodded.

"Common misconception about the South," Elvis said as the color returned to his face. "We are always hustlin'."

Norm backed away from the car as the men climbed out.

"Thanks for the ride," Elvis said as he shook Stick's hand again.

"Did it give you some inspiration?"

"Yes, but I'm not ever doin' that again."

Stick watched as the King of Rock and Roll walked away with a little less strut this time. *He's a Southern boy trying to survive. Just like me. Both artists, doing what we each do best.* He thought about how Elvis wiggled when he sang. *Maybe he feels the music like I feel the car. The electricity—it's ingrained in both of us and creates a spark that's hard to contain—purpose, passion, the stuff of a life well lived.*

Chapter 12

CHARLOTTE, NC
— 1968 —

Earth, concrete, sky. Stick couldn't tell one from the other as gray, brown, and blue all blended like spilled paint in a centrifuge. Number 47 had clipped him on the ninth, and now his car was doing 360s in the middle of the track. Flashes of red, purple, and yellow dodged him left and right. He wasn't dizzy, just needed his car to settle so he could drive. He eased the wheel counterclockwise, hoping to get a handle before the caution flag was thrown. But every time he tugged at the wheel, it released, bopped him on the forearm, and kept spinning the wrong way. *All right, do your thing.* He let go of the wheel completely and held on to the edge of his seat.

After a few more spins, the car's momentum slowed. Stick strong-armed the wheel, and the car came to a rest as Jimmy Chambers passed him. Wasting no time, Stick pointed the car's nose toward the finish line and stepped on the gas, narrowly missing a Plymouth at the back of the pack. He would need to make up time. Thank God the flagger at Charlotte Motor Speedway was a stickler for letting the races play out. Stick would have to make up an entire lap, and that wouldn't be easy. He drove like mad and passed five cars, but the others were just too far ahead. Getting close on the inside lane, he knew his only hope at a top five finish was to weave between the small spaces on the turns. It was risky. The spaces were tight, and one wrong move would send him straight into one of the pilons. But that had never stopped him before.

He snuck around #23, who moved to the right strictly out of fear. Willie was not as easy to pass, and Stick heard the screeching of metal like an untuned violin string as he scrapped past. The space between #42 and the row of posts was almost impossible to see, but Stick knew it had to be there. He got right up on #42's tail and pushed, but the bastard wouldn't budge. Stick maneuvered left, taking off the back bumper. That must have pissed #42 off, because he jerked to the left, daring his competitor to try anything else. But Stick wouldn't be bullied; he doubled down. *May as well thread this needle.*

Stick hit the post. The driver's side panel flew off, tumbling behind the car like cardboard in a twister, leaving him exposed. White stakes were within inches of his body, threatening to be his final grave. Stick's wheel caught the edge of one and spun him across the track, slimly missing five other cars as he ended up near the grandstand. The checkered flag was thrown, and Stick could see #12 had won it by a mile. One, two, three, four . . . Stick counted the cars ahead of him. *I'm five. That'll do. It's still a payday for fifth.* Stick stepped out of the car. The track was a mess: skid marks, cars everywhere. Two men rushed toward him with a stretcher, but when he waved, they stopped and turned back around.

"How exciting!" Mr. Chase, the race promoter at Charlotte Motor Speedway, exclaimed. "All five of you, go sign some autographs. That crowd sure wants a piece of you boys."

Stick walked over to the grandstands, Butch by his side. He saw Willie and gave a quick thumbs-up to make sure he wasn't too mad about the fender. Willie threw his hand in the air and flicked his wrist as if to say, *Please, it's part of the game.*

"Hell of a race, boss. Didn't think you were going to make it, but what a way to squeeze in. The car, on the other hand, has seen better days."

"Yeah, gonna need a new side panel," Stick said, slowing his pace.

"At least." Butch handed Stick a pen as he approached howling fans, scratching and pawing their way to the front of the line.

Amid all the chaos, Stick saw a figure in the distance standing alone at the top of the bleachers. Curvy hourglass hips crammed into dark jeans, a red top, and a headful of wavy hair the color of milk chocolate. She stood with her arms crossed, scanning the crowd. Then she walked slowly, purposefully across the beam, her hips rocking to the sound of aluminum that clattered with each step. Stick's fans called for him to come closer, take a picture, sign a program, but Stick couldn't take his eyes off the woman in red. She descended the stairs, a sexy siren after her prey. She stopped at the bottom and paused a moment before heading to the exit.

"That pen don't work?" Butch asked, handing Stick a marker.

"What?" Stick asked, confused.

"The pen. You ain't signed no autographs."

Stick shook his head, as if to draw himself out of a trance. "Naw, pen works just fine. Here."

He handed the ballpoint to Butch and ran off.

"What? Where—"

"That way," Stick said, pointing.

He realized he wasn't making sense, but he was like a wild animal, attracted to the hunt. He had to find that woman before she got away.

People began to cheer as he entered the parking lot. He put his hands up in a gesture of gratitude, all the while searching for the red blouse. *How did she get away so fast?* He moved in and out of parked cars, a mad man in his hunt. A trunk shut, the rattle of keys. Stick looked to the left. The dark-haired woman whirled her keys around one finger as she climbed in a white Ford Cortina. Stick put his hand up as if to wave, but she didn't stop. *Why would she?* He jogged over as she started the ignition.

"Wait!" he said, desperately tapping on the window.

She rolled it down. "Yes?" Her voice was sultry, slow and lazy like a Sunday afternoon.

"Well, I—" *What the hell do I say now? I chased you all the way out here?*

She stared at him with the bluest eyes he'd ever seen. Hers were a deeper shade than his: deep turquoise, the color of the sea.

"I'm Stick. I just wanted to introduce myself."

"I know who you are."

"But I don't know you."

"Should you?"

Is she playing games? "I would like to," he responded.

"Why?"

For the first time in his life, Stick was dumbstruck. "I, I—"

But then she smiled. "I'm just kidding. I watched you race. You're good."

He looked up and blew a sweaty curl from his eyes. "I've never seen you here before."

"I don't get out much. Annalee," she said, extending her hand.

Stick took it gently and kissed the top. "Nice to meet you, Annalee."

Who am I? Polite and all, kissing her hand?

"Nice to meet you too."

A woman of few words.

"Well, I—can I take you out sometime? How about dinner tonight?" he blurted out, then instantly regretted how desperate he sounded.

She looked up as if thinking. "Don't you need a shower? And a new car? As I recall, yours blew up."

"Right. I am a mess, ain't I?"

"You are. And you almost died in the crash. I think you should go home and rest."

"Oh, that? I'm fine. That was nuthin'."

She set her hands on the wheel. "I have to get home anyway. It's late."

"Well, another time?"

She smelled musky, with undertones of vanilla and hibiscus. Stick breathed her in as he waited for her response. Her lashes were long and curled, her cheekbones high. But he was watching her mouth.

"Maybe."

"When?" The question came too fast.

"I don't know."

Stick leaned in farther. "Will you come back?"

"I may. The race sure was fun."

"I'll leave a ticket with your name on it, if you want."

"Sure. See ya around," she said, starting the ignition.

"I hope so," he said, but she had already closed the door.

Stick watched as Annalee drove off, taillights illuminated, falling in line with the sea of cars exiting. He stood there long after her car was indistinguishable from the others.

Tommy ran up, a stack of papers in his hands. "These—all these people want autographs, Stick. They're waitin'." Flustered, he motioned back to the stands. "Why'd you run off? Too much? I told you it wasn't a good idea to . . ."

But Stick wasn't listening.

Gaffney, SC

A few months later, Stick walked into the garage to see Butch hastily scribbling on a full-sized chalkboard.

"We going to school now?" he asked.

"We gotta chart all our options for cars," Butch said, wiping his face.

"Chart it? You gotta be kiddin', man. There ain't nuthin' to chart. We can talk it out."

"Too late for that." Butch nodded at the back door, where crew members were filing in, all wearing the same Stick Elliott shirts with matching pink logo hats.

Well, look at that, he thought. *Apparently, I'm a brand now.* Stick was touched. He knew his crew believed in him, but the fact that they were willing to display his name head to toe meant they were all in. He just didn't know who had paid for all this merchandise. He certainly hadn't approved such an expense. His momentary pride was displaced by irritation.

"What are you—Butch, what's all this about?"

"Stick, you'd think if a driver was constantly ruining cars—exploding them even—he wouldn't have a sponsor touch him, but"—Butch smiled, showcasing the gap in his top teeth and the dimple in his chin—"we got sponsors out the wazoo. Everybody wants their name on a Stick Elliott car."

"What?"

"You heard me. Look." Butch pointed at the left side of the board. "Howard's Furniture, Anderson's Farm, O. L. Nixon Construction, WSOC."

"The news channel out of Charlotte?"

"Yep, and there's more. These are just the major players."

"Meaning?"

"Meaning those willing to contribute whatever cash necessary to be a sponsor. Your top five finishes at Birmingham, Hickory, and Smokey Mountain Raceway got you noticed. Not to mention that crazy finish at Langley."

Finn piped in. "Man, when you and Willie came round corner four on the final lap, I thought my heart was gonna jump clear outta my throat. I ain't never—"

"So, I didn't pay for any of this"—Stick interrupted, motioning with his finger—"stuff?"

Butch folded his hands in front of him. "Not a penny. You've been a celebrity on your home turf for some time, but now you're one of the top dogs in the South—alongside Petty, Yarborough, and Earnhardt."

"That driver racking it up near Kannapolis?" Stick asked. He'd raced hard against those drivers and knew they were smooth, skilled racers. His own driving style was more rugged, his personality not as polished.

Stick rolled up his sleeves. "Well, I'll be damned. I like the looks of it,

I'll tell you that much." He hesitated, conflicted. "But I'm not sure I want a sponsor. We're doing all right on our own."

"We are, but the boys want to explore this. With sponsors like these, we can choose any car you want. Hell, we can finally get two cars, one for dirt and one with a windshield. I've heard NASCAR's beefing up the rule book, so we might need two separate cars anyway. There's basically no budget."

"Wo-hee," Stick whistled. "Damn. I better take a seat." He sat down in the front row.

Someone plopped a cap on his head. Stick looked left and right at the crew all proudly suited up in his colors, his name. These people were not just mechanics, jack operators, and lollipop men; they were his friends.

"All right, let's get down to business," Butch said. "We got a list of potential sponsors a mile wide. We can take two or be exclusive with one."

The room buzzed. Most wanted the news channel, but there were arguments for body shops, clothing stores, and pharmacies. Butch stood at the chalkboard, looking like a linebacker in a T-shirt that was somehow too big. He crossed his arms and nodded when considering things, every once in a while writing down a good point. Everyone had an opinion, especially Tommy, who couldn't stop talking about all the merchandise.

"Everyone's said their piece. What do you think, Butch?" Stick asked.

"I say we go with Howard's Furniture. They've been around a long time and have standing in this community. It shows we support local businesses. Plus, the Howards have some clout. But we should also accept the sponsorship from WSOC. To have the media on our side would give you exposure. They're in Charlotte, so it's a big deal. NASCAR and all that."

What Butch said made sense, but Stick wasn't sold on it yet. He'd come around to the idea of sponsors paying for gear, logos, even a new hauler, but the idea of someone else owning the very thing he raced in . . . "We should talk about the car."

"All right," Butch said, pivoting.

Stick listened to arguments over Dodge versus Plymouth, Ford versus the new Buick, but he'd already made up his mind. *I'll let them have their say, but this one's mine.*

When the room quieted down, he stood up and faced his crew. "It's a Chevy. That's what we're getting."

Butch raised his chalk to the board. "Don't you think we should make a list? Chart the horsepower, body design, speed—"

"Chevy. It's never let me down."

"But—that new Plymouth—it's a behemoth, fastest on the road. Petty's got one."

"Fastest?" Stick asked. He was intrigued. Speed was the goal, after all.

"Yep, put a Hemi in that GTX, and it's over for everyone else," Butch said assuredly.

Stick stood up and took off his cap, replacing it with the cowboy hat in his lap. He'd been a Chevy guy for a long time, but Butch was smart. He researched the hell out of new cars coming down the pike, so Stick had to at least give it some consideration.

"Okay, so Petty's getting one. Why do you like it, Butch?"

"They call it the Boss. Zero to sixty in 6.6 seconds. Excellent handling, heavy-duty shocks, which you need." He smiled, then continued. "Very masculine. Squared-off corners, four headlights, which they'll go ahead and cover for us. The body is so solid, I could fine-tune the suspension to gain a ton of power and torque. It drives like a dream, fierce and mean but smooth, begging to full-on release to top speed. The GTX suits you. A sleek muscle car with a solid, badass frame and enough power inside to make them other cars look like they're in a footrace. Including the Chevy."

How can I argue with that? Butch knew his shit, and he was a hell of a salesman. Still, Chevrolet had always been reliable, and it would be tough for Stick to trust another.

"What's the Chevy's acceleration?" he asked.

"Zero to sixty in 7.1."

It all came down to speed. And six sure was faster than seven.

"All right, you make a good argument, Butch. Order the Plymouth. I'll be damned if I'll let Petty outrun me, especially now that we all got V8s," he said. "When can I get it?"

"There's a six-month wait on these cars. You need something to drive in the meantime."

Stick began to speak, but Butch interrupted him. "I've got a solution."

"Listening," Stick said.

"There's this cat, always hanging around the track, Arthur Harris, huge race fan. Owns a wholesale textile business over on Twenty-Ninth in Gaffney. He wants to be a sponsor real bad. Thing is, he's got this Ford, a real beauty—Torino. Mostly sits in a garage. He's offered to let you drive it until we get the new one."

"That Torino's a beast," Stick said. "What's the catch?"

"He wants in, just his name on the next car. Real small tattoo on the side panel. Nuthin' else—no profits, no gear, no mentions."

Stick considered for a minute. Sponsors always wanted to brand things, and Stick wasn't up for branding. *I ain't no cow.* But this sounded different. This guy didn't seem to want much, just a little advertisement for his business. *And a Ford, hell, that's . . .*

"I'll do it."

Butch clapped his hands. "All right, we got ourselves a car. I'll set up a meeting with Arthur."

"Naw, just have the car at the track Wednesday. Let's see if it's as good as I've heard."

Stick sat behind the wheel of the Torino and looked out over the elongated muscular hood. Bulkier than his old Chevy, but nonetheless sleek. Stick's large body had plenty of room in the black bucket seat, too.

"He wrapped it for me," Stick noted as he rubbed his hands over the wrapped steering wheel. The black tape allowed him better grip and less heat.

"Yup," Butch said. "Arthur agreed to all the changes, including adjusting the chassis and welding the doors shut."

Stick revved the engine. "Let's see what this thing can do!"

Butch gave him the thumbs-up, and Stick was off. He raced around Cherokee Speedway, tested torque, brakes, sliding capability, and, most importantly, speed. After twenty or so laps, he pulled the car in as his crew ran to its side.

"Ford claims this thing has three hundred thirty-five horsepower, but it's more," Stick said.

Butch furiously scribbled on a notepad. When he finished, he tapped the pen to pad and said, "It's close to four hundred."

"Whoa," Tommy said, and the crew gave an excited cheer.

"I knew it," Stick said. "You can feel that power. And the speed?"

Again, Butch answered. "Zero to sixty in 7.7 seconds. It'll do a quarter-mile drag in a little over fifteen seconds at ninety miles an hour."

"Jesus, this thing has power."

"Yeah, this model's made for racin'. It's got the newly introduced Cobra Jet four-twenty-eight-cubic-inch engine, too."

"It's a beast!" Stick said. "Cancel that Chevy order. I want one of these."

"Well, let's talk about it. Plymouth is making a car that tops at just under two hundred miles an hour."

"These carmakers are really getting behind everyone's fascination with speed, huh?"

"Yeah, especially with the growing popularity of NASCAR."

"People love NASCAR. I'm happy to compete in that circuit, but anybody who knows racing knows it all starts here at the dirt track. Anyway, we'll talk. For now, let's practice." Stick hit the side of the car. "This horse is a winner."

He took another fifty laps, then pulled into the pit when he saw Arthur drive up in a beat-up white van.

"Your girl's fast," Stick said as he stepped out of the car to shake Arthur's hand.

"I knew she was, though I never got up to such speeds. She used to be white, too," Arthur said, pointing at the mud-covered car.

Stick laughed. "We'll get her cleaned up for the race on Saturday."

Arthur clasped his hands together. "I can't wait. You got me some tickets?"

"Course. How many you need?"

"One, maybe two. My daughter may come. She and I don't talk much, but she sure does love racing."

"I'll leave two. And feel free to come to the pit early."

"That's amazing. I will. Better run. See you Saturday, son."

Arthur got into his van and drove off as Stick approached his crew. "What's the weather looking like for Saturday?"

Butch answered, as usual. "Weather's chilly but clear. You should be worried about the roster, not the weather."

"Why?"

Tommy spoke up. "Got a couple of them Florida and Atlanta boys coming up. They want to check you out ever since you've been doing so well in NASCAR. Think they're a little nervous."

Stick smiled a lopsided grin. "Smart. They should be scared. I'm shakin' things up. Them boys won't know what's hit 'em on dirt. This'll be fun. But I better get on now. See you boys Saturday."

I'm the boss of this place, he thought. *And I'm gonna show them how it's done.*

Stick pulled into the pit to see Arthur's van waiting for him.

"Thanks for the tickets. This is exciting," Arthur said, popping the top on a beer. "Feeling ready?"

"Sure am," Stick said, eyeing a woman's coat draped alongside the van window. "Your daughter come?"

"Yeah, she went up to concessions to grab a Pepsi. She don't drink."

Stick thought she sounded like a bore, the churchgoing judgmental type.

"I'm gonna go to my home away from home, put my suit on, and do a couple practice rounds," Stick said, motioning to the refurbished box truck with the flatbed hauler Virgil had helped the crew piece together.

"And I get a front-row seat," Arthur said, sounding like a child meeting Santa Claus.

Stick stepped into the spacious truck and removed his cowboy boots and hat. He pushed his toes into the shag carpet and sat down on a red sofa the boys had bolted to the floor. *A customized bachelor pad*, Stick thought as he interlaced his hands behind his head. Oh, the rendezvous he could have here. Leopard-print curtains enclosed the bedroom area, complete with a large black velvet mattress and pink neon bar sign advertising "nudes." Stick cracked open a Royal Crown soda and guzzled it before slipping out of his suit pants and button-down shirt. He pulled on his white overalls, now emblazoned with the WSOC logo, and started out the trailer door, still buttoning up his suit at the waist.

As he stepped back into the evening air, he saw the back of a woman, bent over, peering into his race car. Her jeans pressed tight against her full bottom. She was wearing red platform shoes.

"Can I help you?" Stick asked.

She turned around, and Stick was met with the same sexy Caribbean-blue eyes he had seen in his dreams the past few months.

"Annalee?"

"Is that a question?" she asked, tugging at her jeans.

"What are you—"

"I see you've met my daughter," Arthur said, coming up behind Stick.

"This—this is your daughter?"

"Yeah, got her looks from her mom, God bless her."

Stick was flabbergasted. *Had she known her father was sponsoring my driving? And why is she staring at me funny?*

"You gonna zip that up?" Annalee asked, her lids lowering as she glanced down.

Stick looked down at his suit. His chest was exposed, the top of his underwear showing. *Well, at least I'm in good shape. Nuthin' to be ashamed of here.*

As he zipped up, he noticed Annalee biting her lip. *No, definitely nuthin' to be ashamed of.*

"You, uh, you gonna watch the race?"

"That's the plan."

Okay, it was a stupid question. What else would she be doing here? But Stick couldn't help himself. He found Annalee intriguing. She didn't fawn over him like every other woman in town. In fact, she stood her distance, giving him nothing to go on. But the way she moved; it was like . . . *She knows what she's doing.*

"You two have met before?" Arthur asked.

"Briefly," Annalee answered.

There was something in her body language and a bite to her words, as if she were waiting for an attack. Stick couldn't interpret the way she leaned back, thrusting her hips forward, yet holding her head high. She flinched slightly when her father spoke, letting one arm drop to her side. *She's not embarrassed by him. It's something else.*

"Well, I better be going," he said, but he didn't move.

Annalee put her hands in her back pockets and stuck her chest out. Arthur must have sensed the tension, because he stood between them and clapped.

"All right," he said. "Go out there and win one for us, boy."

Butch came running over just at the right time. "Stick, let's go!" he said, glancing over at Annalee. He took Stick by the arm and led him away. "That woman's gonna give you trouble, Stick. You need to concentrate."

"I'll be fine," Stick said.

What Butch didn't understand was that Stick was fueled by beautiful women. They were never a distraction, especially this one. She was the sexiest thing he had ever laid eyes on, and he would win because women like that love winners. *By the end of the night, she'll be mine,* he thought, crawling through the window of the Torino.

As Stick revved the engine, he felt the vibration all the way up to his pelvis. The flag dropped, and he didn't wait as he usually did, testing the waters. He punched the gas full throttle right away. This must have surprised the other drivers, because there was chaos on the track. Cars slid to one side as Stick cruised easily in front of them. It was as if they opened the gates for him to take the lead. By the fifth lap, he was outpacing the others by a good quarter mile. He changed gears with a vigor he hadn't experienced in a while. He envisioned Annalee in his bed, and he drove like he couldn't wait to get there. Every turn of the wheel was a curve of her body, every movement of the clutch a thrusting of his. He was sweating, pushing the car to its limits. As he raced under the checkered flag, there wasn't a car in sight behind him.

As the others came to a stop, Stick could only think of one thing. He tried to get to the pit, but the crowd descended upon him quickly. He held the trophy and snapped a few pictures, rushing through posing with Arthur in front of the car. After a few minutes, he whispered to Butch, "Cover me."

Butch stepped out in front of the cameras and began to introduce Arthur as sponsor. He droned on about the car's attributes and Stick's commitment to excellence as Stick ran to the box truck to find Annalee sitting on the steps.

"You! With me, now," he demanded, unzipping his suit.

She didn't budge. *Huh, that's always worked before.*

She stood and ran her fingers along the metal railing leading up to the door. "I know women normally throw themselves at you, but I'm not one of them."

Stick didn't know what to say. "I just—I didn't mean to offend you."

"Oh, I'm not offended. Not flattered, either. You're just going to have to work a lot harder than that." She walked slowly down the stairs and trailed her hand along his shoulder, sending a shiver up his spine. "Good race, cowboy. You really tamed that Ford."

Stick was speechless. He watched as she walked away. *This one's a real doozy. But she'll be worth it.*

Arthur was leaning against the Torino when he turned back around. Stick knew he had been watching the entire exchange. As he walked over, he caressed the side of the car.

"You like this car, huh?" Arthur asked.

"Yeah, she drives real well. Smooth."

"You like my daughter, too?"

Crap. "She, um, she's intriguing."

Arthur gave an exasperated sigh. "Sure is. Never know what's in that one's head, ever since she was a little girl. Stubborn, that's for sure, but a little naive, too . . ."

His words trailed as his mind seemed to drift. Stick didn't know how to respond in the silence. *Is he warning me? Throwing the caution flag before I have a chance to get going? Or does he just want to protect his daughter? Maybe she's been hurt before.*

"I, uh, sir, I didn't meant to—" Stick found himself stuttering for the second time that night.

"Ah, relax, son. You can go after her. I like you. Hell, I think you're the coolest guy around. I would be proud for you to date my daughter. I just think you should know she's unlike any woman you've ever pursued."

Maybe that's just what I need. Maybe he'd met his match with Annalee, the one woman who didn't give in to his charms.

"Thank you, sir. I don't even know if she—well, I'll treat her right, given the chance."

"She needs a good man in her life. She drove the last one away. They weren't married long."

"Married?" Stick had never even considered the possibility that Annalee had been married before. He was getting up there in age but had never considered settling down himself. It wouldn't fit with his fast-paced life, might even ruin his image.

"Yeah, married a rodeo guy real young. I think she was just sad about losing her mother and needed some companionship. It wasn't a good match. He was restless, a bit like you."

"Sir, I'm not—I—" But Stick knew his reputation with women preceded him.

"No need to explain. Hell, if I were you, I'd be sleeping with every young thing that came my way. Annalee's attracted to that bad-boy type, but that's not the type that likes to stick around. She needs stability. She has none of her own."

Jeez. I just want to take her out on a date, not propose.

"Arthur, your daughter is a beautiful woman, and I'd love to take her out. I only have the best of intentions."

Arthur raised off the car and slapped Stick on the side of the arm. "Boy, you're solid marble," he said, shaking his retracted hand. "Have fun. Just know my daughter is different, and I wouldn't blame you if it doesn't last long. You and I, we have greater things to worry about." He raised his arms out wide, but Stick was confused.

"Winning races," Arthur said.

Stick exhaled. "That I can do."

"I know you can. We make a good team, Stick," he said, shaking his hand. "Say, I got some ideas about how we can stir things up a bit. I been studying driving techniques and think I can help you shave a few seconds off your final lap."

Stick didn't like where this was going. *Ain't no way I'm taking advice from this two-bit businessman. Who does he think he is anyway? Just because he owns a sports car doesn't mean he knows what to do with it.* Stick ground his teeth. *It may be your car, but I'm the one behind the wheel.* Stick knew he had to calm down. He still needed the Torino, so he couldn't let his temper get the best of him now. He had to bide his time.

"Yes, sir. Thank you for the opportunity," Stick said, his jaw tight, lips barely moving. "Now, I better get on back to the trailer and get out of this dirty suit."

"Ah, I guess you better," Arthur said.

Stick walked back to the trailer and threw off his racing suit. Standing there in his underwear, he thought about the conversation he had just had. *That man ain't attaching his fame to mine. If he wants to give driving advice, he better get behind the wheel. I'd like to see him try and—*

There was a knock at the door, Butch's staccato five raps.

"Come on in," Stick said, exasperated, and Butch entered, a hop in his step.

"I don't know what you said to Arthur, but he's stoked—"

"I'm done with him."

Butch leaned against the wall. "Why? Is this about his daughter?"

"No. Well, maybe a little, but that's not the main reason. He thinks he owns me!"

"I doubt that, Stick."

"Yeah, yeah, he does. He was trying to give me driving tips. Imagine that. Him teaching me how to drive!" Stick spun around, throwing his hands in the air. "Just because I drive his car don't make me his bitch. Ain't nobody gonna tell me . . ." As Stick talked, he paced, and the trailer shook.

Butch let him finish, then calmly said, "I understand where you're comin' from—I really do—but Stick, we ain't got no other choice right now. The Plymouth's still in production, and unless you know somebody else with a car you can borrow, we gotta stick with him for a while."

Stick stopped, placing both hands behind him on the counter. Butch was right.

"I'll talk to him. Let him know he's part of the team in name only."

Stick's heart rate slowed a bit. "He isn't allowed to make decisions or give advice. He's out of the day-to-day."

Butch nodded.

"And," Stick continued, "he can't come around the garage. I don't want him tinkering with things or giving the crew the wrong idea about his supposed expertise. I got my team in you, Tommy, Finn, and the rest of the boys. You're my racin' family. That's all I need."

Butch smiled.

"What?"

"You said we're a family."

Stick hastily ran his fingers through his hair. "Well, yeah. Them boys have grown on me."

"I'll enforce the rules with Arthur. He may want to come by from time to time to check on the car. It is his, after all."

Stick grimaced.

"But I'll make sure it's when you aren't there. And," Butch said, widening his eyes, "he can't touch the guts."

"Fine," Stick said, happy Butch could be the voice of reason once again.

"That it?" Butch asked, like a parent who'd just settled a toddler's tantrum.

"Yeah, that's it," Stick said. "But, Butch, get that Plymouth, fast."

Butch saluted him and headed out the door. Stick turned the shower on. He needed to wash away the day's grime and figure out how to deal with his insufferable sponsor a little longer. Arthur was trying to insert himself into every aspect of Stick's life, tag along in his fame, become part of his brood. But Stick's family was a tight group: just his granddad, his best friend, and his crew. They supported him, grounded him, and would never let him down. They were salt of the earth, the roots of his tree, and Stick didn't need anyone else invading that space. He paused and grabbed a towel. *Except maybe Annalee*, he thought. *She could really boost my engine.*

Chapter 13

CHARLOTTE, NC
– 1969 –

Stick sat in the WSOC dressing room while a woman in pink-rimmed glasses and giant panda earrings powdered his face.

"Why do I need all this again?" he asked.

"So your skin looks smooth on camera. Everyone does it, even the men."

Stick thought back to the *Speedway* movie set and remembered Elvis's porcelain skin. Had he been wearing makeup? Well, if the biggest sex symbol in the world could have flawless skin, so could he. He just wouldn't mention it to the crew. They'd paint him a pansy.

The woman ran hair goop through his hair and placed her hands on his shoulders.

"There, all done. You're a handsome devil, you know that?"

"Thanks," Stick said, rising from the chair.

He put on a navy suit jacket and walked down the long corridor to the sound stage. He didn't want to do this interview, but Stick needed to play the game. Stick was the biggest headline the town had seen in years;

promoters were now paying him to race at their tracks. Plus, his relationship with Arthur had gone sour after he'd asserted himself too much in Stick's day-to-day business. It all came to a head one day when Arthur suggested Stick hire a more polished crew chief. "Hell, I don't need him to sparkle, I just need him to take care of my car. And Butch is the best there is."

Stick watched as the place bustled with people wearing headsets, directing orders, and shooshing those in the hall. A young college kid wearing a necktie and sneakers approached him.

"You're up in five," he said, tapping on his clipboard. "I'm Dave, stage director."

"Oh, okay. Where do I go? What do I do?"

Dave let out a sigh. "The door that says 'stage.' Go there. Walk out. Sit down. Answer questions."

Smart-ass.

"How long you been here?" Stick asked.

"Six months. I'm an intern, hoping to get a job after graduation."

"Now wouldn't that be great," Stick said, noting the nervous way Dave rocked back on his heels.

"On in five," Dave said again, adjusting his tie. "Remember, you are looking at camera one, directly in front of you. Don't get mixed up with the others."

"Got it. Is it labeled?"

Another sigh. "It's the one in the middle. You've never done this before, have you?"

"Never. Makes me—"

"You're a—race car driver of sorts?" Dave asked, flipping through his papers.

"Of sorts, yes."

"Hmmm, don't know you," Dave said, not bothering to look up.

Stick looked around at all the cables and wires. The lights were making him sweat, or maybe it was nerves. *And this little twerp isn't helping.*

A man in his sixties, almost as tall as Stick, approached. He was wearing a dark-gray power suit, silk paisley tie, and expensive shoes—a man of authority. Stick recognized him as Mr. Weathers, the station's CEO.

"Well, I'll be—it's so nice to see you," he said, shaking Stick's hand.

Stick smiled. "Mr. Weathers, great to see you again."

"Glad you decided to come in. How are you liking that new custom hauler?"

Stick had to admit he did like the new enclosed rig. He'd let WSOC open their coffers for everything except the two cars he now owned. Stick paid for those outright with race winnings and the paycheck from MGM.

"It's great," Stick said. "Car arrives to the track in good shape."

"And you? Bet you arrive all rested in that RV?"

The comforts of the new Winnebago sure were better than the old box truck. Shag carpet and a full kitchen, bathroom, and bed made it a pleasant home away from home.

"You bet. That thing's nicer than my own apartment."

And he meant it. Stick had struggled with accepting such luxuries at first, but he realized he worked hard for it all, attending festivals, music events, even a children's birthday party or two, all in the name of his sponsors. Hell, he'd even done a few shout-outs at the local rodeo. Ever since he'd cleaned out his bank account for the extra car, he was strapped for cash, couldn't even pay his electricity bill at times. Sponsorship dollars were more important than ever.

Stick glanced anxiously toward the stage, and Mr. Weathers noticed. "I know those cameras are nerve-racking, but you'll be just fine. You're just talking to your fans, after all."

"Yeah, I'll be fine," Stick said, trying to appear calm. "I just gotta get this one under my belt, and the next one will be a breeze."

Mr. Weathers turned to look at Dave.

"Who is that?" the boss asked rather loudly, motioning toward Dave.

Dave opened his mouth to answer.

"Don't know him," Stick said with a sly smile.

Green lights flashed brightly, and Stick didn't move. *Sittin' still on* go.

I'll be running my mouth instead of the engine. Ain't that a hoot. Stick's hands felt sweaty, and his heart beat clear up to his throat.

"That's your cue," Mr. Weathers said.

Stick walked out onto a circular stage surrounded by cameras and monitors. *Just like the after-race interviews. That's all this is,* he tried to convince himself. An oval desk stood in the center with two anchors, an empty blue chair on the end. Stick took his seat.

A woman dressed in a bright orange suit spoke first. "Camilla Sagamore here with racing legend Stick Elliott today. Stick's been tearing up the dirt track for years and is doing quite well in the NASCAR circuit as well, with two wins and four top ten finishes so far this season."

She turned to Stick and flashed bright white teeth. "Welcome. How do you do it?"

Stick wiped the perspiration from his brow and looked directly into the middle camera. All his fans were watching; he couldn't let them down.

"Well, I love racin', and I'll do anythin' to win that checkered flag," he said.

The other anchor, a middle-aged guy with thin silver glasses, spoke up from the far side of the desk. "That's true. I've seen some crazy stuff in my life, but you've got to be the greatest driver that ever lived. I saw that race back in Alabama where you won without a steering wheel."

"A fan," Stick said, reaching across the desk to shake his hand.

The anchor was like a ten-year-old schoolboy who had just met his hero. He abandoned all formality and shook Stick's hand vigorously.

"John, why don't you ask Mr. Elliott about his driving style?"

"Thanks, Camilla," John said as he launched into a long list of questions, each prefaced with "as the greatest driver . . ."

Stick quickly became comfortable with the camera and lights, but it was the constant tickle on his leg that distracted him. When John launched into a long diatribe on how his favorite driver had changed racing for the better, Stick glanced under the desk. Camilla had removed her heels and was seductively stroking the tip of her hosed toe against his lower leg. He turned his chair away ever so slightly, but she was persistent. Reaching for a pen across the desk, she grabbed his upper leg, digging her manicured nails into his thigh. He tried to maintain composure as he swatted under the desk.

"Stick, how are you feeling about the upcoming race at Metrolina?" John asked.

Stick had been anticipating this question. "That new track is the best dirt on the East Coast if you ask me. Packed-down red clay. Yeah, I'm looking forward to running, and I hope my Charlotte fans will come out to support me."

Long fingernails tickled around his knee and up his thigh. He gave a little jump.

"See, I can hardly contain myself."

A red light flashed above.

"Well, time's almost up," John said. "Any last comments, Stick?"

Camilla was now playfully inching her fingers near his pelvis. Stick reached under the desk and grabbed her hand, holding it forcefully by the side of the chair.

"Come out and see me this weekend on my home turf, Cherokee Speedway. All proceeds go to the Shriners Hospital."

"Well, you heard it here," John said. "A personal invitation from Stick Elliott himself. Camilla and I are going to take a short break. We'll see you back at the half hour."

They all looked at the camera until someone yelled, "That's a wrap!"

Stick shook his hand loose and stood up hastily. "John, it was nice meeting you."

"Ah, man, this was the best day of my life. See you at the track this weekend."

Camilla removed the microphone from her lapel and ran her hand down Stick's back.

"Pleasure meeting you," she said, slipping a piece of paper into his pocket.

Stick was used to this kind of thing, but not in a professional setting. He crumbled the paper and put it back into Camilla's hand.

"That won't be necessary. Ma'am," he said, nodding before he walked off set.

Stick couldn't believe he'd just said no to a sure thing. Normally, he would have slept with her, then never thought about her again. He had always seen aggressive women as desperate, eager to please, so he took advantage of it, but once he bedded them, there was nothing else. They were boring, pretty faces that would move on to the next superstar or cute farm boy.

Annalee, though—she was mysterious. The fact that she wasn't ready to jump in the sack made her even more appealing. She was different from all the others: a treasure, not a commodity. *She's just like that car that's in front of me—I'll eventually get to her. Ain't nobody better at the chase than I am.*

Gaffney, SC

The Plymouth took longer than expected, but it was worth it.

"Man, look at that beauty," Butch said as they lowered the car from its trailer. "Still can't believe we're getting two."

Electric blue, the Plymouth was sleek and mean, with pronounced edges and silver hood tie-down pins. The Stick Elliott Racing Team logo was emblazed in yellow on both sides.

"Hope she drives as good as she looks," Stick said, running both hands over the hood.

"Oh, she will. This thing's been topping out speed on the test track," Butch said.

"We'll see later tonight. I want to head over to Shelby and give her a run on the dirt there."

"You don't want to try her on asphalt first?" Butch asked. "This one does have glass, you know."

He tapped on the multilayered laminated windshield.

"Nah, if she can handle the dirt, she can handle anything."

"But Stick, her twin is coming soon," Butch said about the windowless version of the same car. "You don't—"

"Don't matter if she gets muddied up. The first NASCAR qualifier ain't for another couple weeks," Stick answered, walking around the car. "Where's the number?"

"You ain't decided on one. You do it, and I'll paint it this afternoon," Butch said. "What you thinking this time? You can't use your old numbers. Gotta retire those."

"Yeah, that'd be bad luck. Let's go with number one. Jimmy ain't got dibs on that one no more," Stick said.

"Number one? That's a little presumptuous, don't you think?"

"Butch, if I have number one painted on the side of my car, everyone will remember me that way. And I'll have to win, because if I don't, the jokes will be intolerable."

Butch exhaled and rubbed his temples until Stick cracked a smile. They both laughed.

"You know I'm right," Stick said, shaking his finger. "I'll live up to the number. You know I will."

"All right then," Butch said. "One it is. I sure as hell hope you know what you're getting yourself into here. You got more damn confidence than anybody I've ever seen."

"Butch, driving's all I've ever known. It's the only thing I'm good at. I'll be number one. You can bet on it."

Shelby, NC

Stick climbed inside his new car at the Cleveland County Fairgrounds. With a blue interior and yellow roll bar, the inside matched the rest of the car.

"Nice touch," Stick said to himself. "Let's see how this baby runs."

Stick had told Butch to stay home. He knew if the crew were there, they would analyze every aspect of the car, clocking his speed, tweaking the tires, and jotting down every mishap. Stick just wanted time to get to know his new car, without all the number crunching. He could tell if it was a good match by the way it felt.

He turned the ignition and noted the quick start-up, the mean sound of the engine. *I like this already*, he thought. Shifting left then up, he gently touched the accelerator with his right foot. He lifted the clutch, and the car began to purr.

"Like a kitten," he said, anticipating a jerky jolt forward as he fully lifted the clutch and jammed the accelerator to the floor.

But the Plymouth took off fast and smooth. Stick rounded the first curve with a fluidity he had never experienced. Even on the dirt track, the car took bumps like a pro, lifting off instead of slouching into them, sloshing through mud instead of sliding around in it. He pushed the pedal down until it tapped against the rubber mats. He passed the stands in a matter of seconds and slammed the brakes near the far wall. The Plymouth's back end twerked around, ricocheting Stick into a tailspin. He leaned into the circle, and all four tires stayed on the ground. He loved this part: the car in a chaotic spin. Stick never felt more in control. The car responded to his every move, his every wish. All around him, red dirt funneled up past the hood like a tornado. Then he came to a stop. The dust died down.

Breathing heavy, Stick hit the steering wheel, "Hell yeah!" he screamed, hipping and hollering. "This is it! Number one, baby! Ain't nobody gonna stand a chance against us, girl," he said, slapping the dashboard one more time.

Stick removed his helmet and dusted it off. "Let's go home," he said as he pulled off the track.

He was tempted to drive past Sunny Slope Farms, where the roads were narrow and winding, but he knew better. He'd made good with the cops in town and promised to keep his need for speed on the track. In return, they promised to support him by stamping Stick stickers on their unmarked cars.

So, he drove the speed limit though downtown, hoping to catch a glimpse of Annalee. When he didn't see her, he drove back to the shop and parked the car in the garage. He sprayed mud off the fender and body, then looked down at his soiled pants, dirty from the track and wet from the wash. He shucked them off, then walked through the dark garage and flipped on a switch. The lights yellowed overhead, illuminating his white T-shirt. *Hell, that's dirty too*, he thought, removing it. As he slid the shirt over his head, he heard a *tap-tap* on the concrete floor.

He rounded the corner and was faced with Annalee, all decked out in a red skirt and tight-fitting blouse.

"Oh!" she gasped. "I didn't know anyone was here."

Stick was aware he was wearing only white boxers, so he tousled his hair. "Um, hi. I was just—I don't normally—"

He noticed Annalee biting the inside of her lip, a slight grin on her face. It was subtle, the desire, her eyes stoic, body relaxed. She reached up and twirled a dark curl around her finger. Stick doubted she was even conscious of the movement.

"You just go tromping around in your underwear?" she asked.

"I—there's a reasonable explanation. Wait, what are you doing here? I mean, I'm happy to see you but—"

Annalee must have sensed her loss of composure, because she dropped her hand by her side and pulled her shoulders back.

"Arthur left the Torino's original valve caps here," she said.

"You call your father Arthur?"

"Yes," she said, looking him straight in the eye. "Butch said I could pick them up." She reached into a brown velvet bag that hung from her shoulder and produced four silver valve stems. "See? Didn't know anyone would be here, undressed."

Stick extended his arm above Annalee on the wall. "Well, it's your lucky day," he said, tightening his muscles and flexing his abs.

Annalee pushed her back against the wall behind her. "Arthur's right. You're too confident."

Her words indicated displeasure, but her body said quite the opposite: the way she leaned against the wall, the visible rise and fall of her chest, a slight blush on her cheeks as she looked up at him with longing.

"I'm just comfortable in my own skin. I'm a damn good driver, and not bad looking either. There's nuthin' wrong with recognizing that." Stick stepped closer to her and doubled down. "Don't tell me you don't like what you see."

Annalee didn't respond right away but rather let her eyes trail from his face down his bare chest, landing on the strip of hair just below his belly button. Her purse dropped, and the valve stems slipped from her hand, clamoring against the concrete floor.

"You're not bad," she said with a laugh.

"Not bad? Then why are you biting your lip again?"

"Habit," she said, carelessly touching a locket that hung from her neck.

"What's that?"

"This?" she asked, rubbing the locket around her fingers. "It was my mother's. She died years ago." Annalee looked down as she opened it up. "It's her, my mother, Audrey, in full Cherokee regalia."

Stick noticed a sudden sadness in her voice. "May I see?" he asked.

She nodded and handed the locket to Stick. He took it gently in his hand and looked at the tiny picture inside. The woman looked a lot like Annalee, with long dark hair and high cheekbones. Her hair was braided and wrapped in ribbon; feathers dangled from her ears.

"She's beautiful," he said, resisting the urge to comment on Annalee's appearance. "She looks strong. She must have been a wonderful woman."

A tear fell from Annalee's eye. *So, she is vulnerable*, Stick thought.

"You know, I lost my mother a long time ago. Actually, I lost her twice."

Annalee took the locket from his hand and closed it, tucking it neatly into her bosom. "What do you mean?" she asked.

"When I was little, she—she went crazy, like insane. She went into a mental hospital. Didn't even know who I was half the time. Then, she, well—she died."

Annalee's eyes softened; her body relaxed. "Who raised you, then?" she asked.

"My granddad. My own father was an asshole. Didn't ever care much for me. Left when I was three."

Stick sensed a change in Annalee's demeanor. She was no longer harsh, protected.

"Your granddad taught you to drive," she said. It was more a statement than a question.

"Yes, out of necessity. He didn't make much at the railroad, so he had other business ventures on the side."

"You mean moonshine," she said, rubbing her hand down the side of her hip.

Stick knew he couldn't answer the question directly. "Just selling something the people wanted."

"And that's what you do now, sell what the people want?"

Stick chuckled. "Yeah, I guess so. But I owe everything to my granddad. I love him. He's all I've ever had, been there for me from the beginning. I would have been holed up in an orphanage somewhere if it wasn't for him. God knows I'd have probably ended up in jail."

Again, Annalee nodded as if reconsidering the man in front of her. She looked at him, her eyes dropping slightly at the corners as if she pitied him. Then, picking up her bag, she said, "You're deeper than I thought, Stick." Taking a step closer to him, she whispered in his ear. "There may be a chance for you yet."

She kissed him lightly on the cheek and walked past him, her hand lightly brushing his shoulder.

"Hey, you forgot the valve covers," he said as he picked them up and walked them to her.

"Thanks," she said, taking them from his hand. "You'll tell Butch I stopped by and we're all settled?"

"Yes, right after I get some clothes on."

"Don't do it on my account," she said. "I like you better without." She smiled and walked out the garage door, leaving Stick stunned again.

She likes me, he thought. He had seen a softer side of her, too. Brief, but it was there. He wondered what had hardened her. Maybe it was the death of her mother, but Stick had a feeling it had something to do with her father as well.

He crossed the garage, thinking how people aren't always who they seem. Annalee was much more sensitive than he had originally assumed. The thing that surprised him most was himself, though: the fact he had gone all his life chasing after things that didn't matter much—women, money, victory. Those things had given him power, established his name, but under Stick's bold, cocky hubris was a man who had a soft side, a tenderness for his granddad, a fierce loyalty to his crew and his friends. With the opening of a single locket, Annalee had opened Stick's heart. She saw him not only for who he was—a man living in the fast lane, swerving in and out of people's lives—but for the man he wanted to be. He wanted to be the man who slowed down and just hung out with friends, taking time to truly understand those around him. The kind of man people could depend on, not only to show them a good time, but to be there through the bad. The kind of man who could love a woman.

Chapter 14

GAFFNEY, SC
– 1970 –

The shrill of the phone jolted Stick from sleep. He picked up his gold-banded watch from the bedside table and read the time: 5:12 a.m. He'd been out late the night before, celebrating after a long drive back from Georgia. His head pounded, so he rolled over and back into slumber as the ringing stopped. The back of his eyelids felt like sandpaper, and his stomach had that queasy feeling like he was stuck on a boat in the middle of the Pacific. He covered himself with only the sheet and fell back into the place where the seas were calm. His breathing slowed, and he felt that moment of consciousness just before the mind dives into deep sleep, a sudden jerk of the body, then peace.

RING!

This time, he rolled over and put a pillow over his head, hoping to stifle the noise.

RING! RING!

What in the world could be this important at five in the morning? He knew Butch was an early riser, getting to the garage around five thirty. Maybe he didn't realize the time. The phone kept ringing, so Stick sat up, scratched his hip, and strode over to the phone in the kitchen.

"Yeah?"

"Stick, it's—" said Butch's voice through the receiver.

"I know who it is. What in the world are you doing calling me at this hour? Do you even know what time it is?"

"Yes, I'm sorry, I—it's your granddad."

Stick steadied himself on the kitchen counter. "What's wrong?"

"He—ugh, we don't know yet, but he's at the hospital. Something with his heart. Finn found him. He went by there to drop some"—there was static on the line—"by the door, and there he was on the porch."

Stick stretched the cord as far as it could go as he reached for the jeans he had taken off by the front door.

"What hospital? Shelby?"

"No, they took him to Spartanburg. It's a good ways away, but they have better cardiologists over there."

"I'm on my way," Stick said, cradling the receiver with his shoulder and ear as he attempted to stumble into his pants.

"Stick, be careful. Don't speed. He's stable. I'm heading over, and Finn's been with him the whole time."

Stick hung up, turned on the sink, and splashed his face with cold water. *If anything happens to that man . . . Shit, I have to get myself together.* He sloshed down a cup of day-old Sanka and washed it down with water, spilling half down his chest. Throwing on a shirt and boots, he got to the door and stopped when he saw his red Chevy pickup parked by the curb. The coffee kicked in, the dizziness dissipated, but he questioned his ability to stay between the lines. What could he do? *I'm a professional driver.* Then he had an idea. He called the police department.

"Boys, I need a favor," he said, explaining the situation.

"We have a patrol car in the area," a voice on the other end of the line said.

Three long minutes later, a police car pulled up, sirens flashing.

"Let's go," a veteran cop with silver hair said as Stick banged on his hood.

"Drive as fast as you can. My truck tops seventy-five, and if you don't go that fast, I'll pass you," Stick said as he climbed up in his truck.

The cop nodded and led Stick out of the neighborhood. The streets were empty as they drove through town, Stick's fingers rapping nervously on the dashboard. When they merged onto I-85, Stick hit the gas and moved to the left, nose to nose with the cop. He made a whirling motion with his hand. *Speed up.* The cop car moved ahead, passing Stick and two 18-wheelers that moved into the emergency lane. *Hang in there, Granddad. I'm coming.*

Despite his granddad's age, Stick had never thought about his mortality. He was a giant of a man, who had always been there for him. He remembered Jake kneeling beside that sycamore tree with a cherry lollipop. "Here, take it." Gene had been five and hiding from the men in white suits. "I know what you saw was scary, but I promise it will be okay. I'll put the lollipop here on the ground, and you can have it if you want. Only if you want." His granddad had sat down while Gene contemplated his options. He'd just seen his mother in her underwear, hiding under a sheet, and those men wanted to take her away. Jake sat in front of that tree for what must have been the better part of an hour, whistling, singing, and licking a butterscotch lollipop. Gene remembered feeling safe then, because his granddad was a big man. Jake wouldn't let the doctors take his grandson away, too. So, Gene eventually came out, gathered his candy, and crawled into his granddad's lap. "It's okay, little one. I'll take care of you. I promise."

Bright lights woke Stick out of his daydream. They were nearing the Spartanburg exit. He followed the cop car to the exit ramp and after a few turns, saw the hospital ahead. A rectangular brick building with white framework, it was the largest building in the area. The cop led Stick right up to the front of the building, where Stick parked between two pillars at the entrance and jumped out.

"You can't—that's not a parking spot!" the policeman yelled, but Stick kept running, tossing his keys behind him.

At reception, a brunette with frizzy hair stopped him. "Can I help you?"

"Here to see my granddad. What room's he in?"

"Who's your grandfather?"

"Jake. Jake Elliott."

"Oh! You're Stick. He's in room two twelve. Up the stairs, down the hall, second door on the left."

"Thanks." Stick jogged down the orange-and-brown-checkered floor and bounded up the stairs before slinging the door open to a dim hallway with yellowed lights cast on white walls like ghosts.

The second door to the left was actually a frosted-glass partition, and Jake lay in a rollaway bed, Butch and Finn at his side.

Butch stood up as soon as he saw Stick. "He's fine. They just gave him a drip, and he fell asleep."

"He was conscious?" Stick asked, noting his granddad's pallor.

"Yes, they think it was a stroke but running tests to be sure."

Stick touched his granddad's hand. It was veiny and dry. "It's Gene. I'm here," he said before turning to Finn and Butch. "Thank you, guys. Why don't you go on home?"

Finn got up and stretched. "Think I will. Guess we'll reschedule that early mornin' meeting?"

"Yeah," Stick said, searching for the right words. "Finn, you saved his life. I will never be able to repay you."

"Ah, I was just at the right place at the right time," he said before grabbing his blue-and-yellow baseball hat from the chair.

"We'll check in on you in the morning," Butch said, pushing out of his chair.

"It's already morning," Stick reminded him.

"Well, we'll check in later, then. I'll say a prayer, too," he said and exited the room with Finn.

Stick looked at his granddad a little more closely now. His olive skin looked abnormally pale, his eyelids a soft purple. His breathing was shallow but constant. He took up the entire length of the bed, his body tucked firmly into a baby-blue blanket. Stick smoothed his hair to the right, just like he preferred it.

The walls were a putrid yellow-green color that reminded Stick of mucus. Covered in a waxy film, the beige floor tile was speckled with brown. He couldn't determine whether it was supposed to be that way or if it was some sort of undeterminable body fluid. *I have to get him out of here*, he thought, noticing a thick needle protruding from a vein halfway up his granddad's arm. He tried to trace the tubal pathway that ran from Jake's body, but there were just too many. Something beeped, and Stick jumped up, looking for the source.

"Oh, don't worry. It's just the drip warning. Time to change," a nurse said from the partition.

"What?" Stick asked as she walked to the other side of the bed and unscrewed a small bag.

She took a clear bag from her oversized jacket pocket and twisted it into place. "Just some fluids," she said, suspending the bag from the silver pole beside the bed.

"Do we know what happened?" Stick asked.

She was middle-aged, starting to show highlights of gray in her otherwise dark hair. She must have been around a while, a seasoned nurse. Good. "Doctors are thinking stroke but not sure yet. They ran some tests. Results should be back soon." She reached for the mint-colored plastic cup on the bedside tray table. "Want some water?"

"Sure," Stick said, sitting down.

She poured from a flesh-toned pitcher, then handed the cup to Stick.

"Rough night?" she asked, cocking her head to the side.

"Yeah, how'd you know?" he asked, taking the cup.

"I've seen my share of intoxication in this ward."

Stick hung his head. He figured he looked pretty disheveled. He took the water down in one long gulp and handed the cup back to the nurse. "May I have some more, please?"

As she poured another cup, he slouched back in the chair and crossed his ankle over a knee. His pantleg was dirtied with oil and grease from the previous night's race. A sniff of his wrinkled shirt revealed a woodsy smell of cologne.

"Nancy, I'll take over," a gray-haired doctor said from the front of the room. "Which Elliott are we treating here?"

"Doctor Hammet. Nice to see you," Stick said, rising to shake his hand. "It's been a while."

Doctor Hammet had been the family doctor ever since Stick learned to drive. He used to make house calls when Stick was ill, and had stitched up his share of work-related wounds without so much as a question about how they occurred.

"You too, Stick. You too," he said, hugging him hard. "I just hate it's under these circumstances."

Doctor Hammet stepped back and pulled a pair of glasses from the pocket of his lab coat. He pushed the tips through his hair and looked down at the folder he was holding.

"He had what we call stress cardiomyopathy. We'll see the extent of damage when he wakes up."

"When can I take him home? He'll want to be home," Stick said.

"We'll need to assess that when he wakes up. Then I can give you a better idea."

"All right, Doc, thanks," Stick said, returning to his chair.

Doctor Hammet checked Jake's pulse and patted his hand. He closed his eyes and bowed his head. After a few moments, he looked at Stick. "I'd recommend prayer."

Stick looked at him, surprised. "It's that bad?"

"It couldn't hurt." Doctor Hammet gathered his folder and stethoscope. "I'll be back in two hours. If he wakes before then, press the yellow button."

Stick nodded as the doctor left the room.

"I won last night, Granddad. It was the most amazing thing . . ." Stick began to recount the night's events, peppering in detail about track conditions. When he finished, he pulled his chair close to the bed, took his granddad's hands in his, and bowed his head.

"God, please don't take him away from me. He's all I got. He—I love him," Stick said, then raised his head and looked around to make sure no one was looking. He pinched the inside corners of his eyes with his thumb and ring finger to stop tears from forming in the ducts. The soft bedsheet felt cool upon his cheek as he lay like a child against his granddad's shoulder. Many nights, his granddad would rock him to sleep when little Gene would weep.

"There, there, little one. Your mama's fine. She's in a place where doctors can help her. She's probably painting or coloring about now. Eating ice cream for dinner."

"Ice cream for dinner?"

"Oh yes, they say it makes everybody feel better."

"Can I have some ice cream?" Gene had asked, walking right into the trap Jake had set for him.

"Do you think it would make you feel better? Happier?"

"Oh yes!" Gene said, sniffling.

"Then we have to get some ice cream."

They'd driven down to the corner store and picked up two gallons, one vanilla and one strawberry, and ate right out of the tubs. After that, Gene fell asleep, content knowing his mama was getting dessert just like he did.

Someone was shaking his shoulder. He lifted his head and saw the nurse.

"You okay, hon?" she asked with motherly concern.

"Yeah, just fell asleep. Occupational hazard," he said, grinning.

The nurse checked the monitors. "By the way, someone left this note for you at the nurses' station."

She handed him a folded piece of paper, stapled together on two ends. As she left the room, he opened it.

Stick, I'm sorry for what's happened to your granddad. He is a good man, I'm told. I will keep him in my prayers, and hopefully God will heal him. If you need anything, call me.

It was simply signed "Annalee," with a phone number below the signature.

"Granddad, I got her number," Stick said, grinning. "You've got to wake up, so I can tell you about this woman."

He turned the paper over in his hands. *She drove all the way out here from Gaffney just to hand deliver this letter? Might just be the kind of woman I want to keep.*

But he was confused by Annalee. It was obvious she liked him; her body told the story. And the letter . . . but she could have stopped in, had reception ring the room. It was almost as if she wanted to remain mysterious. Would she ever give in? Maybe she needed more. Stick couldn't figure it out, but he knew he would find a reason to call her.

The hospital bed creaked. Jake's eyes were still closed, but his right hand began to twitch.

"Granddad?"

His eyeballs fluttered underneath closed lids, and his mouth formed an *O*.

"Granddad," Stick said again, louder this time.

Jake's eyes opened slightly, then closed again. Stick hit the switch on the wall behind the bed, instantly dimming the lights.

"There, that's better," he said, rubbing his granddad's shoulder.

Jake's eyes opened all the way and stared absently. He smacked his lips together, and a low rattling noise came from his throat.

"Are you thirsty?"

Jake nodded. Stick poured a small amount of water and held it to his lips, raising his head with the other hand. His granddad slurped the water, eagerly leaning into the cup. A scratchy voice attempted to form words, but all that came out was a grunt.

"It's okay, Granddad, the words will come. Rest now," Stick said with an air of reassurance, but really, he pitied his granddad.

He pressed the yellow button to call the doctor

"He can't speak," Stick said as soon as Doctor Hammet entered the room.

"That could take some time. Let's run a few tests to see where you are, Mr. Elliott," he said, turning to Jake and taking out a small light pen. "Stick, why don't you head on down to the lobby and take a break?"

"I'll be right back, Granddad," Stick said, probably too loudly.

Stick felt the pressure lift off his chest as he exited the room. As he walked past the nurses' station, a young blonde stopped writing and propped her cheek in her hand, her eyes lifting upward as if in a daydream. The nurse behind the medicine cart pulled at the tie in her hair, letting it tumble down her shoulders in soft waves. Another playfully slid her stethoscope around her neck. They watched as Stick passed, their eyes following his every step. He pulled Annalee's note from his back pocket.

"Do you ladies have a phone I could use?" he asked politely.

The blonde smiled sweetly and lifted the receiver from its cradle. "Dial one to get out," she said as the other nurses gathered near.

Stick turned his back to the nurses and leaned against the counter. He could hear them breathing, smell their perfume mingled with antiseptic. He dialed the number on the note. On the fifth ring, he turned back to the counter to face four nurses standing all in a row.

He reached out, receiver in hand. "Thank you—"

"Hello?"

Stick yanked the phone back up to his ear. "Annalee?" he asked in disbelief.

His audience moaned and sat down in their chairs, one spinning quickly to the other side of the semicircle to gather papers.

"Hi, I got your note. Thank you. I don't know why I'm calling except I needed someone to talk to," he said, almost shyly.

Annalee's voice on the other end of the line was kind, patient, and a little bit sleepy.

"I'm sorry, I just realized the time—"

"It's all right. I can sleep anytime."

"Well, I'm still sorry, but Granddad just woke up. He can't talk yet, but I think he'll be okay."

"Oh, Stick, that's wonderful. Is there anything you need down there?"

"Not really. I just—you know, I thought we connected last time we talked, like we have some things in common."

The nurse sitting closest to the phone raised her eyebrow and clicked her pen.

"So, uh, can I call you again tomorrow?"

"You can call anytime. People always need someone to talk to when they're going through stressful times."

It seemed Annalee was trying to be a friend, but Stick wanted more. He sighed. "Well, thanks, Annalee, and thanks for taking my call. Get some rest," he said. "Bye."

He handed the phone back to the nurse. She put it in its cradle, then asked, "Girlfriend?"

Stick thought this was an awful personal question for a medical professional to be asking. "Not yet," he said, and she smirked.

"Want some coffee?" she asked, pointing to the carafe behind her desk.

"Sure. Black."

She poured a cup of dark watery liquid into a paper cup and reached for a napkin. "Pastry? Bagel?"

"No, thanks," he said, taking the cup.

The coffee was weak, but it was better than nothing. Stick leaned against the far wall and let his head fall back. Since he was young, he had been moving fast, always running from something. He used to run into the woods and hide when his father was drunk—the only way to escape the abuse. He would watch his mother cowering in the corner of their small log house, hiding her face from the objects being thrown around the room. When his father finally left, Stick was glad to see him go, but his mother lost it. She wandered around the house all day, canning peaches and barricading the windows, sure some bad men would come take her away. That last afternoon, Stick had run again because the bad men did show up, just as she suspected. Then Jake taught him to drive, taught him to moonshine, to run from the law. So, Stick kept running, for fear the devil would catch up with him. If he kept moving, nothing could pin him down. No woman could marry him and force him into a life of complacency. No police officer could catch him and put him in a jail cell. No disease of the brain could take over in idle moments. Stick had always believed that what drove his mother nuts was the silence, the fact that she didn't have a life outside her husband. So Stick filled his life with noise, so not even death itself could get to him. He would outrun it as long as he could.

He'd seen his granddad slow down in the last few years, with the dissolution of his moonshining business. Jake's days had become indolent, just meaningless whistling and naps. It's what did him in, Stick was sure.

And now Annalee was a bump in Stick's otherwise smooth road. She made him want to sit down for dinner, have a conversation, take a slow drive. He glanced over at the nurses' desk, their curvaceous bodies stuffed into tight, white uniforms. Their stocking-clad thighs made satisfying sounds, rubbing against each other as they walked. He liked one-night stands: no commitment, no feelings, just sex. He liked being left to his own devices. But now? Something had changed. The flirting seemed frivolous. There was no chase. It was too easy. Annalee, however, was a prize, the checkered flag at the end of a well-fought race. Or maybe he only liked her because she played hard to get. Maybe if he had her once, he may not want her again. But something about the way she made him feel when he called—maybe this would be different.

"Stick, you wanna come back in?" Dr. Hammet asked, his head peering around the doorway to his granddad's room.

Stick chugged the last of the coffee, now cold, and entered the room to find his granddad sitting up, smiling.

"Granddad, you doin' okay?"

"He's doing great," Doctor Hammet said. "Tests came back to show restrictive cardiomyopathy, scarring on the heart. The cause is unknown."

Scarring of the heart? Did he have too much to deal with in his life? The death of his wife, his daughter's incarceration? Raising a grandson hell-bent on doing everything perilously?

Jake muttered to himself, but it was too low and unintelligible for Stick to make out.

The doctor continued, "He'll be fine on his own, no need for medicine at this point. I'll check on him once a week to get vitals." He gave Stick a weak smile. "Sometimes the heart—and this is more of a visceral feeling—sometimes the heart just slows down a bit."

Slowing down. Stick shook his head. "Thank you, Doctor."

Jake made another attempt at speaking, this time with more success. "Home," he said, rather breathless. "Damn it!" he swore, loud and clear, frustrated with his garbled speech.

"I'll discharge you today and see you next Thursday," Doctor Hammet said, writing up the orders. "Take care, you two."

"Let's get you out of here," Stick said as soon as he left, helping Jake into the wheelchair a nurse had brought for them. "I was thinking, when we get you up and about again, I could take you for a ride in the race car."

Jake nodded.

As Stick loaded his granddad's frail body into the cab, he wondered if he could outrun time. Jake got sick because he'd slowed down. He slept, falling into a slumber so deep, he almost didn't make it out. If he could keep his granddad moving, they could blow right past the maladies that came with old age.

Stick revved the engine. "Okay, Granddad, this truck tops seventy-five—wanna see?"

Chapter 15

ATLANTA, GA
– 1971 –

Stick smoothed one hand along the cherrywood bar that stretched the length of the room. Despite its size, there were only four other people at the counter. Everyone else had coupled off, sliding into the high-backed, pin-tucked red leather booths that circled the room. The speakeasy in Atlanta was a den of secrets, patrons gathering to hide from their real lives that bubbled just above the surface of the dimly lit basement. Low whispers, delicate kisses, the spin of a wedding ring as it was pocketed.

Stick had stumbled upon the place after a restless night at a local motel. He'd been on the road for days, picking up wins at Lakewood and Peach Bowl on the way to the big prize at Atlanta Motor Speedway. The crowds at the small-time tracks had been big, the women plenty, but every night, Stick would go back to some cheap motel and call Annalee. They would talk for hours, him mostly about his granddad, her about her mother. She was a good listener, and at the end of every call, Stick would ask to see her, but she always had an excuse. He was confused. Acceptance of his faults, then rejection of his proposal. She would lend an understanding ear, then abruptly end the call. She seemed to trust him yet stayed guarded.

He'd tried to sleep that night in the musty, creaky motel bed, but she was all he could think about: her curvaceous body, her silky Southern voice. So, at two a.m., he had gotten dressed and ended up in the basement of an old carriage house, surrounded by liquor and desperate souls.

"Name's Thomas. What can I do you for?" the bartender asked.

The bartender was dressed in a white button-down with black sleeve garters, a gray vest, bow tie, and charcoal baker boy hat. His upturned mustache curled at the ends, and he sported a pocket watch. Stick tried not to roll his eyes. "What do you recommend?"

"Green Hornet. House specialty."

"Nope. Don't like the color. What else?"

"Harvey Wallbanger?"

"Naw, that's a breakfast drink. How 'bout a shot of whiskey?"

"Got Highland Park and Gillies and Company."

"Give me the Gillies, a good Scottish blend."

Thomas nodded and poured a short glass a quarter of the way.

Stick took a sip. The whiskey was smooth and rich as he rolled it around his tongue. The fruitiness was subtle, unlike the 'shine he was used to, which burst with sweet notes. The Gillies was strong on the back end, a creamy finish with a hint of spice. Stick spun around slowly on his chair and watched the couplings: men and women in love, leaning into each other, others in lust, their tongues locked in a dance, pulling and tugging at clothing. Stick was jealous. He had met the most perfect woman, yet he couldn't rope her in.

"Another," he said.

The bartender nodded and poured. Stick downed this one in one gulp. No one knew him here. Butch and his crew were miles away, sleeping in the RV. Jake was home. And Annalee . . . Well, he didn't know where the hell she was. Maybe she didn't see him the way he saw her. Maybe she'd found someone else. The whiskey suddenly hit Stick, and his eyes blurred a little. He glanced up at the ceiling, etched in gold, and let his pupils trail the dark velvet walls. When he brought his attention back to the counter, there was a woman sitting beside him. She had dark hair that fell just beyond her bare shoulders; her full hips spilled off the sides of the barstool. Stick rubbed his eyes.

"Annalee?"

She didn't respond, so Stick tapped on the bar, an indication he wanted another drink. Thomas poured another shot, this time in a fresh glass.

"Try this," the bartender said. "The best in Tennessee whiskey: Jack Daniels Gold Medal Series. On the house."

Stick looked at him and wondered if perhaps this bartender knew who he was. He didn't ask though. Tonight, he preferred to remain anonymous. As he swirled the drink, he noticed tastes of toffee, rich chocolate, maple, and, oddly, a bit of banana. It finished with a touch of tropical fruit and the smoky burn of a barrel.

"It's good. Thank you." He didn't want to elaborate on the palate in case the bartender asked too many questions about his knowledge of tastes. He turned back to the woman, who now had one elbow on the bar, a finger twirling her hair. Annalee had done that the day in the garage. He said her name again, and the woman turned to reveal sultry eyes and blood-red lips.

"Hello, stranger," she said.

Stick squinted, trying to get a closer glimpse of her eyes, but her long lashes lay in the way.

"Hello," he said as he moved closer, the sweet smell of butterscotch and jasmine hitting his nose.

She moved in close, put her hand on his thigh, and leaned in. She whispered something inaudible to him, but Stick could feel her soft breath on his neck, and it gave him goose bumps. She laughed at everything he said, running her hands up and down his neck, his spine. He had another shot, paid the bartender, and guided her out of the bar. The way her hips swayed in the moonlight sent Stick reeling. He was sure she'd be worth the wait. But what was she doing in Georgia?

As he led her to his room, he fumbled with the keys, so she took them and opened the door, tossing her heels on the spongy brown carpet, along with her top. He said her name again. Beautiful Annalee, so close to the poem his mother used to quote. Annabelle Lee. Sweet Annabelle Lee.

"Why do you keep calling me that?"

The woman's voice broke through Stick's thoughts as he plopped upon the bed. He looked up at her again. The round face, thin lips, brown eyes. This was not his Annalee. How could he have been so stupid to think she would be here, just waiting for him, ready to succumb to his every need? But as he gazed upon this woman, he felt a rise in his jeans, a natural yearning he had ignored for too long. His eyes traveled to her wide hips, now clad only in lacy, white panties. He lay back, and as she climbed on top, he closed his eyes.

Stick's head pounded as light cut through striped window curtains. He sat up and leaned forward, grasping his head. *Fuck, how much did I drink?* He slapped his face lightly with both hands and rubbed his dry, scratchy eyes until the film covering them escaped as tears. He looked around the stale room. His clothes were scattered upon the floor; his belt hung from the ceiling fan. The bedsheets were crumpled, the fitted sheet scrunched and puckered on the right edge. The door to the bathroom was wide open, and he could see into the beige toilet and speckled brown sink. He was alone. Whoever the dark-haired woman was, she was gone.

Stick let his body fall back onto the bed. What had he done? His sexual adventures had always been a source of pride, but now he was ashamed. He'd slipped, given in to his body's carnal desires. He felt sick, last night's whiskey and bar nuts mixing inside his stomach, creating a nausea he deserved. He rolled on his side, picked up the receiver, and dialed Annalee's number. Could he tell her? Would she even care? He didn't know; he just had to hear her voice. But the phone rang over and over, and no one answered. The buzzing shrill played with his mind, taunting him with its *ring, ring, ring, ring*. The chords of loneliness. He slammed the receiver down. *Fuck!*

A knock at the door. Stick sat up. Is she here? Was that her last night after all? *I did have a lot to . . .*

He stood up and, wrapping a sheet around his waist, made his way to the door, which was shaking with the rasp of someone desperate. He opened it.

"Stick, where the hell have you been?" Butch fixed him with a glare and strode into the room like he owned the place.

Stick didn't respond as Butch tossed him his clothes. "Get dressed. I don't want to know," he said eyeballing a black bra draped over the lampshade. "We gotta get going. Got a promo event this afternoon. Get yourself together."

Stick sat down on the edge of the bed. "I fucked up," he said.

"What now?" Butch asked.

"I—well, I kinda slept with a woman last night."

"So, what's new? Why is that bothering you?"

"Because, Butch, I like Annalee." Stick couldn't believe he was admitting this. "I thought we had a connection, but I can't ever get her to go out with me, and last night I got a little drunk. And the woman, well, she looked like—I mean she had dark hair and everything." Stick knew he was rambling, but that's how he felt—lost.

"Stick, it don't matter. Y'all ain't a couple. Don't matter how much you talk on the phone and such. You ain't got nuthin' to feel bad about."

Stick knew his friend was right. What he and Annalee had was, well, he didn't know. It was hard to define.

"Advice from a married man?"

Stick nodded.

"Don't worry about it. I think Annalee likes you. When she's ready, she'll let you know. In the meantime, have a little guilt-free fun."

Stick nodded again. It was just sex, after all. No emotion. He'd always been able to separate the two.

"Now snap out of it. We got some racin' to do, and I need your head clear," Butch said, shoving a cup of lukewarm coffee into Stick's hands. "I'm gonna run 'n get us a couple breakfast sandwiches, and by the time we leave this motel, I want to see the confident lady-killer I've always known."

Stick laughed. "Get outta here, then, so I can get dressed."

Butch bowed and exited the room.

Stick chugged the bitter black coffee like it was penance for his lustful crime. He chucked the cup into the garbage pail and pulled his pants on. *I gotta get my head straight*, he thought. *How is it that this woman has me all messed up? She's just—she's so sincere, so innocent.*

He stood up and wrapped his shirt around the back of his neck, thinking. Annalee had confidence, but was it all a ruse? The day in the garage, the way she talked about her mother, the way she wouldn't discuss her father . . . She was troubled, tethered to a painful past.

He slipped the shirt over his head and walked to the bathroom mirror. Even with bloodshot eyes, dehydrated skin, and a headful of matted hair, he was still good looking. He shook his head, wet a washcloth, and pressed it to his face. He heard the door slam as Butch walked in.

"Ready?" he asked.

Stick nodded. The caffeine had kicked in, and his head was clearing.

"There's a crowd of people waiting at the motel office. Guess word leaked you was stayin' here."

Stick peered out the window to the tiny brick office across the street. Thirty or so men, women, and children, all in Stick Elliott shirts and hats, stood outside the building, paper and Polaroids in hand. A few young beauties in miniskirts and tight leather pants adjusted their bras while others checked their lipstick in their compacts.

"Fast cars and fast women," Butch said, crumpling the brown paper bag he was holding.

That's what I signed up for. Yet I'm worried about one woman, who won't even grab a bite to eat with me.

He slid on his python boots and grabbed his cowboy hat from the top of the television set. "Well," he said to Butch, with a sarcastic touch of impatience, "what are you waiting for? My fans are calling."

"You got it, boss."

Boss. That's right. Stick placed the cowboy hat firmly on his head. *I am the boss of the track. The boss of my life.* He opened the door to the cheers that fueled his zeal. He corrected his posture and threw a wave. *Passion is a powerful thing,* he thought. *When it takes over, it can render a man helpless. And my first passion is speed. Always has been. Always will be. And speed is the kinda passion that doesn't hold you back. It pushes you forward, causing a need for more. I gotta use that, for that is what makes me the best Goddamn driver around.*

He stepped out into the cool morning air, and the crowd rushed toward him, his name on their lips. *Stick Elliott. They'll never forget my name.*

As Stick walked onto the track, he eyed Robby Allister in the corner, bent over his red-and-gold Monte Carlo. Stick thought Robby looked more like an insurance salesman than a hard-charged race car driver, with shaggy brown hair that cascaded into thick sideburns and always smiling. He was the nicest driver around, and despite the fact Robby was his biggest competition, Stick liked the guy.

"Got some trouble?" Stick asked, knowing full well that Robby, a skilled mechanic, had his car in tip-top shape.

"Naw, just rechecking some things. You can never be too careful," Robby said, looking over his shoulder. "Ah, Stick, how ya doin'? Decided to join us today on the blacktop, eh?"

"Figured I'd give you a run for your money," Stick said with a laugh.

Robby twirled the monkey wrench he was holding, then stuck it in the pocket of his jumpsuit. "You always do, Stick. You always do. Still kickin' up at the dirt track?"

"Yeah, that's where my heart is," Stick said as he walked closer to get a peek under the hood. The engine was so pristine, he could see his reflection in its surface. "Robby, nobody's gonna see the guts of this car. Why do you shine it up so much?"

Robby took a clean rag out of his shirt pocket and rubbed black oil from the camshaft. "This car is an extension of me. If I want it to perform, I need to take care of it. I've had the same car for five years."

"Sounds like you're not drivin' hard enough."

"I drive plenty hard, you know that. She's been banged up a few times, but I fix her right up myself. This beauty," he said, closing the hood, "is the only daughter I'll ever have."

Stick looked around. "Hey, seen Willie? He ain't been at many races lately."

"Yeah, saw him down in Virginia last week. He's havin' a tough go. Mechanical troubles, and some of the tracks have banned him."

"That's a shame. He's as good a driver as I've ever seen."

"Yeah, I tried to help him, get him set up with this bigwig who has a fleet of cars just sittin' there, waitin' on the best drivers. But he didn't want it. Said he'd rather drive his own. That at least he'd know when he won, it was his own blood, sweat, and tears that got him there, not some rich man with a souped-up car."

"Don't blame him. Tell him I said raise hell next time you see him."

"Will do."

"All right, Robby. Always fun to chat," Stick said, sticking out his hand. "Have a good race."

Robby shook Stick's hand as he looked him in the eyes. "You too, my friend, but not too good. And don't go bumpin' me around. Just use your speed to pass. No need for tricks."

"That takes the fun out of it." Stick smiled. "See you at the winner's circle. I'll be the one on the podium."

Robby shook his head as Stick hustled back to his car.

Butch looked up from where he was kneeling. "Your tires goin' a little bald. I'm gonna change 'em out."

"Don't."

"What? Why?"

"It's fine, Butch. I'll use it to my advantage."

"Stick, if it rains even a drop, you'll lose control."

"It's not going to rain. WSOC weatherman said so," he said, pointing up to a clear sky. "Besides, I've known those tires were smooth for about a week now. Been practicing with them. I like the way it takes the track."

"Good God. You're crazy, you know that? One loose bolt or bump, and you're going straight to that wall."

Stick pulled a handful of silver from his pocket and put it into Butch's hands. "No parts out there. I cleaned them up earlier today. There's one crack a fourth of the way around, but I've got a plan."

"I still don't like it."

"You don't have to."

Butch hung his head, defeated. "I was thinking—what do you think about six stops for fuel? I figured in speed and length of the track, and that's your safest bet."

"Five," Stick replied. "Six's an unlucky number. I'm not making six pit stops."

"Good God, Stick. I based that on calculations, not superstition. You need six to get you safely through the last leg."

"Will I run out?"

"Probably not, but it'll be close. You should have ample fuel at five, but why risk it? You don't want to be runnin' on fumes at the end. I'd rather top you off at six."

Stick ran his fingers through his hair, considering the proposition. "Five. I'll make it."

Butch took a deep breath. "Okay, but I'm gonna fill it up on the fourth and fifth. You'll be a little heavy, but better than running out right in front of the finish line."

"Fine. I'll deal with the extra weight. Now, let's go. I only have forty minutes to start time and—"

"You've got to go through the rituals," Butch said, snapping his fingers at Finnegan. "Go get Stick's suit and orange candies."

"Yes, sir," Finnegan said, running off.

Stick crawled through the window and fastened his helmet. A new two-way radio was mounted on the dash. *Good Lord.* He had been reluctant to try the radio—hand signals and a good pit board had always done the trick—but Butch was convincing, stating all the best drivers were using them now, and he would be left in the dust if he didn't have one. Not wanting to be viewed as a dinosaur, Stick agreed, even though he thought the static would interrupt his thoughts, not to mention he didn't want Butch in his ear all night.

"Stick, can you hear me?" A voice came through the radio.

"Yeah. How can I turn this volume down if you start jabberin' too much?" Stick asked, half-jokingly.

"Dial on the side, but I would caution against it. We can see things you may not pick up with your limited vision," Butch said.

"Fine, but don't be talkin' the whole time. Just tell me what I need to know, or we're gettin' rid of this thing," he said, tapping the speaker.

"Good Lord, Stick, that was right in my ear!"

Stick laughed. "I'm signin' off for now. Need to concentrate. Lemme know important information only."

"Ten-four, boss."

The pace car drifted along the side and pulled in front of all the cars.

"Gentlemen, start your engines," the announcer said, and the whole place came alive with a rumble that shook the stadium.

They took off, and cars shifted back and forth at a speed of fifty-five miles per hour, a veritable dance throughout the first few laps. As they rounded the corner toward spectators, the pace car moved, and the green flag was dropped. Stick watched as everyone around him went crazy, pushing their cars to full throttle, making moves that would send them to the front of the pack. Stick drove steady, waiting. *No reason to go nuts right now. We got a whole lotta race to go*, he thought. Why burn out gas and tires in the first laps?

"What's your strategy, Stick? You're stuck in the middle," Butch's voice said loudly.

Stick jumped. "Goddamn it, Butch. You scared the shit out of me. My strategy is none of your business. I'll get the job done. Now shut up, or I'm turning this off."

"Ten-four."

Around lap forty-five, Stick decided it was time. He bump-drafted a couple cars out of the way, then slingshot past his teammates. Coming up to Robby at the lead, he broke to the outside lane, keeping pace but not passing. Robby kept drifting, protecting his groove, fully expecting Stick to pass. *Not yet, buddy. Not yet.* He raced in the outside lane for another thirty laps, Butch begging him to come in for a tire change.

Finally, when Stick saw Robby pit, he did too, getting only gas. Finnegan stomped around like a mad leprechaun, spitting profanities because Stick didn't want new tires. The pit stop lasted only seconds, with Robby and Stick pulling out at the same time. Again, Stick went to the outside and found a groove.

With ten laps to go, Stick sped up on the outside, forcing the two cars ahead of him to drift from inside to middle. "They don't know what the hell I'm doing," Stick said.

"Neither do we," came Butch's voice.

Stick laughed.

On the second turn, he was ready. As they rounded the curve, Stick sprinted up the bank as fast as he could, finding the groove he had identified earlier in the day to gain momentum and shoot back down, putting himself several car lengths ahead of the leaders.

"Wahoo!" he yelled as he put the pedal to the floor. "How's that strategy, boys?"

All he could hear on the radio was cheering.

The white flag flowed in the wind, and Stick sped up even more on the curves, his almost bald tires gripping the surface like glue. The crowd was standing now. Stick beat the wheel down the final stretch as the checkered flag waved aggressively. He whizzed past the stadium seats, the people in them a blur of streaked colors.

Then a vibration of the brake, a jolt to the left, the uncontrollable feeling of the car taking over as Stick did a crescent on the track. Robby's red car in his front window meant he was traveling backward. He stuck one arm out the window in a thumbs-up as the other arm strained to gain control of the wheel. Forearm flexed, he tugged and directed the car toward the finish line. *Don't throw the red flag*, he thought as he signaled to the crow's nest.

"Stick? Stick? What's—" Butch's panicked voice said through the radio.

"I'm okay, I'm okay. Don't let them stop this race!" Stick said, trying to sound calm as he put both hands back on the wheel to steer.

"But you're—"

"Don't let them stop the race! The checkered flag is out. No red. No yellow!"

He could see Butch running along the sidelines, hooping and waving at the flag stand.

"Thumbs-up, thumbs-up," Butch yelled, and Stick could visualize him hysterically jumping up and down. "He has control. He has control!" Butch sounded out of breath, but the flagger must have gotten the picture because the checkered flag danced in the wind.

The finish was just yards away, but Stick could see Robby coming up beside him on the inside. *Dammit! He's catching up at exactly the wrong moment.* But if Stick spun the car around, he would lose time, so he went with the momentum of the car and drove backward at full speed.

"Stick! Stick! What the hell are you doing?" Butch was yelling, but Stick ignored it.

He was now neck and neck with a wide-eyed Robby. They blew past the finish line, and Stick broke and turned the car around. The announcer was yelling something he couldn't discern; he could tell by the look on Robby's face he didn't know either.

"What's happening?" Stick asked, putting his mouth close to the radio.

"It's a tie," Butch said.

"A tie?"

"Yeah, think they're trying to decide what to do on account of the fact they've never had a driver cross the finish line backward before," Finnegan's voice said.

"Gimme that," Butch said, and there was crackling on the radio. "Stick, step out of the car. They're trying to figure out what to do here."

Stick took off his helmet and stuck his backside out the car window, then eased himself down. Robby had already made his way over.

"My God, Stick, that was damn amazing!"

"Did what I had to," was all Stick said, shaking Robby's hand. "We tied?"

"Yeah, photo finish."

Officials in NASCAR shirts came jogging over with a stack of papers.

"Hey, guys, great race," a man with a dark mustache said. "We've never had this happen before, so our lawyer is reviewing the rules."

A gray-haired man with a receding hairline and tiny circular glasses flipped through papers. "Checking," he said. He flipped a few more pages, then stopped suddenly, tapped his finger, and said, "There's nothing here that says you can't cross the finish line with the back of the car. Just states the winner is the racer whose fender crosses the finish line first."

"Fender?" said the mustache man.

"The fender is the fender," Robby said. "Front or back. Don't see how it matters."

Stick looked at him with a raised eyebrow. The lawyer pushed his glasses up with his ring finger and waited for his boss to speak.

"So, you're saying . . ." The man twirled his mustache on one end. "You're saying you'd accept a tie, even though this joker came through backward?"

"Not only do I accept a tie, I demand one. And he's not a joker. This man's one of the best drivers I've ever seen," said Robby, putting his hand firmly on Stick's upper arm.

"That *was* pretty awesome. And the crowd—they loved it," said a third gentleman, who, to this point, had remained silent. "They were whoopin' and hollerin' like a bunch a wild mules when he crossed that line." The man pulled a card out of his pocket and handed one each to Stick and Robby. "John DeMoya. NASCAR promoter. We like your style. It's just what we need to spice things up 'round here. As long as it's legal," he added, eyeing the lawyer. "Ain't that right, Morton?"

The bespectacled lawyer nodded his head.

"Now, let's fill the crowd in on the decision, Anthony," he said to mustache man, who shook his head in dismay and walked toward the podium.

The announcement was made, and the crowd erupted once more. Stick could see his pit crew waving towels in the air in celebration. Butch flung off his headset and hugged Finnegan and the rest of the boys.

"Why did you agree to a tie?" Stick asked Robby. "They probably would've sided with you on a technicality."

"It was the right thing to do. You would've beat me had it not been for that tire of yours. And the way you came out of that spin . . . I've never—you deserve it. You should pit for new tires, though. You got lucky this time. You might not next go-round. That wall is awful hard, Stick," he said. "I'd hate to see—"

Stick held up a hand to stop him.

"You've got skill for sure, but you've got to trust your crew. I'm not talking about being reserved, just smart."

Stick considered this, only because Robby was a good driver, and he knew cars better than anybody. *He's right*, Stick thought. *The car is an extension of the driver. Just like a body, it has to be maintained, treated with respect. If I want to get full performance out of this car, I need to treat it well and listen when it needs something. Maybe that's how you get the best out of anything: cars, friendships, relationships.*

Chapter 16

BRISTOL, TN
– 1972 –

The whine of percussion filtered through the stadium noise as Stick pulled into Bristol.

Granddad.

Stick stepped down from his pickup truck and placed the Stetson firmly on his head. Nashville, with all its glitz and glitter, was four hours away, and Stick figured the folks up in this small Tennessee town would appreciate a good ol' boy.

"You're ruining my bad-boy image, you know," Stick said as he hugged his granddad.

The old man felt thin, frail.

Tommy slid out from under the car. "I rather like this music. It's soothin'," he said.

"Soothin'? Hell, if I wanted you calm and cultured, I'd send you to the opera. I need you guys revved up," Stick said.

"Time for that later," Jake said. "These boys think better with my music. Besides, have you looked at this place? Looks like the Colosseum. The way the stadium rises up, it's better suited for a gladiator fight than a car race."

Stick grinned, a smooth, disarming smile. "I'm going to get ready. I better not come back to you boys waltzing around the pit."

As Stick made his way to the RV, he was calm—maybe too calm. Could it be the music? He didn't mind the sway of the violin, the broad vibrato of the cello, but it didn't set the right tone for a stock car race. He stomped his dusty boots on the honeycomb metal of the stairs and stepped inside. *Ain't nobody stoppin' me tonight*, he thought, and he whirled his cowboy hat across the room, landing it squarely on the hat rack. He got dressed quickly and sprinted out, skipping his prerace meal.

The symphony had been replaced by loudspeaker announcements and the waking of engines. Stick climbed in the car.

"Run this car good tonight," Jake said. Jake closed his eyes for a moment, as if he could still hear the orchestra in his head. He put his hand on Stick's arm. "Don't do nuthin' stupid. If the car malfunctions, if you get in trouble, if you—just come in."

Stick couldn't believe what he was hearing. The man who'd taught him to drive fast and do anything necessary to avoid being caught wanted him to be careful? "You g'ttin' soft?"

Jake shook his head. "No. But that crash down in Georgia last week got me rattled a bit. Look, I'm old and, well, I don't need your mileage runnin' out before mine."

Stick didn't know what to do with this version of his granddad. Maybe he was running low on gas, but nothing a little excitement and purpose couldn't fix. As Stick looked at him standing there, though, he knew just what he had to say, regardless of what he knew he would do.

"I promise. I know what I'm doing. I was taught by the best. But I'll be, um"—he couldn't bring himself to say *careful*—"smart," he said finally.

"All right then," Jake said, patting him on the arm.

Stick rolled into the lineup, front row. The flag dropped, and he shifted gears, quickly zigzagging like a bow on a fiddle across the breadth of the track, so no one dared to pass. He ground around the curves, bearing down into the steering wheel. He set the tempo and wasn't letting up, outpacing every other car by at least two lengths.

With twenty laps to go, a persistent rattle sounded deep within the car's body, but Stick pressed harder on the gas. Most drivers would have pitted to diagnose the dry cough, and his crew could get him out quickly, probably duct-taping the loose parts together. But Stick didn't want to win the race by seconds; he wanted to win by a country mile, clock the fastest speed this track had ever seen.

The rattle turned to clatter, and Stick felt the car shake. Ten laps. *Ching, ching, ching.* Nine laps. Tremors migrated through the steering wheel into his hands. Eight laps. *Clank, clank, clunk.* Seven laps. *Sputter, clink, clank.* Number 19 three car lengths behind. Six laps. Joggle, shake. The tires wobbled with subtle movement, and Stick readjusted his hands to compensate. Bent axle joint. Five laps. *Cling, swish, swish.* Four laps. Stick pressed harder on the pedal but felt the strain, the inadequate power transfer to the wheels. Three laps. His whole body shook with the rattling of the axle, but he pressed the pedal and steadied his hands as #19 got closer. Two laps. He felt the strain in his arms as he steered left, trying to avoid the bump on turn two that could rip the axle off for good—*bam!*

The right front tire hit, and the wheel bearings seized, causing the tire to spin out of control. No matter how hard Stick pressed the pedal, the car slowed, rattling and screeching like an out-of-tune instrument toward the inside center railing. Number 19 passed. Then #23, #42, #17 . . . With the railing close, he finally let off the gas as the car spun out, narrowly avoiding metal. He landed in the center grass, right tire ripped off.

He crawled out and stomped the spinning hubcap with one foot. He watched as the other cars completed their last lap. *Lucky bastards.* If only he'd gone in, nineteen laps back.

The checkered flag dropped. The paddy wagon showed up, but Stick waved them off. He may have lost this race, but he sure as hell wasn't climbing up in no cop car or ambulance to be carted away like a bruised-up child. He saw Butch hightailing it across the track in the pickup truck. As he got closer, he saw his granddad in the passenger seat. *Ah, hell . . .*

"You all right?" Butch yelled before he even stopped the truck.

"Yeah, I'm fine." Stick peeled off his helmet and dropped it to the ground.

"What happened?" Butch asked, making his way across the grass.

Jake was behind him, breathing heavily, trying to keep up.

"The axle. It gave way."

"You were ridin' her pretty hard today. Did you let up even once? Hear any noises? Feel—"

"Which one of them questions you want me to answer first?"

"Well, did you know?"

Stick didn't want to tell Butch he could have prevented the blowout if he'd just come in when he first heard the rattle.

"Well, I—" He smiled and put his arms out as his granddad approached.

Jake stepped up and smacked him right upside the head.

"Ow! What was that for?"

"You drove like a damn fool! I saw that side"—Jake pointed at the car with a shaky finger—"shakin' twenty laps back. Don't tell me you didn't know."

"I didn't—"

"Don't you lie to me! You let your ego get in the way of your damn sense. You wasn't satisfied with just winnin' that race. You had to win it bigger 'n anyone else. That's foolish! I didn't teach you to drive that way. No matter what's going on, how fast you're going, you always exercise caution."

"Granddad—"

"Don't Granddad me! That mighta been fast drivin', but it sure as hell wasn't smart drivin'."

And with that, Jake turned and stalked to the car. He squatted to look at the damaged tire, and Stick swore he saw him say a little prayer.

"He just loves you," Butch said.

"I know, but, hell, I—"

"Is it true?"

"What?"

"Was the car shakin'? Did you know?"

"Yeah, I felt it. But, Butch, I thought I could ride it out. I have before."

"I know. Just bad luck this time. We'll get 'er fixed up for next week's race. But you gotta learn to pit every now and then, especially when you sense a problem. You know this car. It's part of you. You got to listen to what it needs. Don't be greedy. Have faith in your crew."

"Okay, I'll think about it." He glanced over at Jake, who was pacing the infield. "I better get the old man home before we have another heart event."

Lawndale, NC

As they pulled up in front of the house, Stick saw a figure on the porch. He flashed his headlights, and she stood up, the curvature of soft beautiful thighs outlined in the light. Annalee.

"Hi," Stick said, suddenly meek. "What are you doing here? And how did you—"

"I heard about the accident," she said, hands on hips.

"Oh, I'm fine," Stick said, but he thought it curious she'd come all the way out to check on him.

"Well, maybe you can talk some sense inta him," Jake said, walking up to Annalee and taking her hand. "You are quite lovely," he said, kissing the top before heading into the house.

"Drivin' dangerously again?" Annalee asked.

"That's all I ever do."

"Well, I guess we better go out for that dinner you promised before it's too late."

"Oh? Are you asking me out on a date?"

I knew it! She wanted me from the beginning; she was just playing hard to get.

"I could use some company, that's all."

Not so tough after all. Stick felt bad as soon as the thought popped into his head.

"I'd be glad to. How about tomorrow night? I'll pick you up at eight."

"I'll pick you up," she said.

"Too fast for you?"

"It's not the speed I worry about; it's the decision-making."

They heard an amen from inside the house, and Stick grimaced. "I know what I'm doing. I'm always in control."

"That's the thing. Even if you're in control, someone around you isn't. You can drive fast and cautiously at the same time. I've watched you. There's no doubtin' you're good, but sometimes you're dumb."

Stick had to admit, he was turned on by Annalee's confidence. He'd never met a woman like her before.

"You're lucky tonight wasn't worse. Next time, you might not be so lucky."

Stick pushed the heel of his pythons into the dirt, thinking of something clever to say, but "Yes, ma'am" was all he could come up with.

Annalee nodded. "Okay. Well, see you tomorrow, eight sharp." She walked past him, and he could smell sweet honeysuckle on her skin.

"Eight sharp. I'll wear my best boots," he called after her.

"Wear whatever you want," she said without looking back. "Boots don't make the man."

"I know a wise old man that would beg to differ."

She stopped and turned around. "What?"

Stick didn't know how to explain his prophetic conversation with the leatherworker without coming across as crazy. "Ah, nuthin'," he said. "Just some old wives' tale—superstition and such."

"Life is hard enough without having to sidestep black cats and throw ash out the window."

Stick loved her practicality but could tell Annalee was pigheaded. He'd never had a woman disagree with him before, let alone stand up to him. But maybe that's what he needed.

Spartanburg, SC

Stick and Annalee sat at a table in the small, dimly lit dining room of Peddler Steakhouse. A small candle flickered atop their corner table and created shadows on the crisp white tablecloth. Stick glanced over the top of his wine list at Annalee. Dressed in burgundy with a deep-red lip, she looked as rich as her surroundings. Her hair, a warm chocolaty brown, was curled, and the smallest bit of her bangs fell seductively over her left eye. The tips of her nails traced the menu, and Stick couldn't help but imagine what that must feel like.

"I'm glad we came here," Annalee said as she put her menu down and leaned back in her wooden spindle chair. Her collarbone glistened, and Stick's eyes wandered down her V-neck. He caught himself and immediately brought his eyes back to hers.

"Me too," he said, and he meant it.

Stick had never been on an official date before; a couple beers and some drunken darts at Nu-Way Lounge didn't count. There had never been much conversation past the usual flirting and small talk, so he didn't know how to act, what questions to ask. He reached down under the tablecloth and placed one hand on his jittery knee. He hoped the quivering rise and fall of his chest wouldn't give him away.

"So, Stick, why do you like racin' so much that you put your life on the line for it?" she asked before taking a sip of water.

"Well," he started, thinking for a moment. "My granddad taught me to drive, and at first, it was the freedom. When I drove, I escaped. All those pent-up emotions and chaos from my youth—when I got behind the wheel, I just let 'em go. I don't know if it was 'cause I really tuned in with the car, my mind focused on one thing, or I was just young and suddenly could go wherever there was a dirt path."

Annalee nodded, so Stick continued.

"Then I think it became about control. After an unsettling childhood, finally, I was the one who could decide my fate." Stick leaned forward, giddy, his speech quick. "When I'm in the car, nuthin' happens if I don't will it. The steering wheel grants me direction, the gas pedal speed. That car won't move if I don't want it to. Despite what you might think, there's a safety in it."

He could have talked more, but he realized he'd been droning on and stopped to wait for Annalee's response.

She leaned forward. "That wasn't the answer I thought I would get."

Stick's heart deflated. He had gone too far, said the wrong thing.

"It was better," she said, and he exhaled. "I thought you would say speed. Men have such a fascination with it, you know. I don't know if it's the power or the thrill."

"It's both," he said and figured it was time to get honest. If he wanted to move things forward with Annalee, he had to be himself. "Speed, of course, factors in there for me. Power, too. There's nuthin' like the feel of pushing something to its limit and having it perform. The speed—that's the fun part. Boys and their toys," he said with a smile and a shrug.

"Honesty," she said with a smile. "I like it."

"I'm about as honest as they get. But what about you, Annalee? All this time we've known each other, and you've never told me what you like to do."

"I don't know. I sew a little. Bake some."

She seemed to struggle with the answer, like she couldn't decide who she wanted to be. Or maybe, Stick thought, she didn't want to reveal it just yet.

"I like antique furniture . . . Don't ask me where that came from. Old things that need fixin' up, broken pieces and worn-out tarnish. I like to strip it and make it whole again. I guess it gives me hope I can fix myself," she said with a laugh, but Stick could tell she wasn't kidding.

He wanted to stop her, ask her who hurt her, but she kept talking about roses, about a chicken named Mr. Jenkins, about her disdain for winter and her love for sweet tea. Stick hung on every detail she disclosed and leaned in farther.

When the waiter came by to refill her glass, Annalee turned to thank him, and Stick caught the slightest glimpse of a scar upon her jawline. There was a lot more to this woman than her beauty. She had a tumultuous past, he could tell. He wondered if that was why he was drawn to her—she reminded him of his mother, an innocent soul tortured by things unseen. Stick couldn't save his mother, but maybe he could help Annalee. He wanted to hold her, take care of her, make everything better. He sat back in his chair. *I can do this. I want to do this.*

Chapter 17

MYRTLE BEACH, SC
– 1973 –

"If you don't slow down, God'll slow you down himself," Annalee said as the wind whipped through her hair.

The traffic by Murrells Inlet was light this time of day, so Stick was showing off a bit. He and Annalee had been dating for a couple months, and this was their first trip together.

"I'll take my chances," Stick said, pressing a pair of loafers into the pedal on Annalee's coupe.

"What if that car ahead of us stops abruptly, and we crash right into it because you were going too fast?" Annalee said, pulling hair from her mouth.

"What if I get struck by lightning? Life's full of danger; I'll ride it till I die."

Annalee shook her head. Stick knew she'd bring it up again later. She always did.

She tapped her foot anxiously on the footboard. "When will we be there?"

Stick didn't know why Annalee was so nervous. Maybe she didn't want people to judge an unwed woman in the South sharing a hotel room with a man she was merely dating. It could cause quite the gossip at Sunday church. They'd spent plenty of nights together, so it couldn't be that. Yet Stick had never even seen Annalee's house. She always insisted on picking him up or meeting him out. Maybe a trip together meant it was getting serious. Maybe she was afraid he was moving too quickly.

"We'd be there a whole lot faster if I could drive the way I want," he joked.

She strummed her fingers on the dash. "Okay, but not over fifty-five."

"Does your car even go fifty-five?" he asked, speeding up.

Her lips formed a slight smile, and she turned her head toward the short, squatty palm trees dotting the side of the road. Stick had learned that look. Annalee didn't want to talk anymore. He wondered if this was normal female behavior; he was on unfamiliar ground, never having been in a relationship before. Did women often retreat inside their own mind, or was this what Arthur had meant by *different*? Was Annalee simply tired of talking, or was there something unstable in her psyche? Stick glanced sideways and noticed Annalee had propped her chin up with her hand as she let the breeze flow through her hair. His mother used to do that—gaze off into the distance, lost in some other place or time.

They rode this way for a while, passing homes, shacks, bait and shell shops. When she strummed her fingers along the side of the car or delicately removed a string of hair from her face, Stick knew she was still present and couldn't possibly be afflicted the way his mother had been. He felt bad even comparing the two when they had so little in common. He made a note to ask Butch about the nature and habits of women. He was married and had surely experienced moments like these. *That's why one-night stands are so much easier*, Stick thought, but Annalee had a pull on him he couldn't explain. He was drawn to her, felt the need to really know her, care for her—a feeling that was starting to grow bigger than his need to run.

They pulled into the Yachtsman, and Annalee's eyes lit up.

"Wow, it sure is tall!" she exclaimed, suddenly alive with wonder.

"Myrtle Beach's first high-rise. You never seen one?"

"No, never been to a city. Never saw any skyscrapers."

Stick loved Annalee's innocence. As strong and stubborn as she was, she had these moments where she was like a child, caught up in the awe of something magnificent.

They climbed out of the car and checked in, and Annalee immediately excused herself.

"I need to use the pay phone," she said, digging quarters out of her purse.

"They have phones in the room," Stick said, holding up the key.

"Oh, that'll be too expensive," she said, then sprinted outside.

He watched as she deposited a few coins and leaned into the receiver. Who was she calling? Her father? He couldn't imagine why a grown woman would need to call her father right away. He decided not to think about it too much, so he flipped through a newspaper in the lobby.

> Previously called Coastal Speedway, Myrtle Beach Speedway is being paved later next year. This weekend's non-Cup points race will be the last one on dirt.

Well, I'll be the devil. Everybody's transitioning to asphalt. Progress was good, but it seemed the powers that be wanted people to forget about racing's hard-charged, criminal roots.

Stick looked back up and saw Annalee through the double glass doors, the heat bending her shape so she became unfocused, a neutral blending of color palettes. For a moment, her dark hair wrapped around her head, clinging to her forehead, and Stick saw his mother, her wild and unruly mane knotted and twisted in the summer sun.

That was when he'd first realized something was wrong. They'd been playing outside, and the heat had been oppressive. Stick drank from the hose, the lukewarm water dribbling down his shirt. His mother was propped up on her elbows in the grass, her head thrown back, face toward the sky. The neighbor's dog barked at a squirrel scampering up the tree. The bell of the ice cream cart rang, and Stick dropped the hose and called for her. His mother was on her hands and knees calmly digging into the ground. When she looked up at him, her beautifully coiffed hair was plastered down. Water spewed from the hose as Stick called her name again, but she wasn't paying him any attention.

"Stick, Stick," Annalee said as she touched his arm. "You didn't hear me?"

He shook his head. The woman in front of him was real. "I'm—I was just thinking—"

"About the race?" she asked. "I know you always get distracted the day before."

Stick nodded, the image of his mother slowly fading. He looked at Annalee's burgundy nails looped around his forearm. His mother's nails had been short, jagged. The dirt—it had stuck to her fingers like glue.

"Dirt," he said. He looked up at Annalee, now patting him on the arm. "The track is dirt."

"That's great," she said. "Should we go take a look?"

Stick stood up. "I'll go alone." He couldn't explain it. He needed to connect with the dirt.

"What? Why?"

He kissed her on the cheek. "You're distracting."

She rolled her eyes and kissed him on the opposite cheek. "See you later, then," she said and walked away.

As he watched her leave, Stick wondered if this woman was a mirage brought on by the coastal heat. The subtlety in her hip sway, her hair—was it curly before? Her sandals made a *flomp, flomp* sound upon the floor. Stick rubbed his eyes, and she was gone.

The nautical-themed lobby was quiet, and he heard only the sound of the watch ticking on his wrist. He walked up to the front desk and rang the bell. Once, twice. Nothing. No one around. Jesus, this heat was stifling. Stick leaned on the countertop and wiped his face with the bottom of his shirt. *Am I just—these things, the people—do I—am I my mother?* Stick considered that Jake had been right, that he had inherited his mother's disease. *It's eating away at my sanity, and I don't even know it. Did she know?* Stick pulled his shirt up again to dab his forehead. *I can't let—*

"Sir! Sir, are you okay?"

The voice jerked him back to reality, and Stick slowly pulled his shirt from his face to see a tanned, sandy-haired woman staring at him from behind the desk.

"I'm, uh, okay. Just hot," he said, figuring he must have looked ridiculous, a grown man with his entire shirt up over his face.

"The air conditioning is broken down here in the lobby. The rooms are fine, though. I apologize for any inconvenience."

"Oh, it's fine. Hey, how far is Myrtle Beach Speedway?" He needed to get out on the track to clear his head.

"Oh, it'll take you about twenty minutes or so. Do you need a map?"

"No, I'm sure I can manage. Thanks."

Stick crossed the lobby, relieved at the permanence of it all. As he exited the glass doors, he walked to the edge of the pavement to the sand and stomped his feet twice. From now on, this would be his connection to reality, when his mind wanted to retreat. The sand, the soil, the dirt—it would keep him grounded.

His tires pressed into the soft track at Myrtle Beach Speedway. A mix of sand and dirt, the driving was slower, not enough anybody would notice, but Stick sure did. The car didn't respond as quickly, either, instead sinking ever so slightly. Twenty laps to go, and Stick was in the lead. Overhead, electrical lines crisscrossed like constellations, and birds scattered, swooping in and out of his view. Stick hated birds. Always had, ever since one pecked him in the head when he was little, and his mom laughed. She wasn't bothered by them, just wandered through the house quoting Edgar Allan Poe, repeating "nevermore," as she washed dishes and swept the floor. He thought they were dirty demons sent from hell, particularly the black ones, especially since there was a slew of them outside the house the day his mother was carted away.

Stick adjusted the clutch and slid the car to the right, just enough to make the back tires spin, throwing sand on the car creeping up behind him. The race had been smooth so far, no surprises, but Stick had been prepared. After sifting the sand in his fingers the night before, he had ordered Butch to deflate the tires just a bit, not so much that the other drivers noticed, but enough to avoid sinking too deep into the track.

He looked up again. *Something's wrong. So many birds. Must be a sign.* He'd avoided all the usual triggers: the color green, lady luck comments, fifty-dollar bills, and peanuts. But nature he could not control.

He tried to forget about the nasty creatures, instead taking a cue from his granddad. He focused on the swishing of the sand, a snare drum. The low, dry sound of speaker static, a trombone. Engine, bass. Five laps to go. He drifted, the seesaw of a bow bearing into fiddle strings. His vision became tunneled. He saw only what was in front of him: not below, not to the side, and certainly not above. If he couldn't see the birds, they wouldn't have a hold on him. The symphony played in his head, guiding him through the finish line, where he sighed a great breath of relief at having come out alive. *The key is to not see the darkness,* he thought. He had done that in many races before, where the dust was so thick he couldn't make out the front end of his car. But as he sat there at the finish line and listened to the cheering crowd, a black bird alit on the hood of his car. It fluttered its wings lightly, then slowly lifted a talon and stepped to the edge, its long black beak almost touching the interior. Stick closed his eyes. *Tap. Tap.* Stick opened them to see Butch's smiling face at the window.

"You gonna sit there all day?" he asked.

Stick pulled off his helmet and checked his hair in the mirror before sliding out of the car and looking around. The crowd was gathering, but he was looking for Annalee. He spotted her yellow sweater over by the trophy stand, jam-packed with reporters. He made a beeline toward her.

"Good idea. Get to them reporters first off," Butch said, tailing him.

Stick saw Annalee nod as she stood just behind the newly built press box. He winked and allowed himself to be enveloped by the crowd, then raised his arm to signal the first reporter.

"What do you think about this track being converted back to dirt?" an older bald man with tortoiseshell glasses asked.

"I love it," Stick answered. "That's what I came from. It will always be my favorite. The dirt is unforgiving."

"Word is they may be changing it to asphalt later next year," the same reporter said.

"Well, that's a damn shame."

"You're still pretty high in points this season. Do you think you can win it all at NASCAR?" another, younger, reporter asked.

"Why not?"

"Well, Petty's good right now. He's almost unbeatable."

"Nobody's unbeatable," Stick said and pointed to a young reporter in the back who had been struggling to be seen.

He cleared his voice and adjusted his hat. His voice crackled as he spoke. "Um, sir, with all due respect, some are saying you gone soft."

"Gone soft?" Stick grunted. "Hell, son, you been payin' attention?"

"Yes, sir, just uh, on account of—some been sayin' your image is tarnished. That you ain't so tough anymore."

Stick was annoyed. "How's that?"

"'Cause you got a girlfriend," the reporter said.

The press pool got quiet.

"Can you confirm?" he prodded.

Stick looked behind him to see Annalee standing there, her arms crossed. "Yeah, I got a woman I'm involved with pretty serious-like."

"Ms. Annalee Harris?" one of the reporters asked, flipping through this notebook.

"Yes," Stick said. He cared for Annalee. No use hiding it.

The younger reporter spoke up again. "So, it don't bother you that she has a kid?"

Stick's eyes darted to Annalee, who had one hand pressed to her mouth. Her eyes were wide, her brow furrowed as if she was about to burst into tears. *It's true.* "That's—what—"

A bird squawked, and Stick's head ticked to the right before setting straight ahead.

"No comment," he said defiantly and locked eyes with Annalee, who had by this time cupped both hands over her mouth.

The beach breeze blew Annalee's hair into her face. The heat blurred her figure, waffling her into the image of another woman. She lowered herself onto the concrete bench and trembled, her hands still covering her face, her hair swept over one eye. What makes the body sway when it's most vulnerable? His mother had rocked like a baby, and he couldn't help but wonder what would have happened if he had hidden under the blanket with her. Could he have calmed her? Spared her from a fate she had all but predicted? *I have another chance*, he thought, *to save the woman in front of me*.

"I'll get back to you boys later," Stick said to the reporters, then pushed his way past the cameras and microphones. He hurdled the concrete wall dividing the track from the stands and with three large steps found himself in front of Annalee. She looked up at him, her face wet.

"Wipe those tears," he whispered. "We don't want the cameras pickin' up on this."

She nodded and opened her mouth to speak.

"Don't say anything," he said. "Everything's fine. We'll talk. In the meantime, we have to act perfectly normal, like I knew all along. Now, stand up. I'm going to hug you, and when we turn around, you have to smile and wave. Can you do that?"

Annalee stood up and grabbed ahold of him, burrowing her head into his chest. When they turned back to the cameras, they waved and clasped their hands.

"Now let's go," Stick said, turning his back on the reporters and escorting her down to the RV, where Butch was waiting with the door open.

Once inside, she sat down and pulled the leopard-print blanket up to her chin. "I need to explain," she said.

"Not necessary," Stick said with a calmness not even he expected. "You were just so enamored with me that you forgot to tell me about your . . ."

"Daughter," Annalee said, pulling the blanket up farther to cover her nose. "Cheryl."

Stick sat down beside her and tugged on the blanket. "If you have a daughter, so do I," he said.

Annalee's eyes widened farther than he thought possible. "You mean you're not mad? I only—I didn't tell you because—"

"Annalee, it doesn't matter. You had your reasons. Or you were temporarily enchanted by my charm. Either way, we don't need to discuss it further." He snuggled under the quilt next to her, and Annalee rested her head on his shoulder. "I'm in this with you now," he said. "On one condition."

She shot back up. "What's that?"

"I get to meet her. Soon."

"Okay, but she's a kid and she might—"

"Be moody? Hate me because I'm not her father? Sounds typical. I'm pretty sure I can charm her into liking me. I did it with you, and you were a tough nut to crack too."

Annalee winced. "Don't be so sure," she said and cuddled closer to him.

Stick liked this feeling of sitting, holding on to life with nowhere in particular to go and no time frame in which to get there. They sat like this for a while in silence.

"Stick, there's one more thing," Annalee said, taking the blanket with her as she sat up.

"There's more?" He drew in a breath. "You hide your secrets well."

"Product of circumstance," she said, fidgeting.

"Tell me. Whatever it is, I can handle it."

"Arthur, he—well, he cut me off. Financially speaking."

"What do you mean he cut you off? He's your father! How could he—" Stick was furious. What kind of father doesn't support his daughter? What kind of man wouldn't protect her?

"I haven't worked at the warehouse in months. The cash stopped. He said wouldn't give me a handout, that I had to work for—"

"His affection?"

She pursed her lips. "It's more complicated than that. Arthur, he's—well, we have a difficult relationship." She shuddered and pulled the blanket up to cover her lips.

"Tell me," Stick said. He wanted to know Annalee completely. The good, the bad, what made her so guarded.

"Another time. For now, I have to figure out how to support myself and my daughter when I have no skills or education or even any Goddamn luck," she said, throwing the blanket to the floor in frustration.

Life ain't got nuthin' to do with luck.

"You've got me," Stick said. "I'll take care of you and Cheryl."

He couldn't believe what he was saying. He'd always seen himself as a lifelong bachelor, and now he was ready to give it all up to support one woman? But he couldn't picture himself with anyone else. He hadn't noticed another woman in months, and the thought of betraying Annalee with another made his skin crawl. She consumed his every thought, his every action. Life in the fast lane suddenly didn't seem so appealing. His heart churned.

"Stick, I can't allow you to—"

"Just until you find a job, something you enjoy. Maybe antiquing. Whatever. I've gotta lot of cash flow coming in. We'll be fine."

At that, she started tearing up.

"Crap." He rubbed at his face. "What did I say wrong, Annalee?"

"Nothing, Stick. You just said *we*." Then the tears spilled out over her cheeks.

He wiped them away, his heart swelling. "I did, didn't I?" He took her hands in his. "We will get through this, together. Whatever you need. I'm here. Think of me as your safety net."

"I've always needed one," she said and kissed him hard.

As their tongues intertwined, he felt something more than passion. A deep-seated feeling that burned, scorching his heart until he thought it would go up in flames. The feeling was beyond adoration, beyond devotion. It was something akin to love.

Chapter 18

GAFFNEY, SC
– 1974 –

Gene looked at the ground below. Frozen solid. He knew if he jumped, he would break a leg, or worse. But it was getting dark, and he was stuck in a large oak tree. He scooched his bottom toward the trunk, hoping he could grab a hold of it and shimmy down, but as he moved, the branch he was on creaked. It was going to break.

He sat perfectly still. He didn't want to startle the bats circling overhead: hairy, hideous creatures that spread their leathery wings wide, revealing ominous veins. The game had been fun enough at the start. His mother had called him her little songbird, since he tended to whistle like his granddad. But then she'd placed him in the tree and said she'd be right back with the camera. That was hours ago. Cold and frightened, he sat on the branch now, hoping he didn't freeze to death before his mother remembered she had a son. Just as the full moon moved directly overhead, Gene decided he would rather die on the ground than stuck up in that tree with the bats hanging upside down in his face. So he jumped. When his body hit the ground, it was like a thousand *daggers of ice jammed into his legs. He looked down at his knees, alabaster skin protruding from dirty, brown pants, and wondered why the caps had shifted so.*

Stick rubbed his legs. Even in the Carolina heat, his joints still ached. The drive to Annalee's was a boring one, so he tended to daydream, calling upon memories of his mother. He'd been thinking about her a lot lately, even more since he'd found out Annalee had a daughter. She'd delayed the official meeting as long as she could and promised today would be the day. He couldn't help but wonder what kind of mother Annalee was. He didn't have much in way of comparison, only a few faded points in time.

As he drove the final mile to her house, he worried that it wasn't normal for a grown man to be stuck in the past so often. He turned the corner and saw children playing in the street, fathers and mothers fussing over them with cups of water, chasing them with the garden hose. He pulled alongside the curb in front of Annalee's house, a one-story gray house with a red door, magenta marigolds lining the walkway, and two large ferns hanging over the small porch. The grass was perfectly mowed, and a tiny gnome smiled mischievously from the bottom steps up to the porch, as if he knew this house's secret. The windows were covered with spear-point wrought iron bars. From the door hung a large cowbell, a pair of men's work boots by the mat. Sitting in a swing on the porch was a porcelain-skinned teen with fiery red hair. Stick stepped out of the truck, rubbed his knees one more time, and smoothed his hair. The young girl pulled down a pair of blue plastic sunglasses and eyeballed him.

"Can I help you?" she asked in a tone that was inquisitive but not entirely apprehensive.

"I'm looking for Annalee," he answered, noting the stark physical differences between Annalee and her daughter.

"She's inside. You here to fix something?"

"I'm, uh, she didn't tell you about me?"

I knew it, Stick thought. *She's still not ready.*

The girl removed her glasses completely. "Who are you?"

Stick stuck his hand out. He figured it was best to make a good first impression, treat her like an adult. Isn't that what teenagers wanted?

"Name's Stick Elliott. I'm here to take your mom to lunch."

The girl crossed her arms and left Stick's hand hanging in the air between them. She pushed her heels off the ground and gave the bench a good swing.

"I'm Cheryl."

"I've heard a lot about you, Cheryl."

"Really?" she asked, genuinely surprised. Then she leaned back and turned her head toward the window. In a bored voice she said, "Mom, there's a man here for you."

A jangle of the bell and Annalee appeared at the door. Stick could see Cheryl's face change to disdain.

"Where'd you get that—I've never seen that blouse before," she said, referring to Annalee's low-cut burgundy top.

Annalee ignored the question and said, "Let me just get my purse." She turned and headed into the house, leaving the door open.

Stick looked back at Cheryl, who was now picking the polish off her toes. He stuck his head inside to see a completely dark interior, minus one low-wattage bulb in the foyer. There was a long, narrow hallway that smelled of baked apples and cinnamon.

"I wouldn't go in if I were you," Cheryl said.

"Oh?"

"She likes her privacy. She would've invited you in if she'd wanted you there."

Stick moved away from the door. "Well, I'd better stay out here, then. Wouldn't want to piss that one off," he said and saw Cheryl crack a smile.

"Definitely not. How long you known her?"

"A while now," Stick said, not wanting to offer more information than necessary.

"But you don't want to say exactly. I get it."

This girl was smart.

"I just don't want to be in the doghouse."

Cheryl laughed.

Annalee reappeared at the door just as Stick was going to ask about the window bars and work boots. She had a brown purse in her hand and dark red on her lips. Cheryl raised her eyebrows. They turned to go.

"Have fun. Keep her out as long as you like," Cheryl called out after them.

"She seems spicy," Stick said as they climbed inside the truck.

"You have no idea," Annalee said. "Just like her—"

Stick started up the ignition. "Father?"

Annalee pursed her lips and grasped the bag in her lap. "Let's go," she said.

It was not the right time to ask about this man Annalee so clearly despised. "Did your house come with bars on the windows? Reminds me of a prison."

He knew immediately it was the wrong thing to say.

"We put 'em up. Makes me feel safer."

"From what?" he asked. "Nuthin' going on in this town."

"From—" she stopped and pulled her purse closer. "Never mind. Where are we going?"

Stick had always known that behind this strong facade was an insecure woman; he just never realized she might be scared.

"Somewhere peaceful."

"Can you elaborate?"

The truck bumped as Stick turned off the main road and onto dirt. "One of my favorite spots. I used to run around down here as a kid," he said, pointing to the thick woods. "I learned to drive here. There's a spot just—" he made a soft turn onto a narrow path and parked the truck behind a kudzu-covered brush. "Here," he said. "Down yonder, there's a creek. Thought we'd have a picnic."

Annalee's face grew dim. "No picnics," she said.

"No?" Stick didn't understand the sudden change in her composure, but he could see that she had retreated into her memory just as he did at times.

"Okay, no picnic. What if we just sat here in the truck and ate the sandwiches I made?"

Her body relaxed a little. "Okay," she said.

Stick reached into the back and gathered the sandwiches, fruit, and sweet tea he'd packed. He laid a dish towel on the armrest and opened the spread.

"Ta-da!" he said, then worried it looked too rudimentary. "Is this okay?"

"It's great," Annalee said and reached for a strawberry.

Stick watched as she took a delicate bite.

"I'm sorry, I just—sometimes I get lost in my head. Stuff from the past." She took another bite, the juice dribbling down her chin.

"Happens to me too. On the drive over here, I saw a bird and it triggered a memory of my mother. How stupid is that? A damn bird."

"It's not dumb. Certain things make me, make me . . ." She closed her eyes. "Nervous," she said finally. She shook her head as if she wanted to shake the picture right out of her mind. "Tell me about your mother."

"She was always a little . . . off. Up sometimes, down others. When I was little, she saw things, things that weren't there. That's how she ended up institutionalized. It was a horrible place. Jake had to drag me in for visits. I would sit quietly, watchin' my mother drool and pick at her hair. Sometimes she would pull handfuls out and give it to me like a present. I ran out a couple times, but Jake would always yank me back, sayin' my mama needed me there. When she was good, we would take her out, drive to the park, and sit on a bench to feed the squirrels or come back to the house for ice cream. Then one day we went to pick her up, and they'd tied her down to the bed, stuck a bunch of needles in her arm, and placed a Frankenstein cap on her head. She'd tried to jump from the roof. Said her little boy was a songbird, and she was gonna teach him to fly." Stick stopped. He hadn't realized how much it had affected him until he said it out loud. "A week later, she was gone. Granddad never told me what happened, only that we wouldn't have to go back to that God-awful place again."

Annalee put her hand on Stick's. "I'm so sorry."

Stick suddenly felt pathetic, less than a man. He straightened up. "But I'm, you know, everything's fine."

"It's okay not to be. I think it's a beautiful thing when a man can open up, admit his vulnerability. Cheryl's dad was not at all like that. He was self-serving, thought he was invincible."

"Sounds like a real asshole," Stick said, feeling more secure in his emotional state.

"He beat me."

A rage Stick had never known existed boiled up in him. *How could a man*—"I hope he's dead," he said.

"He's not."

"Hence the bars on your windows." And the bell.

"Partly. Good news is he doesn't come around much. He's like a plague: once every seven years."

"And it's been?"

"Seven years."

Stick had to protect this woman. "Well, you got me now. I'll beat the shit out of him if he ever tries to come 'round again."

She smiled a sad smile.

"You know what? Let's take a walk," Stick said, stepping out of the truck.

He went around to Annalee's side, but she hesitated. "What is it?" he asked, sensing she was uncomfortable.

"The trees, I don't like them. They—" She stopped and knit her hands together.

Stick thought she resembled a child, scared to jump in the deep end of the pool. He held out his hand. "Whatever it is, I'm here. The forest can be scary, but it can also be comforting. You're gonna have to trust me on this."

Annalee placed one hand in his, and Stick led her through the trees. The leaves were damp, providing a soft cushion to the forest floor. They didn't say much, Annalee nervously noting the occasional chipmunk or rabbit. Stick felt peace in the woods; there was nothing to run from here. Bears didn't gather in these parts, only small critters like foxes and the occasional raccoon, which could be scared away easily with a large stick. Cops never made it this deep into the woods anymore either. The old hillbilly distilleries had been shut down years ago, parts still strewn across the terrain. They approached a clearing, the trees pushed against a backdrop of green. Annalee let go of his hand.

"That's a stone furnace," Stick said, nodding toward a waist-high, cave-like structure built from large stones. "Some animal's taken over," he said, crouching at the opening. "I just wonder what."

The dome-shaped entrance was barred with small logs packed tightly with mud. Inside were twigs, acorns, yarn, leaves, plastic potato chip bags, and various pieces of fabric strewn across the ground and packed into the crevices of the stone.

"I don't wanna find out," Annalee said, backing away.

Stick picked up a jagged rock and banged on rusty piping protruding from the ground.

"That should scare off any creatures," he said.

"I don't much like hairy things, especially creepy ones that burrow in the ground," Annalee said as she exaggerated a shiver. "But this part of the forest is nice, not so closed in."

She followed the piping to a corroded copper pot and two overturned wooden barrels. "So, this is how you make moonshine? Ferment some fruit and pipe it out?"

Stick chuckled. Her knowledge of the process was comical.

"Tell me," she said. "Tell me how it's done." She sat down atop a large sturdy drum.

Stick had never talked about the family business, and for good reason. "What makes you think I know?" he asked slyly.

The space between her eyebrows wrinkled, and one side of her mouth lifted, causing a dimple to appear in her cheek.

He laughed. "Fine. First they take field corn and grind it into meal, kinda like dry grits. Some cheapen it up by usin' horse feed, but that's not pure stuff. Then they soak the corn in hot water, here," he patted one of the copper barrels. "Add some sugar or malted barley, then after some time, the yeast. We—I mean they—transfer it to the copper still to ferment, heating it all the while and stirring occasionally. You gotta use copper, otherwise the product'll taste funny. Then you turn the heat way up. That's the dangerous part, as that alcohol steam escapes through the cap arm." He tapped on the pipe leading from the top of the still. "Don't look like these fellas had a thump keg to force the steam into, so one or two of them probably seared his own skin."

"Is that the thing that makes all the noise?" Annalee asked.

"Yup, it gets pretty loud. Maybe that's why they didn't have one in the woods. Would've drawn the police." Stick motioned Annalee down from the barrel. "See that creek down there? They probably used it to pump fresh cold water down . . ." he said, his voice descending as he trailed the length of the coiled tubing, "into this barrel. This turns the steam into liquid. Then through this . . ."—he shuffled his toes around in the wet leaves, picked up a hose, and held it in the air—". . . and into the bucket here. Then you've got alcohol ready to be bottled and sold."

Annalee had been watching Stick's performance with curiosity. She bent over and picked up a discarded mason jar with a large black *X* on the front.

"What does this *X* mean?"

"That means the finished product was filtered once through, probably a little cloudy. The good stuff is clear as a crystal, filtered two or three times."

"Hmm," she said, placing the jar back on the ground. "Why go through all this trouble?"

"Money, mostly. When the government outlawed alcohol, people wanted it even more, so it drove the price up. You had a buncha people who'd barely scraped by their whole lives suddenly in possession of a skill that could pay.

Most of the people down here at least had been raised on farms. That's all they knew. They'd been experimentin' with cannin' food to get them through the winter. I'm sure many times those preservation techniques failed, and they got some fermented mash that took their woes away. People here work the land 'cause that's all they've ever known, but it ain't easy."

"People like Jake?"

"Yeah, our land's been in his family for years. He tilled it and sold corn, wheat, cotton—whatever he could live off, but it just wasn't enough." Stick stopped. He didn't want to confess to any crimes, but he was sure Annalee already knew.

She leaned back against one of the larger barrels. "I'm pretty sure Arthur's been involved in some pretty shady business dealings in his lifetime," she said, as if leveling the playing field. "I mean, he has that textile warehouse, but I always wondered what was hidden in those huge fabric rolls. He never would let me get too involved in the business. He'd say the warehouse was no place for a woman, and I shouldn't be bothering myself with the books. But I don't know; it always made me think there was something he was hiding. He used to have this old shed at home and wouldn't let no one near it. I wonder if that's where he hid the dirty money."

"You've been watchin' too many movies."

"Maybe," she said, stepping from the barrel. "But—Stick, I know racing's not bootlegging, but it's just as dangerous to me. Do you think you'll always race? I mean, if we're truly in a relationship like I think we are, I have to ask."

Stick could tell the subject had been on her mind, and in fact, it had been on his too. Racing was all he had ever loved, until now. His fear wasn't that it was too dangerous. He was confident in his skill. And it wasn't the money. That had been good lately, better than he'd have at some construction job. It was the lifestyle.

"I don't know," he said. "It's a whole lotta late nights away from you. And the crowds—they're pretty rough. But it's all I've ever known. The one thing I'm good at. You don't have to worry about me gettin' hurt."

"I don't, not really. I grew up around a pretty rough crowd, so I don't mind that. And the late nights, well, that's just a couple times a week. We can work that all out."

"So . . ." Stick twirled her hair around his finger.

"It's the women," she said finally.

He rested both palms on her blushed cheeks. "You have nuthin' to worry about in that department. I've been under your spell since the first time I saw you," he said, stroking her face. "I wouldn't do anything to mess that up."

"That's what they all say."

"I take it Cheryl's father wasn't faithful?"

She shook her head.

"I'm not him. I wouldn't do that, Annalee. I'll never hurt you."

Stick could tell there was more on her mind. He imagined what life must have been like for her, raising a daughter on her own. Just like Jake. Selfishly, he thought of himself in this moment, too. How his father left, how his mother . . .

"Annalee, I'll never leave you."

She sighed in relief, a breath she must have been holding for some time. "Promise?" she asked, like a child searching for parental reassurance, the kind you need when you're four and you ask about monsters in the closet.

"I promise. I promise with all my heart and soul I will never leave you, Annalee."

And at that moment he meant it. Every single word.

Stick sat at his granddad's kitchen table, the scratched Formica top covered in a thick yellow plastic tablecloth that crinkled with every movement. In the center of the table were a bowl of peaches, two cups, and a piece of paper marked with numbers and dollar signs.

"Well, what do you think?" Stick asked, tapping the paper with his pen.

Jake poured another cup of 'shine from a clay pitcher. "It's a life-changing decision."

"I know," Stick said, downing the whole thing at once.

Last week, Annalee had asked him to move in. He spent most of his free time there anyway, but still, it had come as a surprise. She was the type who took things slowly, cautiously testing the water before jumping in. But one night in bed, she'd rolled over and asked him not to leave. "You promised you wouldn't," she'd said, and he couldn't disagree.

As she slept that night, Stick had lain awake, and for the first time in his life really pondered a future that was neither fast nor solitary. He'd watched the moonlight bounce off her chocolate hair. She took quick, short breaths and tossed in her sleep, batting and waving her arms about as if she were trying to escape some invisible crow. When he placed his hand softly on her shoulder, she retreated under the blanket, mumbling in a singsong whisper. He had put one foot on the floor and told himself not to run.

"It does save money," Stick said, selling his granddad—and himself—on the practical issues first. "And she has a garage where I can store tools and trophies."

"You're focusing on the wrong thing, son. Are you ready to make this leap? I know you love her, but are you ready to commit?"

There was no denying it. If he accepted Annalee's offer, he would be living with a woman for the first time since his mother. And what if it didn't work out? He could get in his car and drive. Stick shook his head. No, that wasn't the answer.

"I can't imagine my life without her. But, Granddad, she's got these—these idiosyncrasies that—what if I set her off? Like Mom. What if I'm the problem?"

"That's poppycock," Jake said, stirring the contents of the clay pot with a wooden spoon. "You didn't drive your mama to madness. She was sick with a disease that ate away at her brain."

Stick didn't want to picture his mom's brain, or anyone's for that matter, being eaten away by disease.

"Get that outta your noggin, Stick. You got your wits about you, and you ain't gonna drive nobody crazy. Except maybe me. You been tryin' me since you was yay high," Jake said, holding his hand about a foot off the table. He folded his arms in front of him and leaned in. "Do ya love her?"

Stick nodded.

"You love that girl of hers?"

"She's been hard to get close to, but yeah, I care about her. I'm happy when I'm around them."

"Then do it," Jake said. "She's a good gal. And you could use a woman's soft touch to calm you down a bit."

"I don't know what you're talking about," Stick said with a grin.

It was true: His past trysts had only fueled his ego, the bad boy on and off the track. But Stick had proved himself in the racing world, so he thought maybe it was time to prove himself in the real world, shake his bachelor ways for something more meaningful.

But bars on the windows? Those had to go. If Stick was going to do this, he had to break down every barrier that could stand in his way—only gentler this time.

"I'm going to do it," he said finally. He downed the last of his cup, reached for the pitcher, and downed the last of that, too.

"Thatta boy!" Jake smiled and slapped him on the back. "I knew you'd make the right decision."

"Thanks, Granddad. Now I've just got to get up the courage to talk to one tough teenager."

Chapter 19

MONROE, NC
– 1975 –

Stick pulled up to Starlite Speedway with a petite redhead in the seat beside him. He was nervous about being alone with her—more nervous than he had been with Annalee.

There was too much at stake. Though Stick had told Annalee he would move in, he still hadn't fully pulled the trigger—he felt that he still needed Cheryl's approval. He'd even told Annalee that if Cheryl ever wanted him to leave, he would.

"So, this is where you normally race?" Cheryl asked as she blew a huge pink bubble from the wad of gum in her mouth. "Don't you also drive NASCAR?"

"Yeah, but I prefer these dirt tracks."

"Why?" she asked, rolling and stretching the gum with her fingers.

"NASCAR's a little too shiny for me. I like the ruggedness of the dirt track. It's where I started, where my roots are," Stick said, hoping that would put the questions to rest.

"But wouldn't you make more money in NASCAR? Plus, they're on television."

Stick laughed at that. "Yeah, I guess you're right. But then I wouldn't have as much time to spend with you, now would I?"

Since he'd been around the house more, Stick spent time doing the things Cheryl liked, the things she seemed to have missed in her childhood: baking, playing Scrabble, and watching the occasional banned soap opera.

"I guess." Cheryl shrugged.

Stick parked the RV and opened the divider curtains to check on Annalee.

"You okay back there?" he asked.

Annalee had a bad case of nausea right before they embarked on the trip due to some expired slaw, so she had taken up residence in the back of the RV.

"Yeah," she said weakly as she sat up from the sofa bench. "I just need a ginger ale."

"Cheryl, grab your mama a ginger ale. I need to put on my fire suit," Stick said.

"What's a fire suit?"

"It's a special uniform all drivers wear to keep us from getting burned."

"From what?"

Stick thought only toddlers asked this many questions, but he was glad to answer because it meant she was really taking an interest in the sport. And him.

"If we crash, the cars will catch fire. Drivers can often walk away from an accident, but body burns . . . That's a whole 'nother thing. Before fire suits, we used to dip our clothes in baking soda to make 'em fire resistant."

"Did it work?"

"Don't know, but we thought it did."

Stick crawled through the back, Cheryl right behind him. He gave Annalee a peck on the cheek before retreating into the bathroom, where he stepped out of his jeans and into the white zippered overalls. *My business suit. About as fancy as I'll ever get.* He ran through the semi-banked dirt track in his head, noting the wooden fence that encircled it like a chicken coop. He didn't need to study the drivers tonight; he knew them all by heart. Earnhardt would have been his biggest competitor, but he'd just made his NASCAR debut and probably wouldn't be back on the dirt track anytime soon, especially after he'd spun Stick out in Charlotte, totaling the Plymouth. Tommy had gone nuts and chased Dale with a pistol. So all that was left were some weekend stragglers, a few NASCAR dropouts, and Willie. Stick was pretty sure Willie's eyesight was going bad due to his last few finishes, so all he had to do was stay pretty far behind him, then sneak up on his right.

Instead, what Stick worried about tonight was impressing a cynical teenager. He and Cheryl had grown closer lately, especially after he saved her from Annalee's wrath one night when Cheryl faked sick to sabotage their date. After that, he was her mother's cool boyfriend, and he tried to spoil her at every turn, gifting chocolates, hiding her cigarettes from Annalee, sneaking her a beer every now and then. Tonight, Stick had to seal the deal by being the renegade driver Cheryl bragged to her friends about.

He stepped out of the bathroom. Annalee was sitting up.

"Feeling better?" he asked, hoping she would join Cheryl in the grandstands.

"Yes," she said meekly. "Thank God you didn't eat the slaw."

"Exactly why I never eat mayonnaise before a race," he said. "All right, I'll see you and Cheryl later."

Cheryl perked up from her slouched position on the bench. "You'll give me the signal like you promised, right?"

"Salute and peace," Stick said. "Got it."

He stepped out to find Butch. "How's it lookin'?" he asked. "Willie come round?"

"Good to the first question. That Monte Carlo sure is a muscley thing."

When the Plymouth was deemed unfixable, Stick decided to go back to Chevy. Butch had his heart set on the Chevelle Laguna S-3, a new sleek design with a tapered aerodynamic nose. Stick thought it looked like a spaceship and bet Butch it'd be banned, just like the Charger and Superbird, because it was fast as a roadrunner and had a sharklike design that made the higher-ups nervous. So, the Chevy Monte Carlo it was. Peacock-blue with Stick's signature pink lettering.

"And yes to the second," Butch said, "but he was in a hurry."

"Name of the game, ain't it?"

Butch continued without acknowledging the joke. "Clear day, dirt's packed good. Car's in good shape. Put a new front sticker on the left this morning 'cause that old tire was going a little too bald for me. The stagger's perfect, and you should slip right through those left turns . . ."

Stick zoned out as he watched Cheryl and Annalee make their way up to the grandstands and plant themselves in the high seats, where they would have the best view. He slapped Butch on the back, thanked him, and jumped in the car, pulling up beside Willie, near pole position. Willie smiled and gave a pointer-finger wave. Stick returned the gesture, knowing it would be the only pleasantries they would exchange for the next forty laps. He advanced to the pole and stared up at the crow's nest, waiting for that square of green to start the race.

The flagman gave the go signal, and the rumble of dashing cars was an earthquake of seismic proportions. Stick took a sizable lead early on, Willie in close second. On lap thirty-two, Willie drafted mere inches behind, but didn't tap. *Son of a gun*, he thought, *is he pushin' me?* Stick knew Willie needed the race money as much as he did, so he couldn't figure out his incentive. They stayed this way for a few more laps, Willie stuck like glue to Stick's bumper.

"Damn it, Willie, punch it! Make this interesting."

Stick moved slightly right to see if Willie would take the bait, but as he did, he and Willie both hit marbles, those bits of rubber that shaved off tires. Stick lost control. As he tried to correct his steering, he noticed Willie was spinning too—right toward him.

"Oh, shit!" *I don't want it to end like this, me and Willie both going out in an atomic flame, not in front of—*

The two cars faced each other, and time stood still. Stick could see Willie's face, wide-eyed, his mouth a circle as his hands desperately tried to control the car. Willie's front end grazed Stick's and sent him toward the fence. Stick switched to neutral and steered into the skid as his back right tire lifted off the ground. He slid sideways, parallel to the barricade, and spark skimmed all the way around the corner, finally gaining control of the car. He cleared the fence and headed down the straightaway, his eyes scouring the track for Willie. A yellow flag. *Thank God. Just under caution. Willie's okay.* The pace car entered the field, and Stick saw Willie in pit row. He cut from the line of slow-moving cars and pulled into his pale-faced crew just as a red flag was dropped. *There must be too much debris to clean up.*

"You okay?" Butch asked.

"I'm fine," Stick said as he slid out of the car and headed toward Willie.

"Stick, you're not supposed to get out—where are you going?"

"Just fix the car, Butch. Right side might need new rims, and secure that front bumper," he said as he jogged over to Willie's stall. He walked right up to the side of the car. "Hey!" He hit the side of the car door. "You okay, Willie?"

Willie removed his racing gloves. His left thumb was bent at an angle; blood poured from a gash on his palm.

"Could be better," he said. "Coulda been worse."

"Good Lord! You can't race with that—"

Willie shushed him. "They don't know," he said, motioning to his crew. "I'm gonna finish this race."

"But, Willie, how you gonna drive with that—"

"Good thing I'm a righty," he said, shaking his right hand loose from the glove. "I'll steer with one hand if needed. Don't say nuthin'. You got a clean rag in that suit of yours?"

Stick patted his pockets. He always kept a clean rag for after the race.

He pulled out the white cloth and handed it to Willie, who quickly wrapped his hand and loosely replaced the glove.

"I'll get it looked at later. For now, I got a race to win."

"But—" Stick began, but he knew it was no use. Willie would race, because that's exactly what he would do too. They were cut from the same cloth. "All right, but if you think I'm gonna take it easy on you just because you hurt your little hand, you're mistaken."

"I would hope not." Willie laughed and glanced at the track. "Pace car's back out there. You better get back to your car, 'cause I'm taking off in thirty seconds."

Stick ran back and jumped in his car just in time. The pace car waved him and Willie around lapped traffic then pulled off. Stick had just eight laps to seal the win. Willie stayed close on his tail but fell back a few paces around curves, probably due to the hand. With just five laps to go, a tangerine #6 Chevrolet Chevelle Laguna bumped Willie and sent him soaring to the right. *He's only got one hand. He'll lose control again.* Stick slowed just barely to keep an eye on Willie, who had redirected his car back on the straightaway. That was just enough time for #6 to pass him. *Whoosh!* Right by the driver's window on the inside. *Son of a bitch!* Stick floored the gas and switched gears. He raced up behind the Chevelle and bumped it hard. *Don't mess with me and my friends.* He stuck to the Chevelle's bumper as tightly as he could until he saw Willie right behind him. Willie weaved to the right. *All right*, he thought. *Let's get this asshole.*

Stick stuck his hand out the window and pointed up. Willie slingshot to the right as Stick pressed to the left. *Pick a side, #6. You can't have both.* The Chevelle tried to move toward Willie. *Hell no. Not again. Not for no third place.* Stick adjusted right mere inches and clipped #6's bumper again, which by design was hiked up slightly in the back. The car took a nosedive and scraped the ground, burying its hawkish tip in the dirt. Stick swooped around him and caught up with Willie on the next lap, but when he tried to pass, Willie stood his ground. *Let's see how good you are with one hand, my friend.*

Stick eased left then shot right, but Willie followed his moves as if he had anticipated them, blocking Stick once again. Tapping his fingers on the steering wheel, Stick racked his brain for any weakness of Willie's he could exploit, but he couldn't think of any. *He runs a tight race, even with one hand.* Willie remained in the lead for the final lap. On the last corner, Stick gave it one more push. *If I'm good at anything, it's taking curves.* Since Willie wouldn't let off the inside, Stick shot to the outside groove, so close to Willie that once again their doors lined up. But this time, there was a deafening screech as metal rubbed metal. The checkered flag was flown, Willie and Stick neck and neck. As they crossed the finish line, the only thing that was clear was this was a photo finish. Stick thought about the first time they'd practiced together, how in tandem they were. *I'll be damned. If he ain't as good as I am.* Stick stopped near the paddock and jumped out. Willie ran toward him, his eyebrows lowered, nostrils flared. *Uh-oh.*

"Willie, I—it's racin', man," he said by way of explanation. He didn't want to fight his friend, but he'd put up a fist if he had to.

Willie leaned toward Stick, threw up his good arm—

And hugged him.

"Man, that was the most fun I've had in a while!" Willie pulled back and shook Stick's shoulders. "See the look on number six's face? The way we tag-teamed him? Wowee!"

"Yeah, he was the big surprise of the night, huh?"

"Naw, we were!" Willie looked at the crow's nest. "Wonder if we tied?"

"Well," Stick said, "let's go find out."

They walked across the track, which by now was empty.

"They're reviewing the photos. It was too close to call," a skinny, wiry-haired boy yelled from the crow's nest.

As they waited, Cheryl came marching down the grandstands, Annalee walking slowly behind. Stick looked up and gave the signal. Salute. Peace. He could see the smile on Cheryl's face from afar. Just then the loudspeaker crackled.

"After reviewing the photos, it was determined that Stick Elliott wins!"

Stick looked over at Willie, who was holding his bad hand with the good one, bright-red dripping from the cloth. He deserved to win. He would have if it hadn't been for the hand.

"Congratulations, Stick," Willie said, patting him on the back.

"You drove an extraordinary race," Stick said, then leaned in to whisper. "Now go to the hospital and get that hand looked at."

Willie quickly stuffed the bloody hand into the pocket of his fire suit and nodded as he walked over to accept his second-place trophy. Victory lane was waiting, but Stick had more important matters to attend to. He walked to the grandstands to find Annalee and Cheryl now at the bottom, Cheryl leaning over the side, clapping.

"Great race!" she yelled. "That's my—I know him!" she said to the crowd, motioning to Stick.

He kissed Annalee on the cheek. About that time, Stick saw #6 crawl out of his car and walk toward the winner's circle.

"Excuse me," he said.

Stick was pissed as hell at this beginner who thought he could wrangle with a bull. He clenched his fists and started toward him, but when he heard Cheryl's cheers, he stopped. Looking back, Annalee's face was filled with horror. She knew what he was about to do. *I can't let her see me beat another human being. It's too much for her. Not after all she's been through. She needs a protector, not a bully.* Stick, already close to the third-place finisher, stuck out his hand.

"Good race," he said, and the driver shook his hand warily.

"Ralph's the name," he said.

Stick leaned in close, grasping Ralph's shoulder with his other hand. "I don't give a rat's ass what your name is, son. You try something like that again, and I'll beat you with the sharp edge of a screwdriver."

The driver recoiled. "But, sir, I learned it from the best."

Stick narrowed his eyes.

"I learned it from you."

Stick was flabbergasted. *He looks up to me*, he thought as he eyed the young driver. He looked back at Cheryl. *And she does too.*

Stick turned back to the driver and cleared his throat. "Well, good—" He stopped. He wouldn't jinx this boy. "For you," he finished. "Now you better get on. Third place comes with a bit of cash."

Ralph took that as his cue to leave and jogged off. As Stick made his way to the winner's circle, he looked around for Cheryl and Annalee but didn't see them. Annalee never much liked the fanfare, so he figured she had gone to sit down. He quickly accepted his trophy and took his victory lap with a beauty clad in red, white, and blue on the hood of his car. She curved her hips and stuck out her chest to get Stick's attention, but for once he didn't care. When the ceremonial lap was over, he slid out of the car and was met by the scantily clad blonde.

"Hey, handsome. Whatcha doin' after the race?" She stood close and put one finger in the pocket of his fire suit. He felt a tingle on his hip.

Man, they're getting more aggressive, he thought. Stick removed her hand from his pocket and inched back. "I'm going back to my RV to rest," he said, hoping that would ward her off.

She stepped closer and whispered in his ear. "Want some company?"

The hair on the back of his neck stood up. She smelled of rose water and hair spray. He looked at her as she ran her tongue across the inner rim of her lips. Her cool skin was porcelain, plump, and dewy, her cheeks dimpled. Her eyes were . . . brown. A boring shade of hollowed brown.

Stick smiled. "Thank you, ma'am. With all due respect, I must decline. There's a woman in that trailer I care about a lot. I'm goin' to her now."

Stick walked quietly back to his RV, desperate to see Annalee, the blue-eyed goddess who had stolen his heart. He found Cheryl waiting by the door.

"Hey!" she said enthusiastically. "That was the coolest thing I've ever seen!"

"Thanks, kiddo."

"Kiddo?"

Damn. Maybe she didn't want to be referred to in such a childish manner. "Sorry, I—"

"My father used to call me kiddo," she said, her lip pouting.

Stick's heart sank. He felt bad for Cheryl, who never really had much of a father figure.

"The difference is," Stick said, "I'm here. And I ain't goin' nowhere."

She looked up at him.

"If that's okay with you?" he added.

"Yeah, it is. It's very good." She turned to walk away but stopped. "And Stick?"

"Yeah, kiddo?"

"Stop beating around the bush and move in already."

She smiled, then skipped off to join her friends.

Stick shook his head, flabbergasted. *Well, I'll be damned.* Stick paused by the RV door and looked over at the track, still brimming with fans: women in tight tops with their tits all shoved up, twirling their hair as they lingered around drivers and news cameras. *They'd latch on to any one of them guys as long as they were winnin'.* That was the first moment Stick realized he had grown weary of that superficial dance. He stomped his muddy boots on the mat and walked inside to find Annalee sitting at the foldout kitchen table. She had changed into a turquoise blouse, her hair neatly braided to one side. Her hands were placed atop the table, and she kneaded them anxiously as she did on race days.

"You feelin' better?" he asked. Stick felt bad he didn't have time to focus on her earlier.

She held her thumb and forefinger up. "A smidgen," she said. "The ginger ale settled my stomach."

"Good." He turned the yellow chair around and straddled it, casually placing his forearms on the backrest. "I just ran into Cheryl, and she gave me the go-ahead to move in."

"She did?" Annalee asked, stupefied.

"Yeah, I was as surprised as you are now." *Here we go.* "So, I guess this is happening." He clasped his hands together and grinned.

"I guess so," she said, averting her eyes up and to the right.

Is she second-guessing this? Because if she's—

Annalee grimaced. "I'm pregnant."

Stick's first reaction was to jump up, but the sudden movement caused his knees to ache, so he sat back down. For a second. *She's pregnant. That means*—He stood up again, slower this time, and leaned against the wall.

"You mean—"

"Yes."

He was going to have a child. Stick had never thought about being a father, never even knew he wanted to settle down. Hell, his life was a series of chases. *What if I let them down, do something that messes the kid up?* Would the pressure of loving someone cause the kind of heartache his granddad had experienced?

"Stick, say something." Annalee looked like she was about to cry.

He sat down again, this time beside her. "I—I'm thrilled. Really, Annalee. I just—ya think I'll be a good father?"

"You're a good man," she said. "So yes."

His eyes searched hers. Could she be so sure?

"Does anyone know?"

"Not a soul other than you."

Stick went from zero to sixty in two seconds. His body felt alive with excitement, pride. He leaped up, the aching in his knees a distant memory, and threw his hands wide. "I want to tell everyone!"

"You're not worried it'll hurt your image?"

"I don't care. I'm so happy."

And he was. Stick had spent most of his life running. It was time he focused his attention on staying put. All the birds and bad luck in the world couldn't ruin this moment for him. He gently touched Annalee's still-flat stomach and felt a pulsing thump.

"And for the record, I never doubted my boys could swim fast," he said, to which Annalee laughed and rolled her eyes.

No more runnin' for me. We're havin' a baby. My baby. Will he look like me? Or—A sly smile crossed his lips. *I can't wait to teach him how to drive.*

Chapter 20

SPARTANBURG, SC
– 1976 –

The maternity ward was set up like a track: triage in the middle, where the crew waited and nurses, orderlies, and doctors rushed around gray concrete in multicolored pajamas, passing and bumping into each other without so much as a "sorry." Stick sat outside Annalee's room, staring at a mural of a sweet-faced sunshine smiling at red flowers and purple bunnies. This part of the hospital looked as if someone decided life was worth celebrating with bold hues instead of the sickly green and brown of the rest of the building.

Stick rubbed his hands together, mostly because of nerves, but also because Annalee had been gripping them so hard during contractions, he thought she would rip them right off. The medical crews had raced into the room just as Annalee let out a blood-curdling scream that Stick had only heard before in horror movies. She had jerked her knees to her chest and arched her back, her round stomach expanding toward the ceiling like a watermelon ready to burst. Then something did burst. Stick didn't know what, but suddenly there was water everywhere, all over the bed, dripping to the floor. He jumped back, and the nurse shooed him out of the room.

The door was closed. The blinds shut. Stick sat right outside the door and could hear Annalee growling.

A rotund little nurse with a properly twirled bun waddled over to him. Her face fit perfectly within the circle of sunshine, rays emanating from her outline.

"You okay, hon? You're as white as a ghost."

"First time," he said, his knees bouncing.

"Ah, always happens with first-time dads. With the second one, they're out here smokin' cigars and such." She placed her chubby hands in front of her stomach. "She's fine. Hurts like hell, yes, but no other way to do it."

The heavy breathing and the agonizing screams stopped abruptly. Was the silence worse? He looked up at the nurse, who was smiling.

"Wait for it," she said calmly.

A cry. A loud, high-pitched exclamation.

"What was that?"

"That was your baby. The most beautiful sound on earth."

Stick jumped up. He wanted to see him, hold him, make sure everything was okay.

"Give 'em a minute," the nurse said patiently, her piggie nose scrunching up in delight.

"I'm not good at waitin'," he said, snapping his fingers in rapid succession.

"Good things come to those who—"

"Not in my profession, they don't. You'll get clobbered up if you wait around." Stick glanced nervously toward the window. *What's taking them so long?*

The door opened.

"You can come in now, sir," a nurse said as she removed bloody gloves.

Stick rushed into the room.

Annalee didn't even notice him. Her glistening face hovered inches above a tiny blanket cocoon. As he neared, he could hear her humming. He placed one hand on the bedside.

"Hi," Annalee said as she lifted the blanket to reveal the baby's face. "Meet your little girl."

Stick's heart seemed to skip a beat; his stomach fluttered. Of course, he had considered the possibility of a girl, but his gut had told him otherwise.

Cerulean eyes stared intensely back at him, not batting one single long black eyelash. She was perfect. He reached out to touch her, and a tiny hand grasped his finger. He would protect her forever.

"You won't believe this," Annalee said pulling the blanket down even farther to reveal a headful of dark, coffee-colored hair.

"She has so much!" Stick exclaimed, then leaned down to kiss Annalee.

"I know. Cheryl barely had any when she was born."

An administrator walked over, toting a clipboard. "Take your time," she said. "But I'll need a name before we can take her back to the nursery."

Annalee and Stick looked at each other as the woman left the room.

"Well, do you want to hold her?"

Stick didn't want to admit he was terrified. He'd never held anything so delicate. "Yes."

Annalee slid the baby into Stick's arms. He didn't want to move for fear of tripping or . . . The baby squirmed and blew a bubble. Stick held her tight to his chest. He could feel her warmth, this tiny little thing who was his to nurture and love. He wanted to savor this moment, pause time so he could hold his little girl forever.

"Your granddad is on his way with Cheryl. We'll want to name her before they get here," Annalee said.

Stick sat down on the edge of the bed to steady himself. "Audrey, after your mother?"

"Viola, after yours?"

"No, I think that would be bad luck."

"Right," Annalee said. "What about Gena, after you?"

Stick had never felt like a Gene. He didn't even know where that name came from. "That's pretty, but I could see her as a teenager like, 'Dad, did you have to make my name so close to yours?' Let's keep thinking. Something angelic. Because—look at her, Annalee! She's a gift from God."

Stick had never been religious, but he was overwhelmed with emotion. He wanted to laugh. He wanted to cry. He wanted to scream. He wanted to pray. He wanted to do it all at once.

"Angela?"

"No, that sounds like a clerical worker at the DMV. Something—"

"Evangeline, Ariel, oh why didn't we think of names earlier? Seraphine, Olivia, Jane. What about Jane? I like it."

"Too plain. What about Jana?" he said. "I like Jana." Just then the baby cooed. "She likes it too."

"Jana it is then."

"Jana Marie." Stick looked at Annalee.

She nodded. "It's settled then. Welcome to the world, Jana Marie."

Stick sat there for another hour, just staring at his baby girl. When Jake and Cheryl arrived, he gave them space but stayed close, hovering at the foot of the bed.

"She's beautiful, son. Congratulations." Jake's face brightened with the wrinkly parentheses of a granddad's smile.

Stick watched Cheryl, the way she stood with her legs crossed, hands upon the bed railing as if it were the only thing guarding her from a steep mountain drop. Her face, the blank expression of an apprehensive teenager about to embark on a journey she was unsure of. She was scared of this newborn but wouldn't admit it. Stick knew this must be tough for her, having been the only child for so long. Here he'd come and changed her whole life. He had to assure her it was for the better.

"A house full of women," he said awkwardly, struggling for the right words. He cleared his throat as they all turned to look. "Who knew I'd end up with two daughters?"

Cheryl's eyebrows lifted, and the edges of her lips turned up. She uncrossed her legs and reached out to touch the baby's blanket.

"All right, little sister," she said and laughed as Jana gripped her finger.

"I brought my best cigar," Jake said. "Me and the new father are going to celebrate."

Stick hesitated. He didn't want to leave Jana, but Jake took him by the arm.

"She'll be okay." Then in a whisper, "Give the girls some time, time to bond."

Stick followed Jake to the smoking room. Jake lit a cigar and handed it to him. "I remember when your mother was born," he said. "Greatest day of my life. I was scared too, don't get me wrong. Felt I wasn't prepared, but it'll come to you. Always does."

Jake had been a good parent. To him, to Viola.

Stick pushed his hair back. "What if I mess up?"

"You most certainly will. At some point. Everybody does. Love her and be there for her. That's enough."

"I will always be there for her," Stick said. "I was even thinking we could bring her to the track on race nights. Annalee could keep her in the RV."

"You don't think that'll be too loud for a baby?"

Stick hadn't thought about this. Maybe he should reconsider his line of work after all.

"Granddad, do you think I should get a regular, you know, nine-to-five? Isn't that what you're supposed to do when you have a kid, settle in a bit?"

Stick figured his granddad would jump at the chance to tell him to quit racing.

"Listen," Jake said. "You've done about all the settlin' you're ever gonna do, son. As much as I—" He paused, swept his eyes up to the right a moment, then continued. "You love racin'. Don't quit. You'd be bored to tears in a normal job. Most fathers are gone all day anyway, then get home just when the kiddos are going down for bed. You'll be home most of the day and gone when the baby's sleepin' anyway."

"Good point," Stick said, puffing on his cigar.

It didn't take much to convince him not to retire from the track, but he did wonder if small-town races would pay the bills with a new baby in the house. "Should I go back to NASCAR? More money for diapers and all."

"Boy, you went from quittin' to takin' on races. What's goin' through your head?"

"Everything. I don't know. I want to make more money for my new family, but I want to be there for them, too."

"That is a tough one. I was lucky enough to be able to work with you there, but your daughter, she's gonna want somethin' different. NASCAR's the way to go these days. Them purses are pretty big. You can't give yourself up completely when you have a family. That girl will learn the meanin' of life by seeing you do what you love."

For a backwoods moonshiner, Jake sure was wise. Stick had to find the right balance between money and family, without losing himself in the process.

"Don't think too much right now, son. Just enjoy the moment," Jake said and took a long, intentional draw of his cigar.

"Wait—you shouldn't be smoking. Not after your—did the doctor say you could smoke?" Stick asked.

"Didn't say I couldn't," Jake said, taking another puff. "I've done it for years, after every batch goes out. Kinda a ritual of sorts, like when sailors christen a new boat with a bottle of champagne."

Stick decided not to ruin the moment by giving his granddad a lecture, so he let it slide, but made a note to talk to Dr. Hammet later.

"Granddad," Stick said, dropping ashes in the cylindrical can against the wall, "was there anything about Mama you noticed when she was young, you know, like—anything I should look out for?"

"Stick, Jana will be fine. But no, your mama wasn't any different than any other kid. Kids're crazy things when they're little, runnin' around, talkin' to themselves, talkin' to imaginary friends. They do the weirdest stuff. One time, I saw a kid at the park eatin' sand. The point is, there's no way to tell. Your mom's disease, it creeped up on us." He sighed, closed his eyes, and took a deep drag, held it there, then blew the smoke out in a series of short puffs. "Don't worry. The chance that—well, again, Jana will be fine. She has two loving parents. Your mother didn't. She lost your grandma early, then your no-good father. Doctors say it was probably just too much for her to handle. But you and Annalee, you have so much love to give that baby. And you'll always be there for her. I know it. I can see it in you."

"Thanks," Stick said.

His granddad had come a long way in his thinking. Either that or he was playing cool, so he didn't scare the shit out of Stick. Stick smashed his cigar into the tray and bear-hugged his granddad.

"I'm thinking of puttin' my original number back on the car, baby pink and all. An homage to my daughter."

"I like that," Jake said and took one last puff of his cigar before tossing it into the trash. "Let's go see that baby."

Stick grabbed his granddad around the shoulder with one arm. They walked this way down the brightly colored hall, nurses and orderlies passing them left and right. There were cries, laughter, alarms, screams. Clear bassinets whizzed by, blue and pink cocoons inside. *Babies really are born into chaos,* he thought. But in the air, there was a lightness, a happiness you could see in the nurses' faces. The relief in a mother's sigh, the joy in a new father's eyes. It was as if they all knew that among the mayhem that is the beginning of life, it only took a single breath for everything to be okay.

They paused at the window to Annalee's room, the blinds now open. Stick could see Annalee holding Jana, Cheryl planting tiny kisses on the baby's forehead. All the fuss around him, and Stick didn't care. He was in no hurry.

Chapter 21

LINCOLN, AL
– 1977 –

It was foggy out, but the image was clear. A dark-skinned man stood perfectly still by the side of the road, a cowhide drum in one hand and rattle in the other. A tomahawk was attached to a brown leather belt at the side of his buckskin leggings. He had long hair that was shaved on the sides and braided in the back and deep-set eyes that matched the seriousness of his countenance.

Stick heard Talladega was built on an ancient Indian burial ground; he just wasn't sure what he was seeing was real. Ever since Jana was born, he had been worried about becoming the kind of parent his mother was, afraid that if given time, his brain, too, would manifest images and sounds that weren't visible to anyone else. He hadn't wanted to race at Talladega anyway, on account of the track's jinx, but Butch had talked him into it since the Cup Series finishers received huge winnings. Still, Stick couldn't get the series of strange events out of his mind.

Five or six years back, drivers had arrived to find their brake lines cut and sand in their gas tanks. Then there were the deaths. At least three drivers and one fan had died, all under peculiar circumstances. But what scared Stick most was when Bobby Isaac pulled out of a race because he heard voices telling him to go home. People thought he was crazy, but years later, he still stuck to his story, convinced the voices saved his life that day.

So as Stick eyed the man standing by the side of the road, he couldn't help but wonder if it was a sign. He paused a moment, thinking he should hightail it out of Alabama. The man's lips turned up at the corners, and he began to beat gently on his drum. Stick shivered and drove right into the speedway.

Butch and the crew were already there in garage eleven, setting up shop.

"Please tell me you saw that Indian out by the road?" he asked.

"What Indian?" Tommy asked, deadpan.

Finnegan swatted him with a dirty rag.

"He's kiddin'," Butch said. "Of course we saw him. Girl at the ticket booth said he's there before every race, blessing the track."

"How nice of him," Stick said, relieved. "How's it lookin'? No sand in the fuel tank?"

"Naw, everythin' looks good. How you gonna deal with that bankin'?" Butch asked, nodding toward the track.

The track was 2.6 miles, longer than Daytona, but the banking on all turns was severe: thirty-three degrees. Normally, he would use the steep incline to his advantage, shooting up then back down to increase his lead and scare the other drivers, but not today. Not at Talladega.

"I'm gonna leave it alone."

"Good," Butch said, as the rest of the crew let out a sigh of disappointment. "What about that slight fifth turn in front of the main grandstand?"

"That's where I'll risk a little, give the audience a good show. I always wondered why they curved the front stretch so in that area."

"Why did they do anything with this track? I swear it's—" Finnegan started.

"Finn!" Butch warned. "Speeds been fast lately, maybe because it's such a damn long track."

"Always a good day to break a record. What is it here, anyway?"

Tommy piped in, "Two oh eight."

Stick spread his lips into a mischievous smile.

"Oh, Lord," Butch said. "I know that face."

"It's the face of a winner," Stick said. "Plus, I promised my little girl."

"You promised your toddler? Oh boy, you shouldn't make promises like that. If you don't win, she'll never let you forget it," Butch said. "Did you tell her we painted the number pink just for her?" He stepped aside so that the fancy, powder-pink seven was visible.

"Sure did, and told her it was in honor of her birthdate."

"Cute," a voice behind him said, and Stick whirled around, ready to punch some hick for making fun of his race car.

"Robby, you son of a bitch! You racin' today?" Stick asked, holding his hand out to his old friend.

Robby had aged, and not as well as Stick. His brown hair had patches of gray on the sides above his ears, and his nose wrinkled when he talked.

Robby took Stick's hand and shook it, patting him on the arm just above the elbow. "I'm racin'. Took a year off from NASCAR to focus on my family for a bit, but I'm back. You better watch out."

"You hear that, boys? Robby says I better watch out."

"Then you better," Tommy said.

"Whatcha drivin' these days, anyway?" Stick asked.

"Dodge."

"Eddie and Mike switched to Dodge too. We'll see how it handles."

The loudspeaker crackled as it did when the announcements would begin.

"Better get goin'," Robby said. "See you in second place."

Stick laughed and gave a thumbs-up. If he was to lose to anybody, he'd want it to be Robby.

While fans settled in with their seventy-nine-cent hot dogs and lukewarm beer, Stick changed and walked to the car. A cold breeze blew past him, and he shuddered. There was something eerie about this place. He didn't know if it was the Choctaw by the road, the creepy way the oaks twisted in the sky like giant skeletons, or the fact that in the time he'd been standing there, he'd seen four black birds circling Robby's car. But despite all this, Stick crawled into his freshly painted Chevy and lined up for the race.

Stick did as always: drove a row back, watching, calculating his move. Then, he passed nearly a third of the field. This time, the song that filled his head wasn't the usual heart-pounding strum of instruments or the searing of a fiddle; it was a song his granddad played once, and only once, after his mother's funeral: "Isle of the Dead." Why that particular song filled his brain at that very moment, Stick was unsure, but he couldn't shake it.

He glided the Chevy to the front of the pack, and Robby was right behind him after having completed a lengthy pit stop. He knew his friend would try to make up time by passing him on the next turn. He just hoped he would play it smart. This was not the track to be pulling stunts and tricks. He shifted close to the inside, knowing Robby would try that first. As he approached the turn, Stick hugged the corner so tight, nothing could get through. Robby moved to the outside lane, flat up against the car in front of him. Stick made it through the turn still in the lead. As he sped down the curved frontstretch, he looked into the grandstand. He didn't know what made him do it; he typically never took his eyes off the track. But there, for a split second, he saw the Indian right up against the wall that separated apron from track. The man was playing the drum, the beat the same as the one haunting Stick's mind. *How can that be?* Stick must have taken his foot off the gas pedal for a millisecond, because Buddy Baker's black-and-silver #28 shot past him. Stick maneuvered to the left and pressed close to #42. Hot on his tail was Robby, who moved farther left. There was a gap about a foot wide between #42 and a red Chrysler #17. *Don't do it, Robby. It's not worth it. Not on this track.*

Turn one was coming up, and Robby moved to the far right. *What is he doing?* That wasn't his usual position. Stick knew Robby would never ricochet up the bank; it wasn't his style. He was a smart driver, always had been. The sky was turning gray, and it looked like rain. Stick hoped it would hold out the final ten laps. At the beginning of turn one, Robby surged up the bank. *What the hell is he doing? He's*—Shit. Shit. Shit. The climb was swift, one fluid motion, and Robby soared to the top. The back wheels lifted off the ground a little and—*swoosh!*

Robby's car was airborne, a hunk of metal flipping and flying through the sky—and barreling toward Stick's car. Imagining the complete destruction of Robby's car hitting his, Stick pressed the gas pedal to the floor and rammed into the car beside him, pushing himself and four others out of harm's way. They skidded into the infield just as Robby's car landed right side up at the bottom of the bank. It spun like a top before rolling onto the driver's side. There was no fire, no smoke.

Stick stopped the car and climbed out. The silence in the stadium was so stifling, so eerily quiet, that Stick looked around to make sure the crowd was still there. People stood in the stands, hands over their mouths, some covering their children's eyes. A dog someone had brought began to howl, a confused lonely cry. Stick scanned the audience for the Indian. He didn't know why he had to find him, he just knew he did, maybe to prove to himself he was really there. But the man was gone. An ambulance honked, and Stick realized he was standing in the way. Four paramedics rushed to the car, each one turning his face away when he reached the vehicle. One dropped his head as he walked slowly back to the truck. One sat on the ground, his face pale, his eyes glazed. Another threw up in the grass alongside the track. The fourth, a tall, calm-faced man, walked toward Stick, both arms outstretched, ready to push back on the crowd that had formed. They weren't even trying. A murmur spread like a wave. Robby was dead. Stick knew it. He had known it all along. The birds, the song, the Indian. The fucking beating of the drum.

Greenville, SC

The funeral procession was slow. *Robby would have hated this*, Stick thought as he curled his fingers in a perfect ten and two position around the steering wheel of his granddad's Ford. Leading the line of black cars were two county cops. Stick's lip curled. *Ironic. A bunch of bootleggers led down the road by the very cops who chased us.*

Jake shifted uncomfortably in the passenger seat, and Stick knew what he was thinking: *This could have been you.* Over the past few days, Stick had lost sleep over it. He couldn't help but ponder his own mortality. One minute you're invincible, a young racer in your prime with nothing to worry about except what kind of beer you'll have or which beauty to kiss. Then, someone taps you the wrong way, a lug nut pops, lightning strikes, your heart stops. Robby hadn't known when he crawled into that car it would become a death trap. He'd raced a hundred times before and landed safely at the finish line. *Why did he bank it?* He'd never attempted that before. Why didn't he play it safe and—*There ain't nuthin' safe about racing. That's why we do it. The surge of adrenaline, teetering on the edge of peril, that thin line between life and death.*

Stick glanced in the rearview mirror at Annalee and Butch. His friend stared with glassy eyes out the window, Annalee straight ahead at Stick. The procession stopped in front of Sunset Cemetery, and people flowed from their cars. Stick held Annalee's hand and walked the narrow grassy path to Robby's final resting place. He noticed Willie standing at the edge of the crowd over by an oak tree, hat in hand. Annalee nodded as Stick broke her grasp and joined his friend.

"How you holdin' up?" Willie asked, a soft sincerity in his voice.

Stick felt nauseous, like someone had drilled a hole in his stomach and pulled his entrails out. He began to sweat even though the outside temperature was barely sixty-five degrees.

"I don't know, man. This is rough. Makes me wonder what the hell

I'm doin'," he said as he placed one hand on his chest to subdue his runaway heart.

"You're fulfilling your passion."

"But it might kill me," Stick said, and he was suddenly aware why that bothered him so.

Jana. Annalee. Cheryl. He loved them. He loved them so much his heart ached.

"And so could a million other things. Hell, half my life I've been dodgin' bullets. Quite literally. You too."

The sunken tightness in Stick's chest, the gnawing in his stomach, the pressure that squeezed at his temples, the shake of his normally steady hands. Fear. Stick had never experienced such intense anxiety before, not even when his granddad was hospitalized. The fear had taken over his body, hijacked his gladiator frame, and reduced it to a mere man.

"You okay, Stick? You look white. More so than usual," Willie said as he put his hand upon Stick's arm.

"Yeah, I just—I got a daughter now, Willie, and—"

"You're scared."

Stick bowed his head as if the emotion were a badge of shame. "Yeah."

"That's normal. Happened to me when I had my first kid. And it doesn't get any better. You're scared because you're no longer in this world alone. You got people dependin' on you. People you love, and that's the scariest emotion of all. You can't give up your passion, Stick, but you can drive smart."

Jake had been right again. "My granddad has said that to me many times," he said, shaking his head. He needed to readjust his perspective.

"Winnin' is still the goal. Speed the catalyst. But we don't have to play bumper cars with our lives anymore, Stick. We just gotta go 'round a circle faster 'n anybody else."

Stick was grateful for Willie's wisdom but unsure how he would put that into practice on the track. Maybe he would cut back on the races, go in for a few more tire changes, bump draft a little less often, listen to Butch a little more.

"Bottom line is somethin's gonna get us, and we can't predict it. We're all on this earth for such a short period of time. I don't know about you, but I want to spend mine behind the wheel of a race car."

And that's the heart of it. How do I want to spend mine? Stick knew the answer, and it wasn't an easy one. He wanted to speed up while slowing down. He wanted to spend more time with his daughter, but he also wanted to be fully present on race days, focused on the thrill of competition, the enchantment of speed. *I just have to find the right balance.*

The preacher began to read the Lord's Prayer, so Willie and Stick made their way over to the tombstone, but not before Stick took his friend by surprise and hugged him.

"You're a good friend, Willie," Stick said, a tear threatening to drop. Willie gave him a sad smile and hugged him right back.

At the prayer's finish, Robby's casket was lowered into the ground, and sobs filled the air. Annalee had found her way to Stick's side, along with Jake and Butch. She laid her head on his shoulder as fresh dirt was shoveled into the grave. Drivers who had never shown emotion before wept. Stick glanced at Willie, who had a tear in his eye. They were all thinking the same thing: Robby had returned to where he started, to the very thing every man there had in common—dirt.

Chapter 22

LAWNDALE, NC
– 1979 –

Tiny cowboy boots hung over the edge of the red Radio Flyer as a fluffy pink dress lifted in the breeze.

"Hold on tight!" Stick said, as he pulled Jana down the road to Jake's farm.

She squealed as a smile spread across her face, revealing small pearl teeth with a gap in the middle. Her hands gripped the sides of the wagon as it bumped down the rocky path. The apple trees were in full bloom, pinkish-white flowers not yet yielding fruit. Annalee had taken Cheryl to Love Valley for the day, so Stick promised Jana a fun day at Granddad's.

"She's in the lead! Will she do it? Will she take home the trophy?"

He got low to the ground and pushed Jana, holding onto her legs so she wouldn't fall out.

"There's the finish line! There it is!"

Jake stood by the front porch waving a checkered dishcloth. Stick guided Jana under, then picked her up and held her high.

"She wins! She wins!"

She burst into giggles, and they all laughed.

"And what is the prize?" Stick asked Jake.

He pulled a Snoopy stuffed animal from behind his back and handed it to Jana. She hugged it tight. She toddled to sit on the bottom step of the porch, cuddling her new toy. Her lips were moving as she lifted the dog's ears and whispered inside. She picked a berry off the bush beside her and held her palm up to Snoopy's stitched mouth. Jake chuckled. Stick did not, worried as he always was about behavior that might indicate her inheriting the mental illness that ran in his family.

"Ah, son, she's playing," Jake said. "That's what kids do, play make-believe. Hell, that's practically all they do."

Jana stood up, babbled something inaudible to Snoopy, then turned and said, "Me want juice."

"See there?" Jake said. "She's smart. Already stringing words together."

Stick was happy to hear all this. He wanted to enjoy his daughter, not constantly worry whether she would develop some crazy mental illness later in life.

Jana tugged on Stick's pantleg. "Dada, juice."

She looked so small there, so dependent, so vulnerable. He would do anything to make her smile. "How about a milkshake instead?" he said, lifting her off the ground.

"Yes!"

"You wanna go?" Stick asked Jake.

"Naw, I'll stay behind. Kidney's bothering me a bit today. I'm gonna go get a little drink myself and lie down."

Jake took a lot of naps lately, sometimes falling asleep in the chair while watching cartoons with Jana.

"I think drink's the last thing you need," Stick said without thinking.

"Not that kind of drink. I closed it down. Don't even make any more for myself. Doctor's orders."

"Huh," Stick said. "It's really come to an end."

It made Stick kind of sad. He knew there was no need for distilleries anymore. Southern Comfort, wine coolers, and peach schnapps were readily available at any roadside gas station. And something called "light beer." Stick refused to try that one. His granddad's business, while entirely illegal, had been fun. It had paid the bills, taught Stick some pretty valuable lessons in driving, and been the thing that bonded them together. Without the business, Jake would have worked overtime at the railroad station, and they would have barely seen each other. Stick was grateful for moonshine.

"It has," Jake said with an air of nostalgia. "It was one hell of a ride."

Jana put one hand up to her mouth and pointed at Jake, eyes wide to Stick. "Ooooh," she said, forming a circle with her mouth, drawing out the Os.

"Grandpop said a bad word, didn't he?"

Jana nodded.

"We'll keep that one a secret, okay? Extra whipped cream if you don't tell Mommy."

Jana clapped her hands together. Stick took that as a yes.

"All right, we'll get going, but we'll be right back."

Stick hated leaving him by himself, but the old man was stubborn and refused to get a live-in nurse. At least he got around fairly well most of the time and had all his faculties for such an old fart.

Stick drove slowly with Jana in the truck. He placed his arm across her tiny body every time they turned or hit a bump in the road. He thought about Robby and the family he had left behind. Did he think about them as he was dying? Stick couldn't get the picture of Robby's car out of his mind. He'd seen his fair share of accidents in his day, but that one was unnervingly violent. He had backed off racing in the months following, too upset by the whole thing. He'd supplemented by collecting appearance fees at local fairs and such, but he knew he would have to get back on the track soon.

A car pulled up beside them at the main light in town. A thirty-something in a trucker's hat reached across his car to roll down the passenger window.

"Stick Elliott!"

Stick waved.

"Stick, you gotta come back, man. We all miss you out there. Racin' just ain't the same without you."

"Thanks, man," Stick said but was happy when the light turned green.

He waved as the guy beside him stepped on the gas, no doubt trying to impress his idol.

Truth be told, Stick did miss the track. He just needed a comeback plan. He wasn't afraid to race. He knew Robby's accident was a combination of bad decision-making and the Talladega jinx. He'd race, but not at Talladega. Never again.

They pulled up to the Mighty Moo. Stick ordered a vanilla milkshake with extra whipped cream and chocolate sauce for Jana and iced tea for himself. He paid, put his change in the tip jar, and handed the cup to Jana, who immediately began sucking down the frosty goodness.

"You wanna go see Uncle Butch?" Stick asked.

Jana nodded and continued working on her milkshake.

When they pulled into the garage a few minutes later, Butch was leaning against the garage door, smoking a cigarette. His square body was more circular now, his gray T-shirt pulling tight against his belly.

"Since when do you smoke?" Stick asked, getting out of the car and going around to the other side of the truck.

"Since the accident. It was—well, I figured if someone as good and clean-cut as Robby can go just like that"—he held up one hand and snapped his fingers—"then I may as well do all the things I've been avoiding all these years. God knows it don't make no difference."

Stick opened the passenger door and picked up Jana. Her face was covered in whipped cream, and her dress was dotted with chocolate sauce. She waved when she saw Butch. He immediately crushed the cigarette under his foot.

"Well, hey, pumpkin," Butch said, his voice changing to a cheerful tone. He leaned into Stick as they got close and whispered, "Arthur," then nodded toward the garage office.

"What's he doin' here?"

Annalee's relationship with Arthur had always been tense. Stick didn't know why, only that it had something to do with her ex-husband. Arthur had always been decent around Stick, albeit a little strange. They didn't see him much, especially after Jana was born. Stick trusted Annalee's instincts on the matter and figured she would reveal the reason in due time.

"Don't know. He's been lingerin' for a while now."

When they walked inside, Arthur saw them and came right over.

"Well, I haven't seen you in a while," he said, poking Jana gently on the arm.

She giggled.

"Whatcha got there?" he asked, pointing to Snoopy.

"Woof woof."

Arthur smiled and tickled her before turning to Stick. "Stick, when you gonna get back out on the track?"

"That's what I came here to talk about."

Butch smiled. Stick knew he had been waiting for this moment. The day-to-day garage work was boring to him too.

"We can go in the office," Butch said.

Stick hoped Arthur wouldn't offer to watch Jana. He didn't want to tell him no, since he was her granddad, but if Annalee found out, he'd be in a heap of trouble.

"I better be going," Arthur said, much to Stick's relief. "Got a big shipment coming in from out of country."

Stick thought about what Annalee had said about Arthur's business dealings and wondered exactly where that shipment was coming from.

"Wave bye to Papa," Stick said.

Jana waved. Arthur blew her a kiss.

"Hope to see you out there soon," he said as he walked away.

"Dodged that bullet," Stick said.

"What's the—"

"Don't even ask, 'cause I don't know. Now, let's go talk about my return."

They went into the office, a crammed space that smelled like motor oil. Jana sat at the desk with some paper and a bucket of crayons and began to scribble.

"You ready to go back? I'm thinkin' we start at Cleveland or Cherokee. Back to your roots," Butch said excitedly.

"Good idea," Stick said. "But there's gonna be some rules."

"Uh-oh," Butch said.

"Uh-oh," Jana repeated.

The men laughed. She'd been a little parrot lately.

"No green anywhere. Not in the car, not near the car."

"Got it. No green. Let me guess, same prerace meal, no well wishes, and no black cats. Does that cover it? You've always been superstitious, Stick; we all know that."

"Yeah, but even more so now since—" He paused. "If anything, and I mean anything, feels off, I'm not racin'. No questions asked."

Butch nodded.

"And I'm not racin' Talladega ever again."

"You know that takes you out of NASCAR Cup Races, then?"

"As a matter of fact, I'm not racin' anywhere that was built on top of a gravesite. It's just too spooky."

"How are we supposed to—" Butch gave up and wrote "No graves" in his notes. "Fine, but I've got some rules too."

Stick sat back in his chair. He'd expect nothing less from his best friend.

"If you need to pit, you gotta pit, Stick. Enough of this trying to squeak out a couple more laps." Stick opened his mouth to speak. "And, and—" Butch said, putting his hand up. "If I say the car's not ready, you're not racin'. Period."

"Under what circumstances might that be?" Butch tended to get nitpicky with the condition of the car.

"If I think it's not viable to drive, I get last word."

Stick opened his mouth, but once again Butch intercepted him. "This sport's hard on these cars, especially the way you drive. They need maintenance in between. And sometimes, *sometimes*," he emphasized, "the car ain't worth salvagin'. It needs to be rebuilt or exchanged."

Stick knew Butch was just nervous, looking after his best interest. "Fine, but this is not a license to get a new race car whenever you damn well please."

Butch was aghast. "What? I would never—"

"I'm jokin'," Stick said. "But you can be overly—"

"Those are my provisions. No negotiations. Or you can get another crew manager. I'm sure Finn would love to take over."

"God no. Okay, fine. You get last word on the car. But be reasonable. You know I've driven with underinflated tires, loose steering wheels, all that before."

"I know. Safety only," Butch said. "Now, I'll call the promoter down at Cherokee. There's a qualifier in two weeks. When should we send the press release?"

"Few days before. Gets 'em hyped up more."

Jana turned around in the chair and started crawling down backward, awkwardly holding a crumbled piece of paper in one hand. She shoved it into Stick's lap. It was a rectangle with a few rounded corners sitting atop four circles. Inside the rectangle, another circle, this one perfect, intersecting with two diagonal lines. Stick turned the paper around to Butch, a quizzical look on his face.

"Did you draw Daddy in a race?" Butch asked sweetly.

"Yes."

"You want Daddy to race?" Stick asked, to which she nodded and crawled into his lap.

"You should bring her to the daytime races at least. We can give her some earmuffs to stifle the noise. Would be good press. She could take a victory lap with you when you win."

"Win!" Jana repeated.

"Yes, Daddy will win for you, sweetheart," Stick said as his heart melted. "First time she's ever said that word."

"Well, get used to it, 'cause we are gonna do a lot of winnin' around here," Butch said, standing up.

Gaffney, SC

Stick's first race back was an absolute disaster. A snowstorm had come through two days prior and deposited a few inches. Granted, it was nothing like the Great Southeast snowstorm of '73, but snow was rare enough in the Carolinas that it crippled the whole area. Everyone was shut in their homes, and talk of canceling the race circulated. In the end, Bill Cash paid a bunch of teenagers four dollars apiece to sweep off the seats and sprinkle the steps with some salt. There wasn't much to be done about the track, though. It was a sloppy mess.

Stick arrived at Cherokee Speedway at a quarter past six. It was still cold out. The temperature had dropped every night since the storm, causing the leftover snow slush to refreeze. The track was a mixture of sloshy mud and hard, crunchy ice. Cash had decided to put the till out there to break up some of the frozen stuff, so the cars wouldn't go slipping and sliding. It had been a good idea, but now the track had deep ridges, and Stick was pretty sure half the cars were gonna get stuck in it like quicksand.

Butch pulled up in his own pickup truck, a heavy-duty Dodge with a thick chain roped around the hitch.

"I hope you don't get stuck, but if you do"—he banged on the side of his truck—"Bessie's ready."

"You named your truck Bessie?"

"Yup, and she's gonna save your ass if necessary. Sure you don't want to bag this one? It's gonna bottom out your suspension at the very least."

"Don't see how we can. This is my big comeback. People are expectin' me to race tonight."

Butch stepped out of the truck, and his feet sank into the mud clear up to his ankles. "Christ. This is gonna be bad." He walked with overexaggerated steps to the car. "Where's Annalee and the munchkin?"

"In the RV, keepin' warm."

"Good. So, there are no heats tonight. Just the main event. Called 'em off on account of track conditions. Half the drivers didn't show up anyway."

"They're scared."

"Or smart. Speaking of, Finn's not gonna make it. He's stuck tryin' to fix electricity at his mom's house. She's been without heat since yesterday, and those kerosine lamps are dangerous."

"We got a fill-in?" Stick asked. He wasn't anticipating problems; he just wanted to make sure that if he had to take a pit stop, there were enough hands on deck to get him out quickly.

"Merle from over at Scooters Garage."

"Does he know what he's doin'?"

"Yeah, worked with a couple rookie drivers down at Midway. He'll be fine."

Stick sighed. A messy track and one man down—were these signs? He looked around the track. *Nah, look at these boys.* A couple had deflated their tires so much they looked like fat jelly rolls. A yellow Buick rolled off the trailer with the biggest set of ridged tires he had ever seen. He wasn't even sure they were legal, and from the puzzled looks of the officials, they didn't know either. A few of the teams stacked up fifteen sets of replacement tires, the limit. What good would that do if their guy's car was wedged down in the mud?

Butch hit Stick's arm with the back of his hand. "Look." He pointed to a driver trying to put chains around his tires, which was illegal.

The officials abandoned the monster car and went running over, yelling and waving their arms in the air. Stick felt reassured. These weren't signs. They were all in the same sinking boat. If anything, he had the advantage here. He had experience driving in all sorts of conditions, on all sorts of terrain. He just had to take it steady and not do anything stupid.

"Did you hear me?" Butch asked. "I said you're gonna win this one. These fools don't know their head from their ass."

"So, I win by default?"

"Any way necessary." Butch laughed. "You might want to wear the brown suit tonight."

"Naw, I'm going with the white," he said as he walked to the trailer. "I want 'em all to see just how dirty I'll get to win."

"But—"

"I'm kiddin', Butch. I'm gonna use good sense. I'm not gonna drive stupid."

"This driving's stupid," Stick said an hour later as he watched the crew change out his tires to heftier ones.

The cars had sloshed around so much that the race was halted halfway through so they could re-salt the track, but Stick doubted that would make any difference.

"I don't know about these tires, boys," he said. "Look a little bloated to me."

"Y'all just keep bangin' into each other out there like a bunch of bumper cars. I'd like to keep this car as intact as possible," Butch replied.

"I could raise the suspension?"

"I'm doin' just fine," Stick said. "This ain't mud boggin'."

"Yeah, probably a waste of time. None of y'all goin' top speed anyway. Just drive in a straight line like you did in the Florida sand."

"I am drivin' straight, but the track's an oval, in case you haven't noticed."

Tommy and Merle snickered. Stick looked around and began to laugh, a hard belly-rolling laugh.

"What's so funny?" Butch asked, standing up from his crouched position by the left front tire.

"We all look like a bunch of pigs covered in mud." He had to pause to collect his words. "May as well go roll around in it; we ain't gonna get no dirtier."

A bolt making an *urrrk* sound signaled the last tire was screwed into place. The entire crew stood up.

"Oink, oink," Merle said, and they all burst out laughing right alongside Stick.

"Seriously, somebody take a picture. This is the most ridiculous thing I've ever seen." Stick wiped mud from his cheek.

Tommy grabbed the Polaroid they kept around for quick promos. "Get in there, boys," he said.

They all pushed together as he snapped the photo. Tommy waved it in the air. "This one's goin' up on the garage board for sure."

Despite the frustration of the race, this was the most fun Stick had had in a while. Something about hanging out with his crew, shootin' the shit, covered in what looked like, well, shit—it made Stick happy. This was stock car racing in its truest form: a down-and-dirty display of speed and all the crazy driving that came with a bunch of rednecks trying to have some fun on a Friday night.

An official, a squirrelly man with a headset that dug deep into his balding head, came sprinting over and would've landed face down in the mud if it weren't for Merle grabbing his arm at the last minute.

"I'm comin' 'round to consult with the top drivers. Seems the powers that be want to shorten the race by twenty laps."

"Shorten it, why?" Stick asked.

"Well, y'all are having a hell of time out there. And the fans are gettin' slapped with so much mud, we're gonna have to hose 'em down at the end."

Stick glanced over at the stands. The fans were having a good time, dancin' and drinkin', hootin' and hollerin'.

"Looks like they don't mind it too much," he said to the official, who was busy trying to wipe mud off his hands.

"Is it a yes or a no?"

Stick looked around at his team, who just shrugged.

"It's fine, whatever the other boys want to do," he said, thinking it wouldn't be a bad thing to get Jana home early.

He could see her tiny face pressed against the window of the RV, creating fog with the breath coming from her upturned nose and rose lips. He waved. She waved back. *God, that girl melts my heart.*

The loudspeaker crackled on again. "Tonight's race will be shortened by twenty laps, due to driver safety," the announcer said.

"Driver safety?" Tommy raised one brow and scratched his head.

"Yeah, they coulda come up with a better excuse than that," Stick said. "Ain't never been nuthin' safe about stock car racing. That's part of the—" He stopped, remembering Robby's accident. "Well, may as well have some fun with it."

He glanced over at Butch, half expecting him to say something about being cautious or driving smart. He might have been thinking it, but he didn't say it.

"I could stand to see some excitement, quite frankly. So far, it's just y'all slingin' sludge around the track," Tommy said.

Merle nudged him with his foot. An attractive woman wearing a T-shirt stretched tight across her large breasts was making her way down the stairs of the grandstand.

"I'd pay to have her muddied up," Tommy said. "We could get y'all off the track and start a proper mud fight, whaddy'all say?"

"Yeah," Merle said, his mind wandering to places Stick didn't want to know about.

"Eyes on the prize, boys," Stick said.

"My eyes are on the prize, boss," Tommy said, almost drooling.

Stick laughed and climbed back in the car. There were only ten laps left in the race, so he'd have to make the best of it. As they started up again, #27 got stuck right away, but it was on the side of the track, so the race didn't stop. Stick forced the gears, causing his back wheels to spin, much to the delight of the fans. The green Chevy #34 behind him got a face full of mud pie, which he spat out the window. Number 4 tried to speed up but turned the wheel too much and ended up buried on the first inside turn. Stick chuckled and trudged right through that mud like he owned it. When he crossed the finish line, he was several laps ahead. After the last few cars trickled in, Stick pulled his goggles and helmet off and put his hand up to the flag stand, motioning for them to wait. He walked clear across the track to the RV. Annalee came to the door with Jana, followed by Cheryl, who wore a Stick Elliott trucker hat.

"Win!" Jana said, holding her arms up in the air.

She was wearing a white-and-yellow dress that made her look like a daisy.

"Give her to me," Stick said, both arms outstretched.

"Stick, it's cold and filthy out there," Annalee said, pulling a shawl around one shoulder.

"Oh, Mom, seriously, it's fine," Cheryl said, then looked at Stick. "Those other suckers didn't stand a chance in hell."

"Language!" Annalee said as she covered Jana's ears.

"She's heard worse," Cheryl said, then winked at Stick as she retreated back into the RV.

"Bundle Jana up," Stick said to Annalee. "I brought a coat. It's behind the blue chair."

Annalee sighed and disappeared back inside. When they returned, Jana's legs were covered in black tights, a pair of brown cowboy boots on her feet. Her dress was covered completely by a black coat that was way too big for her.

"Really, Stick? Where did you get this?" Annalee asked, spinning Jana around.

On the back of the coat, written in light pink cursive, was his car number and the words "Daddy's Little Girl."

He smiled at Annalee and reached up from the bottom step. "Give her to me."

"I don't know, Stick. She'll catch a cold without a hat."

"Hand me my cowboy hat," he said.

"Which one?"

"The tan one. It's in the closet by the hall."

Annalee handed Jana over to Stick, disappeared, and came back a minute later with a tall Stetson.

"Stick, this thing's huge," she said as she handed it to him.

He plopped it on Jana's head, and it fell over her eyes. He took it off, rolled up the rag he had tucked in the loop of his suit, and stuffed it in the top of the hat. He placed it back on Jana's head. The hat stood tall, but it didn't fall.

He grinned and hustled back across the track to a cheering crowd. A beauty queen stood by his car, dressed in black and white for the occasion, a tart smile on her lips, probably because her outfit was covered in dirt. The race promoter handed Stick the trophy, which he balanced on the hip opposite his daughter. He posed for a picture, then gave the trophy back to an official. The beauty queen stood beside them for another round of photos, and when they finished, she leaned in to kiss Stick on the cheek. Jana put a dimpled hand up and squished it into her face.

"No," she said, pushing the girl away.

Stick gave a lopsided smile and tickled Jana. "You wanna go ride in the race car?"

"Yes!" she said excitedly, forgetting her disdain for the beauty queen.

"A victory lap!" the announcer said. "Joining Stick Elliott will be his daughter, Jana."

The whole place cheered, and Jana waved with both hands. Stick handed her to Butch momentarily while he crawled inside. Butch handed her gently through the window, and she sat in Stick's lap.

"You drive," he said, and Jana put both hands on the wheel.

Stick kept one hand on the bottom of the wheel, invisibly steering as they made their way around the track. It was the slowest he'd ever remembered driving. He didn't want the mud to splash up on his little girl, but mostly, he wanted to take his time and enjoy the moment. She giggled the whole way around and, forgetting she was "driving," took her hands off the wheel to wave at her mother, Butch, the crew, and finally the fans. They came to a stop by the finish line, and Tommy came over to help her out of the car.

"Down," she said.

"I don't think she likes me much," Tommy said, waiting for Stick to crawl out and take his daughter back.

"Down!"

"No, she just wants down," Stick said.

"But the mud—" Tommy glanced over at Annalee, who had both arms crossed as she stood outside the RV.

"Put her down," Stick said. "She's a kid. She wants to play."

"You do it," he said, holding Jana out to Stick. "Annalee looks fightin' mad over there."

Stick backed up just far enough that Jana couldn't reach him. "Why do you think I want you to do it?" he said with a smile.

Jana wiggled and repeated her demand until Tommy relented and put her down. She immediately sat down and pushed her legs straight out. Stick averted his eyes from Annalee to his crew, gathered near the winner's circle. They all began to laugh, and Stick thought what a sight they must be. He looked down at his own suit, once white, now covered in thick orange splatter. Then he sat down right beside Jana and smeared mud right on her cheek. She smiled. The press gathered round and began to snap photos of the two of them.

"Play dirt, Daddy," Jana said with a sweetness he couldn't resist.

Stick smooshed his boots farther down in the mud. He stuck his hands all the way in, too.

"That's all I've ever wanted to do, honey."

Chapter 23

CHEROKEE COUNTY, SC
— 1980 —

A human fence encircled the race car: eight crew members in gray jumpers, one old man in overalls, and a stunning woman in peacock blue. Annalee had her arms linked with Jake on her right and Butch on the left. Jake's arms were intertwined with Tommy's, his stance wide. Butch averted his eyes. Finnegan and the rest of the crew completed the chain around the car.

"Well, what have we here? A little protest?" Stick asked, mocking his friends and family. "Hey, honey," he said softly to Annalee. "Where's Jana?"

"Runny nose. Cheryl's got her at home." She glanced around at the crew. Jake spoke first. "You can't drive in this race."

"Oh, really?" A smirk spread across Stick's face.

"The car ain't ready," Butch said, an argument that had been repeated over the last few days.

"Smoke keeps shootin' up from the engine, and the left side's a little wobbly," Finnegan said from the other side of the car.

"And there's a clankin' in the back we can't figure out," Tommy added.

"Not to mention you hit your Goddamn head in last week's race and clear near passed out. You probably got a concussion, but you're too stubborn to get it checked out," Jake piped in.

The momentary loss of time had spooked Stick a bit, but when he'd come to, nothing hurt. He figured he would count his blessings and move on.

"I told you to fix the car," Stick said.

"We tried. We did a full inspection. It runs clean most of the time, but it still ain't right. Not all the time," Butch said as he released his arms and shoved his hands down in the pockets of his tan carpenter pants.

"Nuthin's perfect all the time," Stick said.

He could manage a clackety car. It was poor decisions that caused problems, and he wouldn't make those. Not now. Not with his family on the line.

"It's too danger—" Tommy said, but Jake interrupted him.

"You ain't right! You 'bout near totaled that car last week, and we found you delirious. You ain't thinkin' straight."

But I am thinking clearly. Stick had originally been unnerved that he'd rattled his brain a bit, so he'd quizzed himself the past few weeks with dates and such, testing his accuracy with the nightly news. David Brinkley had all but confirmed Stick's brain was in working order.

"And Annalee says you been havin' headaches."

Stick looked at Annalee, who shrugged nonchalantly. It was true, but that was probably from lack of sleep. Jana had been in their bed lately, and Stick couldn't fall asleep for fear of rolling over and squishing her. He didn't want to seem weak, so he'd been popping Tylenol by the handful. Annalee must have noticed.

"I'm fine!"

"You might be," said Butch, "but this car's not. I don't think it'll last the race. I need another week or so with it, to run diagnostics."

"And while you're busy runnin' tests, I ain't makin' no money," Stick said.

The bills had started to pile up as Stick got used to supporting three other people. He needed to race to make ends meet.

"But you'll be alive," Annalee said.

"Christ, you guys are overreacting. I've driven races with three tires, a blown-out carburetor, and I don't know what else, and y'all scared of some unexplained noises? I told you to bring the car down and—"

"We did, but we think it's best if you just sign some autographs, let fans pose with the car, that kinda thing," Butch said.

"This car's not a Goddamn prop. What am I gonna say when the fans ask why I ain't racin'? 'Cause no excuse is gonna be good enough. They'll think I'm a pussy. I'm racin', so y'all better get outta my way."

He started toward them, and Jake nudged Annalee. She shook her head ever so slightly as he huffed.

"Granddad, don't get her involved!" Stick roared.

Annalee kneaded her hands. Stick lowered his voice to a reasonable volume. "I'm racin', and that's that." He rolled his eyes as he inched closer to the circle. "I promise"—he looked at Annalee—"if anything feels off, I'll come in."

"And if you see smoke," Butch said, walking toward him.

"I'll come in."

"And if the car stalls?" Butch asked, like a parent prompting his kid to say thank you.

"I'll *come in.*"

"If anything at all rattles or otherwise feels—"

"I'll come in!"

The chain began to dissemble, each crew member breaking off to inspect the car one more time. Annalee walked past Stick, pausing to whisper, "Be"—she hesitated—"good."

Only Jake remained in front of the driver's-side door.

"I promise," he said, to which his granddad nodded and stepped away from the door.

"Get this thing ready," Jake said to the crew. "Or I'll have all your asses."

There was a collective "Yes, sir" as the crew hustled to check the tires, steering, under the hood. Annalee wandered off somewhere, as she often did before races. She had to get away from the pit to ease her nerves. Stick readied himself in the usual manner, choosing high-paced bluegrass over the Mozart record his granddad had gifted him. He washed his face with a white towel and ate a few candied orange slices. After pulling his fire suit on, he opened the bottle of aspirin, took two, and walked out the door.

Despite an unsettling beginning, it couldn't have been a more perfect night at Cherokee Speedway. The air was chilly, the sky clear. The rain had come two nights prior, so the dirt was tightly packed, meaning there wouldn't be much dust.

Stick lined up in the front row and lowered his goggles, which tinted the sky a brown hue. He shut off the two-way radio, so he could focus on the subtleties of the car without chatter from the crew. There would be no symphony of the mind today, no music directing his moves; just man and machine, synchronized as one. He let out a hiss as the car started up. The hum of the engine was on beat with his heart. Exhaust blew from the tailpipe as he exhaled. One by one, he wrapped the fingers of his right hand around the steering wheel, then extended his arm and leaned back. His well-worn python boots hovered above the gas pedal, ready to strike.

Go!

And strike he did. Stick bolted with such fury the back tires lifted for a second. He bolted down the track as the other cars jutted from the start line, a jumbled mash of hubris and grit, all vying for glory. The older drivers stayed out of Stick's way, having learned the hard way over the years, but the younger drivers had something to prove. They each wanted to be the one who took out a legend. So Stick thought it cute when #42, a boy with a bit of hair above his lip, tore along the inside lane like a dingo in pursuit. One swipe of Stick's front fender and the boy lost his nerve. The next twenty laps were like babysitting. A newbie barreled his way through the pack, listlessly shifting, scanning a space he could slither his way into. Stick saw it coming and lined up beside another car so tight you couldn't see daylight between them. Then, just as the newbie retreated, Stick took off. He tried to crawl the wall in turn two—no doubt something he'd seen Stick do—but lacking the skill, he ended up sliding and crashing at the bottom, creating a hell of a mess and requiring a caution flag.

Fifty laps in, Stick was annoyed with the constant stop in play. "It's a race!" he yelled at the flagger. "My grandmother drives faster than this!"

Stick pulled in for a pit stop and immediately felt the upward motion of a tire jack, the sound of a drill. Butch ran over to the driver's-side door.

"You gotta smidgen of fume comin' from the front left," he said. "I woulda told you that, but you turned off the—"

"We ain't drivin' fast enough for that to be a concern."

"I know, but—"

"It's just a little. I'll keep an eye on it," Stick promised.

A tap on the hood meant the car was done. Butch stepped out of the way as Stick cruised back into moderately moving traffic. The "go" flag made a welcome appearance.

"I'm done with these ingrates." Stick took off, scaling the wall on the second turn and cutting in front of all the other cars.

It was time to strengthen his lead and teach the young boys a lesson. He drove with such force he was soon ten car lengths ahead of the rest. The bit of smoke emanating from the hood had turned into a solid stream of pressure, which Stick could feel reverberating through the tips of his boots. Tonight's race was just seventy-five laps, and Stick intended on finishing, no matter what was spewing from the car's orifices. At lap sixty, the cage rattled, and at seventy, the hood popped open, blocking Stick's view.

I'll be damned if I'm going in now. I've won races blind before.

He knew Butch would be pissed, but he was going to win this race, even if the whole car fell apart right there on the track. He scanned his periphery. No one was near him, but there was a faint emerald streak to the far back left. *Asshole. You can suck my—*

Stick adjusted the throttle and forced the gas pedal down. He aggressively shifted gears, and the front hood flapped like the mouth of a gator. Sizzling currents jumped from the car like fireflies. The chassis wobbled, the tap of percussion. Or was that his heart? Beating—the sound inside his body melding with the ones outside. He couldn't tell the difference. The loud scrape of metal dragging. His body low to the ground. *Pop!*

He was airborne.

Stick removed his hands from the wheel—there was no use in steering upside down. Twisting through the atmosphere, Stick tumbled around like a rag doll, his body thrown against surfaces he could not distinguish. His neck whipped, trying to stabilize its bobbing head. And all through this, Stick's knees ached. He thought it was a peculiar thing, to feel achy joints during such a horrific tumult. Like having a headache in the middle of an avalanche, a stomach pang while caught in the winds of a hurricane. Which is how he felt now. Stick wasn't sure where his body would land and how intact it would be when it finally did. He just prayed it hurt less this time.

Chapter 24

CHEROKEE COUNTY, SC
– 1980 –

Tap. Tap. Tap. Ripping, screeching. Ringing in his ears.
 Dust. Coughing.
 Lids opened. Orange. Gray, black. The cloud was gone. He was, it was all too—
 Head pulsating.
 Click.
 Pulling. Falling. A heap of tangled body.

Chapter 25

LAWNDALE, NC
– 1939 –

Jake had found him lying on the cold hard ground. Gene had passed out after seeing his kneecaps all distorted that way.

"Gene, Gene! What—"

The shrill of his mother's voice. "My baby! What happened to my baby?"

She must have been in the bathtub, for she ran to his side completely naked, minus a cloth around her matted ponytail. A yellow scarf. He remembered the color. It was the color of caution.

Chapter 26

CHEROKEE COUNTY, SC
-- 1980 --

D*rip. Drip. Tick, tick, drip.*
Sweat droplets collected in his dark, unruly brows. Others stung his dry, cracked lips; tasted salty on his tongue. Heat radiated through every surface, penetrating the skin.

Drip. Drip. Tick.

"It's gonna blow!"

Robby.

Another voice, louder. "Somebody get him outta there!"

Even closer: "Goddamn heap of metal—I can't!"

Stick shifted his body to relieve the pressure on his neck.

Not Robby. Me.

Dust. Red clay. A gas pedal.

I'm alive.

He struggled up from the floor and hit his head on the steering wheel. The roof of the car was dented and pressed to within an inch of his scalp.

Turning to the side, he saw boots with metal tips. A tan arm through the small opening where the window used to be.

"Stick! Grab my hand. You gotta get out. There's fuel leaking. This car's gonna catch fire."

It was all worth it, Stick thought as his eyes closed again.

Chapter 27

LAWNDALE, NC
-- 1939 --

He was floating, legs dangling above the ground in the cradle of arms as he looked at the sky. Stars flickered, winking at him like they knew a secret. It was peaceful.

Chapter 28

CHEROKEE COUNTY, SC
— 1980 —

Tick. Tick. Pop.

He woke to sparks, like fairies caught in a violent dance.

Zapping skin.

Musky sulfur.

Stick eyeballed the exit. It was too narrow. Rolling onto his stomach, shards of metal dug into his forearms and elbows.

"He's too big! There's not enough room!"

Trapped.

Stick slid to the other side as the car shifted.

"Wait! Stick, don't move! You're too—the car might roll."

"Get him outta there, Butch!"

"I can't reach! It's too—"

"Well, rip the son of a bitch roof off that car!"

"How am I supposed to—the hammer! Hand me a hammer!"

"That's not gonna—"

"I'm gonna knock the roof up and get him out!"

"Stick, close your eyes. There's gonna be shrapnel. Might wanna cover your head, too."

Stick tucked his head clear into his lap and squeezed his eyes shut.

Chapter 29

LAWNDALE, NC
— 1939 —

Gene's body was numb. He watched as the stars disappeared, the black night sky replaced by a speckled ceiling. His body began to thaw from the warmth of a fire. That's when the pain returned.

He cried out in horror. His whole body felt like it had been smashed against a brick wall, especially his knees—

"Put some clothes on!" he heard his granddad yell.

"I need to call for help," said the terrified voice of his mother.

"No! You can't. They'll—they'll—"

A rustle, shouting.

"They will take you away!" There was desperation in Jake's voice.

Gene felt a warm set of hands across his forehead. "He's coming to. Put on a dress. I'll take him to the hospital."

"Good idea," his mother said, and Gene could hear her shuffle out of the room.

"You're gonna be okay, little one," Jake said, but Gene could tell by the way his voice trembled that his granddad was scared.

Gene was wrapped in some sort of woolen quilt and carried back out the door. The hard leather seats of Jake's Ford were cold and cracked. Gene pressed his head against the window, his breath creating a halo of fog. He couldn't see much, just a yellow scarf flying through the air as his mother sprinted toward the car. A dark, black creature circled overhead, blocking the twinkling stars.

Chapter 30

CHEROKEE COUNTY, SC
– 1980 –

Sparks popped and sizzled on his skin, jolting him back to the present. Vapors burned the delicate membranes of his nose.

"Hurry up! There's a fire near the back."

"I have to move this jagged edge, or he's gonna get cut up."

"If you don't move faster, we're all gonna be blown to smithereens!"

Who's—they should just leave me here. It's been a good run. What am I—this heat's makin' me outta my head. What about Annalee—Cheryl—and Jana? I gotta get—how the hell? I can't even—

Snap, snap, snap! A series of piercing sounds. Specks of brilliance, sparklers in a dance.

*I can't let my boys die saving me. The girls I'll miss; they'll be okay. So, this is how it . . . always knew I'd die in my car anyway. Best place to be. The smell, it's—*Stick felt woozy again. *Here it goes. Death's not that bad. Hell, I been askin' for it all my life.*

Chapter 31

SHELBY, NC
– 1939 –

His eyelids burned with the starkness of light, and a strong smell hit his nose. Vinegar—no, turpentine. He didn't know. The night sky with its multitude of faintly luminous bodies was gone. He guessed a wish was out of the question, though he could use one right about now.

A clear mask descended over his face, covering his mouth and nose. The last thing he saw was his own breath, this transparent essential element presenting itself in front of his very eyes.

Chapter 32

CHEROKEE COUNTY, SC
– 1980 –

Stick felt hands all along his arms. He rolled onto his stomach and shimmied out, his knees buckling as he tried to stand. Four guys dragged him along the dirt to the other side of the concrete wall.

The car exploded in a fireball; white clouds replaced by solid black plumes. The heat made him gasp, and he realized he had been holding his breath.

"Guess we'll retire number seven," he said, slumping onto the ground. He looked over at Butch, who was red as a beet, sweating profusely.

"Nuthin' rattles you, does it?" Butch asked, hunched over, trying to catch his breath.

Stick shook his head, but his heart was beating faster than usual and his stomach churned—the inexplicable sense of relief paired with exhilaration. He'd always thought that with all he'd been through, a fiery car crash was a hell of a cool way to die, but after seeing Robby's accident, he wasn't so sure. He was grateful nothing hurt, except the twinge of a headache radiating from the base of his skull.

Butch made his way over to Stick and bent down. "We're gonna run outta numbers if you don't stop wreckin' cars."

"Nah," Stick said, shaking his head.

The sound of fire truck sirens howled in the distance as Stick tried to stand.

"Sit still. You need hydration," said Butch.

"Good idea. Bring me a beer," Stick said with a grin.

Tommy rolled one over so when Stick opened it, the brownish-golden liquid spewed, foam pouring from the top. He placed his mouth over the bottle like a water fountain. Hops tasted sweet on the back of his tongue as he took the towel from his pocket and wiped his forehead. Black ash. *I must look quite the sight.* His fans gathered near the retaining divider to get a closer look at their hero, the driver who defied all odds.

"Gimme somethin' to write with," he said to Tommy as he tried to stand.

His knees were a little sore, but that was nothing new.

"Stick, you're not gonna sign autographs after all that, are ya?" he asked, handing him a pen.

"Why wouldn't I?"

"Because, well—you need to get checked out and—" Tommy sputtered as Stick walked off.

If he remained upright, everything would be okay. His head hurt, but he'd been able to walk away, unlike Robby. *I have to keep moving.*

As he approached the fans, men cheered and pumped their fists. Women batted their lashes and adjusted their tops as he strode over, pen in mouth for good show.

"Oh no you're not." Annalee's voice filtered through the crowd as she pushed her way through and grabbed Stick by the arm. "You're comin' with me."

"Yes, ma'am," he responded and turned right back around.

"This is *not* funny," she said, smoothing his hair. "You're goin' to see a doctor."

"I'm—"

"Stop being an idiot," Jake roared, appearing seemingly out of nowhere. "I told you—Good Lord, Stick, you scared us to death!"

"Hey, Granddad." Stick smiled a schoolboy grin.

"Don't you 'hey, Granddad' me! If you weren't so big, I'd put you over my knee and—AH!"

"Whoa! No need to go there," Stick said as he stopped and put his hands up.

Annalee pushed him forward. "All your granddad is trying to say is—"

"When you take a tumble like you did, you need to stop being so pigheaded and get yourself checked out!" Jake flailed his arms in the air.

Stick saw his granddad, fear in his eyes, and it reminded him of that frigid winter's night. The night his granddad had saved him—the first time. Jake was just a scared old man protecting his grandson.

"Okay. I'll go," Stick said, "but I'm going out for a drink first. I think I've earned it."

"Goddamn it, son." Jake shook his head and walked off, clenching his fists.

Stick looked at Annalee. "I'll be home soon. And I'll be quiet. I won't wake Jana."

He hugged Annalee, then left her standing there, adorned with a bright red scarf. Had she been wearing that before?

"Come drink with me," Stick said to Butch, who was gulping down a large cup of ice water. "Just one. I promised Jake I would take you with me."

Butch slammed his cup down on the ground. "I'll do anything for you, Stick."

"Good," Stick said, massaging his head. The pain now radiated across his entire skull. "Get me an aspirin, too. I got a hell of a headache."

Two beers in and the headache wouldn't dissipate. The neon lights at Clancy's caused his eyes to blur a little, and the back of his neck felt hot.

"I think you got a fever," Butch said, twisting around on his barstool.

"Why would I have a fever after an accident? Don't make no sense. My ears always get red when I drink."

"Yeah, but your whole head don't. Stick, you need to go home, go to the hospital. You promised Jake."

"I'd have to agree," the bartender said, wiping the inside of a glass with a white cloth. "You don't look so good."

"Fine," Stick said, shoving a ten-dollar bill across the counter. "But I ain't goin' to no hospital."

Butch rolled his eyes up and sucked his lips in. "I ain't gonna argue with you. But I'm leaving, and you're comin' with me. I'll take you home, let Annalee talk some sense into you."

Truth be told, Stick was happy to go home. Despite the fact he'd only had a couple drinks, he knew a hangover coming from a mile away. He hadn't been drinking as much since Jana was born, so maybe his tolerance had gone down. *Funny*, he thought, *a bootlegger who can't hold his liquor.* But Stick had nothing to prove, not to Butch.

"Fine," he said.

Butch whirled his keys around his forefinger. "All right, let's go, boss."

Stick climbed into the pickup truck and leaned his head against the window. This time he didn't have to blow on the pane: The heat from outside fogged the window right up.

"What's that feeling like you've been somewhere before?" he asked.

"Déjà vu?"

"Yeah, I'm having déjà vu," Stick said.

His hands were sweaty and swollen. He unbuttoned the top of his shirt, wet with perspiration. When they pulled into Annalee's drive, he could see all the lights in the house were off except one.

"Got them bars removed, huh?" Butch said.

"What?"

Stick thought Butch had been talking about the roll bar. Then he realized his friend meant the jail bars on the windows.

"Yeah, I'm here now. Ain't nobody comin' round to mess with my little family."

"Need help gettin' out?"

Stick waved his hand dismissively and walked to the front door. He stepped inside to find Annalee sitting at the kitchen table, staring at the clock.

"Been waitin' up?" he asked. It was sweet she cared so much.

"Yes," she said as he walked into the light. "Good Lord, you look awful!"

Stick doubted that. He never looked awful. Disheveled, yes, but never awful. He glanced in the oval mirror that hung on the wall. His face was speckled red, splotched and crawling with patches of white, like a flat rash. Veins popped from his temples in gnarled cords. *What the hell?* At first, he thought he'd been seared by the heat of the crash, but someone would have treated him had he suffered burns. And he would've felt it, surely. Maybe it was the alcohol. He did tend to get a ruddy complexion anytime he drank, or got too much sun for that matter, his Irish blood rushing right to the surface and tinting his cheeks and nose with the rosiness of a thousand capillaries. *Or maybe I'm just exhausted.* Stick rubbed his eyes, which he noted were pink and dilated.

"I'm fine. I just need to lie down."

He wasn't fine, but nothing a good night's sleep couldn't cure.

"Oh no you don't," Annalee said. "You're going to the hospital."

"I just want to lie . . ." Stick walked back toward the bedroom, the hallway looking longer than usual, warped on one side. *Am I—what's going on?*

Annalee grabbed his arm and stuck a thermometer in his mouth before he could say another word.

"One oh four! Jesus help me. Stick, you're burning up."

He sat down on the edge of the bed and tried to pull his boots off.

"I'm calling Dr. Hammet," she said, rushing down the hall just as Cheryl entered the room.

"You look like shit," she said stoically, leaning against the doorframe. Or was the door leaning? It was oddly shaped, bent.

"Stay outta there!" Annalee yelled as she ran back to the room. "Dr.

Hammet says he probably has the flu. It's been going around. Jeez, what a night. What else could go wrong?"

Annalee put one hand over her mouth and nose and pushed Stick down onto the bed with the other. She poured some children's liquid Tylenol down his throat, then ran to the bathroom and turned on the faucet. Stick had never had a woman fuss over him in such a way before. He smiled.

Annalee came back into the room and placed cold washcloths on his forehead, which seemed to quickly absorb the heat emanating from his skin.

"You just need to rest," she said, closing the door, her face shadowed with fear.

That's what I said, he thought, but now that he was in bed, he couldn't sleep. The pain in his head was obtrusive, the heat all-consuming. So, he lay there, staring up at the ceiling and wondering why he'd never noticed the popcorn-like indentions. His neck started to grow stiff, rigid and unmoving—probably from the whiplash. The first time he'd felt pain like this, when he'd jumped out of the tree, it had been cold; so cold his fingers and toes had gone numb. Now, he lay there sweating, praying for a drop in temperature that could dull the pain in his head and spine. *Surely, these are just normal aches from the accident*, he thought. *If anything was really wrong, I'd know it. You don't walk away from an accident like that only to die later.*

The alcohol had worn off, and now his knees began to ache, too. He felt a fullness in his bladder, so he sat up. The bathroom was so far away, but he didn't want to call Annalee to help. He stood and waited for the rushing in his head to stop before he made his way to the dimly lit bathroom. As he pushed the door open, the room began to spin, a slow nauseating unevenness. *Boy, what did they put in those drinks?* Stick reached for the sink and fell. The cold, hard floor was welcome upon his cheek.

"What—Stick!" Annalee yelled, and all he could see were the tips of her red toenails. "You're bleeding!"

"My neck, it hurts—" he said.

He was hovering again, this time on a soft pillow of white.

Chapter 33

SPARTANBURG, SC
– 1980 –

Damn bright lights. I'm in a—why do hospitals always smell like a jar of pickled vegetables?

The gurney bounced along the floor to a room the color of vomit. Among the men and women in matching outfits, stethoscopes around their necks, charts in their hands, was a single black bird, sitting by the window. Stick thought it looked awfully terrifying and wondered if he was mistaken and it was a bat. He shuddered and averted his eyes, but when he did, the room spun again. He squeezed his eyes shut, and when he opened them, they settled on a cockroach in the corner of the room. It crawled up the side of the wall, its long wings flat against an almond-shaped body. Stick looked up. A brown substance was splattered along the ceiling.

"This place is disgusting," he said.

Annalee was suddenly at his side. "He's talking!" she said as if this were a revelation. "Stick—oh, Stick! You're at the hospital."

"Well, this is the dirtiest hospital I've ever seen. Just look at all these cockroaches."

Annalee patted his arm as a doctor shone a penlight in his face.

"His pupils, they're—"

Stick couldn't hear the end of people's sentences. It sounded as though they were whispering or covering their mouths to blunt the words.

A pair of hands lifted up his head, turned it to one side. Pain streamed down the entire length of his body.

"Ooww!"

"Does that hurt?" a voice asked—not Annalee's, probably a doctor's.

Yes, dumbass. It hurts, Stick meant to say, but the words wouldn't come out. He blinked twice.

He felt Annalee's fingernails gently scratching his arm in assurance. He looked back at the window. The black bird was still there, hopping around on the sill. *Why are there always birds around when bad things happen?*

A nurse entered and stuck a needle in his arm, then fastened it down with tape. Another attached square sticky pads to his chest, while another put a cuff around his arm that squeezed tightly every minute or so. They placed ice packs all along his body, so he felt like a cadaver lying there, cold and exposed.

His head kept squeezing, a pulsating sensation like fire trying to escape. It built up in his forehead and rushed down to his ears, pushing against the drums, so the only way to relieve himself was to pull on his lobes, allowing the heat to funnel its way out the opening. When he reached up with his right hand, his arm was pulled down by some cord, causing an array of alarms that made his headache worse. He lifted his left hand instead and was instantly pricked deep in the crevice of his arm by a needle.

Stick looked down, and upon seeing his body crawling with tubes, cords, and measures, he began to panic. *Why am I hooked up like a science experiment? I have a little fever and headache, and they're treating me like a curiosity, a freak.* Rage started to boil but something else too: a tingling, shaking feeling that Stick remembered from his youth, from the days with his mother. Fear. *Is this what they did to her?*

He remembered her sitting upright in that small wooden chair, her chin drooping slightly to the left, sickly orange stains surrounding her laugh lines. She'd had bruises on her arms and scaly skin from burns near her collarbone. Her hair had been missing in patches. She hadn't tried to look up, not even when he walked into the room. She hadn't moved.

Stick raised both arms again, setting off another set of alarms. He grabbed at his hair, just to make sure it was still there.

A bespectacled doctor came rushing over in a tizzy. "Don't! Mr. Elliott, don't pull," he said in a stern voice.

But Stick wanted out of there. He would not be relegated to a hospital bed. They would not do to him what they did to her. He pulled at the snakelike cords stuck to his arms, but the wires became tangled. He sat up and threw the ice off the bed, crystals crashing and cracking on the floor.

"I'm going home!"

The white lab coat rushed to Stick's side in an attempt to subdue him. *The men . . . they're coming to get . . . the lab coats, they're going to medicate me into a zombie so they can perform their cruel experiments. Not on me, they won't!*

Stick pushed as hard as he could, and the doctor fell to the ground. Before he could get both feet on the floor, a team of men in green suits were upon him. They held him down, which made him punch and kick harder, the wires whipping against his bare skin, blood squirting from his forearm. *Where's Jake? Why isn't he stopping this?*

Stick glanced over at the window, and again there was the black bird, sitting with its head cocked to the right.

"Demon!" he pointed and felt a hard jab in his other arm.

The bird must have summoned darkness, because Stick's field of vision began to narrow. A slow creeping of blackness tunneled its way into his eye sockets until there was but a dot of light left. He struggled to see, trying to hold on to the image of Annalee, a yellow scarf flapping as she screamed.

"Leave him alone!"

Chapter 34

SPARTANBURG, SC
– 1980 –

The pressure was intolerable. *Did they shock me? Open up my skull? Sear into the fleshy parts of my brain with a blowtorch? Are they operating? Am I supposed to be awake during this?*

Stick tried to move his body but found he couldn't. Probably anesthesia. *But I shouldn't be conscious if they're—who told them they could—*

Stick opened his eyes, the only part of his body he seemed to be able to control. The lights in the room were dim, not bright like an operating room. And it appeared no one was around. He couldn't move his head due to the pain, but in his periphery, he caught a glimpse of a hand.

"Who—" he muttered, the words not coming easily.

What did they give me?

The face of an angel came into view.

"Stick, you're awake," Annalee said. "He's awake!"

She had been crying, he could tell, her face wet with tears, smudged with mascara.

"I'm here," she said and patted his hand, which seemed to be anchored down.

"What's—what's going on?" he asked, as surprised as she was that the words came out clearly.

"They had to—you were fighting." She paused. "You punched the doctor," she said, and he detected pride among her sadness.

"Why—can't move," Stick sputtered. "Am I—" *Paralyzed?* The last word wouldn't come out.

"They strapped you down," another voice filled with worry, sadness. Granddad.

"You was fightin' mad. They had to. Never seen you so wild," Jake said, and Stick could feel him bedside.

They tied me down? Is that what they did to my mother? What kind of hospital am I in?

Questions came, but the words would not. The clock on the wall counted the seconds as Stick darted his eyes around, trying to get his granddad within his field of vision. As he moved his eyes far left, the pain returned. He winced, then gripped and tore at the bedsheets with his fingers.

A third voice. "He's feeling some intermittent pain, but not much. We loaded him up with—"

Fuck! Intermittent pain, my ass. It feels like a Goddamn freight train pummelin' through my brain. Am I sick with some disease that'll drive me mad?

"Granddad," Stick said.

I think they heard that one.

He felt a warm hand on his chest, then his granddad spoke as if he could read his mind.

"Don't you worry," he said. "You ain't gone mad." He paused, and Stick heard him swallow hard. "Not like your mama. You're . . . You'll be okay." There was a crack in his voice, barely perceptible, but there.

Annalee cleared her throat.

There's something they're not telling me. He could feel it in the room, a heaviness pervading every corner, lingering in the air like an unspoken curse.

"Can we speak outside?" asked the third voice, a man of authority.

"You go," Jake said.

Stick heard the door close and felt pressure on the bed as Jake sat down. The throbbing in his head subsided. It was as if some magic had pushed the pain from his brain through his body, down his veins, and out through the tubes. He tried to smile.

"Remember that time down by Grassy Pond when we came upon that cow pasture, the one with the bull?"

That's when you taught me to drive.

"Yeah," he muttered. His voice was low, buried in his throat. In fact, he felt stuck, trapped inside his own body. Every part of him wanted to move, release whatever was holding him down. Run. Scream. Scratch his nose, which was itching so terribly.

His granddad was still talking. "And you just flew through those cow patties, shit flying everywhere, and charged right at that bull. Biggest one I'd ever seen . . ."

There was a bug on the ceiling. It crawled in and out of the tiles, weaving through space, traveling anywhere it wanted. There were probably more of them up there, hiding, marching from room to room. Stick was jealous.

"That's when I knew you'd be the best." Jake had ended the story, and Stick was sad he missed it.

He was tired anyway, and a certain calm had replaced the anxiety he had felt. The door reopened, and he heard Annalee's footsteps, the *click-clack* of her heels slow and deliberate. The bed sprung up, the man beside him gone. It was then Stick heard his granddad weep.

Chapter 35

SHELBY, NC
– 1949 –

Gene was up to his chin in corn, the yellow tips grazing his face as he whizzed through. He should have rolled up the window, but he hadn't thought of that; not when the police had surprised him when repacking 'shine that had come displaced.

He'd been rushed from sleeping in on account of sampling too much product the night before. The rooster had woken him up, so he hadn't had the cover of night this time. He hadn't woken his granddad, either. It was better if he didn't know. He'd packed the trunk too quickly, trying to get out before Jake woke for his morning coffee. If he'd lost even one jar, his granddad would be on him like white on rice. He'd deduct it from Gene's pay, and Gene would get a hell of a talking to, so he'd had to stop.

Now here he was, deep in the maize, unable to see the end. He could hear sirens in the distance, but the trouble was, he didn't know which way they were coming from. He plowed through Mr. Becker's farm, sure he'd have to pay later. But dealing with Mr. Becker would still be better than explaining all this to his granddad. He charged through the stalks and decided straight ahead was his best bet. He was pretty sure there was a creek at the end of the cornfield. The police might be waiting for him there, but he'd bet money they wouldn't go through the creek.

But I will.

The speedometer on the old Ford was broken, but Gene figured he was going at least 125. He hunkered over the steering wheel, peering through stalks that had stuck themselves like glue to his windshield.

The creek. Lights. Three police cars. It all came into view as he exited the field like a bull released from its pen at the rodeo. There was only one thing to do: jump the creek.

Gene hit the edge, the back tires bouncing as he was launched across.

"Ah, ha, ha!" He hipped and hollered as he became airborne. *This is fun.*

The back end of the Ford hit the ground with a bang. His rearview mirror revealed baffled police standing by the creek bank, mouths agape. One even laughed.

The sweet smell of muscadine filled the air.

Chapter 36

SPARTANBURG, SC
– 1980 –

Stick's eyeballs flickered inside their sockets. He couldn't see a thing, but his hearing was somehow magnified. He heard Annalee sniffling. She was close. Jake and another—was it Butch?—whispered a little farther away.

"It's cryptococcal meningitis. Doc said there's no cure," Jake was explaining.

"What do you mean no cure? They can't give him nuthin'? They're just throwing the red flag?"

Definitely Butch. His voice was worried, more than usual.

"There ain't nuthin' to give him, except stuff to ease his pain. He slipped into a coma 'bout an hour ago. They don't think he'll ever come out of it."

Is this some sort of trick? The doctors want to keep me here so they can control—Mama. Did they—what will they do to me?

A fourth sound. A squawking so terrifying it could only be that of a vulture or raven. It was close to his ear. Who let that damn bird in?

"It's eatin' up his brain, takin' over. Earlier he was rantin' about bugs and such. Things that weren't there."

But they were! You didn't see them because you weren't looking up, which I can't do now either.

Another sound—indistinguishable.

How many—who—what all's in this room? Where's my daughter? Is she—she can't see me like this. She'll be—

A blackness wrapped its way around his body and entered his mouth, which he was sure was hanging open. It twisted and coiled its wretched fingers like vines as it burrowed into his brain, infiltrating the deep recesses where his thoughts and memories lived. It reminded him of kudzu, the way it overwhelmed everything in its path, slowly becoming part of the organisms it invaded until the hosts no longer recognized themselves.

Chapter 37

LAWNDALE, NC
— 1938 —

The windows were wrapped in rope his mother had painted green. Where she found that much and how she got it painted, Stick didn't know. He'd been playing by the creek all day and came home after stepping on a mound of fire ants. Wiggling and shaking his shorts, he'd stopped dead in his tracks when he saw his mother, balanced on a ladder, hammering the ropes in place. She wore a flowy blue dress that picked up when the wind blew.

"That'll keep 'em out," she said as she stepped off the ladder to greet Gene. "Why, you look awful! What are those red marks all over your legs?"

"Fire ant bites," he said, flicking another one loose.

She sprang into action, tossing the hammer haphazardly into the bushes. "Take your pants off!" she yelled.

Stick started toward the house.

"Not in the house! Here."

Gene removed his shorts.

"Underwear, too," she said.

"Here? People will see me," he said, even though there was no one around.

Viola began to tug at Gene's waistband.

"Mama, stop. Mama!" Gene wriggled and spun out of her grasp as she chased him around the yard.

"What in tarnation is goin' on here?" Jake yelled from the open window of his car parked at the curb. "Viola, stop messin' with that boy." He got out of the car and stepped between the two.

Viola sat down in defeat. She pulled at blades of grass but kept one eye up at Jake. Gene thought she looked like a scolded child, Jake towering over her. But despite his size and obvious authority, Granddad had a kind face, a tender heart.

Jake threw Gene's shorts back at him. "Get dressed." He looked up at the house. "Why is there . . . redecoratin'?"

"It's to protect us from intruders," she said as if it was a perfectly normal thing to do.

Jake ushered Gene into the house, gave him a tube of calamine, and told him to apply it all along the bites. "And change your clothes," he added before heading back outside.

Gene sat at the kitchen table applying the chalky pink lotion to his legs. His mother was in the bushes, trying to locate the hammer she had thrown. He saw Jake take her gently by the arm and lead her to the porch. They sat down on the steps together, Jake's arm around her shoulders. Gene couldn't hear what they were saying, but when they finished, Jake got up and began to pull the ropes from the windows. Viola stood there a while, nervously biting the skin around her fingers. Then she picked up the green paint bucket and poured it over her head.

Chapter 38

SPARTANBURG, SC
– 1980 –

Voices. Jake, Butch. They were whispering.

"You can't leave me, Stick."

Annalee.

"You ain't never slowed down your entire life. It's not a—it's not a caution flag. It's black and white. It's—"

He tried to visualize Annalee. Dark hair, blue eyes. She had been wearing a yellow scarf.

"You have to get up. Get up! Get up, damn it!"

Lights on. Lights off.

Chapter 39

SPARTANBURG, SC
– 1980 –

Annalee sat in the sunshine. Stick noticed the slightest touch of auburn on the tips of her hair. Jana busied herself with the wagon, pulling Snoopy along the sidewalk, gathering flowers and weeds. She was wearing Wonder Woman Underoos, red boots, and a little gold headband stuck up like a crown from her dark hair.

Annalee was talking, but Stick was busy making sure Jana didn't get too close to the road.

"Stick, did you hear me?" she asked, slightly irritated.

"Uh—"

"I said I'm pregnant."

Stick swung around. Annalee had pulled her shirt up slightly, her barely swollen stomach revealed in the sun. A long dark line ran from her navel to below her skirt, like rust on worn-out farm equipment.

"We're gonna have a—"

"Yep, another one," she said as she leaned back on both elbows, smiling.

Stick glanced at Jana, who had squatted near the grass to pick up a ladybug. She spoke to it gently, and he wondered what on earth she could be talking about.

"Oh, Annalee, I'm so happy," he said, touching her stomach. "Jana's gonna have a sibling."

Stick was happy, but he wondered how he could possibly have more love to pass around. He loved Jana more than anything. She was the spitting image of Annalee, and smart, to boot.

"Me too, but Stick? I'm not sure I can do this on my own. With you being gone so much. And Cheryl's a teenager now. She doesn't want to sit at home watchin' kids. What if I can't handle it?"

Stick figured Annalee's hormones were just getting the best of her. "Jana can start preschool over at the church. And I'll help as much as I can," he reassured her.

But she was still uneasy. He could sense it. She's worried I'll leave, and she'll be stuck with three kids. That's why she overreacted last week at the race when I signed that woman's chest.

"Annalee, you're a great mom, and me, I told you I'm in it for the long haul, whether you like it or not."

Jana ran up then, balancing the ladybug on her fingertip.

"Daddy," *she said as she placed her tiny hand in his.*

The ladybug crawled onto his palm, and he shivered just to make Jana laugh. Stick didn't like creepy-crawly things, but this one was beautiful. The polka-dotted red body opened to reveal long clear wings. It fluttered, then flew off.

"Aww," *Jana sighed.*

"Don't worry, sweetheart, they always come back."

Chapter 40

SPARTANBURG, SC
– 1980 –

"Come back! No, no, no! Come back!" Annalee was screaming at the top of her lungs, a hysterical, terrifying scream.

The pressure in his chest weighed a thousand tons, his body a puddle of molten lead. He was stuck in a dark tunnel, plastered to the ground.

A booming sound in the distance and a tiny glimmer of light.

His body couldn't move, but his soul did. Drifting toward the light, he felt the ground shake beneath him, and as he looked back, he saw shadows around his lifeless form. He kept going, faster now, to find the source of the light. Was it a wishing star? Something high up in the universe that could explain all this nonsense?

As he neared, Stick realized there were two lights, round and yellow. Headlights. And they were headed straight for him.

Chapter 41

SPARTANBURG, SC
-- 1980 --

Stick was traveling backward, the cops in hot pursuit. The headlights of the black Ford were like the eyes of a wild beast in the dead of night. Stick stared straight at them, his eyes burning. He didn't need to look behind him. He knew these roads like the back of his hand. Gravel flew and dust pillowed around the car.

He remembered the bull, the one that had been in the pasture the day his granddad taught him to drive. That thing had glared at him, daring him to cross its territory. Its nostrils had flared as it picked up one hoof. Then it charged, and Stick's instincts kicked in. He put the car in reverse and drove as fast as he could backward, that damn bull chasing him around the pasture. Stick saw a fence behind him and knew beyond that fence was a ravine so deep, they'd never come out alive. But Jake never said a word, just held on tight and trusted his grandson. Just as the wooden slats came within a foot of the car, Stick whipped the wheel around, and that bull went charging clear through its enclosure.

Now, the tree cover was thickening, and Stick knew what was coming next. The road just past Thompson's farm turned from gravel to red clay. And beyond that, a bank so covered in moss that only he knew the drop on the other side. A fifty-foot plunge right smack down to the depths of Broad River. This time of year, it would be cold, even if you survived the fall. And yet, the yellow headlights kept pushing him toward it. Just before the dip, Stick flashed his lights in rapid succession, then quickly turned the wheel to the left, the car spinning on the dirt, blocking the cops from descending the ravine.

The Ford smashed into the side of Stick's car, and he knew the moonshine would be ruined. He paused, just for a second, to look those policemen in the eyes. The horror, the gratitude, the emotions were all there on their faces. He waited for their expressions to settle before sharply turning the wheel and stepping on the gas. He knocked off a hubcap and side mirror as he raced down the dark road, speed his only desire.

The policeman, the trees, the stars, the sky—it all disappeared. All that was left was Stick at the wheel, laughing as he kicked up a sea of red dirt.

EPILOGUE

Stick Elliott's cortege wrapped around Shuford-Hatcher Funeral Home and all the way down the street. Dale Earnhardt, Cale Yarborough, Toy Bolton, and Buddy Smith were in attendance after requesting services be postponed by one day so they could race in the Atlanta Journal 500. My father, Stick Elliott, was laid to rest in the red clay dirt of Gaffney, South Carolina, just days after Halloween, 1980.

Born Gene Hampton Daves to Viola and Wade Daves, Stick was raised in Lawndale, North Carolina, by his granddad when Wade abandoned the family and Viola began to suffer from mental illness. Granddad Elliott was a railroad security guard and would carry a large nightstick, which he would run along the sides of the train cars to scare off train hoppers and hobos. Everyone called him Big Stick, so when he would bring his grandson along, Gene became known as Little Stick. The name stuck and would be his racing name for years.

Stick was honing his driving skills way before he was legally qualified to do so. He was barely fourteen years old at his first race, though he was driving well before that, hauling moonshine and evading cops through the Appalachian Mountains. With a loaded-up Ford, he would dash through the rough terrain and backwoods country roads filled with twists and turns, rocks and mud, kudzu vines, and steep drop-offs. But driving wasn't just a fun pastime; it was a necessity.

Stick drove whatever he could get his hands on, crafting race cars out of salvaged vehicles and junkyard parts. As the years went on, he wrecked cars, and money ran thin. He sold all his belongings in the '60s to compete in NASCAR. "I thought I could make it on my own," he said in a newspaper interview, "but . . . it cost 301.5 acres, five houses, five tractors, and nine mules." That's when he decided to race other people's cars, including Toy Bolton's and Ralph Earnhardt's. He even joined a team at one point, racing alongside Wendell Scott, NASCAR'S first Black racer.

Stick was a phenom: a hard-charging stock car driver who had such control it was almost as if man and machine were one. He had a knack for keeping the car in the groove lap after lap, never wavering under pressure, and tore up tracks across the South during the '50s, '60s, and '70s. He was feared behind the wheel so much that many drivers just moved out of his way and let him pass. His driving was aggressive, often pushing the limits of the car and the track in such a way that he would leave officials befuddled, searching through rule books. At Daytona, he passed cars in grass on the inside of turns and ended up on the front page of the papers. I remember a story from my childhood in which his steering wheel came off completely at the end of a race, and somehow, he managed to coast to victory. At another race, he skidded in on three tires.

During his career, he had over four hundred victories. He was known to win four races in a weekend and sometimes two in one night. He entered the Winston Cup Series from 1962 to 1971, with ninety-three starts and a few top finishes, but he always preferred the dirt track, where fans would gather in droves just to see him race. Local drivers didn't give much thought to the other competition if the "Master of Dirt" was on the track. They knew Stick would take curves like a bolt of lightning, slam into the rear of any car, and scale the concrete wall just to get that checkered flag. Promoters would pay him to show up because they knew the crowds would follow. He was a showman, a handsome country boy with a steel foot. He'd arrive in his Wranglers, snip-toe boots, rodeo buckle, and cowboy hat, and the ladies would swoon. But the men liked him too. His rugged, no bullshit, charismatic personality appealed to everyone. He was at the same time a heartbreaker and a man's man, the John Wayne of racing.

That was the Stick Elliott everybody knew: a fierce competitor on the track and a good ol' boy off it. As soon as he exited that car, he had a smile on his face and a respectable handshake for those who competed with him. NASCAR Grand National Series driver Toy Bolton said, "He [Stick] would give you the shirt off his back." He was a real stand-up man, even befriending the cops who chased him. He loved to joke around with the other drivers, psyching them out before a race with a sly comment, hiding their tools, or painting funny faces on the sides of their race cars. On one occasion, he even stuffed a hot dog into a driver's tailpipe, causing quite the pop when the engine started.

Stick raced with the best of them. Together with Ralph Earnhardt, the patriarch of the Earnhardt dynasty, they became known as "Kings of the Last Lap." In fact, in 1973 when Earnhardt suffered a heart attack, he chose to put Stick behind the wheel of his #8. Stick won eighteen races in a row after that.[1] The Intimidator himself, a young Dale Earnhardt, raced against Stick too. The story goes that in the final lap, Dale clipped Stick and scooted past his spinning car for the third-place finish. One of Stick's crewmen angrily stormed toward Earnhardt as he climbed out of the car and fled the track. The next weekend, Earnhardt showed up to the track again. Stick stared him down, then said with a grin, "You know, son, you might just make a driver yet."[2]

Stick became the driving instructor for Charlotte High Performance Driving School, providing instruction to James Garner for the Grand

---

1   Jimmy Dearing, "Ken Schrader, 'Stick Elliott' Among NDLMHOF Inductees at Florence Kentucky August 8th," STLRacing.com, *St. Louis Motor Racing News*, August 4, 2009, https://www.stlracing.com/community/index.php?threads/ken-schrader-stick-elliott-among-ndlmhof-inductees-at-florence-kentucky-august-8th.134645/.

2   Jay Busbee, *Earnhardt Nation: The Full-Throttle Saga of NASCAR's First Family* (Harper, 2016).

Prix, the Smothers Brothers, and the King himself, Elvis Presley. Stick impressed so many with his driving prowess that he was signed as a stunt double in Elvis's MGM movie *Speedway*, during which it's said Stick terrified the King when he took him on a harrowing ride around Charlotte Motor Speedway.

The Stick Elliott legacy continues to this day, with a dirt track race held in his honor every year at Cherokee Motor Speedway, his induction into the National Dirt Late Model Hall of Fame in 2009, and subsequent inductions into the Hall of Fame at Cherokee and Carolina Speedways. In 2014, Stick was featured in a fictional book by Aaron L. Carter called *Boyhood Adventures*, and most recently, he was highlighted in Dale Earnhardt Jr.'s documentary series, *Lost Speedways*, on Peacock.

To many, he was one of the best drivers who ever lived, his fame and skill the stuff of legend. But to me, he was a father, and a damn good one at that. I remember his ruddy red hands holding me tight, lifting me up like an airplane only to swoop me down and plant me softly on our shag carpet. I remember his smile, which covered his entire face, and the way he loved my sisters and me just a little too much. Once, when I was three, he brought home a van filled to the brim with stuffed animals. When my mother questioned this huge display of affection, he replied that he didn't know which one I would like, so he'd bought them all. When I was four and my twin sisters were two, he pulled up to our brick ranch house with a tarp-covered trailer hitched to the back of his pickup truck. With a grin, he opened the tarp to reveal a souped-up bicycle, to which my mother protested I wasn't old enough to ride. "Oh, that's not for Gena. That's for the twins. This," he said, yanking back the blue tarp like a magician, "is for Gena." There in the back of the flatbed was an ATV, built out of spare parts from the garage. Needless to say, my mother forbid it, but my father took me on it anyway.

My mother, three sisters—including my oldest half sister, whom Stick treated as his own—and I spent many nights at racetracks, tucked inside a custom RV, munching on SpaghettiOs and Swanson TV dinners. We became immune to the noise, the roar of the engines a gentle lullaby that rocked us to sleep. Sometimes, if the race finished early enough, I got to ride with my father for a victory lap, my tiny, dimpled hand waving to the cheering crowd. My mother would get upset when Dad would let us play in the clay because "that red dirt don't come out of nuthin'."

And she was right. She would take us home and scrub us clean, but our white porcelain tub would forever sport a red ring. I miss that stain. It was a reminder my father was still slinging dust on the backstretch. It wasn't a fiery crash that took him at such a young age, as most people assumed would happen; it was cryptococcal meningitis, a fungal disease that took over his brain. He fought hard. But in the end, Stick Elliott lost, and our house of four women was left in the dust. All my sisters and I have left of him are the stories, the photographs, and the memories of one of the greatest men on and off the track, a man the world lost much too soon.

This book, while fictionalized in parts, is my tribute to him and a life well lived, a way to keep him and his hard-charging spirit alive.

ACKNOWLEDGMENTS

My gratitude overflows, so buckle up.

First, I am thankful for my dad, Gene "Stick Elliott" Daves, for being the kind of man worth writing about. He barreled through life quickly, but boy did he leave a lasting impression on many.

To my mother, who was in love with my dad her whole life, even after his ended. I thank her for doing the best she could to raise me and my three sisters on nothing but food stamps and whole lotta grace. Times were difficult, but Mama taught me grit and I am forever grateful.

To my sisters April and Dawn, for putting up with my nerdy bossiness our entire childhood and loving me despite it.

To my oldest sister, Tammy, for helping raise me. She and my brother-in-law, Terry, sacrificed a lot, and I appreciate them both more than they will ever know.

Piero, your beautiful smile started us on this journey. But it's your heart that sealed the deal. Thank you for believing in me.

Massimo and Giovanna, you are the best part of my life. Period.

To my editor Sara Quaranta, thank you for your positivity and patience throughout all the early edits.

To Dee and everyone at Greenleaf, thank you for your hard work and enthusiasm.

There are many people that supported me throughout my early life. Whether it was used books, hand-me-down clothing, a bag of groceries, or just a kind word, I am grateful for each of you. So thank you to Ruth, Papa, Archie, Vicki, Lori, Kelli, Fred, Nancy, Earl, Thomas, and to the man who was the greatest storyteller of all time, Uncle Jake.

And finally, bless the readers of books for opening your minds and hearts to a small-town country girl with a story to tell.

ABOUT THE AUTHOR

Raised in Gaffney, South Carolina, Gena Elliott became homeless at the age of ten, following the sudden death of her father, Stick Elliott. She became the first in her family to get a college degree and soon after worked for the *Spartanburg Herald Journal*, a *New York Times*–syndicated newspaper, as writer and copy editor. She currently resides in Florida, where she enjoys reading, the outdoors, and, of course, NASCAR.